WAVE WEAVER

WAVE WEAVER

FIVE FORCES BOOK TWO

MICHAEL HARDCASTLE

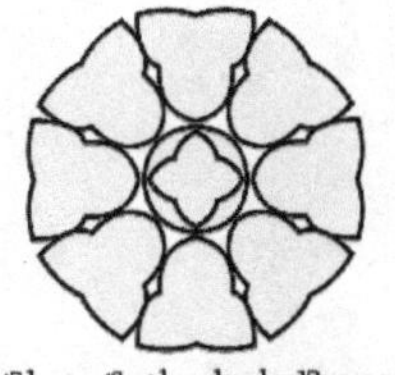

Glass Cathedrals Press

WAVE WEAVER

The following is a work of fiction. Any names, characters, places, and incidents are the product of the author's imagination. Any resemblance to persons, living or dead, is entirely coincidental.

ISBN 979-8-9942517-2-0 (paperback)
ISBN 979-8-9942517-3-7 (ebook)

Published by Glass Cathedrals Press.

www.hardcastlewrites.com

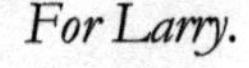

For Larry.

CONTENTS

R. Maeldon
SILGARIA
MIRKWALD
Mulruhm
L. Mulruhm
Kir Doon
Kir Mala
COLDREACH
MOUNTAINS
THE EVER WOOD
CROWN LAKES
Asaj
Ashborne
Banam
Sylphren Wood
Hollow
Mahab
Nuzibah
Levent Hills
Aen's Hollow
Mountains
Gede
TAMOR
Mirkwald R.
Flint
R. Aldria
L. Lagdo
Thorpe
Raith Crossing
ALDRIA
Fivewells
Savo
Nadell
Lembalt
Appencourt
Palmoor
Farhaven
Lembalt Archipelago
Finger Isles
Rigel
Falport
THE RUNE LANDS
BASTON SEA

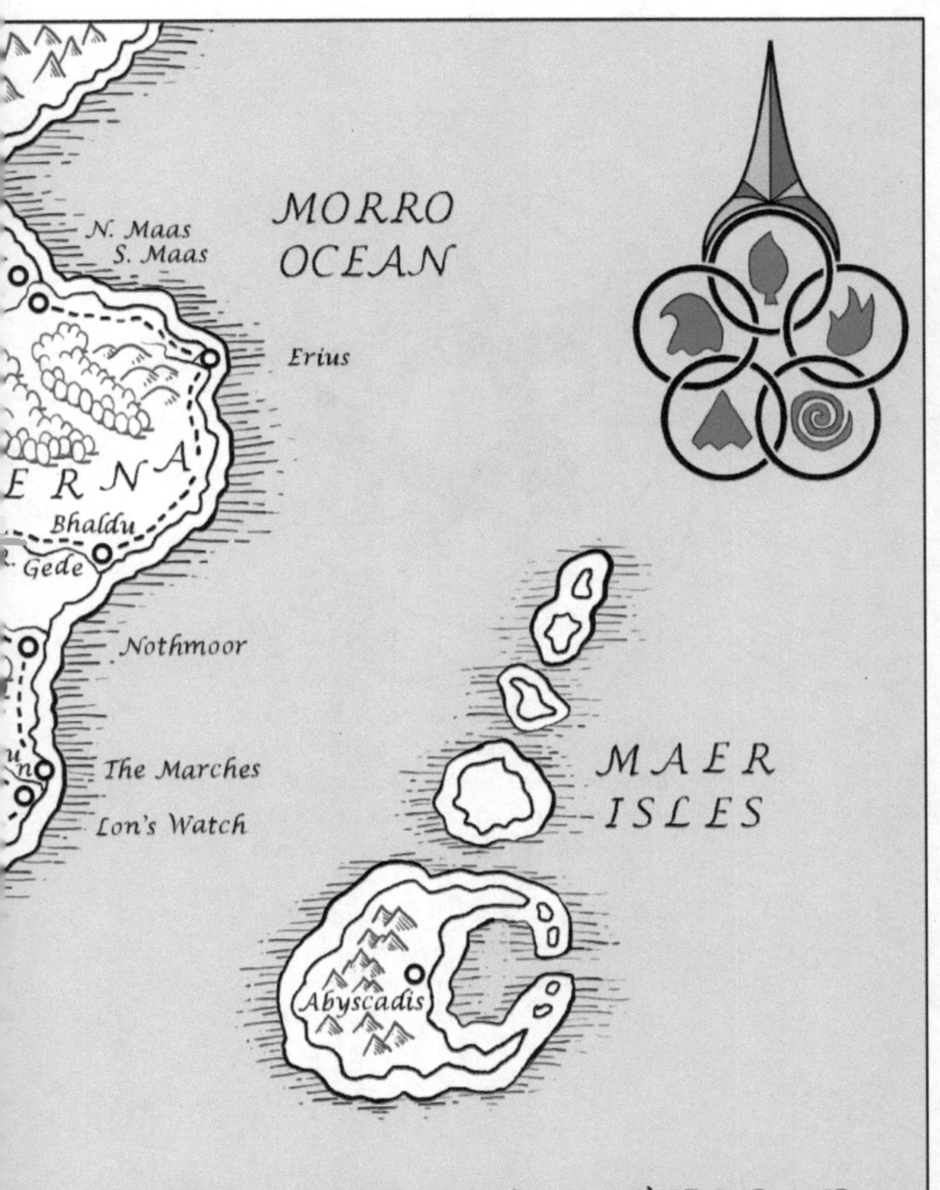

MORRO
OCEAN
N. Maas
S. Maas
Erius
ERNA
Bhaldu
Gede
Nothmoor
The Marches
Lon's Watch
MAER
ISLES
Abyscadis
ALDRIA AND ITS ENVIRONS

Root enhances Flame, as wood feeds the fire.
Flame enhances Aether, as heat warms the air.
Aether enhances Stone, as wind shapes the rock.
Stone enhances Wave, as banks guide the river.
Wave enhances Root, as rain fuels growth.

Root consumes Aether, as trees break the wind.
Aether consumes Wave, as the sky drinks the sea.
Wave consumes Flame, as water quenches fire.
Flame consumes Stone, as fire melts iron.
Stone consumes Root, as the axe hews wood.

Chapter 1
Ripples

JAYN ELDRAGOR HAD STOOD only once upon the shore of the great Morro Ocean. She had not dared to swim. Barefoot in the sand, she walked to the edge and let the waves lap over her feet. She felt the cold water glide around her ankles, the gentle ebb and flow, the subtle pull of the tide, connecting her to something vast and unknowable. In that moment, she understood what it meant to be a Wave Weaver.

She still remembered that experience weeks later as she stood on the stone platform and closed her eyes. She shifted her feet and let the ripples of energy swirl about her. She felt the weight of Thalia Moldo's hands upon her shoulders. Wave subsumes Stone, just as the river is channeled by its banks. It was just a metaphor—and maybe not the only possible one—but it was a useful metaphor. Jayn let the Stone flow through her. *Flow* wasn't the right word. Wave flowed. Stone grew. Either way, the crystalline pattern of yellow light that wasn't really light Blended with the ripples of Wave and became something new.

This time Jayn didn't flinch when the sliding wall reached her. She leaned into it, putting all her body weight against it, though she could not slow its movement. Even with Thalia behind her, they both began to slide. Jayn ignored all this as much as she could and focused on her lacing. The shield needed to be a very particular shape. If she could just get it in the right place and set it before… Her left foot slid over the edge. She still had a couple more seconds.

Thalia pulled her hands back just before they fell, cutting off the supply of Stone, and Jayn's lacing dissolved into nothing. They had learned from the last attempt that it was less painful to land separately than together in a tangle. She waited until the rope net stopped bouncing and swaying before opening her eyes.

Weaver lights set along the walls of the black stone chamber illuminated the strange series of platforms that hung suspended above her. She could not see the moving wall that had pushed her and Thalia off their platform, but she heard a low grinding sound as it retreated. This was the final challenge of the Gauntlet, and if even one person fell, the whole five-member Training Pentad had to start over.

The rope net bounced and swayed again as Shilo Lorn and Ryn Silverbell jumped down from where they had been waiting, one platform behind Jayn and Thalia. The net didn't move at all when Pavel Talvor glided down on a cushion of Aether. He'd made it farther than any of them. Normally someone would have groaned or grumbled by this point, but they were so close to the end that no one's resolve had broken.

It was impossible to maintain any grace or dignity crawling on your hands and knees along a web of thick ropes. Eight weeks ago, that would have bothered Jayn. Now she didn't care. Or she wouldn't have cared if it wasn't for Pavel Talvor. She glowered up at him as he walked easily across the swaying ropes toward the iron ladder that would take them back to the start of this final obstacle. He tucked his thumbs into the pockets of his gray trousers and even whistled a few bars of some melody as he strolled along the rope, swirls of white Aether keeping him balanced. There was a reason Aether Weavers made the best dancers and acrobats, though he was neither.

Jayn had mixed feelings about Pavel Talvor. The one-time thief was a decade older than the rest of the Pentad, though still handsome in a rugged and unkempt way, but he was beyond arrogant and often infuriating, a criminal with questionable morals. Still, when creatures from the pit had overrun Falport six weeks ago, he had fought bravely. Amidst the chaos, they had found themselves alone together for much of that long night. They had fought back-to-back at times and kept each other alive. If—or more likely when—they found themselves in peril again, she knew she could trust him, and yet…

"Come along, children," Pavel said, peering down at them with his idiot grin. Jayn and the others had made it halfway to the ladder, but he was already back up on the starting platform.

Everyone had learned not to encourage him, so Jayn and the others kept their heads down, moving forward until they rejoined him at the beginning of the room. The Gauntlet, an essential and frustrating part of Watchkeeper training, consisted of a series of stone chambers, all housed within an enormous tin warehouse. The chambers were open on top, but a flat ward of Wave served as a sort of ceiling that the recruits were not allowed to cross, and high above that lay the actual slanted ceiling of the warehouse.

Beyond the Wave ward, Captain Nyssa Lahmeer stood atop the thick wall. The setup allowed her and the other attendants who took turns guiding them through the Gauntlet to move freely and track their progress without having to participate in the trials themselves.

Nyssa regarded each of them as they stood catching their breath. "Now might be a good time to retire," she said. "The sun has surely set."

Jayn looked at her teammates. She saw the same grim determination in their tired faces that she still felt. Thalia spoke for the group. "We'll give it one more shot."

Jayn nodded in agreement. More often than not, Thalia spoke for the Pentad. Jayn felt on some level that she herself should have taken on leadership of the group. After all, Jayn was the daughter of Anyse Eldragor, Aldria's Fourth Pentarch. Jayn was a member of the first echelon of society and would someday be a Pentarch herself, if everything went to plan. Still, she didn't begrudge Thalia the role.

Thalia Moldo was a natural leader, though she didn't seem to know it. She was level-headed and pragmatic and had an ease with people that Jayn envied more than anything. Jayn did not like most people. The two of them could not be more different, even in appearance. Thalia stood a full foot taller, with broad shoulders and well-defined arms, a physique earned from years spent as a redsmith's apprentice before joining the Watchkeepers. She had lush, curly black hair and a rich tan complexion, while Jayn was slight and pale.

"Very well," Nyssa said. "Just remember, no group has ever finished this chamber on their first attempt."

Thalia grinned. "We can break that record at least."

"Technically," Pavel said, "this is only our seventeenth overall Gauntlet run, and the record is twenty."

Thalia shook her head. "Those were twenty attempts in four weeks. We've been here for eight. It's not the same."

Their schedule had been disrupted a mere two weeks into Watchkeeper training when Kobolds raided the compound, blew up the smithy, and killed dozens of Watchkeepers and nearly 200 citizens and city guards. The cleanup took weeks.

Jayn nodded in understanding. She too had wanted to break the Gauntlet record, but it wasn't a fair comparison. Though their Gauntlet attempts had been suspended for over a month, the Pentad had resumed training sooner than Jayn had expected. The surprise attack had given everyone within the Watchkeepers a heightened sense of urgency. No one understood why the Kobolds had attacked, where they came from, where they went, or if they would attack again. The organization needed as many able-bodied Weavers as they could get. Jayn's group had trained for much longer than whichever group had set the twenty-run record, and they were the only Training Pentad in memory to have faced actual combat and mortal peril during training. With all their experience, it would have been surprising if they *didn't* complete the Gauntlet in under twenty runs.

"Plus," Jayn said aloud, "all the Pentads before us also had to clear the mirror chamber."

The missing Runeform had also delayed their resumption of the Gauntlet. On top of all the other destruction wrought that day, a group of humans who were inexplicably working with the Kobolds had stolen and then somehow destroyed a Runeform that had been part of the Gauntlet. Apparently, the Council of Masters had spent a full week debating the best way to remedy that situation. Eventually, they had decided just to leave that room empty. When the Pentad reached the mirror chamber, they simply walked through to the next challenge. It was a strange reminder of all that had changed that night.

Pavel sighed. "There will be a gigantic asterisk in the ledger either way, but we won't be setting any sort of record if we don't get going." He gestured to the obstacle course of sorts that lay before them. Nothing was moving now; it wouldn't activate until they moved forward.

"Fair enough," Thalia said. She turned to face Jayn. "How close were you?"

Jayn frowned. She wanted to say that she almost had it. Instead, she shook her head. "There just isn't enough time. Or I'm not fast enough, not yet. If we're going to get this tonight, then we have to come at it differently."

Thalia nodded. "If we're not using the shield bridge, then how else can we cross the gap? Pavel can cross no problem, but none of the rest of us are making that jump."

"Maybe Shilo?" Pavel said. "She can use her Flame strength and chuck the rest of you across." He mimed an overhand throwing gesture.

Shilo grinned but shook her head. "I can't use that kind of force without breaking bones. Plus, I would be stranded, until that wall pushes me off the edge, and then we'd all be back down there."

Jayn glanced over the side of the platform. The actual bottom of the chamber lay hidden in shadows, but the fall to the safety net was still far enough to be jarring.

"Well," Pavel said, "if the shield bridge is the only way, how can we do it differently? How do we make it work?"

"Can you make it from farther back?" Thalia offered.

"No," Jayn said. "There's nowhere else close enough where I also won't get knocked down. I don't have that kind of range and certainly not enough energy left."

Watchkeeper recruits kept long hours and were only allowed to attempt the Gauntlet after a full day of training. Jayn had learned to chug water every chance she got, but by now her mouth was dry, her lips were chapped, and her temples throbbed with an all-too-familiar dehydration headache. Wave Weaving drained moisture from her body, so she had to be cautious and deliberate with every lacing she made.

Shilo cleared her throat. The curly-haired Flame Weaver was naturally shy and often made such preambles before venturing an opinion. "Maybe we can give Jayn more time. Maybe we can slow down the wall."

"How so?" Jayn asked.

Shilo gestured to the group's Root Weaver, who had been characteristically quiet the whole time. "Master Nox has been teaching Ryn and me about different ways to Blend Flame and Root. Basically, it all comes down to the transference of energy. Everything possesses something called dynamic energy. That's what Master Nox calls it. When an object isn't moving, it stores that energy. When the object moves, the energy is released. By Blending Root and Flame, we could convert the moving energy back into stored energy. Basically, we could stop the wall, or at least slow it down. It could give you the time you need." Shilo immediately lowered her eyes after saying all that. She toyed with the bulky locket around her neck, which contained no keepsake but a hunk of coal.

Jayn smiled. Shilo Lorn had come a long way since joining the Watchkeepers, though she still too often doubted herself. Born into a family of fishermen but with a gifting that meant she would never make it as a sailor, Shilo had grown up believing herself to be a failure. Jayn sometimes wondered if there had been a cosmic mix-up somehow, and she and Shilo had received the wrong gifts. As a Wave Weaver, Shilo would have made an excellent sailor, and as a Flame Weaver, Jayn could have fulfilled her dream of serving as an officer in the Standing Army. Of course, then neither one would have become a Watchkeeper. Jayn had come to appreciate her own abilities, but she still felt the occasional pang of jealousy when she saw Shilo in action.

"I've heard of that," Jayn said. "There are talented Flame Weavers in the Standing Army who can stop an arrow in flight."

"It's worth an attempt," Pavel said. "Do you two have enough juice left for that?" He looked at Shilo and Ryn in turn.

"Sure," Ryn said, "but are we allowed to tamper with the obstacles like that?"

Pavel scoffed. "Why not? That thing is part of a Runeform, so it's in—uh, indestructible."

He didn't need to explain the hesitation. For a thousand years since the Burning, as far as anyone knew, no Runeform had ever been damaged or destroyed, until six weeks ago when that mysterious Pentad of rogue Weavers shattered that mirror. It wasn't the only long-held notion to be shattered that night, though no one outside of Jayn's Pentad knew the other part.

Pavel craned his head back to look up at Nyssa. "What do you say, Captain Lahmeer? Is that within the rules?"

Nyssa studied their group for a moment before responding. "It is allowed, though draining a Runeform like that is not an easy task. Still, you are permitted to try."

Thalia shrugged. "Let's see what happens."

Pavel crossed the short gap from the first platform to the second. Each section hung fixed in the air without any visible supports. Runeforms came in all shapes and sizes and could do many miraculous things. They were all created over a millennium ago and predated recorded history, as history had reset following the Burning, which among other calamities had involved the global destruction of all written books and records.

As soon as Pavel's foot made contact, the platform sprang to life. The first challenge was not unlike an obstacle course Jayn had seen at the Standing Army's training camp outside of Savo. This platform was just wide enough for five people to walk abreast, but it was interrupted by thin pillars spaced along its length. Various-sized beams stuck out at different heights along each pillar, and the pillars all rotated in sync, creating a spinning maze of stone. Pavel didn't wait. The Aether Weaver danced his way through the whirling stone forest. The others followed as best they could.

This first challenge was tricky but not impossible. It took agility and timing, and eight weeks of weapons training and conditioning with Mistress Lane Whitcomb had prepared all of them for such a task. The stone beams weren't spinning fast enough to cause real damage, but if you weren't careful, they could sweep you off the edge. As she dodged her way through the course, Jayn saw Ryn jump back from one pillar swinging toward him, only to be caught by the one behind. The sandy-haired boy twisted and caught the beam that threatened to push him off the platform. He hung on as it swung him out over the edge. She couldn't wait to see if he managed to ride it back around. She had to keep moving.

She reached Pavel just behind Shilo and a little ahead of Thalia. A few moments later Ryn joined them. This was the only place they could stop to catch their breath, but there wasn't much room. They stood with their backs pressed against a five-foot stone wall, only inches away from the spinning beams. Thalia gave them a few seconds to recover before saying, "Let's go."

They all clambered over the wall. There was no room to stand atop it, and the far side presented a steep slope down into empty space. They allowed themselves to slide, got their feet under them, and jumped across the gap onto the next platform. This one was smaller, only about ten feet long, with a bigger gap between it and the next one. Pavel sprinted across and easily cleared the gap with an Aether-enhanced leap. None of the others could do that.

This platform also activated as soon as they landed. A massive stone block to their right hovered next to the slab they stood on, forming a right angle with it. A movable wall was set into the block in the same way a paper box slides into its lid. With a low grinding noise, this wall began to push out across the platform. When it reached the edge, they would have no place to stand. The top of the wall rose a few inches shy of the Wave ceiling, so they couldn't climb atop it either.

Shilo dashed forward, stopping halfway across the platform. She turned and slapped her palms against the advancing wall, as forking streaks of red Flame swirled around her. Ryn grabbed her shoulders and vines of Root erupted from his stomach. Jayn couldn't tarry to see if their lacing actually slowed the Runeform down. She dodged around them, with Thalia on her heels, and stopped at the edge.

Mistress Agia Bellos, the Watchkeepers' Wave master, had taught Jayn and Thalia about shield bridges earlier that week, and now it was obvious why she had. Their utility was limited, and they were generally impractical in most real-world situations. Still, it was a clever concept. A shield, formed by Wave and hardened into solidity by Stone, was most often used defensively, to keep things in or out. Only the Weaver who created the shield or an Aether Weaver who knew what he was doing, could destroy it. Of course, any set lacing would eventually dissolve on its own, though powerful ones could last for weeks.

Jayn's shield only needed to last for a handful of seconds, which made it easier to form, but it also had to be the right shape. A rectangular-shaped shield would never work, because no one would be able to walk across it. The surface of a shield was slippery—Mistress Bellos had called it "frictionless." Your foot would gain no traction, like stepping onto an impossibly slick frozen pond. You might be able to slide your way across, but you were just as likely to slide off into the pit. Sliding couldn't be avoided, but she could direct the slide.

Thalia's Stone merged with her Wave. She didn't think about the advancing wall as she focused on forming the perfect-shaped vessel. Most Wave Weavers only created cube- or dome-shaped wards, but only a lack of imagination constrained them. Jayn anchored one end to the edge of the platform and extended it out until it reached the next one. Wards could be extended across empty space, but they had to be connected to something solid. She modeled her shield after the slanted wall they had just hurdled. It rose sharply, though not too high, before gradually sloping down to the far platform. She even gave that long slope a concave surface to keep them from sliding over the sides.

Only once it was set did she glance to her right. The moving wall had come within inches of her and was still advancing, though much more slowly than last time. "Go," she said to Thalia. The Stone Weaver didn't hesitate. She couldn't climb up the steep side of the shield, so she jumped up and over and slid across to where Pavel waited. Jayn spun around. "It's set!"

Ryn's heels hung over the edge of the platform, as he stood behind Shilo, feeding her Root. Shilo kept channeling Flame into the wall—or was she siphoning energy out of it? She turned her head, perspiration beading on her face. "You first!" she called.

Jayn nodded. As soon as Shilo cut off her lacing, the wall would resume moving at its regular speed. Jayn turned and jumped onto the shield, easily clearing the steep rise and sliding headfirst toward the next platform. If any non-Weaver had seen her, she would have appeared to glide through thin air. To her eyes, the transparent shield was a shimmering web of dark blue light that oscillated between fluid ripples and a complex pattern of geometric tessellations.

Thalia helped Jayn regain her feet, and the girls turned to see Ryn and Shilo sliding almost on top of each other across the gap. They landed in a tangle on the solid platform, and a moment later, the shield bridge burst like a popped bubble and vanished without a sound. It had done its job.

This small platform offered them a genuine moment of rest, as nothing had activated when they reached it. Another short gap, easily hopped, led to the final leg of the obstacle. Beyond that lay a simple black stone ledge and a ladder that would take them up to the top where Nyssa already waited. They needed to finish this in one shot. That last lacing had nearly drained her.

"Your hands are still glowing," Thalia said.

Jayn turned back to the others. Indeed, Shilo had released her Flame lacing, but her hands still glowed with an internal light. Luminescence was a natural byproduct of Flame Weaving. Shilo looked at her hands. "It's all the energy I drained from that Runeform," she said, a strange sense of awe in her voice. "It was so… immense. As soon as I started, I didn't think it would work… But I guess it did."

"Good job," Jayn said, genuinely meaning it. Shilo had already expended a great deal of strength throughout the Gauntlet. Several of the rooms had been shrouded in darkness and required Shilo and Ryn to make Weaver lights for illumination. It was difficult to compare different types of Weavers, but Shilo may have been the strongest of all of them. Certainly, she had the deepest reservoir. Well, it was between her and Ryn. The unassuming, scrawny Root Weaver was a powerful healer, and he had undoubtedly saved her life on that blighted long night. In fact, the boy had pulled everyone in this room back from the brink of death at one point or another, including himself, as miraculous as that was.

Shilo smiled but then grew serious. "I'm not sure what to do actually. I can't hang onto this for much longer, but releasing it all... could be dangerous."

"It may come in handy on this next bit," Pavel said, gesturing toward the final obstacle. "On the last attempt, when it was clear Jayn wasn't going to set her bridge in time, I activated this one, just for a second, to see what it would do."

The platform before them was long and narrow. It ran between two floating stone walls, each set far enough back to leave a large gap. Dozens of gray spheres were affixed to each wall. By way of demonstration, Pavel extended one foot across to touch the platform. As soon as he did, the spheres came to life. Each one shot across to the other side, touched the opposite wall, and then rebounded. They bounced back and forth like so many rubber balls, though they never sped up or slowed down. Each time they bounced, their trajectory changed, seemingly at random. They were large enough and fast enough that a hit from any of them would likely send someone flying off the narrow path that lay between the walls, back into the net below. After a few moments, Pavel withdrew his foot.

"Simple enough for me," he said.

Jayn glanced at Ryn. "Deflection wards?" she said.

He nodded. "Sure. Of course, I can't set one on myself."

Jayn studied the obstacle again. How could they possibly get Ryn across?

"Possum ride," Pavel said.

"What?" Jayn asked.

"You know, possums." He pointed over his shoulder at his back. "They carry their babies on their back."

"What's a possum?" Ryn asked.

Pavel sighed. "I'm saying I can carry you on my back and run us through."

"Oh," Ryn said. "You can do that?"

"I can try. What about you? You still got the juice?"

Ryn studied each of the girls in their group, no doubt calculating how much Root it would take for three deflection wards and weighing it against his reserve. They all had to be close to their limits.

"I won't need one," Shilo said, clenching her still glowing hands into fists.

"Right," Ryn said with a nod. "I can try."

They had been working together long enough that they needed no further discussion to implement the plan. Jayn reached out her hands toward Ryn, and he grasped her forearms. She summoned her last bit of Wave, though she would reserve a small portion. If she allowed herself to be drained completely, she might black out. Supplying was easier than wielding, as it required no active thought. A spectral green oak tree formed around Ryn. She sent lines of Wave into its roots, tinging the tree a blue-green color, almost the same shade as the Morro Ocean. He sent branches out toward her and Thalia simultaneously, demonstrating the impressive level of mastery he had achieved in such a short time. Flickers of light swirled around Jayn and Thalia as Ryn set the wards and released his lacing. He staggered as he took a step toward Pavel.

Pavel grabbed his arm to steady him. "Easy, kid," he said. "We're nearly there."

"We got to be quick," Ryn said. "Those wards won't hold long."

"I'll go first," Shilo said, in a surprising moment of self-assurance. Or maybe she just couldn't hold the siphoned energy in any longer. She dashed forward, tucking her arms in close and bending her head down as swirling red lights surrounded her. She made no attempt to dodge the spheres that began flying back and forth. She didn't need to. Each time one made contact, there was a flash of light, and the ball rebounded off her.

"Right," Pavel said, watching her. "Let's do this, kid." He squatted down and Ryn hopped on his back, wrapping his arms around his shoulders and his legs around his waist. White light swirled down from the top of Pavel's head. He dashed forward, moving slower than he would have unencumbered, but still faster than most people. Aether gave him increased agility as well as a preternatural spatial awareness. He seemed to understand the trajectory of each flying ball and could dodge, duck, or jump his way past it, even with Ryn on his back.

Jayn glanced at Thalia. The deflection ward made her appear slightly blurry. They both nodded. Jayn jumped the gap and ran, with Thalia on her heels. There was no telling how long the wards would hold, but she just had to trust that they would. She kept her eyes fixed straight ahead and did her best to ignore the whizzing spheres. Even as tired as he had to be, Pavel still managed to show off. He jumped over one low-flying ball and then actually landed on another one in midflight, kicking off to get more height.

His buffoonery was a welcome distraction from the constant near misses the deflection ward created. True to its name, the ward altered the paths of the flying spheres just enough to miss her, or barely miss her. She felt the whoosh of air as they passed all around her, occasionally grazing her just enough to feel it, but not enough to hurt. When the spheres passed directly in front of her, it was hard not to hesitate or stop, but if she did, Thalia would run right into the back of her. She didn't know what would happen if two deflection wards collided, but likely they would both end up falling. Jayn was reminded of her first time testing a deflection ward, when Mistress Hinter, the former Root master, had gleefully chucked wooden blocks at her. No one had seen Gwen Hinter in six weeks. She had vanished with the Kobolds that night, apparently by choice.

Then Jayn was across, standing on the black stone ledge with the rest of her Training Pentad and panting to catch her breath. They were all exhausted, but every one of them was beaming. "Right," Pavel said, sticking out his fist with his little finger extended.

"No," Jayn said. "Absolutely not. That is so stupid." She laughed while she said it.

"Come on," Pavel said. "This is our thing. We have to do it."

The others were laughing now too, but they all extended their hands, grasping each other's pinkies and forming a circle with their fists. Pavel counted to three, and they all said, "Pentad!" like a bunch of idiots.

Overhead, Nyssa applauded. "Well done," she said. "Now climb on up."

It was an eerie sensation walking out of the room that housed the Gauntlet along the tops of the walls that divided the different chambers. Every time they had failed their previous attempts, they had been forced to retrace their steps back through the completed chambers. Now it felt as if they were walking along the clouds, staring down at the earth where mortals toiled below.

They climbed down the ladder back into the first chamber and hesitated before the exit. A banner hung on one wall, depicting the relationships between the Five Forces. Each force was represented by a different colored shape arranged around a white circle. Stone enhanced Wave, Wave enhanced Root, Root enhanced Flame, Flame enhanced Aether, and so on, in a never-ending circle. Crisscrossing black lines in the center represented all the ways in which the Five Forces could not interact. Stone destroyed Root. Root destroyed Aether. Or so everyone believed. So everyone had been taught.

"What are we going to do now?" Thalia asked. "I mean, will we still have to run the Gauntlet next week?" Today was Foamsday, the fifth day of the week, and they would not have regular lessons again until after the weekend.

Nyssa shook her head. "Not unless you want to. Starting next week, your afternoon schedules will look a bit different. Each of you will begin lessons on wielding your complementary forces."

Jayn smiled. She would start working with Root and Stone on her own, unaided by Ryn or Thalia. Soon she would be able to wield two forces at the same time, creating her own shields or deflection wards.

Nyssa held up a cautioning hand. "A word of warning though. Each of you is a gifted Weaver in your own right. However, aptitude with your natural gifting does not always translate to success with complementary forces. It may be a struggle." She pointed to Jayn and Shilo. "Root is especially challenging for almost everyone."

They all nodded, though a quick glance around showed Jayn that they were all still eager to begin that training.

"Now hurry off to dinner before they toss whatever has been set aside for you."

Nyssa ushered them out and turned off toward the officers' dorms, while the Training Pentad angled their steps toward the towering black Citadel at the center of the Watchkeeper compound, which housed the dining hall, among other things.

The moon rode high overhead, amidst a sea of stars, shining down upon a warm night as the seasons turned from spring to summer. Despite the aching in her bones and the dryness of her throat, Jayn felt elated. She did not want such a night to already be over. "So…" she said, dragging the word out so everyone would know what she was about to suggest. "Secret Training?"

They groaned.

"Come on, just for a little bit. I don't want to go to bed yet."

No one spoke up, though Pavel's stomach growled audibly as if in protest.

She laughed. "After dinner, of course."

The head cook, who was surprisingly well informed about everything going on within the compound, must have anticipated that they were going to finish the Gauntlet that day—or else would need plenty of consolation if they failed. She had left a veritable feast waiting for them in the dimly lit dining hall, kept warm on Flame-laced heating pads. They all ate heartily, though no one as much as Pavel. Continuous Aether Weaving drained the body of the energy that food imparted and made him ravenously hungry. Jayn chugged about a gallon of water in between mouthfuls of food.

The food definitely helped, but they were all sore and weary. Still, Jayn managed to convince them to follow her down into the forgotten storage room in the Citadel's dusty basement for a late-night round of what the group called Secret Training. It was an uninspired name, but no one had come up with a better term for the clandestine gatherings the group held most nights after the end of their official Watchkeeper regimen. There they could practice things that, while not explicitly forbidden, would have raised too many eyebrows and questions if the Watchkeepers knew about it.

"All right," Pavel said, once he had secured the door, and Ryn and Shilo had lit the room with a single Weaver light. "Let's make it a short session. We still have chores in the morning… I'll never get used to saying that."

"What are we going to try?" Thalia asked, deferring to Jayn, since she had insisted on meeting.

She looked at Ryn and then Pavel. "I think they should try the Blending."

Pavel groaned. "No, come on. We've tried that for ages. It only worked the one time."

"But it *did* work," Jayn said. "We *think* other Blendings might work, but this is the only one we know for sure can happen. It did happen, didn't it?"

She looked at the men and at Thalia. They had witnessed it or been a part of it. Shilo and Jayn had been unconscious at the time, but the others never wavered in their conviction, and she had come to believe that it indeed must have happened, as impossible as that was.

"Fine," Pavel said with a sigh. "You want to give it a go, kid?"

Ryn only nodded. He moved over to the corner where he had concealed his small knife behind an empty crate. Recruits were not supposed to carry weapons on the compound, even a little whittling knife. Ryn did not hesitate to draw it from its leather sheath and make a shallow cut along the back of his forearm. No Root Weaver could heal his own wounds, except for Ryn, who could achieve it through his unique Etching. Except, he still could not deliberately activate his Etching. The cut on his arm would eventually heal spontaneously, but it could take hours. Only once had he been able to heal himself in a different way, when he could not afford to wait, when Jayn and Shilo were dying from Kobold poison.

Pavel placed his hands on Ryn's shoulders, as a Root tree grew up around the boy. Pavel released a steady stream of Aether. Root and Aether were opposing forces. They did not Blend. Root consumed Aether, just as trees break the wind. As Ryn had pointed out, it was a weak metaphor. But it was just a metaphor, a poetic image meant to help recruits understand the ways the Five Forces interacted. Root wasn't really tree roots. Aether wasn't really the wind or the force that animated living things, as the element was alternately believed to represent. Still, it was an accurate metaphor, or it always had been. Indeed, Root did consume Aether. The wispy streaks of white light dissolved upon contact with Ryn's tree.

How then had Ryn managed to Blend the two opposing forces? He'd described it a thousand times. In his moment of desperation, he had created a new metaphor. Wind stirs the leaves. Ryn's lips were moving now as he reached out for the Aether, and she knew he was chanting it. Wind stirs the leaves.

"Wind stirs the leaves," she said beneath her breath, willing it to work.

She saw it happen. A narrow shoot of Root reached for the Aether. The white light quivered, but it held. The tendril of Root wrapped around the Aether, absorbing it and turning a lighter shade of green. It held for only a second, and then the Aether frayed away into nothing. But it had held. And Jayn had seen it. She could not doubt it. It was an impossibility, a genuine miracle. But it had happened. And if that could happen, it meant that any Blending was possible, *anything* was possible. It meant that someday, somehow, Jayn Eldragor might still become a Flame Weaver.

Chapter 2
Mushrooms

RYN STILL DID NOT KNOW what to make of the new Root master. Granted, Alton Pembrim had been in the position for only about a week, but he was proving to be even more eccentric than his predecessor. Ryn had also only known Mistress Gwen Hinter for a short time, but she had seemed likeable enough. Initially, he had a hard time believing that she had been willingly working with the Kobolds, but as the weeks rolled by with no sign of her, alive or dead, that appeared to be the only explanation. Others within the Watchkeepers simply stopped talking about her, like she had never existed.

Ryn's Training Pentad had mulled the mystery over more than once. On the night the Kobolds attacked Falport, Shilo witnessed Mistress Hinter stabbing another Watchkeeper to death before slinking away into the night. Perhaps she had not known how brutal the Kobold assault was going to be, but rather than come forward and confess her role in the plot, she chose to murder a fellow Weaver and flee, either alone or with the other unidentified humans who had aided the Kobolds.

In the aftermath of the attack, Ryn volunteered with the other Root Weavers in caring for the wounded. Mistress Hinter had forbidden him from healing until he'd been properly trained, but with hundreds of wounded and maimed citizens, guards, and Watchkeepers, they needed all the help they could get. He learned much in that long week. When performing triage on such a scale, Root Weavers had to be coldly calculating. Healing multiple serious wounds was extremely draining. Those with minor injuries were only given Rootbalm to ward off infection and a pain-numbing tea. They faced longer recoveries, and many would be left with scars, but true healing had to be reserved for the more grievous cases.

Indeed, the goal seemed to be to use Root as little as possible, in order to help the most people. Fully restoring a victim on the verge of death would completely drain most Root Weavers, so Ryn learned how to perform a partial healing, focusing only on the most severe injuries and leaving the rest to be treated with medicine and time. Root Weavers also did what they could to make an injury easier to heal through Weaving. Stitching a wound closed with a needle and threads of silk helped, as did setting a broken bone back into position before lacing it.

It had been tough to Dowse victims, see in his mind's eye everything wrong with them, and then decide what if anything needed to be done. It was hard to move on when he knew someone was in pain, but after he blacked out on the second day from using too much Root, he learned his lesson. The hours he spent unconscious were hours he could have been helping others. After that, he spent every waking moment he could in those large white tents they had set up on the lawn of the Watchkeeper compound.

Those field hospitals looked more like greenhouses than sickrooms, with all the plants. Draining energy from vegetation helped Root Weavers conserve their own strength. A team of servants hauled out the shriveled brown husks and replaced them with a steady stream of fresh plants. They used mostly greedvine, a climbing plant Ryn had not heard of before. It was considered a pest in most places because of how quickly it grew. If left unchecked, it could take over an entire garden. The Watchkeepers kept a dedicated greenhouse for cultivating the plant on long trellises that could be easily transported for such times of need.

Pavel had come up with a theory that the Kobolds had a fast-acting poison on their claws. When he and Ryn had first met Captain Nyssa Lahmeer, her Pentad's Root Weaver had died suddenly after receiving only a scratch from a Kobold. Other events from that time also suggested the existence of a poison or venom. Ryn shared this concern with the Root Weavers treating the victims, yet none of them had been able to definitively identify a poisonous agent in the blood of any of the wounded. It was true that many died before they could receive treatment, some of injuries that should not have been life-threatening, and scratch marks from the Kobolds were unusually resistant to Rootbalm and prone to infection, but no one could confirm an actual poison at work. It was one of the many mysteries that still remained from that night.

Eventually, everyone who could be helped had been, and the Stone Weavers had sealed up the breach in the city wall and begun work on restoring the destroyed smithy. Then Ryn's group resumed their training schedule. For several weeks, various other Root Weavers within the organization had filled in for Mistress Hinter, teaching Ryn and Jayn as best as they were able, until finally the Council of Masters decided on a new Root master: Alton Pembrim.

Master Pembrim had not been among the volunteers who filled in to teach lessons, but Ryn had seen him in those hospital tents.

Master Pembrim was strange. Ryn had heard the Root Weaver cadets say more than once that Pembrim behaved more like a Scholar than a Watchkeeper. Scholars had a reputation for being eccentric. Pembrim spent most of his time in a cellar near the greenhouses, where he grew and cultivated mushrooms. He wore thick spectacles and was always squinting whenever outside, as if unused to the harsh light of the sun. He perpetually had dirt under his fingernails, and his dense black hair grew in a frizzy mass around his head. Pembrim's mood alternated between an intense and excited passion for his work and a dull uncommunicative despondency, switching seemingly without pattern or reason.

He was in his dull and silent state now, as he worked alongside Ryn making Rootbalm, following a joint lesson with Jayn. Ryn didn't mind. His thoughts were also elsewhere. That afternoon he would begin his new set of lessons with the Wave and Flame masters. He had never even attempted to wield a force other than Root, so he was eager to begin.

"What do you know about detection?" Master Pembrim asked.

It took Ryn a moment to respond. The question had been asked without warning or context. "I'm sorry?" he finally managed to say.

"Detection. It's one of the less flashy facets of Root Weaving. Has no one taught you about that yet?"

"No, I don't think so."

"Hmm. Well, under the circumstances, such omissions are inevitable, I suppose. Put down your mortar."

Ryn had been grinding up a mixture of rindwort and kind-marrow into a paste to serve as a simple basis for Rootbalm. On their own, the herbs were good for treating fevers and infections, and Root greatly enhanced those properties. He set down his mortar and pestle and turned his attention toward Master Pembrim.

Pembrim cleared his throat and seemed to take a moment to put his thoughts together before continuing. "When you Dowse someone, you make a connection to their… essence, their lifeforce, their soul—whatever you want to call it. You gain an awareness of them that goes beyond normal perception. Detection is simply Dowsing from further out. You don't pick up on anything close to what you get from Dowsing. Mostly, it's just a sense of where something is. Relative location. Do you know what I mean?"

Ryn nodded. "Yes, actually. I think… Well, I didn't know what was happening at the time, but I think I have used detection before. For about a year before I found out I was a Root Weaver, I was able to sense where silverbells were buried in the woods where I lived."

Ryn winced after saying that. He had only recently understood how sheltered his life had been in those woods. He'd been raised by his herbalist aunt, and his education had been sparse and sporadic. He'd had almost no understanding of what Weaving even was until he met Pavel. Ryn's second name, if he had one, had been among the many things Aunt Marla neglected to teach him, and so, when he joined the Watchkeepers, Ryn had to make up a second name for himself. He realized now how strange it sounded to say he had a knack for digging up silverbells, when his second name supposedly *was* Silverbell. If Master Pembrim recognized the coincidence, he made no comment, thankfully.

"Interesting," he said. "Generally, when an Etching manifests, that is the first real sign of being a Weaver, yet your gifting was operating on some level for a year. I suppose, of course, that if you were never injured during that year, you would not have known you could heal yourself."

Ryn had never made the connection, but it made sense hearing it from Master Pembrim. Just because he had only become aware of his Etching that day in the woods when Kobolds attacked him and left him for dead, that didn't necessarily mean that was the first day it could have activated. Weavers without unique Etchings had to be tested to know if they had the gift, though there were often other signs. If a fisherman's son took to the water as if made for it, he would be tested for Wave Weaving. If a young girl was naturally graceful or fearless in climbing trees, she might be tested for Aether. A child could not be tested until mid- or late adolescence, however, because that was when the gift fully materialized or activated.

Ryn only had a moment to think about all that before Master Pembrim continued. "It makes sense that you were able to pick up on such a mushroom, however. Personally, I don't care much for the taste of silverbells, though interestingly they are impossible to cultivate and can only be harvested in the wild, which is what makes them so expensive. One of the many mysteries of mushrooms. Animals, of course, are easiest to detect, but you also pick those up with your eyes and ears, so it's easy to miss the extra layer of perception. Plants are barely perceptible to most Weavers, so mushrooms would stand out."

Ryn's forehead wrinkled at that comment. "Are… mushrooms not plants?" he asked.

Master Pembrim laughed but without condescension. Despite his strangeness, Pembrim was a patient teacher. "No, though I understand why you might think that. If you ever Dowse a fungus, that will become readily apparent."

"What are they then?"

He shrugged. "They are simply their own thing. You have animals here and plants there," he said, gesturing to the right and left, "and then you have fungi somewhere in the middle. They are like plants, but equally like animals. They are very strange, which is why they have always fascinated me. I am also somewhat of an expert on detection, which is why I bring it up. It's a skill worth developing. Apparently, I haven't told you this yet, but I have an Etching of my own. My detection ability is far more advanced than any other Root Weaver. Follow me."

They were working in a shed that Mistress Hinter had also previously used for lessons, a comfortable space crammed with everything an herbalist would ever need. Master Pembrim walked to the open door. He gestured toward the nearest greenhouse. "In that building you will find eight humans, all Watchkeeper cadets, as well as 120 plant specimens, representing forty-one different species. I can't even begin to count the bugs, but none of them are harmful to the plants." He paused for a long moment, before adding in a softer voice. "Did you know that in an acre of healthy soil, there are as many as a million earthworms?"

Ryn's eyes widened. "You can sense all that?"

Master Pembrim nodded. "It makes a fun party trick, I'll tell you that."

Ryn wondered what sorts of parties Master Pembrim went to. He also wondered if the man had actually counted all those earthworms before. He asked neither of those questions. "What about Kobolds? I mean, I think I've also been able to sense their presence before. It started the first time I encountered them. Back in the Sylphren Wood that day, there were three standing behind me, and I could sense their presence before I turned around."

"Hmm. That's even more interesting. It makes sense that they would have stood out to you though. You were a Weaver for a full year before you realized it, so by that point you had a pretty good sense of what belonged in your woods and what most definitely did not." He sighed. "Those Kobolds are a big fat question mark. I wish we could have taken one alive. You've never Dowsed a corpse before, have you?"

"Um… Yes, actually."

Pembrim grimaced. "Sorry. I won't press for details. No doubt you were hoping they might still be alive. There's nothing more disheartening as a healer than finding that dark void. It's not completely empty, however, if you have the stomach to look close enough. You can still get a sense of what once comprised the body and how those parts might have worked when still animated, if you know what you are looking for. You don't get nearly as much as you could from a live specimen."

Ryn wasn't sure what Master Pembrim was going on about. The question about Dowsing and dead bodies had stirred up some unpleasant memories he tried to push aside. Was Pembrim saying that he had been Dowsing Kobold corpses? Ryn tried to form a question, but the man was already moving briskly along. He seemed to be climbing from his slump back into a more loquacious frenzy.

"Since you clearly have the aptitude for it," he said, "we're going to start honing your detection skills. It has a lot more uses than just finding mushrooms. We'll start by trying to tune you into humans. They give off quite a big presence. It's hard to tell people apart at any distance, but you should be able to home in on people you know very well, such as your Pentad members. Think about how useful that could be in the field, huh?"

The remainder of the session passed quickly, though the next one in which Ryn mainly fed a stream of Root for Shilo to manipulate under Master Jalen Nox's supervision dragged on. Still, Ryn ate quickly at the lunch hour, eager for the new slate of afternoon classes. The second half of the day was divided into three sections. First, Ryn would learn to channel Flame back with

Master Nox. Then, he would tackle Wave under Mistress Agia Bellos. The third slot of the day would alternate between more weapons training and conditioning under Mistress Lane Whitcomb and lessons covering the laws of Aldria. Watchkeepers helped maintain civil order within the nation, so they had to know the rules that governed it.

Ryn found that first set of afternoon classes ultimately disappointing. He had worked with Master Nox before, so he knew the man to be stern and unemotional but not harsh or abusive in his teaching, as his brusque demeanor initially suggested. Flame Weaving began by envisioning a Flame within your chest, which at first seemed a subtle distinction from Root, which formed in the pit of your stomach. The difference became apparent after a long hour of trial and error.

Ryn wanted to master Flame because he wanted to be able to fight. He nearly died in his first encounter with the Kobolds. He would have died if not for his Etching. Then in short succession he witnessed three other Kobold attacks, including the massive raid on Falport. Each time he'd been a helpless bystander, able to do little more than heal the survivors in the aftermath. He was a short, scrawny kid and not much good in a fight, though Mistress Whitcomb had been training him in using and throwing knives and had recently started him on the bow. Flame could give him a decent shot at winning his next confrontation. He didn't know how or why, but he knew with a sickening certainty that he would face Kobolds again someday.

Master Nox must have sensed some part of Ryn's resolve, because he was quick to caution him about expecting too much. Most Root Weavers could learn to generate heat, useful for making a spark to light a candle, or for Blending with Root to make orbs of light, but few could throw the powerful punches that Flame

Weavers were famous for. Even if they could, Master Nox was quick to remind Ryn, a Root Weaver's place was not at the forefront of a fight. The Pentad must work to keep their Root Weaver out of the fray, so he can heal them after the battle. Ryn tried not to be stymied by that argument, though it was perfectly reasonable. By the end of their hour together, Ryn had conjured a few red flickers of Flame, but he couldn't do anything with it. Not yet.

The second session with Mistress Bellos was equally disheartening. He'd had few interactions with the Wave master since enlisting, and Ryn was still trying to get a read on her. She quickly informed him that she would not bother teaching him any Wave lacings. If he wanted to try his hand at wards, he could talk to Jayn or Nyssa in his own time. The sole purpose of teaching him Wave, she informed him, was so that he could Blend it into his own Root lacings, a role currently filled by Jayn. Weavers had the most success picking up the force that enhanced their inherent gifting, so he was optimistic. Indeed, before their hour was up, he could reliably summon lines of Wave, even though it started bizarrely in the soles of one's feet.

Blending two forces together proved too challenging for that first lesson. Creating a lacing of Root came almost automatically to him now, but envisioning Wave on top of that required a new level of mental focus. If he was able to generate ripples of Wave at all, his Root tree would vanish in the process. It was as if he needed to be able to split his mind into two separate sections. Still, Mistress Bellos assured him that it was a promising start and offered a rare smile.

The third lesson on the laws of the land, while important, was boring, though he did rejoin his Training Pentad for it. Mistress Bellos taught the class. She was the most senior of the Watchkeeper

Weaving masters, so she took on extra tasks such as this. The first lesson focused largely on the legal distinction between minor and major crimes, using theft as the main example. Ryn and his friends had to avoid looking at Pavel to stop themselves from bursting into inappropriate laughter. The group's Aether Weaver had built some reputation as a thief before straightening out his ways. Pavel sat leaned back in his chair, listening to the lecture, affecting the most innocent look he could.

Ryn learned from the group's discussion at dinner afterward that none of his teammates had experienced much success with their complementary forces either. Still, no one protested when Jayn suggested once again that they sneak down to the Citadel's basement for some Secret Training. This early in the evening, plenty of servants and other Watchkeepers still bustled around the massive black-stone building, so sneaking down into the basement unseen wasn't always easy, but they'd had plenty of practice.

They began their Secret Training, as they often did, by attempting to recreate the impossible Blending of Root and Aether. They did not succeed. Ryn thought over what he had learned that day. "Maybe we can come at this a different way," he said.

Pavel sighed, shutting off his flow of Aether. "I'm open to suggestions," he said.

"What if you taught me how to use Aether?"

Pavel raised an eyebrow. "You think that would help?"

"Any Weaver can learn to use any of the Five Forces. Lots of people have told me that."

"True," Thalia cut in. She and the other two girls had been watching Ryn and Pavel's attempts. "However, while you might be able to create a small amount of Aether, it's unlikely you'll be able to create any lacings with it. That's why the Watchkeepers don't bother teaching us opposing forces."

"There are exceptions," Shilo said. "I've seen Master Nox use Stone to repair training dummies."

Ryn nodded along to their comments. "I don't need to make any Aether lacings," he said. "I just need to generate enough to combine it with my Root."

Pavel smirked. "Oh, so you're just trying to get rid of me, then, is that it?"

Ryn shrugged. "I think it might simplify the process. They keep telling us that so much of Weaving is believing that what you are doing is going to work. I know that Root and Aether can Blend, so if I'm controlling both sides, it might be easier."

"So, I'm the problem, then? My doubt is stopping the Blend?"

"Well..." Ryn lowered his eyes. "Do you believe it will work?"

Ryn had learned that most anytime Pavel acted indignant, it was merely for show. Now he seemed to grow more serious at that question. He mulled it over before responding. "Maybe you are on the right track, kid. I saw it happen. I was a part of it, so I shouldn't have reason to doubt it. But then... Well, when you see something impossible, you have to find a way to rationalize it, to make it make sense. Like maybe that was just a fluke, or some strange distortion of reality caused by Thalia's luck charm."

Clearly, Pavel had given the events of that night a lot of thought. It made sense. At the time, Ryn had only begun to grasp the rules that supposedly governed the Five Forces, but the others had all grown up knowing them. They knew that Root and Aether didn't mix, just as the sun rises in the east and never in the west. It was a law of nature that Ryn had violated. They all had needed to find a way to come to terms with it. Ryn was glad that they had handled it so well, and that no one had felt moved to report him. He had known from the start that they would have to keep what he had done a secret, though he couldn't exactly say why. Blending

Aether and Root was not a forbidden act; there was no need to forbid things that are impossible, but it felt like a forbidden act. He worried that the Council of Masters would react in fear and anger if they found out about it. Of course, more likely, they would simply not believe that it had ever happened—in the midst of the chaos and madness of that night, Ryn had just imagined the Blending. That certainly made more sense than him altering the fabric of reality.

A long silence fell over the group. Ryn knew they all must be thinking back on the events of that long night. Pavel broke the quiet by saying, "But I will teach you Aether."

"Thanks," Ryn said. He knew this would not be easy. He couldn't even Blend Root and Wave yet, and those forces *wanted* to mix together, but he could make a start.

Thalia smiled and regarded the others. "And what about the rest of us?" she said, affecting cheerfulness to lighten the mood.

Shilo only shrugged. She looked tired, more so than usual at this time of night. Perhaps she had pushed herself too hard in her attempts to learn Root and Aether that afternoon.

Jayn chewed her bottom lip before responding. "I think Ryn might be onto something. We've tried every other Blending with no success, but we know it has to be possible. Logically, we can't assume that Root and Aether is the one exception that happens to work. If those two can Blend, then we must also be able to Blend Root and Stone, or Wave and Flame, or any combination."

"So," Thalia said, "you think we should all try learning to wield our opposing forces?"

"It might help. Certainly, it will be hard, but what we're doing now just feels like running our heads into the wall. This afternoon when Master Caston was teaching me Stone, I asked him… Well, not about any of this, but…" She cleared her throat before continuing. "You may all remember that before I found out I was a Wave Weaver, I was hoping to manifest as a Flame Weaver. My parents and all my grandparents had that talent, so it seemed reasonable to expect it. I failed the test for Flame. I couldn't brighten the candle. Then I tested for Wave, and I passed. If I had tested for Root or Stone then, I would have failed. However, now I can at least begin to create those forces, and with practice, I know I could also learn to brighten a candle with Flame. So, I asked Master Caston why only the test for Wave worked back then and why it was impossible for me to envision Flame."

That was a good question. Ryn had never thought about it like that, and a quick glance around the group told him the others were also curious to know what Master Caston had told her.

Jayn smiled as she continued. "Well, he gave me another metaphor. He said the Five Forces are like a treasure that is buried underground, but someone has dug a hole down to it. It is a narrow hole, and we can only just reach our arm down into it. For most people, the hole does not exist, and they cannot access any of the Five Forces. However, Weavers can just barely get their hand in to touch a part of it. Whatever part lies closest to the surface, that is our inherent gift, the force that dictates what type of Weaver we are. I tried to reach for Flame, but there was too much dirt in the way. Then without even trying, my hand found Wave. Or maybe you could say my foot fell into the hole."

Thalia laughed. "That does make sense," she said.

"Then he went on," Jayn continued. "He said each time we reach into that hole, we widen the gap, and it gets easier. Eventually, more of the treasure gets exposed, and we can begin to touch the complementary forces. That's also why the Watchkeepers taught us to Blend with each other from the start of our training. We each know where our piece of the treasure lies, so in a sense, we were showing each other how to get there. Master Caston said that if I tried, I could probably begin to dig in a deliberate way, to claw my way down and underneath the treasure, where the opposing forces lie. Of course, he was quick to remind me that the Watchkeepers would not bother to teach me Flame or Aether. Watchkeeper training focuses only on the practical."

It was a good metaphor. Ryn wondered how far you could take it. Could someone excavate the treasure completely? Would they then be able to wield any of the Five Forces at will? Probably, such an ability would take a lifetime of practice to achieve.

Thalia nodded along. "I think we should try it. The Watchkeepers are teaching us the complementary forces, so if we drill in opposing forces on our own, well, we will be widening that gap. That should be useful even if it doesn't lead to success with new Blendings."

Shilo cleared her throat and said without raising her eyes, "Jayn, if you want, I could try teaching you Flame."

Weeks ago, Ryn would have missed it, but he saw Jayn conceal a smile. He knew some part of what it would mean to her to master Flame. He glanced around the group. "I'll teach Root to anyone who wants to try it," he said. "I still think we also need to work on creating new metaphors. That will help with the Blendings. Water quenches the flames, that's what they tell us, so you need to think of a way in which Flame would help Wave, and then believe it."

"That is a tough one," Thalia said.

"Yes," Pavel said. "Water and fire famously don't mix. Hmm, what about..." He scratched the black stubble on his chin and then said in his best affectation of a wealthy gentleman, "The furnace warms the bathwater?"

Ryn couldn't help but laugh at that. Jayn cracked a sly smile but said nothing. She really must have wanted to learn Flame, if

Pavel's jibes at her high-class background couldn't arouse the usual response from her.

Chapter 3
Pains

SHILO LORN WASN'T SLEEPING WELL. Often, she found herself lying awake at night, staring up at the white plastered ceiling. Hers was the top bunk in the room she shared with Thalia and Jayn. Back home when she couldn't sleep, she would slip out of her room and sit at the end of the family dock, staring up at the stars and listening to the waves lap against the pilings. Here she could not do that. She did not want to disturb the other girls by climbing out of bed, and she didn't know where she would even go if she did leave her room. So, she just lay there, staring up at the white expanse of ceiling, wishing it held stars.

Master Nox was the first to notice her growing fatigue, or at least, he was the first person to say something to her about it. This was during her morning session with him, on the third day of their new training schedule. "Rough night?" he asked, after she failed to suppress a yawn.

She shrugged. "I just had trouble staying asleep."

He nodded. Master Nox was a short but solidly built man who kept his hair cropped close to little more than black stubble. He spoke in a soft voice with hardly any inflection, but Shilo liked him. He had sought her out in the aftermath of the Kobold attack to make sure she was all right. He had also given her the locket of sorts that she now wore around her neck. No mere trinket, it housed a lump of coal, an important source of strength for Flame Weavers. Master Nox reminded her in many ways of her father. She wished her father were here in Falport. She wondered how things were back in Palmoor and resolved to write to him soon. She had not written home since shortly after the attack on the compound, letting them know she was all right. She had received letters from both her parents, as well as her younger brother Lou, but she had not yet written back.

Master Nox hesitated before responding, which was rare for him. "Your time so far with the Watchkeepers has been… less than conventional, and I know how taxing training can be even under normal circumstances. I may not be the best person to talk to, but you should talk to someone. You haven't been focusing, and frankly, it seems like you're not really trying half of the time."

She could not meet his gaze. "I'm sorry. I know what you mean." She looked at her hands. "When I joined the Watchkeepers, I saw it as a way I could help people, to make the world… safer somehow."

"And you no longer see it this way?"

"It's not that. I just… I look at someone like Ryn, with his amazing gift. He's helped so many people already. There wasn't much I could do after the attack, but I volunteered where I could, and I saw Ryn day after day healing people with the rest of the Root Weavers."

"Hmm, so you wish you were a Root Weaver and not a Flame Weaver?"

"Not exactly. What I can do… I guess it just scares me sometimes. I don't want to hurt people."

As Master Nox had repeatedly told her, Flame was not inherently violent, yet its most practical use was in fighting. Flame Weavers aren't stronger than regular people. They don't throw their punches any faster or harder, but Flame amplifies the force of the impact and gives the illusion of superhuman strength. On top of that, Shilo's unique Etching allowed her to impart something else, a kind of energy generated by thunderstorms and magnetic rocks, what Master Nox called static energy. The first time it manifested, she had sent a grown man flying through the railing of her family's fishing boat. She didn't know if he had survived that punch. She hadn't meant to do it, but he was a pirate. If she hadn't hit him, he would probably have killed her father, or one of her brothers, or her. The second time she used her Etching on someone, she knew what she was doing, and she had meant to kill. She had punched a Kobold named Kalo, who seemed to be their leader. If he had been a human, or even a regular Kobold, he would have died, but Kalo was something else, a Kobold who was also somehow a Weaver. She didn't regret either punch. Kalo would have killed her and all of her friends if she hadn't stopped him. Still, she had never set out to be a killer.

Master Nox allowed a long silence to elapse before speaking. "Let me show you something," he said. He walked out into the center of the room, away from the training dummies. He was always barefoot in his dojo, and Shilo had learned to take her boots off and leave them by the door as well. He took up a sparring stance and nodded to her. She stood opposite him, putting her hands up as he had taught her.

Then he hit her.

The Flame sprang from his chest and wrapped his arm before she knew what was happening. His right hook swung around her guard and struck her in the shoulder. She fell to the ground under the force of the blow. She lay stunned for a long moment before she realized what had happened.

It didn't hurt. In fact, she had barely felt the punch. Why then had she collapsed? What kind of lacing had he used? She tried to sit up but couldn't. Her left arm wasn't working. Leaning to the side and using only her right arm, she managed to push herself up into a seated position. Her left arm hung useless at her side. It was like she had slept on it wrong the entire night, but with none of the tingling or dead-weight heaviness that came with such a numb limb. Sensation had vanished completely from her arm, as if it wasn't there. She looked up at Master Nox, who stood at attention with his arms folded behind his back as if nothing had happened.

He grinned when he saw her puzzled face. "Don't worry, feeling will return in a few minutes."

"What did you do?"

"I should have taught you this much sooner. I admit I've been focusing too heavily on testing your Etching. It is fascinating, but as you've realized, it will seldom be practical in the field. If the stars are kind, you may never have to face Kobolds again. Most of your time as a Watchkeeper will be spent tracking down rogue Weavers, and the goal will be to disable and detain, not to kill. The numbing lacing I just used will help you do that. At full force, it will leave your opponent completely paralyzed below the neck for up to half an hour. It will do no lasting harm either." He paused and then grew more serious. "If fate wills it though, and you find yourself confronting Kobolds again, do not bother with half-measures. Use your Etching and do it without regret."

She nodded, then looked again at her lifeless arm. She poked it with her right hand. "When the numbing wears off," she said, "will you show me how to use that lacing?"

He nodded and offered his hand to help pull her to her feet.

Learning that lacing boosted Shilo's mood, and she managed to hold onto that feeling throughout the day. After her lesson in Master Nox's dojo, she joined Pavel in Master Flint's spacious training room to practice Blending her Flame into Pavel's Aether. Since the Kobold attack, Pavel had become intensely focused and serious during training, though he was still lazy and sarcastic outside of the classroom. Master Trevor Flint was an energetic old man who was always smiling. He showed them an unusual defensive lacing. The pinkish light created by mixing the two forces enshrouded Pavel's body. Anyone who touched Pavel while the lacing was in place would experience a sharp, stinging sensation. Shilo did not volunteer to test its effectiveness, as apparently it could be quite painful, but Master Flint assured Pavel that his lacings were correct.

Then she returned to the dojo to train with Ryn, the quiet but sweet Root Weaver. This was another lesson in principle and not in practice, because it could be dangerous. Root Weavers could mask fatigue so their subjects wouldn't feel tired, but the fatigue would still be there below the surface, and if they pushed themselves too hard, they would collapse. Blending Root and Flame was all about energy transference, and a lacing could be used to actually restore someone's energy without the need for rest, though it required sapping it from someone else. Master Nox spent most of the lesson cautioning them on the dangers of such a lacing, but he also explained the benefits. A messenger carrying a vital communication might find her horse flagging before reaching their destination, so she could share some of her own vitality with her steed, ensuring the message arrived in time. Still, Shilo found herself wondering when she would possibly need such a lacing.

After lunch, she trained with the peculiar new Root master. She would have to build her proficiency with Root before she could attempt to learn healing, so she simply tried to generate enough Root to Blend with her Flame and create a Weaver light. She had been practicing making such lights with Ryn since the beginning of their Watchkeeper training. They were often paired together for morning chores, traveling around the compound and replacing the lights that had burned out. If she could make Weaver lights on her own, that would be a useful skill in the field. She came close to wielding both forces simultaneously, which Master Pembrim assured her was a good sign. He said if she could pull off creating a Weaver light by the end of their first week together, it would be a good indication that she might also be able to pick up healing, a rare accomplishment for Flame Weavers. She was eager to take on the obvious challenge. She wanted to be more than just a fighter.

Then it was back to Master Flint, this time without Pavel. She was getting better at envisioning Aether. It involved imaging a stream of wind blowing straight down upon the crown of your head, which was hard, because actual wind never really blew in such a way. She could reliably form flickering strands of white Aether, but she couldn't do anything with it yet, and she certainly couldn't generate Flame at the same time. Master Flint was chipper and encouraging as always.

And then it was up to a room on the second floor of the Citadel, her stomach growling from the strain of generating Aether, despite not actually using it. Mistress Agia Bellos drilled her Training Pentad on the laws they would be helping to enforce.

Towns of any size employed a guard that did the bulk of local peacekeeping. Smaller villages such as Palmoor only had a sheriff who could recruit volunteer deputies as needed. Town and village councils settled local disputes between citizens, and traveling justices weighed in on the thornier matters, while big cities employed a magistrate, a role somewhere between a mayor and a justice.

The Watchkeepers were an added layer of security on top of all that. A village sheriff could handle the local drunks, but if that drunk was also a Flame Weaver who wasn't afraid to throw punches, or if he joined up with other Weavers to form a gang and exploit his non-Weaver neighbors, then that sheriff might send for the Watchkeepers. The Gray Guard, as they were sometimes called, maintained outposts across Aldria. Pentads also actively patrolled the countryside, looking for signs of rogue Weaver activity before it got bad enough for someone to send for help.

Generally, the Watchkeepers did not involve themselves with matters that concerned only non-Weavers, though it became tricky when gangs contained a mix of both kinds of criminals. An illegal gambling ring, for example, might employ Flame Weaver bouncers. Mistress Bellos spent most of the lesson stressing the need to cooperate as much as possible with local authorities and not step on any toes, especially if the Watchkeepers had not been sent for.

Then came dinner, and of course, after that, Jayn insisted they all slink off down to the basement for what her friends called Secret Training. Three days in, Shilo was already regretting her offer to teach Jayn to wield Flame. The spunky blonde was determined to master it, though as yet she had not summoned a wisp of Flame. Shilo knew Jayn all too well. Eventually, probably soon, her iron resolve would falter, and then she would get mad. And probably yell at Shilo. It seemed inevitable, though Shilo longed to avoid that.

She studied Jayn as the girl balled her fists and attempted to envision a glowing fire inside her chest. Shilo willed her to succeed. She hoped she could succeed, and soon.

On the other side of the small dusty room, Thalia and Pavel were arguing about something. Shilo tried to keep her focus on Jayn, but once she became aware of the others' voices, she couldn't help but listen.

"Start over," Pavel said. "What exactly did it look like? I'm still having a hard time imagining it."

Shilo knew exactly what they were talking about. It was one of a set handful of conversations they had run through dozens of times in this basement, and though Thalia sighed in exasperation, she clearly wasn't done rehashing this particular topic. "It looked like a barn owl," Thalia said. "You've seen those, you know what a barn owl looks like. Only it was bigger than any bird I've ever seen, bigger than a man, big enough to pick up Kalo and carry him away. And it didn't have a beak like a bird. It had lips and a nose, and round human eyes, but completely black."

Pavel shook his head. "You're sure that is what you saw?"

Thalia threw up her hands. "Yes! Lots of people saw it flying over Falport that night. Captain Lahmeer said she saw it. They saw it too." She gestured toward Shilo and Jayn.

Shilo didn't love reliving her memories of that night, but doing so would put off Jayn's inevitable tantrum, so she took advantage of the opening. "Yes," she said, turning away from Jayn and toward the group. "It was just as Thalia described."

Jayn grumbled something, but it sounded like an agreement. Apparently, she wasn't going to protest the disruption to their practice, which Shilo silently thanked the Maker for.

Pavel scratched his chin. He needed a shave. And a haircut. Wavy black hair framed his long, angular face. "People in town are saying it was a Drake, and I suppose maybe it was. I just didn't think Drakes were real. They are found in the oldest surviving legends, so maybe they did exist back before the Burning, but not now. At least, they shouldn't exist."

Ryn spoke up. "Maybe it wasn't a Drake," he said. He stood leaning in the corner, his hand covering a cut he'd made on his arm in another attempt to activate his Etching. "There was the other creature…"

"The bear?" Pavel asked.

"Well, it looked like a bear," Ryn said. "We only saw it briefly as it was coming out of the… portal or whatever that was."

Pavel pressed the heels of his hands against his eyes. "All right, let's start again from the top, the very top. Put aside the speculation. What do we know for a fact?"

Thalia sighed again, though she herself had often prompted a discussion of that strange night, and she was the first to answer Pavel's question. "Kobolds attacked Falport. They also attacked the Watchkeeper Citadel. At least a dozen humans were working with the Kobolds, including a full Pentad of rogue Weavers, one of whom was working as a servant here in the compound."

"Why?" Pavel asked. No one answered. "What was the goal of the attack?"

"You said no speculation," Jayn said, finally joining the conversation.

"Fine, but what did they do that we know about? Other than try to kill everyone, of course."

"The mirror," Jayn said. "Sometime prior to the attack, the rogue Weavers stole a mirror-shaped Runeform. Based on what we overheard at the Fish Dock, the acquisition of the mirror was something they had to do—or wanted to do—before launching the attack. Then at the same time Kobolds were attacking the city, the rogue Weaver used the mirror to… do whatever it was Thalia and Ryn saw them doing in that warehouse."

"They opened a portal," Ryn said, his tone flat. His gaze seemed unfocused, as if he were looking back now on whatever he saw that night. "It had to be some kind of portal."

Pavel flicked his wrist in a dismissive gesture. "Let's back up. What do we know for a fact about the mirror?"

"That's your part," Jayn said, scoffing. "You got the explanation straight from Captain Lahmeer."

Now Pavel sighed. "Yeah, but she basically didn't know anything. The Watchkeepers were using that mirror as part of a simple puzzle. Nyssa said, the more you looked into the mirror, the more things changed. At first, it would just be a normal reflection, but then the images in the mirror would stop matching the people and things outside of the mirror. You might walk to the left, but your reflection would walk right or not move at all. Then, if you kept looking, the person in the mirror would look less and less like you." He shook his head in disbelief. "Nyssa said that one time her reflection was missing an arm, like it had been amputated."

"So what does that all mean?" Thalia asked. "If you'll forgive the speculation."

Jayn leaned forward on the crate she had been using as a chair. "Different possibilities," she said. "Maybe different ways your life could have gone, if you had made different choices."

Pavel nodded. "Or maybe different versions of yourself. Some Scholars have speculated that our reality is just one of many, possibly infinite, realities. Maybe the mirror was like a window that let you look into those different worlds. And maybe the window could be turned into a door. Maybe it was a portal…"

The silence stretched longer this time before Thalia spoke up. "I saw the same thing that Ryn saw. The mirror was glowing. All five of the Weavers were sending lacings into the mirror." She raised a hand before Pavel could protest. "I know! No lacing uses more than two forces, but that's certainly what it looked like, an unbelievably complex lacing using all five forces. We saw that big hairy creature walk out of the mirror."

"The bear?" Pavel asked. "And it also had a human face?"

Thalia shrugged. "I think so. We only saw its face for a moment as the mirror was breaking."

"*If* the mirror broke," Pavel said, raising a finger. "Perhaps it just appeared to break. You admit, everything was happening very quickly at the time. None of us has seen the mirror since. We can't say for a fact that the Runeform broke." He didn't have to say that Runeforms can't break. That was another one of those immutable laws of nature they were all starting to question.

Thalia ignored the objection. She was clearly also thinking back to that time, striving to remember more details. "The mirror made this droning noise when the creature was coming out," she said. "We only climbed up to see that last one, but before that I had heard the droning noise more than once. Call it speculation, but I think we can assume that the owl creature also came through that portal. No one saw it until after the rogue Weavers started using the Runeform."

Pavel nodded. "It's a fair assumption. How many times?"

"What?"

"How many times did you hear the droning noise? How many times might they have used the portal?"

She shook her head. "A few. Definitely more than twice. I didn't know what it was at the time, so I didn't know I needed to be counting."

"Five," Ryn said.

All heads swiveled to look at him. The rest of this dialogue they had rehearsed countless times, but this was genuinely new information.

"How do you know?" Thalia asked as gently as she could. "You were unconscious most of the time when they were using the mirror."

Ryn stared into empty space for some time before answering. "I don't know. Even though I wasn't awake at the time, I could still hear… voices. I didn't remember any of it at first, but it's starting to come back to me… I think there were five."

No one responded right away. Probably, like Shilo, they didn't know what to say to such a vague and confused statement. This time Jayn broke the silence.

"I think he's right," she said, drawing everyone's focus. "When that owl creature showed up, before she carried Kalo away, she said something to him. It was something like… 'The Five have come.' It didn't mean anything at the time."

Thalia nodded. "Maybe she did. That does sound familiar."

Shilo tried to think back to that moment but couldn't recall the details. Kalo had stabbed her, and she had used her last remaining strength to fight him off. She'd been in and out of consciousness after that. She had only a vague memory of some great winged thing flying overhead, but somehow, she did remember its face.

Pavel shrugged. "Five is a good assumption anyway. Everything comes in fives. So, the Kobolds and the rogue Weavers went through a great deal of trouble to steal the mirror, use it as a portal, and summon five of these human-faced creatures from the Maker knows where, before they all completely vanished."

"Speculation!" Jayn said, raising a finger in imitation of Pavel. "Maybe the portal was used five times, but we don't know what came through. Maybe only two of them were creatures with human faces."

Pavel laughed. He always enjoyed a clever comeback, even at his own expense. "Fine," he said. "They summoned two man-faced creatures and as many as three other unknown entities."

Jayn's smile faded. "There was something else about that owl," she said. "When it showed up, Kalo didn't want to listen to her. He wanted to stay and finish us off, but the owl made him listen. He submitted to her."

Pavel frowned too. "That Kalo was no joke. He's clearly in charge of at least some of the Kobolds, but if this man-faced thing is in charge of him, then we definitely don't want to mess with any of them."

Thalia slowly shook her head. "Even if all our speculations are true, we still don't know the answers to any of the really important questions about what happened that night and why it happened."

Shilo nodded in silent agreement.

After that, no one felt much like continuing their Secret Training that evening, and the guys and girls headed to their separate dorms. Shilo was feeling better about her abilities after her lesson with Master Nox, but now she had another reason not to sleep at night.

Chapter 4
The Scholar

THALIA MOLDO WORKED THE BELLOWS, watching Korin from the corner of her eye and doing her best to match the other Stone Weaver's pace. The work was exhausting, but Thalia was no stranger to back-breaking labor. She wished Master Caston had constructed this strange clay furnace under the covered roof of the smithy. The immense heat radiating from the furnace was harsh enough without the late spring sun beating down on her neck. Despite all that, Thalia enjoyed the work. Korin was a few years older than Thalia. She was reserved but dependable, and Thalia liked working with her, though they weren't quite friends.

After what seemed like ages, someone tapped her on the shoulder. She didn't even look to see which cadet was relieving her. She merely straightened her back and took a few staggering steps away, while the new Weaver stepped in to replace her. Korin also stepped away as another fresh pair of arms took her place. Thalia followed Korin to the water barrel—not one of the ones used for quenching metal—and let her drink from the ladle first.

After quenching her own thirst, Thalia clasped hands with Korin, a common gesture in Master Caston's smithy that conveyed a number of meanings. In this case, it meant "Thanks for your help" and "See you later."

Korin strolled away, while Thalia turned to look back over the partially rebuilt smithy. During the Kobold attack, someone working with the Rogue Weavers—possibly the traitorous Mistress Hinter—had blown up the Watchkeepers' marvelous smithy in order to put a hole in the city wall and allow Kobolds into the compound. Master Caston still wasn't sure what had caused the explosion; it took a lot of force to break through a Stone-strengthened and Wave-warded wall. The smithy, with its dazzling array of forges and anvils, had been Thalia's favorite place in the world, and its destruction had grieved her almost as much as the loss of many of her fellow Watchkeepers that night. Maybe that was a bit of an exaggeration.

Master Rohan Caston, who oversaw the smithy, had taken the destruction surprisingly well. With the loss of most of their materials and sophisticated tools, Master Caston had taken his students "back to the basics." Thalia and her Training Pentad were the only new recruits currently among the Watchkeepers, but many cadets who had completed their training remained within the compound, either because it was their assigned station or they were pursuing advanced lessons with one of the masters. This was especially common among Stone Weavers, as the breadth of smithing and crafting could not be fully covered in a mere six months.

As they slowly rebuilt the smithy and acquired what tools they couldn't make themselves, Master Caston had spent the last several weeks teaching them the history of crafting, from the early days after the Burning right up to the current age. He seemed to enjoy the little history lessons. He'd taken them all down to the rocky beach outside of Falport one weekend to forage for flint, so they could craft spear- and arrowheads with improvised stone and wooden tools. They learned how Stone could be used even in such rudimentary creations.

The existence of Runeforms and certain ancient monuments suggested that people alive before the Burning had achieved technologies far in advance of what people could create today. All that knowledge was lost in the chaotic centuries following whatever cataclysm destroyed that civilization. Still, Master Caston taught them, if Stone Weavers didn't exist, people today might still be sharpening flint to hunt for their dinners. Stone gave its users insight into whatever materials they worked with. They could understand and manipulate the underlying structures of matter, which drove them to continually build and innovate, allowing metallurgy and other lost arts to be rediscovered at what Master Caston considered to be an impressive rate. Maybe that was true, even if a thousand years on, civilization had still not returned to what it had once been. If they could only rediscover how to create Runeforms, Thalia felt, then they could do anything.

Master Caston also used the wide open field created by the explosion to run a series of projects and experiments he claimed he never had the space or time for before. That was why Thalia and the other Stone Weavers were taking shifts working these two large bellows attached to this unusual furnace. A third Weaver stood on a raised platform, using a simple Stone lacing to help separate impurities from the slabs of iron currently being melted over a bed of white-hot coals. As Thalia watched the gouts of fire rising from the furnace and felt the intense heat even from this distance, the master Stone Weaver himself came to stand beside her.

He nodded to her in greeting. "Good morning, Thalia. Putting in a shift before your morning chores, I see?"

"Yes, sir. I'm happy to help, and I'm curious to see how this whole thing turns out." She paused before adding, "Tell me again why this is better than a regular furnace?"

He laughed. "Trust me, you'll know why once you get your hands on this steel. This is a traditional technique I learned in Iscerna. The clay itself is imported from there. None of the clay you get around here has the right properties. It couldn't handle the heat. The way we forge steel in Aldria, it is not nearly as refined as Iscernaen steel. Too much slag. This steel will be purer, and better than that, it can be hardened with no loss of durability."

She remembered a detail he had mentioned when they were building the furnace. "But this thing can only be used once?"

"Oh yes, we will have to smash it apart to get the steel out. Of course, clay being what it is, it could be rebuilt again, though I doubt Commandant Lahey will have the patience to let me keep mucking about with this kind of stuff too much longer. But that's why we're making such a big batch. It should be done this weekend. I can't say exactly how much this will yield, but I'll definitely make sure you get a piece."

She nodded. "Thank you."

He looked sideways at her for a moment before continuing. "I am curious though, have you given much thought to what you want to make?"

She dropped her gaze, staring at the dusty ground that had once been covered in grass. "Well, I was hoping that you might have time to help me forge a knife."

"Ah," he said.

She nodded. Master Caston knew of her ambition to be a bladesmith. Her father had been a bladesmith, making knives for hunters and cooks, before a short-lived commission with the Standing Army had gotten him killed. Her father's legacy had driven her toward smithing, long before she knew she was a Weaver. Still, they had yet to cover blades in her time so far as a recruit. She was not one to question her master's approach, so she had patiently waited for when those lessons would come. This was the first time she had directly asked him to teach her bladesmithing. She didn't know how he would respond.

After what seemed a long pause, he said, "I never met your father, though I was familiar with his work. He made excellent blades, and I don't just mean they were good for a non-Weaver. I think a knife is a good choice for steel of this quality, and I would be happy to teach you."

"Thank you," she said.

"Of course. Now, you should probably hurry to the dining hall if you want any breakfast before you have to begin your actual assigned chores."

She knew a dismissal when she heard one. She smiled to herself as she made her way across the lawn toward the towering black Citadel. Few people were out and about this early in the morning, though she did pass one woman, curiously dressed not in Watchkeeper gray or the green uniforms of the servants, but in a fine blue riding dress. Thalia nodded politely to the woman as they passed, but then she stopped in her tracks. She turned to see that the woman had also paused to look back at her. It took Thalia a moment to remember the name.

"Miss Bellain?"

The Scholar smiled. "Thalia Moldo, the redsmith's apprentice, though now a Watchkeeper, I see. I'm surprised you remember me."

Thalia made a strangled sound of bewilderment. "I'm surprised you remember *me*, Miss Bellain."

"Please, call me Mina. You taught me how to use the Rigel fountain, not something I am likely to forget."

Thalia wanted to protest that but knew better than to say anything. The Scholar had clearly known everything about the Runeform fountain that day she had appeared outside Master Foster's redsmith shop. Thalia had not told the woman anything she had not already known, so clearly now she was just being polite by giving Thalia credit. Immediately after her encounter with the Scholar, Thalia had discovered her Etching. Amidst the chaos her luck Etching had created and with everything that followed, she'd given little thought to her encounter with Mina Bellain. The woman had asked the prophetic fountain an oddly mundane question: "What will I have for dinner?" In response, Rigel had said…

For a moment, Thalia almost forgot everything her class-conscious mother had taught her about manners and proper behavior. So sudden was her desire to run off and find her friends, that she almost forgot all about Mina Bellain standing in front of her. She had no idea how she had reacted or what emotion her countenance had given away. She did her best to remain calm and slow the thumping in her chest. She coughed, pretending to clear her throat, as if that could cover her reaction.

"Well, Mina," she said finally. "It was a pleasure seeing you again, but I'm afraid if I don't hurry off to breakfast now, I will miss the meal entirely."

Mina laughed and waved her hand in dismissal. "Of course, I won't keep you. I'm sure we'll have a chance to catch up later."

Thalia barely managed another polite nod before turning to rush toward the dining hall, where she hoped her Pentad would still be. Only her deeply ingrained sense of propriety kept her from sprinting.

"Secret Training," she said as she strode up to the table. She had no stomach for breakfast anymore.

Jayn arched an eyebrow. "What, right now?"

Shilo's forehead furrowed in concern. "We all have our morning chores though."

"We can be a few minutes late," Thalia said, keeping her voice low. "It is somewhat urgent."

Thankfully, no one protested further, or they didn't want to draw unwanted attention in the crowded dining hall. They made their way silently down into their basement meeting room, and no one spoke until the door was shut.

"You know," Pavel said as he slid the bolt into place, "if we want to keep having these secret meetings, we have to come up with a better codename than 'Secret Training.'"

"The name was your idea," Jayn said.

"I don't think so. I'm much better at coming up with codenames than that."

Jayn only sighed before turning to Thalia. "Well, what did you need to tell us so urgently?"

Thalia felt a bit foolish now. Maybe her sense of urgency had been overblown. She certainly could have waited till their usual meeting time to tell them about the Scholar. Except, why was Mina here, within the Watchkeeper compound? She said she would have time to catch up with Thalia later. Did that mean she was staying here? Regardless, Thalia had called for this meeting, and so now she had to explain herself. It took her a moment to gather her thoughts. She did her best to meet their gazes.

"On my way here, I ran into this Scholar."

Pavel reacted to that last word in such obvious disgust that Thalia stopped short. He must have realized what he had done, so Pavel forced a smile and said, "Sorry, I'm just not a fan of Scholars. They're far too nosy and are best avoided."

"Right," Thalia said. "Well, I actually have met this particular Scholar before, briefly, when I was still Master Foster's apprentice. With everything that's happened the last few months, I'd forgotten all about it, but seeing her just now reminded me of something that happened. Something important, I think."

Jayn still looked confused, but she nodded in encouragement. "Go on."

"Master Foster's redsmith shop is on the same square that houses the Rigel fountain, so one night while I was closing up, this woman, Mina Bellain, she came over to the shop and asked me what I knew about the fountain. I told her everything I could, but she seemed to know it already. That's when I guessed she was a Scholar. Others have visited the fountain before, of course. I was always curious to hear whatever questions people came to ask the fountain and what the fountain would say, though it was mostly nonsense, so I went with her up to the fountain. As a Scholar, she could have had any number of important questions, but she asked something rather strange. She asked Rigel to tell her what she would have for dinner."

Pavel burst out laughing. This was especially odd, after his initial disgust at the mention of a Scholar. Everyone looked at him. He threw up his hands. "No, I'm sorry. I still don't like Scholars, but that is a very clever question, especially if you are trying to test the extent and limits of the Runeform's apparent prophetic abilities. If it told you, 'Beef stew,' then you could do everything in your power *not* to eat beef stew, just to see if you could change your fate. I wonder…" He trailed off, shaking his head. "But, of course, I'm betting Rigel told her something else entirely."

Thalia nodded. "It said, 'Only those who have tasted deadly poison and survived can stop the… the something.'"

"The something?" Pavel asked.

"I've been trying to remember. It was something I've never heard said like that before with a definitive 'the' in front of it. The Rending. The Sundering. Something like that. There was something in the way Rigel said it… It reminded me of how people say, 'The Burning.'"

"Deadly poison?" Jayn asked. "Are you thinking the prophecy was talking about us and the Kobold poison?"

Thalia could only nod. Each of them at one point or another had been scratched by Kalo or another Kobold. They believed a Kobold's claws could carry some kind of fast-acting venom and only Ryn's healing had saved them from death.

"I don't know," Ryn said, shaking his head. "We don't know for sure that the Kobolds had poison on their claws. None of the healers found any signs of it."

Pavel scoffed. "It's still the best explanation, I maintain. It's possible that not all Kobolds carry the poison, or maybe they can choose whether or not to inflict it. When we were first attacked in the Sylphren Wood… The way Nyssa's Root Weaver died, it had to be poison or some other toxic substance on their claws. Then the way the Kobolds tended to ignore those of us who had been scratched… Those attacks did something to us, marked us in some way that stuck with us even after healing. Nyssa said the same thing. When she went out into the streets of Falport, the Kobolds didn't want to fight her until she attacked them. It actually helped keep her alive." He paused. "Though of course, if we are being technical, none of us 'tasted' the poison."

"Wait," Jayn said, her eyes half-closed in concentration, as if trying to remember something. "What you just said…" She turned to Thalia, a sudden urgency in the set of her jaw and her narrowed eyes. "Think back to that moment when the owl with the human face came for Kalo. What do you remember her saying? What exactly?"

Thalia thought back. Their conversation the other night had already begun to jog her memory. "When it first showed up, the creature was yelling. It told Kalo to stop, to leave us alone. It said… 'The Five are through. We are headed for…' the Reach, I think?"

Jayn nodded. "Yet, but then she picked up Kalo, and as she was flying away, she looked back at us with that hideous human face. Do you remember what she said then?"

"It… or she said, 'We will remember…'" What had the owl said?

"Those who bear the Mark," Jayn said. "We will remember those who bear the Mark."

A silence fell over the group.

Jayn chewed her lip. "What Pavel said… that the Kobolds marked us somehow, it made me remember that moment."

Pavel scratched his chin. "Those who bear the Mark… Those who've tasted poison… Even if that's all about us specifically, where does that leave us? Somehow, we have this destiny to stop something probably rather bad from happening? What had Rigel called it, again?"

It came to her then. "The Rivening," Thalia said. "He called it the Rivening."

Pavel shrugged. "I've never heard of it, and I've read my fair share of ancient prophecies. Rivening… Riven just means to tear or rip. What could that be? Regardless, if we don't know what it is, we don't need to spend too much time worrying about stopping it." He paused, looking at each of them in turn to ensure they were listening. "I will tell you this much. We all need to stay as far away from this Scholar as we can. If Rigel gave her that prophecy… and maybe there's a chance it might be about us, then it can't be a coincidence that she is here, right now, in the compound. A Scholar would not be here without permission from Commandant Lahey. Something about the Kobold attack had to have piqued her interest, and likely she will pry out every single detail if she hasn't already. She'll know about the stolen mirror. She'll know that Kalo is a Weaver, and she'll know the theory we put out about the poison. She'll find out how involved the five of us were in everything that went down that night, and probably she will want to interview us." He paused and looked at each of them again. Thalia had never seen Pavel so serious. It scared her. Pavel spoke slowly, putting deliberate emphasis on each word. "Under no circumstances should any of us tell her anything about that night that we haven't already told the masters. In particular, we can say nothing about that Blending."

Shilo was the first to speak into the silence that followed that pronouncement. "Isn't that a little much? Do we really need to be so worried about this Scholar? Maybe she could help us."

Pavel leveled his gaze at her. Shilo lowered her eyes. "No," Pavel said. "We absolutely need to be worried. You have no idea how much power the Academy of the Ways has, even here. If this Scholar hears even a rumor about what Ryn and I did that night, you will never see us again. We'd wake up in some dungeon underneath the Academy. They would force us to perform that Blending over and over again, so they could understand it. If we couldn't do it, they would find a way to make it work, even if it meant slicing Ryn open. Listen to what I'm telling you. The Scholars worship knowledge above all else. Something like what we did, something that is supposed to be impossible... They would slit each other's throats just to be the first to make that kind of discovery."

After another long pause, Jayn cleared her throat. "Well, even if things are not quite that dire, I still agree with the principle. There's a reason we didn't tell the masters about that Blending. We certainly don't need to tell this Scholar about it. Ryn used his Etching to heal himself. Then he healed me and Shilo. That's still the story."

Thalia couldn't say exactly why they had kept the Blending a secret so far, but somehow it had felt like the safest course of action. She nodded. Then she sighed. "Well, if the bottom line is that we need to avoid attracting unwanted attention, then we probably shouldn't be any later to chores than we already are. Sorry for dumping all this on everyone first thing in the morning. Let's meet up again tonight and talk it over some more, all right?"

No one could argue with that, and the Secret Training dispersed. They really did need a better name for it.

Chapter 5
Etchings

DESPITE THE UNUSUAL START to the morning, Ryn soon felt things slipping back into the normal routine. This was Foamsday, the fifth day of the week and the end of the traditional work week, a concept still new to Ryn. Individual days had meant little in his life growing up in the Sylphren Wood, except for Sundays when the Aen's Hollow church held its weekly services. Ryn had sometimes attended those services, though his aunt Marla never went.

He and Shilo were paired together for morning chores. They went through some of the outbuildings spread around the main Citadel, replacing Weaver lights that had burned out. Soon they would be able to handle this chore solo, assuming each could master simultaneous control of Root and Flame, but for now they worked together. Neither was particularly skilled at making conversation, and both were quieter even than usual that morning. No doubt Shilo was also reflecting on everything Thalia had shared and Pavel's dire warning about this Scholar. Still, long stretches of silence didn't particularly bother either of them, and Shilo offered a weak smile as they parted to head to their morning classes.

Ryn met Jayn at Master Pembrim's shed near the greenhouses. She seemed unaffected by the morning's revelations, though perhaps she did show a keener interest in the day's lesson and asked more questions than usual. They had spent most of the week learning a particularly challenging lacing that could partially shield someone from the effects of a Flame-enhanced punch. The individual would still feel the blow, but the shield could diminish that added force. Though Root on its own enhanced Flame, Wave consumed Flame, so to create the canceling effect, Wave had to be used more prominently in the lacing. Master Pembrim told Ryn to allow the two forces to Blend but not to mix completely, a concept he still couldn't quite grasp. Their failed attempts didn't seem to fluster Jayn, and when that hour was up, she left with a wave and a nod.

As soon as Jayn left, Master Pembrim said, "Follow me," and set off at a brisk pace across the lawn. Ryn fell into step behind him. The Root master often moved their lessons to different locations, but they did not head in one of the usual directions toward the greenhouses or the cellar where Pembrim grew his mushrooms. Instead, they headed straight for the Citadel, an impressive black building composed of spires and arches.

Stranger still, they walked around to the side entrance that led into the dining hall. The morning sun slanted through the high arched windows, leaving a pattern of light and shadow along the wooden tables and benches, all empty at this time of day. Noise spilled out from the opening above the counter that led into the kitchen, as the head cook and her staff were already at work preparing the midday meal. Master Pembrim led him across the stone floor toward the sound, and they entered through a door by the counter.

The cooks, busy with their various tasks of kneading bread, stirring simmering pots, or chopping vegetables, ignored the master Root Weaver and his student. Master Pembrim navigated through the bustle, clearly familiar with the flow of this particular kitchen. Ryn followed, doing his best not to get in anyone's way. An opening on the far side of the room led to a hallway lined with doors, each likely opening into a different pantry laden with dried and preserved goods. It took a lot to feed all the Watchkeepers and their servants.

They stopped at the last door on the left. Master Pembrim turned the knob and stepped inside, passing through a shimmering wall of Wave into a dim room. Many wards were designed to keep people out, but this clearly wasn't one of those. Ryn hesitated only a moment before following. A shiver passed through his body as he entered the room, though the ward itself did not cause it. This pantry was remarkably cooler than the hot humid kitchen behind them. It felt like the seasons had turned back to winter in a single moment. He looked back at the ward.

"A clever lacing," Master Pembrim said. "It doesn't actually make the room colder, but it insulates it and prevents the normal transfer of heat. The ice makes it cold."

Indeed, large blocks of bluish ice lined three walls of the narrow pantry. They should have been quickly melting in this late-spring heat, and indeed a drain had been set in the floor to handle such runoff, but the ground felt dry beneath Ryn's boots.

Master Pembrim slapped the palm of his hand against one of the blocks. "Harvested in the ever-frozen Coldreach Mountains and floated down the River Aldria, a miracle of modern technology and Weaving. It's great for keeping perishables from going off, though I have commandeered this particular ice room."

We must cross over and head for the Reach, Ryn had heard one of the man-faced creatures say, or he dreamed he had heard that. Did the Reach mean the Coldreaches, that range of towering peaks to the north that separated Aldria from Silgaria? He had no time to dwell on that now. The ice room was crammed not with racks of meat or wheels of cheese, but large irregular-shaped bundles wrapped in white sheets. They were bodies, Ryn realized, kept in this room to slow the process of decay.

Master Pembrim walked through the narrow aisle between corpses to a metal counter on the far end, where another body lay beneath a loose sheet. "Come have a look," he said, throwing back the covering. Ryn instantly recognized the corpse as a Kobold. They were all Kobold bodies. Of course they were. All the humans slain in the battle had been burned or buried weeks ago. They would not have been preserved like this. Ryn picked his way through the rows, careful not to bump any of them. He felt an irrational need to keep quiet, as if they might still wake up, though they had been dead going on seven weeks now.

He stopped a few feet short of the corpse on the table. The creature was clearly dead, though its leathery gray skin showed no signs of decay. Its eyes were closed, its thin lips pealed back to reveal sharp teeth. Those marked it as a predator who exclusively or mostly ate meat. Ryn kept his eyes fixed on that grotesque face, reluctant to look at the cavernous hole where the creature's chest and stomach had been. Master Pembrim had apparently cut it open with some precise and sharp tool and removed most of its organs. It made sense that someone would want to dissect a Kobold to learn more about the creatures, but it still felt grisly and macabre.

"You can step closer," Master Pembrim said. "I can assure you, he is long past hurting anyone."

Ryn did inch a little closer, but he shifted his gaze to Master Pembrim, who stood peering down at the cadaver. "Why are you showing me this?" he asked.

"Death is the other side of life. As a healer, it's important to understand the full cycle of life, from birth and growth to death and decay. The body cannot sustain itself without the deaths of other things." He seemed to be waxing philosophical, a common occurrence. He spoke as if to himself. "Death occurs when the body forgets how to be a body."

"What?" Ryn couldn't keep himself from asking.

Master Pembrim glanced at Ryn before returning his gaze to the corpse. A slight smile crossed his lips. "That's just my personal theory anyway. I may be wrong, but it helps explain how healing works and why some things are harder to heal. A cut from a sword across the stomach is certainly a dramatic injury, but assuming the Root Weaver has enough energy, the wound is quickly mended. Healing is just reminding the body how it works. The skin and muscles know how to knit themselves together. Even bones know what shape they're supposed to take.

"It's the internal things that are harder. Many illnesses are caused by tiny creatures that invade the blood or lungs. Fevers and coughs, these are just the body's reaction to the invaders. A healer can't remind the body not to be sick in those cases, because the body already knows that. He can strengthen the body's ability to fight and mitigate the symptoms, but the body itself must still destroy the invaders. An old or weakened body cannot fight as hard and may still succumb, even with the best healers. For the same reason, you cannot stop aging. You cannot remind a body how to be young; it only knows how to be its current age.

"Harder still are sicknesses that come when the body turns on itself. Tumors often form when part of the body forgets its proper function or attacks itself. Healing can be worse than useless then, if it makes the tumors grow, though rare Etchings sometimes occur that allow a Root Weaver to correct even those kinds of disorders… Apparently, there is a woman among the Maer who possesses such a talent, and she offers her services freely—for those who can afford passage to Abyscadis."

Ryn nodded along to the explanation. It made perfect sense. Mistress Hinter had told him about the sicknesses and diseases that resisted healing, but she had not explained the reason why in such a succinct way. "I never thought about it like that," he said.

Master Pembrim glanced at him again. He seemed slightly startled, as if he had forgotten Ryn was there, but then he gave a curt nod. "Yes, well, not to give you a big head, but you are among the more powerful Root Weavers I have had the pleasure of working with, at times too powerful from what I've heard. Probably you can blast through pesky little infections and biologic invaders without even noticing. It may surprise you to learn, but even most Guild healers would be powerless to help a victim infected with a fast-acting poison, for example."

Ryn overcame his revulsion to look at the body then, especially the hands, with their long black fingernails pointed like claws. "Did you find signs of poison?" he asked. Of course, Master Pembrim had heard Pavel's theory about poison; all the Root Weavers and probably every other Watchkeeper knew it by now. Maybe that was part of why he was studying the bodies.

Master Pembrim shrugged. "No, but that doesn't mean anything. These Kobolds have such strange anatomies, and you get so little from Dowsing a body after death. Half of the organs I've pulled out of this corpse, I couldn't even tell you what they do. It's possible they could have a gland for creating venom. Their fingernails are surprisingly porous. They're all male, all the ones we have. If I had a female specimen, it would give us a fuller understanding of the species." He sighed. "Really, there are a lot of things about these creatures that just don't make sense."

"Like what?"

"The blood is the main thing. It's blue, for one, and it's way too acidic. It foams up when it touches the air, and if you get any on your skin, it causes a burning rash. They shouldn't be able to survive with blood like that. In fact, as soon as they die, their blood starts to eat away at them from the inside. It took too long for me to figure that out, so by the time I had the bodies drained, so much had already been lost to deterioration. I don't know, it's like these things are from another world. They just don't make biological sense in this one."

Another world. It would explain some things. A few years ago, Kobolds did not exist, or so it seemed. Then they started popping up, first as rumors in the Coldreaches, before they started appearing all over Aldria. Perhaps, they came from the same place as the man-faced creatures that seemed to be their leaders. There had to be another portal somewhere in Silgaria or some other gateway that the Kobolds could pass through but not their leaders. Ryn filed all those ideas away to tell his friends later. He had another question for Master Pembrim just then.

"When these Kobolds were attacking," he said, "something else happened that was a little strange. One of them came after me, and in the moment, I had no way to defend myself, so in a sort of desperate act, I Dowsed the Kobold." It had been Kalo, the Kobold Weaver.

Master Pembrim's eyes widened, and a sudden light came into them. He had spoken so far with a philosophical aloofness, but now he was genuinely excited. "You did? You Dowsed a living Kobold? What did you see? What do you remember? Anything could be helpful."

Ryn shook his head and held up a hand to stop the questions. "I'm sorry, but it only happened for a moment. Mostly, it was bewildering. As you said, it was completely different from a human. I only bring it up because when I Dowsed the Kobold, he reacted strongly, as if I had hurt him somehow."

"Perhaps you did."

"How can that be? I've been warned so many times to be careful with healing, because you can do more harm than good, but how is that so? What you said about tumors makes sense, but how else can Root be dangerous?"

"How can Root be used to cause harm, you mean?"

"I suppose," Ryn said. Then he quickly added, "Not that I want to, of course."

Master Pembrim made a dismissive wave with his hand. "Of course not. It's a good question, and one that not every Root Weaver wants to acknowledge. The truth is, Root can be used to kill."

Ryn tried not to gape. "What? How could that be?"

Pembrim smiled. "I'm told you first used healing when you had basically no training, and you did it successfully more than once before you received formal instruction here. It is in many ways an intuitive leap, once you understand Dowsing. When you see disorder in the body, you naturally want to correct it, to bring those disrupted systems back in line with the rest. However, if you were… given over to evil impulses, let's say, you could affect the opposite result. You could hinder someone's ability to fight off infections, or you could prevent a wound from healing. With enough concerted effort, you could overwhelm the heart and shut it down. When the heart stops beating, death quickly follows."

Ryn shivered again, though this time not from the cold. "Do Root Weavers really do that?"

Pembrim shrugged. "If you believe in wild rumors, supposedly there is a secret brotherhood of Tamorine Death Weavers, who carry out such assassinations. I've never given the idea much credit. Such a lacing would have to be done in close proximity to the victim and would take time and a great deal of energy. Dowsing is in many ways an intimate connection between two minds. To gain such a profound awareness of another person and then to snuff out their life like that… I imagine it would be permanently damaging to the soul. No, any real assassin would just use a knife or an arrow far more effectively and efficiently."

Ryn swallowed, his throat suddenly dry. He had a strong desire to run from the room. All this talk of death and the piles of corpses around him filled him with unreasonable dread. Master Pembrim put a steadying hand on his shoulder. This sudden contact surprised Ryn more than anything; it seemed so out of character from Pembrim. Ryn looked up and the Root master seemed to hold him in place with his dark eyes.

"Steady as it goes, Ryn," he said. Clearly, Ryn had not been able to hide his shock and revulsion. "There's a reason I'm telling you all this and showing you this. You really are a gifted healer, and I expect a lot from you someday. Death and life are like the two sides of a coin, and you have to understand and appreciate both." He paused and lowered his gaze. "Still, I'll let you go a little early today. I recommend you take a walk in the fresh air before you head to your next lesson."

Ryn could only nod, as he pushed aside a dozen different questions. He turned and left Master Pembrim alone with all his corpses.

Jayn closed her eyes, picturing a flame flickering in her chest. She had come a long way since that first failed testing for Flame. She had mastered or begun to master all the basic Wave wards and several that required a Blending with Stone, not to mention her own invisibility Etching. She was starting to use Stone herself, as well as Root, though she could not create lacings with either just yet. Now she needed to learn Flame. From there, she could perhaps match Ryn's achievement of Blending two opposing forces. She needed more than just a new metaphor. She needed an idea for a new lacing. Blending Wave and Flame was pointless if she couldn't do anything with it. What would such a lacing look like? What would it do? Wave was the force of stability; Flame, the force of chaos. Wave Weavers created wards; Flame Weavers generated energy. What would a Flame-enhanced ward do? Energize those who passed through it? Or disable them?

She was getting ahead of herself. First, she needed to master Flame. She imagined the flickering red fire inside her spreading, growing to surround her. She opened her eyes and concentrated on the candle before her, one of three set carefully in a tin tray on an overturned barrel. Ryn stood to her right and Pavel to her left. She couldn't help noticing from the corners of her eyes the flickers of red light dancing around the two men. She knew she should be focusing on brightening the candle, but she had to glance down at herself. Though she had felt it forming, she was still relieved to see flashes of red hovering around her gray shirt.

This broke her concentration, and the lights vanished like smoke, but it didn't matter. She had done it. She could summon Flame.

"Very good," Shilo said. She stood opposite her three Flame students, her eyes darting between each of them, but she met Jayn's gaze to say that. Shilo was being deliberately careful around Jayn. Jayn knew what the girl was doing, of course; Jayn had been a bit impatient in the past, exhibiting something of a bad temper. Shilo stepped gingerly to avoid upsetting Jayn, though she didn't have to—not anymore, Jayn hoped.

The candles to either side of Jayn lit up brighter, as Pavel and Ryn succeeded in their elementary lacing. Jayn tried not to sigh. It was ridiculous to compare herself to the two men. Their giftings were complementary to Flame; it was only natural they would pick it up faster than her. She stepped away from the group and arched her back to stretch. It had been another long day at the end of a long week.

Thalia sat on a crate on the far side of their little closet. She smiled at Jayn. "Maybe we can switch it up now?" she offered.

They'd spent the first half hour of this Secret Training session rehashing the hurried conversation from that morning. Pavel reiterated his warning to give the Scholar a wide berth, though he refused to elaborate on his reasoning. Clearly, he'd had a bad encounter with the Scholars in the past. Probably, he had stolen from them. Ryn told them what little he had learned about the Kobolds from Master Pembrim, who was apparently studying the bodies. That seemed fitting with the man's character. Jayn couldn't decide whether she preferred the strange new Root master or Mistress Hinter, even knowing she was a traitor. Ryn's comments put them dangerously close to revisiting the night of the attack yet again, which no one seemed eager to do, so someone had suggested they resume their actual Secret Training.

Jayn shrugged. She looked at the two men. "You two want to try your Blending again?" Failing another attempt at that might humble them some.

Pavel shook his head. "Not really. It's been a long week."

Jayn didn't fight him. Probably, they should all just go to bed. Tomorrow would be a lighter schedule, though they still had an extended round of chores in the morning. Still, she wasn't quite ready to give up on the evening just yet. She had been thinking a lot about Etchings, and she decided to ask a question that had been needling at her recently. "Fair enough," she said. "Actually, I think we might be going about this wrong. Wouldn't it be better if we focused on helping Ryn activate his Etching?"

Pavel quirked an eyebrow. "Isn't that what we've been doing?" he said slowly.

"Not at all. Ryn's Etching doesn't use Aether. It's like how Thalia and I can create a shield using Stone and Wave, but Captain Lahmeer can make a stronger one using only Wave, because that's her Etching."

"Oh," Shilo said. "I never thought about it that way. So, you're saying that what they did using Aether and Root, anyone could do that? Well, anyone who could wield Root and Aether and make them Blend?"

"In theory, yes. It's another way to achieve what Ryn should be able to do through his Etching using only Root."

"Yeah," Ryn said. "I think she's right. Or that's how I look at it, anyway." He paused. "Except, the thing I still don't really get is, when my Etching does activate, it doesn't use Root. Well, of course, I guess it does, but it's just automatic. I don't have to create a Root tree first, yet it still can drain energy from the plants around me."

"He's right," Thalia said. "That night when Kalo attacked him… I was there the whole time while his body healed itself, and

I never saw any lacings. Actually, my Etching works in a similar way. If I don't control it, anything I work on will pick up the luck enchantment. I can feel the energy leaving my hands, but I can't actually see it the way Stone normally works."

Jayn shrugged. "That's just how it is. Some Etchings are automatic, while others are not. Hmm, does that mean Ryn can never consciously activate his Etching? I suppose you can't really make a direct comparison between his and yours."

"Except…" Shilo hesitated before continuing. "Except, it seems like all Etchings are automatic the first time they're used, doesn't it?"

"What do you mean?" Jayn asked.

"Well, my Etching is kind of like yours. I can create it by concentrating and using a Flame lacing, but that's not how it worked the first time. I didn't know anything about visualization or lacings. I just threw a punch, and that pirate went flying. I didn't use Flame, at least not the way I use it now. When I first started learning with the Watchkeepers, I could see my own lacings right away, before I could see other people's. I didn't see anything like that that day on the boat."

"So what are you saying?"

"I'm just wondering why it was automatic that first time and not now. Why was the first time easier than every other time? Like, what would have happened if I hadn't joined the Watchkeepers and if no one else came to teach me about Weaving? Probably I wouldn't have learned to control my Etching like I can now, but I have to imagine I could still use it again. If the pirates came back, or if I was in some other danger, surely, I would be able to throw that kind of punch again. Except, I would never think to close my eyes and imagine a fire inside my chest. I would never see the lacings, but my Etching would still work, just like Ryn's and

Thalia's can still work without thinking. It's like…" She paused long enough that someone else could have spoken, but no one did. "It's like my Etching only works the way it does now, because the Watchkeepers *told* me that's how it's supposed to work. I believed them, and that belief became reality."

"It never stops," Pavel said, slowly shaking his head, his gaze unfocused. After a moment, his eyes locked on Ryn. "What you did that night, kid… You pried out a stone from the very foundation of the world, and now everything is crumbling."

They all fell silent after that. There's no telling how long that silence would have lasted, because it was soon shattered by a knock at the door—the door to the disused storage room in the basement of the Citadel, where none of them were supposed to be.

Chapter 6
The Commandant

THE MAN WHO CALLED HIMSELF Pavel Talvor looked at the four kids who comprised his Training Pentad. Every one of them appeared stricken with fear or guilt. He sighed and took the few steps necessary to reach the door. These kids had a lot to learn about the benefits of lying. He turned the bolt and opened the door.

"Ah, Captain Lahmeer," he said in greeting. He'd made a quick mental list of all the possible people who could have knocked, and she had been near the top, though that may have been down to wishful thinking. "How are you this wonderful evening?"

Nyssa Lahmeer craned her neck to look past him. "I see you're all here," she said. He admired that neck—the graceful curve of it—as well as her deep brown eyes and her beaded braids that clinked together like tiny windchimes as she moved.

"How might we be of service?" He kept his tone smooth and casual, betraying none of those thoughts. Sure, Nyssa was beautiful, but this world was full of beautiful women. She was a decorated officer within the Watchkeepers, while he was a lowly recruit, and that created a separation between them—in her eyes at least.

She sidled past him to fully enter the room. She took in all of the nervous-looking teenagers in a dusty closet with a sweeping glance. "So," she said, the ghost of a smile on her lips, "where's the booze?"

The kids all exchanged confused glances. Thalia began to protest.

Nyssa held up a hand. "No need to explain. I was a recruit once too. My Training Pentad had a spot like this, only it was up in one of the spires." She pointed upward. "We all have to unwind somehow." She surveyed the kids again. Jayn at least had managed to control her expression. A crease formed between Nyssa's brows. "Still…"

Pavel laughed to get her attention back on him. "Oh, I would love to have been here back then. I'm sure Recruit Lahmeer and I would have been good friends."

She frowned at that comment, but at least her focus was back on him. He didn't trust any of the others to spin the lie they needed. Pavel had been lying successfully for most of his life, and he knew the best lies always involved as much truth as you could get away with. That made them easier to remember too. "We are admittedly a little dry at the moment, but your assessment is mostly correct. Sadly, this lot has not yet learned how to shut things off completely. While we should have been griping about all the teachers we don't like, instead we were having a bit of a philosophical debate on the nature of Etchings. Sounds tedious, I know, but Shilo here had some good points."

Nyssa folded her arms. "Etchings, huh?"

Pavel couldn't trust the others to pick up the lie and run with it just yet, so he kept right on talking. Fortunately, he had established himself as a bit of a blathering fool with Nyssa already. "Actually, perhaps you can give us some insight. Why do some Etchings seem to be automatic or even unconscious, while others require concentration?"

Nyssa shrugged. "That's a question for a Scholar, I suppose. Although it figures you five would have an interest in Etchings, since each of you has one." She glared at Pavel on that last bit. Probably she had found out about his Etching from Master Flint. Pavel had kept it a secret when he first met Nyssa, though not for any particular reason. Secrecy was his default impulse.

He smiled. "Of course, but we were also wondering why every Etching seems to be automatic the first time it works. Take your shield Etching, for example. Now it takes you a full minute of concentrated effort to make a shield of any substantial size, but what about the first time you used it? Did it take a minute then, or was it more… instantaneous?"

She frowned and got a faraway look in her eye. Pavel felt a little bad then. Etchings tended to manifest when one was a teenager, often in response to a pressing need. Whatever caused a young girl to suddenly need an impenetrable shield could not have been good. Still, giving her something else to think about would take her mind off of wondering what they were really doing down here. She shook her head. "I suppose it did happen right away that first time, but what of it?"

"Well…" Jayn said, stepping forward. Pavel didn't move to stop her; she was the next-best liar in their Training Pentad, and Nyssa would be more likely to buy the cover if it wasn't just Pavel selling it. "What if you could still use your Etching instantly, without having to stop and visualize it? Shouldn't that be possible?"

"That is an interesting point, I suppose." Nyssa paused. "How did you get on such a topic? Are you sure you haven't been drinking? Or imbibing something else?" Jayn began to protest, but Nyssa quieted her with a wave of her hand. "It doesn't matter. You all need to come with me."

The kids looked worried again. Thalia spoke up. "Are we in trouble?" To her credit, she kept her tone neutral.

"What? No, nothing like that. Commandant Lahey needs to speak with all of you."

"The commandant?" Jayn couldn't hide her surprise. "Why?"

Nyssa sighed. "Just, come on. We're late enough as it is, since I had to track you down. I tried to catch you coming out from dinner. No one is in trouble though."

They all filed out behind Nyssa. Pavel noticed Ryn discreetly tossing his knife into a straw-filled crate near the door. None of them were supposed to carry weapons in the compound, a rule that had not been changed even after Kobolds overran the place.

Pavel cleared his throat when they reached the base of the stairs. "How did you find us, by the way?"

"Master Pembrim," Nyssa said over her shoulder as she began to climb. "He's spent long enough with Ryn and Jayn that he can pinpoint them anywhere in the compound, thanks to his Etching." Pavel had heard about the new Root master and his talent, though he had not yet met the man.

Jayn spoke up next. Despite her many admirable traits, the girl feared getting in trouble with authority maybe even more than the others. "Why exactly does the commandant wish to see us?"

"He will want to explain that himself. I guess none of you have really met him yet. Normally, he likes to meet with new recruits earlier in their training, but we've all been a bit busy with everything that's happened. When we get in there, stand at attention and don't ask any questions, unless he gives permission." She paused. "He's not someone you need to fear, but... Just be on your best manners."

No one asked any questions after that. Pavel had made identifying the commandant a priority early on during training, though he had kept a careful distance from the man. Pavel had only seen him a few times, strolling purposefully across the lawn or through the halls of the Citadel, with a train of attendants at his heels. Nyssa's warning matched with everything he had heard about the commandant, a gruff, no-nonsense man who radiated authority, even from a distance. At the third-floor landing, Nyssa turned and led them down a hallway. Night had fallen outside the windows, but Weaver lights illuminated the Citadel with a sallow glow. Pavel knew that Commandant Lahey's offices were up on the fifth floor, but this level held several different meeting rooms. Nyssa stopped before one such chamber and knocked on the heavy oak door.

"Enter," a booming voice said within.

Pavel and his Pentad shuffled into the dim room, lit by a single Weaver light on the far side. They lined up side-by-side where Nyssa indicated with a nod, their hands crossed behind their backs and their chins level.

Commandant Hiram Lahey was not alone. The leader of the Watchkeepers sat on one side of a narrow wooden table. His gray tabard was trimmed in black, and three black bands wrapped the sleeves of his shirt, but otherwise the uniform was the same as theirs. He even wore a shiny red pin on his lapel to indicate he was a Flame Weaver. His wiry black hair, parted at the side, had weathered mostly to gray, as had his bushy eyebrows. With his square jaw and steady gaze, Hiram Lahey could have easily passed for a general in the Standing Army.

Pavel had never seen the woman sitting across from Lahey before, but he knew at once who she must be. The silk dress, the studied neutral expression, the barely concealed sense of superiority—this woman had to be a Scholar. Pavel's father had been a Scholar, and he knew the type all too well. What had Thalia said her name was? Mina Bellain. Clearly, this was her. If more than one Scholar had come to the Citadel, they were all in trouble.

She rose smoothly to her feet and turned to smile benignly at them before looking back at the commandant. "I've kept you long enough," she said. "I will leave you to your recruits."

Lahey rose to shake her hand. "Let me know if we can be of any further service to your studies, Miss Bellain."

Mina Bellain's eyes lingered on each of them as she left the room. She smiled at Thalia but said nothing. Pavel needed to figure out what this Scholar was doing here, but that would have to come later. As the door clicked shut behind her, he turned his full attention to the commandant. Though he hid it better than the others, Pavel did want to know what they were doing here. If he alone had been summoned, there could have been any number of unpleasant reasons, but all five of them? Probably it was nothing bad.

Nyssa stepped forward, her boots squeaking on the polished stone. "Commandant Lahey," she said. "Presenting Pavel Talvor, Jayn Eldragor, Thalia Moldo, Ryn Silverbell, and Shilo Lorn, as requested." She gestured to each of them as she spoke, and Lahey quickly surveyed the group. Pavel had no doubt the man would remember each name and face.

"Thank you for coming," Lahey said. "I apologize for not meeting with you recruits sooner, but my attention has been focused elsewhere. You are all aware of the continuing threat posed by the Kobolds, on top of mounting tensions with Tamor. I have been back and forth to Appencourt far too often of late. I regret that I was there and not here when Falport was attacked. However, I am told that your Pentad performed admirably throughout the ordeal. I commend you for that."

Though Nyssa had warned them to be quiet, that clearly necessitated some response. "Thank you, sir," Jayn said in the level tone of a soldier. The others nodded. That seemed to suffice.

"That is part of why I called you here tonight. I am told that two of you were with Captain Lahmeer in the Sylphren Wood during the first documented attack on humans by Kobolds. When my masters and officers gave their full accounting of everything that happened here the night of the incursion, each of your names came up more than once. It seems you collectively managed to be present at several pivotal moments that evening. To get to the point, the Hall of the Assembly will be holding a formal hearing soon to discuss the ongoing Kobold threat. It has been decided that you will travel to Appencourt, alongside Captain Lahmeer, to testify about the attacks."

Pavel glanced at his teammates, who were all exchanging confused looks.

Lahey's thick eyebrows rose a fraction of an inch. "Is there a question?" he asked.

"Respectfully, sir," Jayn said, "but why us?"

"For the reasons already stated. I will also tell you that the Hall specifically requested you five. Your involvement was included in the full report sent to Appencourt." He paused. "Personally, I believe that the lords hope they can get more… straightforward answers out of fresh recruits than they can from my masters and officers." He made a dismissive wave with his hand. "It comes down to a lot of political nonsense you needn't worry about."

"Sir," Pavel said, hoping the window for a question hadn't closed. "With respect, why now? It's been two months."

Lahey nodded solemnly. "Indeed. The Hall is clearly taking the Kobolds seriously to be moving this quickly." He spoke without a trace of sarcasm. Pavel would have laughed if they had been anywhere else. "Take the weekend to prepare," Lahey continued. "You will be excused from your regular chores tomorrow, and you will leave first thing on Flaresday. Tomorrow, I will sit down with each of you individually to hear your accounts of everything related to the Kobolds. But for now, while you are all here, I want to give you some general instructions on how you are to conduct yourselves when you get to Appencourt."

He paused to look at each of them, ensuring he had their attention, before he continued.

"First, you must stick exclusively to the facts. As much as possible, volunteer no opinions. There are many things we still don't understand about these enemies, and no doubt you have all speculated about their means and motives. You need not share such speculations with the lords of the Assembly. Don't be afraid to say, 'I don't know.' This is especially important when it comes to the more… sensational events of that evening. With regards to the other creature or creatures you may have witnessed that night, report what you saw as faithfully as you can, but do not share any theories you may have formed regarding their origin or intent. Understood?"

This was not an invitation to speak, but Pavel decided to press his luck anyway. "You are referring to the Manfaces, sir?"

"Manfaces?" Lahey asked, his head tilting slightly.

"The giant animals with human-like faces." Pavel glanced at his teammates. "We've taken to calling them Manfaces, for lack of a better term." That wasn't true. Sometimes Pavel lied simply because he thought it would be funny.

Lahey nodded. "Yes, I am referring to the *Manfaces*, as well as the Kobold with the black armor. I would make no mention of anything he did that might have resembled Weaving."

"Sir?" Jayn said. She waited for his nod before continuing. "If I understand your meaning, you wish us to… withhold information?" Clearly she had wanted to say "lie."

"Perhaps I need to make myself clearer," he said in a brusque tone that meant none of them should try interrupting him again. "I am not instructing you to lie before the Hall. If they ask you directly about something, then by all means, answer truthfully. You simply should not *volunteer* anything beyond what they ask. If you must know, we have decided to reserve information regarding the suspected Kobold Weaver as a sort of trump card. There is a concern that the lords may wish to mount an… insufficient response to the Kobold threat. They may underestimate the danger these creatures pose. If they need further incitement to action, then Captain Lahmeer will disclose that particular detail, but you will leave that decision to her discretion. Understood?"

This was not a question. They all nodded and murmured, "Yes, sir."

He studied each of them once more before continuing. "One last thing. None of you should say anything about the possible motives or whereabouts of the former Watchkeeper Gwen Hinter." Even Nyssa, who had been staring levelly at the wall, reacted in surprise to that pronouncement.

"But sir…" Shilo managed to say, despite the obvious panic in her voice. Pavel understood why she would feel compelled to speak up. She alone had witnessed the former Root master killing a fellow Weaver before disappearing into the chaos of that night.

Her testimony was the sole basis of the Watchkeepers' conclusion that Hinter had fled the city of her own accord, with all the guilt that implied. Shilo was too innocent to willingly lie about such a thing.

Lahey raised a hand to stop any further comment. His tone softened slightly. "I understand your reluctance, Miss Lorn. If the Hall asks you directly if you saw Gwen Hinter kill someone that night, then you must of course tell them the truth. They are unlikely to do so, however. Gwen Hinter has been reported only as missing. They may ask if you saw her that night. I know from the reports that you and some others saw her shortly after the explosion in the smithy. Tell them about that encounter. If at all possible, we would like to keep her suspected betrayal out of the public record. Can you do what I have asked you?"

It took Shilo a moment to respond. "Yes, sir," she managed to say. "I will try."

He nodded. "Good. I don't want any of you to think that we are not taking the search for Gwen Hinter seriously. We are making every possible effort to locate her. We simply prefer to deal with this matter internally. I'm sure you can all understand."

He took several moments to look at each of them once again. Pavel kept his chin level and met Lahey's gaze, betraying no emotion.

"That's enough for now," Lahey said. "Captain Lahmeer will assist you with the necessary travel preparations. I will send for each of you at some point tomorrow. The interviews will start in the morning but may continue into the afternoon. I want to know everything that you know or remember about that night. You are dismissed."

They followed Nyssa out of the room. She walked them all the way back to the dorms, so they had no chance to discuss what had happened openly. This wasn't good. For several reasons, Pavel had no desire to appear before the Hall of the Assembly in Appencourt. Still, if the kids stayed in line, they could keep their secret and their freedom.

In the aftermath of the Kobold assault, first Nyssa and then several of the masters had debriefed them. They'd told almost the entire truth—everything from the Kobold Weaver named Kalo to the Manfaces that emerged from a portal. They'd told just one lie. One very important lie. It wasn't time to worry just yet. When a lie made more sense than the truth, few would question it. Pavel would remind Ryn of that tonight when they were safely back in their rooms. He hoped Jayn would do the same with the girls. They would tell their lie to Commandant Lahey, and then he would send them to Appencourt, where they would lie to the Hall of the Assembly and maybe even the five blighted Pentarchs of all Aldria. The man who called himself Pavel Talvor knew that he could do it, and he would do whatever it took to make sure the others could too.

Chapter 7
Preparations

"AND THEN THE GIANT OWL swooped down and picked Kalo up in its talons, and they flew away," Jayn said. "After that, I passed out, and sometime later Ryn revived me with his healing."

Commandant Hiram Lahey studied her. He sat with his elbows on the table and his fingers steepled below his chin. This was the same room he had called them to last night. He'd sat through her account without comment or any visible reaction on his stoic face. From his comments yesterday, he had clearly read everything the first Watchkeepers to interview her had written down. Nothing she said had surprised him; she had been careful to say nothing surprising.

Commandant Lahey allowed the silence to stretch, no doubt hoping she might say something else to fill it. Jayn remained quiet; she had learned the silence trick long ago from her mother. Finally, he nodded. "I commend you for sticking strictly to the facts. You clearly took my advice to heart, though of course you could have been more forthcoming with me."

She ignored the invitation. "Thank you, sir" was all she said.

"Now, I understand your mother is a Pentarch, the fourth I believe."

His sudden shift caught her off guard, as did his feigned ignorance. He knew exactly who her mother was. She kept most of that from her face and all of it from her voice. "Yes, sir. My mother is Anyse Eldragor."

"Will that be a problem? Of course, I doubt any of the Pentarchs save the first will take part in the hearing, but I'm sure your mother will wish to see you."

"No, sir, it will not be a problem."

He studied her a moment longer. "I'll be blunt, Miss Eldragor. We seldom get recruits from the so-called first echelon of Aldrian society, let alone the child of a Pentarch. You are also very young to have joined the Watchkeepers. Am I wrong for inferring there may have been a falling out?"

Now she understood his line of questioning. She couldn't fault him for his conclusion. She had enlisted shortly after turning sixteen, the minimum age for joining the Watchkeepers. She shook her head. "With respect, sir, you are mistaken. My mother fully supported my decision to join the Watchkeepers."

"I am glad to hear that, then. Well, that about covers it. Will you excuse me for a moment?"

That surprised her too. Shouldn't he have dismissed her and called for her next Pentad member? Instead, he rose from his seat, moved around the table, and left. Jayn turned to look at the door as it closed behind him. She heard the deep rumble of his voice as he spoke to someone. Then the door opened again, and the woman from last night, whom Thalia had identified as Mina Bellain, the Scholar, slipped in.

Mina offered a broad smile. She had the fair skin and straight dark hair of northern Aldria, though one could never assume origin based on appearance. Whatever distinctions between people groups may have existed in the ancient past, the Burning had jumbled everyone up, so while many dark-haired, pale-skinned people still resided in north Aldria, this Scholar could have just as easily been from Tamor or Iscerna. People came from all over to join the Academy of the Ways. Mina's accent certainly gave nothing away. She spoke with measured formality. "Good morning, Miss Eldragor," she said. "Might I have a moment of your time? The commandant has graciously granted me permission to speak with you and your Pentad."

Jayn tried to conceal her surprise. Pavel's dire warning about Scholars had made her cautious. The coincidence of the prophecy Thalia had overheard and what had happened to Jayn and her Pentad also made her uneasy. Still, she couldn't refuse to speak with the woman when cornered like this. Perhaps Pavel had overstated the risk. Scholars mostly had a reputation for being eccentric but harmless. Jayn pushed aside the queasiness in her stomach and smiled back. "Of course," she said.

Mina made a bowing gesture almost like a curtsy. "My name is Mina Bellain of the Academy of the Ways. Most would call me a Scholar."

"I—it's a pleasure to meet you." Jayn had wanted to say she had heard of Mina through Thalia but thought better of it. Doing so would have led them straight to Rigel's prophecy, and Jayn would not be the one to bring up that topic.

In the end, Mina asked her only a few questions, none of them related to poisons or prophecies. The questions she did ask still unsettled Jayn.

"Tell me about the Kobold called Kalo," Mina said as soon as she was settled in the chair the commandant had just vacated.

Jayn tilted her head. "What would you like to know?"

Mina's cheerfulness never wavered. "Well, as you can imagine, I am very curious about the report that this Kobold may have been a Weaver."

She really had stuck her nose in as deep as she could if she knew that much. If neither the Hall of the Assembly nor the Pentarchy had learned that detail yet, how had she found out? Clearly, Commandant Lahey trusted this woman, if he gave her access to the Citadel and his records. She couldn't be much of a danger. Either way, Jayn had to cooperate, or at least give the appearance of cooperation.

She shrugged. "I'm not sure what he was. Certainly, he was different from the other Kobolds who attacked the Citadel."

"How so?"

"Well, he was taller, for one. Most Kobolds, at least the ones I saw, are my height or shorter. This one was tall. He would have been tall even for a human. The others wore leather trousers and vests, but he had a full set of black leather armor."

"Yes, I gathered as much from the reports. What I am most interested in is his apparent Weaving."

Jayn spent most of her time deliberately not thinking about that. When his dark lacing had enveloped her, it had paralyzed her somehow. She hadn't fallen over, and yet she couldn't move. She was stuck there, her feet barely touching the ground, powerless and defenseless. He could have killed her so easily. He would have killed her if he had been less sadistic. Instead, he had dragged his claws across her face and stabbed them into her stomach, leaving her to die from his poison. Though Ryn had healed the wounds so that not even the trace of a scar remained, she still remembered them. For weeks afterward, she would find herself absently running a hand across her cheek or over her stomach. She still had nightmares about it. She could not tell all that to Mina Bellain, but she had to give the Scholar something.

"It didn't look like Weaving," Jayn said. "I'll grant you it was something unnatural, but not any lacing I've ever seen." An idea came to her then. Maybe information could flow both ways. Scholars studied the Five Forces far differently than the Watch-keepers and probably knew much more. "I'm curious, Miss Bellain. Do you know of a lacing that can paralyze someone? Not like the numbing blows a Flame Weaver can deliver, but actually freeze someone in place where they stand? You are a Scholar. Have you ever heard of such a thing?"

Probably Mina didn't want to say yes or no to that. Scholars never wanted to show their ignorance, but they were also reluctant to share their knowledge with those outside the Academy. Still, she couldn't refuse to answer the question either without shattering her pleasant and agreeable façade.

Mina's affable expression never faltered, but it did take her a moment to formulate a response. "Perhaps such a lacing could be affected through one or another Blending, yet if the reports are correct, and the Kobold's Weaving appeared as black shadows and not colorful light, then we might assume it came from some other source, entirely separate from the Five Forces. That is what I find so interesting."

Jayn suppressed a smile. A vague evasion and a quick shift to a more astounding idea to distract Jayn. This Scholar was good, but Jayn had been taught by the best. The brief interview ended peacefully, though neither woman gave away more than she wanted. Jayn hoped that someday some circumstance might put

Mina Bellain across a negotiation table from Jayn's mother—if Jayn could watch from a safe distance.

Ryn told Commandant Lahey the truth—as much of it as he could. He made a few omissions. He made no mention of the conversations he may or may not have heard in his mind when he had passed out near the portal. He told only one lie, near the end. It was an easy lie to tell, Pavel had reminded him last night and again that morning. No one could suspect the truth when the truth was impossible. The lie made more sense, was more believable. It's what people expected would have happened.

"I was bleeding badly," Ryn said. "Shilo and Jayn had been injured as well. If I waited for my Etching to kick in on its own, well I might have died before that happened. The falling debris had nicked an artery." Ryn had learned all about arteries and veins and the rest of human anatomy from the Root Weavers. He swallowed once and then told the lie. "So, I concentrated, and I finally activated my Etching. I healed myself, and then I was able to heal the others." Ryn sighed. All the talking had made his throat dry.

Commandant Lahey said nothing. He studied Ryn's face, his eyes inscrutable beneath those bushy eyebrows. Ryn didn't know what else the man wanted.

"I only made it work that one time though," Ryn found himself saying. "I've tried using my Etching again since, but it hasn't happened… It still works on its own of course. If I cut my arm, eventually the cut heals after an hour or two… The window seems to be getting shorter… I don't know why it did work that one time. I guess with all the pressure and urgency of the moment, that's why I could do it. I've heard that's how it works sometimes."

Finally, Lahey nodded. "Yes, that is true," he said. "Your Pentad was lucky to have you there. I'm sure in time you will gain full mastery of your Etching. Remember also what I told you about sticking just to the facts when you are in Appencourt. No need to volunteer too much."

"Yes, sir. Of course."

With that, the interview was finally over. The commandant excused himself but asked Ryn to wait a moment. He went outside and the Scholar came in. Jayn had warned Ryn about this. He had passed her on the stairs on his way to this meeting. Still, with all his nervousness about talking to Lahey, Ryn had forgotten all about it, until he saw Mina Bellain step through the door.

"Tell me about your Etching," Mina said after introducing herself and taking a seat.

He thought she might go straight to the poison, but this question was just as dangerous, if not more. Before he left home, he had viewed Scholars as beings out of fairy stories and legends. They were wise and clever and could outwit any foe with their secret knowledge of the universe. That was clearly an exaggeration, but Ryn knew all the same he could not expect to match wits with this woman.

"No need to be nervous," Mina said, with an encouraging smile that didn't quite reach her eyes.

Ryn took a deep breath. He had gone in a matter of weeks from living in the woods with his aunt to living in a big city with thousands of strangers. In that time, he had learned one valuable lesson about interacting with others. No one took you seriously if they thought you were an idiot. Ryn knew he was ignorant of most things, and ignorance is often mistaken for stupidity. He had come to accept people thinking he was stupid, as it offered a quick route to gaining knowledge. He leaned on that now, gladly showing his ignorance to this woman. A wise and learned Scholar would never suspect a rustic idiot could have unlocked one of the hidden secrets of the universe.

He told her so much of the truth that his few omissions and one lie were mere bumps in his rambling, disjointed story. He started with the first attack in the Sylphren Wood, playing up his fear and revulsion toward the Kobolds. The emotions were genuine, but if he presented himself as a coward, that would likely also help her to overlook him. He emphasized his total confusion upon waking to find his wounds healed and the forest around him drained of life. He spent a long time describing those desiccated trees.

He made no mention of any poison the Kobolds might have inflicted, and she never asked about it. Though she had prompted him only to talk about his Etching, he made plenty of digressions, covering details she no doubt already knew about, from the killing of Nyssa's Pentad to aspects of his training here in Falport. When he finally got to the lie, he told it in an even more muddled way than he had explained it to the commandant. By that point, he hoped, she would be too annoyed by his terrible storytelling skills to suspect anything he said might be a lie. It seemed to work. He hoped it worked.

Thalia sighed as she emerged from the Citadel into the warm sunlight. Though it was just past midmorning, she was already tired. She was glad that Jayn had warned her that Mina Bellain would be stepping into the interviews. In the end, the Scholar had asked her nothing about Rigel's prophecy or Kobold poison. Her questions focused exclusively on Thalia's luck Etching.

Thalia had taken a bit of a risk when she began telling her story. She still wasn't sure if it had been wise, but pointedly ignoring their shared experience with the Rigel fountain might also have drawn Mina's attention. Thalia had already acknowledged that she remembered meeting Mina that time. So, Thalia began her story of discovering her Etching by saying, "Actually, it started right after I met you. When the Rigel fountain gave you one of its usual nonsense answers, and you left, I went back to close up the redsmith's shop. That's when one of our customers showed up, carrying a broken kettle."

She went smoothly on from there, explaining how she had come to join the Watchkeepers and how Master Caston had helped her learn the limits of her gift. If she imbued any object with her luck enchantment and gave it to someone else, that person would experience two days of uncommonly good luck, followed by a day of bad luck—the recoil that many powerful enchantments carried. She made no further mention of the Rigel fountain, and she hoped her gamble had succeeded. She had acknowledged that she of course remembered Mina asking the Rigel fountain a question, but she downplayed any significance the Runeform's answer might have held. Either way, she couldn't take back her words now.

As she made her way across the lawn, she considered what further preparations were needed for the trip to Appencourt. Three sets of saddlebags had been delivered to her shared room with the other girls, and she'd been instructed that she could take nothing more than what would fit in the bags or that she could comfortably carry on her person. Though they would be traveling along the safest and most well-maintained road in Aldria to reach the capital, Watchkeepers never traveled without weapons. She would have to see Mistress Whitcomb for a staff; she had developed the most proficiency with that weapon.

Master Caston intercepted her before she could reach her room. "There you are," he said. "Have you finished your interview with the commandant?"

"Only just," she said, gesturing back toward the Citadel.

"Excellent, come with me."

"Where are we going?" she asked as she fell in line beside him. He seemed more animated than usual.

"Well, I heard about your upcoming outing to Appencourt. There is no way I will be able to keep the other Stone Weavers from using up all the Iscernaen steel while you are away, so if we're going to make your dagger this weekend, we better get started."

Thalia smiled. After her run-in with the Scholar and all the sudden attention from the commandant, she had forgotten all about Master Caston's steel-making project. She knew from watching her father as a child the long hours needed to forge a finished blade from ingots or rods of steel. She would have hardly any time to pack for their journey, but she didn't think twice about following Master Caston toward his partially rebuilt smithy.

Shilo squeezed her legs as Nyssa Lahmeer had shown her, and the mare took a few reluctant steps forward. Apparently, Shilo was the only one in her Training Pentad who had never ridden a horse, so after her long and nerve-wracking interviews with the commandant and the Scholar, Shilo had gone to the stables for a rudimentary lesson with Nyssa.

Shilo had not often interacted with Captain Lahmeer, and those moments had never been one-on-one. Shilo found the Wave Weaver to be a patient teacher who gently corrected problems with Shilo's form or technique. Properly caring for a horse was an involved and complex process, but Nyssa was quick to explain that their goal today was just to make sure Shilo wouldn't fall out of the saddle on the road to Appencourt—or be too sore for it. Shilo was surprised to learn that if you wanted to ride all day and be able to walk afterward, you couldn't just sit on the horse. Good riding form involved putting more weight on your legs, in more of a crouch than a sit. It wasn't easy, but Nyssa kept reminding her of its importance.

Still, Shilo knew it would be a long four days riding to Appencourt, and she wished they could sail upriver instead. She'd grown up on boats and preferred them far better as a means of transportation. Perhaps, they would take a boat on their return to Falport, but fighting upstream against the current was labor intensive—requiring several polemen or assistance from a team of mules walking alongside the river—and would take twice as long as riding, so few people did it. It couldn't be helped. She would certainly be sore from four days of riding, but Shilo had no fear of falling out of the saddle. If she could hang onto the rigging of her father's sloop during a summer storm on the Baston Sea, she could stay atop a horse.

"Good," Nyssa said, as she watched Shilo steer the mare around the fenced-in pen near the stables from atop her own gelding. "Make sure not to saw on the reins. A steady hand is all it takes."

The lesson soon ended, and they handed the horses off to one of the grooms in green livery. "One more thing," Nyssa said, as they walked away from the stables.

Shilo glanced at the tall Wave Weaver, hearing some hesitancy in her tone.

"About last night," Nyssa said. "How are you feeling about what the commandant said about Gwen Hinter?"

Shilo frowned. Everyone called that woman Gwen Hinter now, never Mistress Hinter or the Root master. Despite everything that happened that night, despite almost dying at the hands of Kalo, witnessing Gwen Hinter stab that Watchkeeper had filled Shilo with the greatest sense of dread. Everyone expected a literal monster like Kalo to be evil, but no one expected that from a Watchkeeper, let alone a member of the Council of Masters.

Shilo slowly nodded. "I understand the commandant's point," she said. "I see how it could be damaging to the whole organization."

"It isn't just about saving face," Nyssa said, clearly choosing her words carefully. "Everything is being done to find her. If she surfaces anywhere in Aldria, there are enough eyes and ears out there that we will know about it. Disclosing her involvement with the Kobolds could affect more than just the Watchkeepers. Word is already out that humans were working with the Kobolds, but right now the public assumes they were all lowlifes from the fringes of society. If people knew that a highly placed, well-respected member of the Watchkeepers was involved, it could cause panic. The implication is that anyone could be working with the Kobolds, anyone could be a traitor. Your neighbors, your relatives… We want to avoid that kind of panic."

Shilo hadn't considered all that. It was a chilling thought. They really couldn't know how many people were involved. They didn't know their goals or what they wanted. They knew nothing.

Nyssa put a comforting hand on her shoulder. "Try not to worry about all that. Keep your chin up and stick to the plan. It shouldn't take more than two weeks, and then we'll be back here in Falport to complete your training."

Shilo nodded. Maybe four long days in the saddle wouldn't be too bad. If she was exhausted, it would be easier to fall asleep at night.

Nyssa Lahmeer answered the knock at her door. "Agia," she said in greeting, and ushered her mentor into the room. Her dorm in the officer's barracks was a bit untidy just then, as she was in the process of packing for the trip to Appencourt, but she knew Mistress Agia Bellos wouldn't care.

"So," Agia said, "you are heading back out."

Nyssa shrugged. "It's just to Appencourt and back. It should be a fairly dull outing."

"One certainly hopes so." Agia studied her face. Nyssa suspected she knew the reason for this visit. She knew Agia worried about her.

"I'll be fine," Nyssa said. "I'm ready to get back out in the world."

"I think you may be. I suppose it might not matter either way. After what happened to your Pentad, we hoped keeping you here would give you space and time to heal, away from the world. And then the whole world came crashing down on all of us…"

Nyssa nodded in understanding. It took the Kobolds invading Falport for her to realize just how much the loss of her Pentad had affected her. Every Watchkeeper had fought to defend the city, but Nyssa had thrown herself into the fray with total disregard for her own life. Part of her had wanted to die in that battle. Now she wasn't so sure. Now, she thought, she might want to live.

Nyssa patted her mentor on the shoulder. "I appreciate your concern, Agia, I really do. The truth is I'm no longer so eager to go back on field duty. I'm coming around to this whole teacher thing.

I would like to stay and see Jayn Eldragor and the rest of her Pentad through their training at least."

Agia smiled. "I told you you'd make a great teacher." Her smile took on a more mischievous slant. "Even that rogue Pavel Talvor seems enamored with your teaching."

Nyssa scoffed and gave her a slight shove. "Don't start with any of that now."

Agia threw up her hands to protest her innocence. "I'm not saying anything. He certainly is confident though."

Nyssa had to shake her head at that. "No, he's arrogant, not confident. It's easy to mistake the two, but I've found that arrogance is often a cover for a lack of confidence."

Agia laughed. "You are a wise woman, Nyssa Lahmeer."

Pavel slid the loose pane of glass from its casement and set it carefully against the wall. He was halfway up the staircase that led to the top of one of the Citadel's many spires, at the point where it rose from the main roof of the building. The dust on the stone steps told him no one else ever came up this staircase. Still, he stopped to listen before climbing out the window.

He moved carefully around the thin tower to the far side, placing himself near the edge of the building. The roof here had only a slight slant, falling down to a tall ornate crenellation that ran around the eaves of the Citadel. Here no one could see him from the ground or any of the other spires. No Watchkeeper would find him here, but one being could. He had to wait only a few minutes, leaning against the side of the tower, before Corvus alighted beside him, his claws making a mechanical clack on the stone roof.

"There you are, old friend," Pavel said.

Corvus gave only a bird-like croak in reply. Corvus was a Runeform, created over a thousand years ago and far older than any kingdom or country in existence, and yet the crow-shaped mechanical creature had taken a shine to the man who called himself Pavel Talvor. Pavel didn't understand it, but he was grateful for it. Corvus was his only true friend; the Runeform knew all of his secrets, the truth behind all his lies, but Corvus would never tell.

Pavel sighed, looking up at the wispy clouds drifting across the sky, as the sun sank to the west. "I'll be heading to Appencourt the day after tomorrow, if you can believe it. Will you be tagging along?"

"No way!" Corvus crowed.

Pavel laughed. "I know the feeling, buddy." He let his mind wander for a bit. Aloud, he said, "Four years and eleven months. That's how long I got left on my sentence. Ten months and three weeks now. Thirteen months to a year… That makes… sixty-three months, minus a week. I'm not sure I can make it that long."

"You should leave. Go now!"

"I thought you might say that." Pavel sighed again. "No, I guess I'll have to see it through. I'll get my slate wiped clean, and then it's farewell, Pavel Talvor. Hello… Well, I got just under sixty-three months to come up with my next name. I'll stick around till then. Someone has to keep those kids in line. They're all impressive Weavers, but not a lot of good sense among them."

Corvus made no reply to that. He busied himself pretending to preen, even though he'd never lost or gained a single feather in a millennium. Pavel watched his pretend bird for a while, before returning his gaze to the sky.

"Still," he said, "being Pavel Talvor isn't all bad. I've never asked you, but… What do you think about Nyssa?" He was careful asking questions like that around Corvus.

Corvus cawed and took off, but as he spiraled overhead, gaining altitude, Pavel heard him say, "You should marry her!"

Pavel closed his eyes and leaned his head against the stone wall. He would never be the marrying kind, and he knew that nothing Pavel Talvor did could last more than five years. Once his service to the Watchkeepers ended, Pavel Talvor would cease to exist, and the man behind the name would head back out into the world. Nothing could keep him from his destiny of finding the lost and legendary Five Crowns. Nevertheless, hearing Corvus say those words still hurt.

Chapter 8
The Appencourt Road

JAYN HAD NO REASON to feel nervous. She'd grown up in and around Appencourt, and she'd been away in Falport for less than a season. True, she'd never testified before the gathered Hall of the Assembly, but she had spent many a tedious hour during her childhood sitting in one of the balconies overlooking the Assembly Room, before her mother's appointment to the Pentarchy. She knew exactly what to expect in this hearing, yet she still felt uneasy as she made her way toward the field by the stables.

She hoped to one day have a seat in the Hall of the Assembly. She was of course already known to the lords and ladies of the Hall, but only as the Fourth Pentarch's daughter. She had made polite conversation with them at dinner parties and dances, but she had never formally testified before the Hall. However this hearing went, people would remember, and if she hoped to return to the Hall as a duly elected lady someday, she needed to make a good impression now. The journey would take four days, and she would use what time she had to make sure her fellow Pentad members knew how to act, so they didn't embarrass her. Pavel and Ryn would need the most help, for very different reasons.

Jayn joined Shilo, Thalia, Ryn, and Pavel, who were standing by and watching as Captain Lahmeer oversaw the grooms and servants who were busy cinching saddles and securing travel bags. The road to Appencourt was lined with villages and inns, so they needed little food or any of the gear required if camping were expected. They would need grain for their horses, as grazing was limited along the populated road.

Movement across the yard caught Jayn's attention. Mistress Lane Whitcomb approached, flanked by two assistants carrying armloads of weapons. Mistress Whitcomb oversaw all the physical aspects of Watchkeeper training that didn't involve Weaving, and she also maintained the organization's arsenal of weapons.

Mistress Whitcomb always wore divided skirts rather than trousers, as it allowed her a fuller range of movement. A lifetime of training outdoors had aged and wrinkled her face like old leather. She nodded to Jayn first. "Eldragor," she said, "I have a bow and some steel-tipped arrows for you." One of the assistants handed over the small curved bow and its quiver. Whitcomb hesitated before continuing. "I maintain that you should stick to the bow as long as you are able, but in a scrape, you may want this." She nodded to the other assistant, who handed her a sword.

Jayn smiled at that. When she had first started training with Mistress Whitcomb, the woman had dismissed Jayn's preference for the sword, citing Jayn's lack of height and reach. Still, when disaster had struck the Citadel, Jayn had found a sword and done well with it. Fighting alongside Pavel, she had killed a dozen of the monsters, which had been strong and ferocious but strangely had little competence with their own weapons.

She shifted the bow and quiver awkwardly to one hand as she took the sword. Thankfully an attentive stable hand came to help her. She handed him the bow and arrows but kept the sword. He took them over to the gray pony that had been assigned to her. It looked like a good mount, but she would inspect it in a minute. She slid her sword partway from its scabbard to examine it. It was a single-edged Iscernaen-style blade, like the one Captain Lahmeer wore at her hip. It came with a belt that she strapped around her waist, securing the blade to her left side. She would of course take the belt off for riding, but she wanted to get a feel for it now.

Mistress Whitcomb moved down the line. Pavel needed nothing from her. He already wore his two bladed weapons strapped across his back. They were relics from before the Burning that he had "salvaged" during his old life as a "treasure hunter," both designed to disarm his enemies or shatter their weapons, but Jayn knew from experience that he could use them to put down Kobolds when needed.

Shilo received a staff, and Jayn expected that Thalia would also get one. Instead, Mistress Whitcomb handed over an impressive-looking poleaxe. Thalia was taller and stronger than most women, and with the added reach and versatility of the poleaxe, she would be formidable. Most women in the Standing Army used some kind of polearm to compensate for their generally smaller size and shorter reach, though Jayn had never cared for such weapons. She'd trained in the sword like her mother, though of course she'd hoped to inherit the added power of a Flame Weaver.

Mistress Whitcomb knew her students well, which is why she had not given Shilo anything with a blade. Despite being a Flame Weaver, the timid fisherman's daughter still had no stomach for violence. She would rather whack away with a staff than use anything that could slice or stab her foe, even though a wooden staff could be just as deadly, especially swung by a Flame Weaver.

Ryn received a decent-sized dagger, which he strapped to his belt alongside the garden trowel that he inexplicably liked to carry around. He also wore a strange satchel swung across his chest, with little canisters studded along the strap. Mistress Whitcomb also gave him several smaller knives that were balanced for throwing but had good leather grips. She had spent a week teaching him how to sew little pockets and straps into his shirts and trousers. Throwing a knife was almost always ineffective in combat but could help in a pinch. As the group's only reliable healer, Ryn would not be expected to take part in a fight, but if anyone did manage to get past the others, he had to be able to defend himself in close-quarters combat. Producing a knife from up your sleeve and hurling it at your foe was unlikely to do any real damage, but it was a compelling distraction likely to create enough of an opening to draw your real dagger and find a spot up under the ribs to stick it. Assuming Ryn had the stomach to do something like that.

Indeed, he seemed to pale at the sight of all the weapons being doled out. "Is all this really necessary?" he asked Mistress Whitcomb.

She laughed, no doubt hearing the trepidation in his voice. "It is and it isn't," she said. "If the stars are kind, you will have a nice, lovely ride to Appencourt and back, enjoying the early summer weather, with nary a need to draw a blade. Still, you are Watchkeepers, and it is important to look the part, for the citizens you pass on the road, as well as the lords of the Assembly."

"Well put," someone said, coming up behind them.

Jayn flinched. She'd been too distracted by the shiny steel to hear anyone approaching. She turned to see Mistress Agia Bellos carrying a small wooden box. The Wave master nodded to each of them. "Though you are still recruits who aren't even halfway through your training, you must still present yourselves as full-fledged Watchkeepers."

Her tone was telling. Apparently, not all of the masters had been in complete agreement over the decision to send Jayn's Pentad to Appencourt. Jayn wondered again why she and the others had been singled out. There had to be more to it than what Commandant Lahey had said.

Mistress Bellos laid a hand on the box's lid but hesitated. "Think of this as a bit of theater. The Hall is expecting Watchkeepers, so that is what they will see. These are being loaned, not given to you." She opened the box, and the early morning sun glinted off the five metal pins resting on a velvet cushion.

Mistress Bellos handed them out without any of the words or ceremony that would likely accompany the official presentation of the pins at the completion of their six months of training. Still, Jayn couldn't help but feel a sense of accomplishment as she undid the clasp and stuck the pin through her gray tabard just above her left breast. The blue pin was shaped like a cresting wave, identical to the ones worn by Mistress Bellos and Captain Lahmeer, signifying a trained Wave Weaver. Sure, their training wasn't yet complete, but they had done more to earn these pins than most recruits.

Mistress Bellos tucked the empty box under her arm and regarded them all as they adjusted their pins or hefted their weapons. "Now you certainly all look the part. See that you act it as well. Look to Captain Lahmeer for guidance. You are to defer to her in all matters." She paused and looked at each of them again to emphasize the point. Her gaze seemed to linger on Pavel the longest. "Now, this little outing should take no more than about two weeks, but that is still valuable time away from your training.

Given the unique experience you have already gained, you will not have to make up those missing two weeks, *if*—" She raised a finger to stress the emphasis on that word. "If you continue to practice your lacings every day. Be sure to continue practicing with your complementary forces as well. Help each other out with that."

Jayn suppressed a smile. They would have continued helping each other even if they'd been ordered *not* to do so.

"Furthermore, the experience you will gain in Appencourt should be an acceptable substitute for the lessons you will miss on Aldrian law. You will see the governance of Aldria firsthand. Now, I wish you luck and safe travels on your journey. May the stars guide you and the Maker watch over you."

She nodded and left, as did Mistress Whitcomb and her assistants. Jayn moved to her little gray mare and stowed her sword. She held her hand out for the pony to snuff and stroked its neck. The others stowed their weapons and familiarized themselves with their mounts. Shilo had also been given a pony that could have been a sister to Jayn's. Nyssa had a tall piebald gelding that was mostly black, except for its white muzzle and a few splotches on its sides. Ryn had a bay mare, while Thalia and Pavel had geldings whose coats were closer to chestnut brown.

Jayn didn't love that she and Shilo had been saddled with similar mounts. Shilo had never ridden a horse until two days ago, while Jayn had been in a saddle since she was old enough to hold the reins. She told herself that she'd been given this small, seemingly docile pony because of her size, not any slight against her horsemanship. They were borrowing these mounts from the shared Watchkeeper pool. There was no need to give her a large gelding that someone else might need more. Captain Lahmeer had been given a lot more horse than was strictly necessary, but perhaps that was another bit of theater to distinguish her as the leader of the group.

"Here you all are," a new voice said.

Jayn had been about to swing herself into the pony's saddle. She turned to see who had come upon them now. Her heart sank as she saw Mina Bellain wearing a red riding dress and leading a dappled mare toward them. Apparently, she had stabled her horse in the city. The fact that she had retrieved it and led it back into the compound could mean only one thing. Why on earth would Mina Bellain, of all people, want to join them on the ride to Appencourt? If she had meant to return to Lon's Watch, she would have ridden east out of town, while they would be heading north out of the Appencourt Gate.

Over the weekend, Jayn's Pentad had found time for a brief meeting—this time in a spot Pavel had found up one of the spires rather than their accustomed room in the basement. They'd compared notes on the interviews with Commandant Lahey and the Scholar. Everyone had stuck to the agreed-upon story of Ryn's healing himself. Mina had asked them all different questions, ranging from their Etchings to Kalo to what Ryn and Thalia had seen in that warehouse. Curiously, she'd asked none of them about the Kobolds' poison or the Runeform fountain's supposed prophecy. According to Pavel, that only proved she *was* investigating the link between the Kobolds and the prophecy. It explained her interest in their particular Pentad, he reasoned. Jayn had not been so sure, but maybe Pavel was onto something.

"Miss Bellain?" Thalia said. "How can we help you?"

There was nothing but pleasantness in Thalia's voice, but Jayn had known her long enough to detect the unease beneath the surface. She didn't even need to look at the others to know that none of them were pleased to see the Scholar. She made everyone nervous, especially Pavel.

If Mina picked up on any of that, she did not acknowledge it. She only smiled. "Well, as fate would have it, I also have business in Appencourt. When I heard your party was heading out today, I decided I should take advantage of the escort. Not that I expect any trouble here in the Golden Lands, but one can never be too careful, times being what they are."

"Of course, Miss Bellain," Nyssa said, nudging her mount forward, already in the saddle. "It would be our honor as Watch-keepers to escort you."

Mina's smile only broadened as she craned her neck to look up at Nyssa. "You are most gracious," she said, "but please, call me Mina." She swept her gaze to include all of them. "All of you should call me Mina."

Many people believed that the Golden Lands were named such because of the rich trade that flowed through that wedge of Aldria anchored by Falport in the west, Lon's Watch to the east, and Appencourt in the north. Indeed, the commerce here generated most of Aldria's wealth. The country's geography made its port cities—the biggest being Falport—uniquely positioned as hubs of international trade. Aldria's alliance with Iscerna brought in quality steel, silk, and other textiles, while trade with the Maer gave them access to the exotic spices and goods from the mysterious lands across the vast Morro Ocean that only the Maer Tallsails could navigate. Tamor had lost all that access when Aldria defected, which was a main reason they still resented the split some 200 years later. They could only take part in the ocean trade by using Mirkwalders as middlemen. Though Mirkwald remained officially neutral, they tended to side with their much larger neighbor to the southwest.

Still, it was not the flow of coin that had first given the Golden Lands their name. That became apparent when the traveling party, now consisting of seven members, rode through the Appencourt Gate and the city fell away to reveal miles and miles of farmland stretching out to the east. On their left, the River Aldria followed the road for a time before turning away, replaced by a sparse woodland. The acres of "golden" wheat, barley, rye, and oats, among other crops, were the true namesake of this fertile stretch of land and the lifeblood of Aldria. Grain was the main draw for the Maer ships. They had little room for farming on their rocky islands, though they had managed to cultivate sea oats on Abyscadis, which was the name of both their largest island and their only true city.

Jayn explained all this—or much of it anyway—as they rode. She addressed herself to Ryn, who was the most forthcoming about his ignorance and eager to learn, but she spoke loudly enough that the others might hear her. The busy and almost constant traffic along the crushed-gravel road meant that they could only ride two abreast. Nyssa led the group, with Mina at her side. The Scholar seemed content for now to chatter away with Nyssa and more or less ignore the others. Thalia and Shilo rode behind them, with Jayn and Ryn next, and Pavel taking up the rear.

A rider in a hurry could make the journey from Falport to Appencourt in under two days of hard riding, but they were not in a hurry. They would make it in about four days, though Nyssa informed them that they had a full week until the hearing, giving them plenty of time to rest and prepare once in Appencourt, even if unexpected delays arose.

They rode for hours, passing miles of mostly uninterrupted farmland. The villages in this part of the country were spaced no more than half a day's ride apart, and little red-brick taverns with rooms above the bar were more plentiful than that. They stopped at one such establishment once the sun had reached its zenith. By then sweat had begun to run down her face and the small of her back. The days were getting longer and hotter as the summer solstice drew nearer. Summer Feast, though not as big a holiday as Winter Feast, was still a major occasion in Appencourt, but they would likely be back in Falport by then.

Jayn and her Pentad members sat at a wooden table set out in the shade of a broad oak tree away from the road, while Nyssa went into the tavern to buy some lunch. Mina followed her inside to arrange her own meal. Jayn and the others exchanged quick glances, hunched their shoulders, and leaned in closer. This was their first moment alone since the Scholar had unexpectedly joined them.

"Tight lips," Pavel said, holding a finger to his mouth. "Absolutely no Secret Training while she's with us."

That was too obvious to require a response. "But why is she here?" Jayn asked instead.

Pavel shook his head. "Doesn't matter. We keep our cool and don't attract any unwanted attention. Don't give her any reason to suspect we are not anything but what we seem."

Suddenly a bird dropped from the sky and alighted on Pavel's shoulder. Jayn, who'd been sitting across from Pavel, leaned back and gasped. Pavel merely glanced at the crow. It wasn't a crow. Jayn had forgotten all about Corvus, Pavel's miraculous pet Runeform. She'd seen it only twice before. The creature tended to avoid entering the Watchkeeper compound, but now that they were free of the city, it apparently had no problem dropping down into their midst. The bird-like thing cawed and nibbled at Pavel's ear. It had unnerving eyes that glowed with a constant blue light, lighter in shade than Wave wards.

Jayn smiled as she shook her head. "What were you saying just now? Don't attract unwanted attention?"

Pavel tried ignoring the bird-thing, until it bit down on his earlobe and made him flinch. He flicked a hand at it. "Go away, Corvus," he said.

"As you wish!" Corvus said in its raspy voice. It spread its wings and beat at the air but only rose high enough to hop over Pavel's head and land on his other shoulder. It made a crackling noise, almost like laughter.

Pavel sighed. "It can't be helped. As well informed as she is, I'm sure she already knows about Corvus. He might be a good distraction for her, to get her mind off whatever else she thinks she knows about us."

The tavern's doors hung on rusty iron hinges, so they had plenty of warning when those doors swung open. Nyssa emerged first, followed by two barmaids. One carried two fistfuls of mugs, while the other had a large platter piled with rounds of bread. Each of them got a mug of what was likely watery yellow ale and a loaf. The bread had been hollowed out and filled with a hearty soup, packed with stringy beef and slices of carrots. Mina came last of all, carrying a ceramic teacup.

"I had a big breakfast," she said by way of explanation. Then she noticed the Runeform on Pavel's shoulder and her eyes widened. "Ah, is this the famous Corvus I see?"

Pavel shrugged. "That's him, all right. Don't call him famous. It'll give him an ego."

Mina smiled. Corvus tilted its head to regard her. She tilted her head back at him and smiled. "It's a pleasure to meet you, Corvus," she said.

"Pleasure to meet you!" Corvus said. One of the lords in Appencourt had a large red bird he kept in his home. It delighted all the lord's guests with its ability to repeat a few words and phrases. Corvus's echoing of Mina's words reminded Jayn of that bird. While the bird was simply a mimic, Corvus was something more. There seemed to be a genuine intelligence behind that voice.

"So it does speak," Mina said, turning her gaze to Pavel. "What does it do, precisely?"

"Not a whole lot, really," Pavel said. "Mostly he just keeps me company."

"Ah, but there must be more to it than that. Every Runeform was created with a specific task or purpose in mind. A man who travels with three of them should know that."

Pavel raised an eyebrow. "Three? Corvus is the only one I got right now."

"Your blades, I mean."

Pavel started to protest, but she waved a dismissive hand.

"Oh, I know," she said. "People like to call them relics or artifacts, but to my mind, weapons like that are really just another kind of Runeform. They are unbreakable, no?"

She waited, so after a moment, Pavel nodded.

"That's a defining characteristic of Runeforms," she said. "Maybe your blades don't talk or help the grass grow, but anything created before the Burning that we could not create today through any combination of technology or Weaving, in my book, is a Runeform. Tell me, Thalia, can any enchantment keep a blade sharp for a thousand years?"

Thalia clearly wasn't expecting to be called on, but she stammered for a moment and then said, "Well, no. You could make one unbreakable or undullable for a time, but with the recoil, it would eventually break."

Mina nodded. "Unbreakable enchantments with no recoil. That's knowledge that was lost with the Burning, yet you carry those miraculous blades on your back. No doubt, you've thought about how they were made and why. No doubt, you more than anyone have thought about why Corvus was made."

Mina made remarkable points and raised interesting questions, all masked by an air of bland pleasantness. Jayn couldn't help but wonder what Corvus actually did and why Pavel kept it around. During the chaos of the Kobold attack, Corvus had seemed to help Jayn's Pentad members find each other, and it had even warned them about Kalo.

Pavel scratched the black stubble on his tan face. "You are right, of course," he said after a moment. "I have thought about it." He tilted his head to look at the bird-like Runeform on his shoulder. "As near as I can figure it, I believe Corvus was created to be a companion, like a real pet bird but with more intelligence. He can carry a conversation from time to time." Corvus looked down its beak back at Pavel. Pavel glanced at Mina. "I will warn you though, he takes a while to warm up to strangers, so you might not get much out of him."

Corvus squawked and took off, though he didn't go far. He landed on a low-hanging branch of the oak tree overhead.

"Well," Nyssa said, spreading her hands, "it will make for a good conversation topic on the road, but let's eat up for now, yeah?"

No one had touched the bread bowls or the ale yet. Jayn and her Pentad murmured their agreement. Mina made no further comments during the brief meal, but every time Jayn glanced over, she saw Mina staring up at Corvus with something almost like a smile on her lips.

To Jayn's surprise and relief, the Scholar did not attempt any further conversation with her group until they stopped for the evening in a little village called Bellwater. The village had no visible belltower or any flowing water—though you could sink a well almost anywhere in the Golden Lands and strike groundwater—but that's how it always seemed to be in little villages like this. The names never seemed to have any connection to the places themselves. It did have a sizable inn called The Bellwether. Inns here were always much larger than you would find in similar-sized villages elsewhere, given the high traffic on this road. They had large stables, plenty of rooms, and a big great room that came with a warm meal and, more often than not, entertainment, along with the sense of security found in prosperous little villages. One needn't fear any of the locals might steal your goods or slit your throat as you slept.

Entertainment that night in The Bellwether's great room was provided by two young men who could have been brothers. They wore red vests over their laborer's clothes. One played the flute while the other juggled. The best that could be said of the performance was that it was easy to ignore. The road-weary Pentad sat at a long table in the corner, while Mina and Nyssa arranged rooms and ordered dinner. They'd already handed off their mounts to the stableboy, who seemed somewhat competent.

When Mina joined them at the table, shortly after Nyssa, she turned and surveyed the half-filled room. "You can tell a lot about the mood in any country from spending an evening in any inn like this," she said.

"What's the mood here?" Pavel asked. He seemed determined to show Mina that he was in no way intimidated by her.

"A little tense," she said, taking a seat. "People are still worried about Kobolds, of course, but after two months with no sightings, fears are beginning to wane there. So people are falling back to the perennial fear of aggression from Tamor."

Before she left to join the Watchkeepers, Jayn had heard some rumblings of concern over Tamor among the lords and ladies of Appencourt. Since then she'd had a lot less access to the general news of the country, or really she had not sought it out, focusing entirely on her training instead.

Nyssa nodded in agreement. She didn't seem particularly bothered by Mina's presence in their party, or she hid it well if she did. "Last I heard, Tamor still has its forces marshalled near the Mirkwald River, supposedly on training exercises. The magistrate in Nadell can't be too happy about that, even with reinforcements from the Standing Army."

Nadell, the westernmost city in Aldria, sat in a precarious location. At the mouth of the Mirkwald River, they had first pick of the strange but valuable goods the Mirkwalders pulled out of the vast and supposedly haunted Ever Wood. However, that river also served as the official border between Aldria and the Tamorine Empire, and raids across the river were not uncommon, at least historically. Nadell also lay north of the treacherous Lembalt Archipelago, home to pirates and Tamorine privateers. The lord who sat in the Hall for Nadell always seemed to have dark circles under his eyes.

"Still," Nyssa said, directing her question to Mina, "do you think anything might come of it? Tamor likes to make a big noise, but it's been well over a century since they've made any earnest attempt to retake Aldria."

Mina tilted her hand from left to right, as if to say it could go either way. "I'm no expert on Tamor, but we can't judge Tamor as it is now by the Tamor of old. Ever since the first King Lemuel had the audacity to declare his kingdom an empire, the nation has become far more unpredictable." That had been some fifty years ago, and Mina didn't look much older than forty, so she clearly had some working expertise on Tamor for such a ready response. Lemuel's son sat on the throne of Tamor now, calling himself Emperor Lemuel II. "Far more fanatical too," Mina added after a moment.

"Well," Nyssa said, "let's hope the Hall will take decisive action to deal with the Kobolds, so we can all turn our focus back to Tamor, if need be."

"I agree," Mina said.

Then their dinner arrived, and they didn't talk of much else of consequence after that. The sun had set by the time they made their way upstairs to the rooms. Nyssa, Jayn, and Thalia had a room that contained a single large bed. Jayn didn't much like the idea of sleeping so tight, but she supposed it was better than camping outdoors.

After Nyssa left them for her accommodations, Thalia waited a few minutes and then went and fetched the boys from their smaller room. Pavel clearly wanted to keep talking about the Scholar, but Thalia reminded them all that they still needed to practice their Weaving, as Mistress Bellos had instructed them.

They couldn't think about attempting any of what they had taken to calling "forbidden" Blendings, though that word wasn't entirely correct, but after some discussion, they settled on a tact that would help them with such Blendings in the future while still providing cover should Nyssa or Mina stumble in on their practices.

The room provided little space for standing, so they all sat in a circle on top of the bed. First, they envisioned Root. All five of them. A small green tree sprouted quickly around Ryn. After some effort, Jayn and Shilo summoned theirs. A Root tree could look like any tree really, but both girls modeled theirs after Ryn's, which he said was based on a crown oak. Thalia and Pavel could produce nothing, but that was expected. Still, they tried for about twenty minutes, with Ryn offering what few tips he could. Then they moved onto Flame. All five of them.

It was a little unorthodox, but not inexplicable. Watchkeepers weren't expected to learn to handle any of their opposing forces, but they were welcome to try—on their own time. If they were all practicing together, it wouldn't single any one of them out as attempting something unusual or impossible. They could explain it away as an attempt at team building or a fit of youthful enthusiasm. So they reasoned.

Jayn could reliably summon Root and Stone, though she couldn't make any real lacings yet. She managed a few sparks of Flame but got nowhere with Aether, which didn't bother her. No one could master all Five Forces, but of course it was still a major stretch to try for four. It was ambitious, she knew, but Jayn Eldragor was a woman of high ambitions.

Chapter 9
The Scribe

SHILO SAT HER MOUNT as best she could. A full day of riding had made her sore in places she had never felt before. She had slept reasonably well at The Bellwether inn, despite being crammed into a bed with Thalia and Jayn and despite everything else, but she still dreaded another day of riding and the two more days that would follow that. No one spoke much, as the excitement of setting out on a journey gave way to the tedium of travel.

The first half of the day passed without incident. Shilo had been given a docile pony, which seemed content to follow the horse in front of it and needed little guidance from her, which was just as well, because she still barely knew what she was doing. Traffic bustled up and down the Appencourt Road, though those heading south would have called it the Falport Road. Shilo's party passed several rolling merchant caravans, pulled by bulky draft horses and guarded by bored-looking mercenaries in leather jerkins, as well as smaller carts pulled by mules and carrying the last of the spring harvests, heading in whichever direction the farmer thought would get him a better price.

At noon, they stopped and took shelter in a small stand of trees beside a gurgling stream just off the road. They ate the hard bread and dried meat they had packed and fed the horses oats from canvas feed bags that strapped over the horses' muzzles. Captain Lahmeer had been giving Shilo pointers throughout the trip on how to care for her mount. Shilo walked around the trees, stretching her legs as she munched on a hunk of bread. Tiny pink and blue flowers bloomed wherever they could get sunlight, and dragonflies zoomed around, hunting smaller insects. It was a lovely spot, but the break was far too short, and soon she was climbing back into the saddle, her legs already protesting.

She was so focused on maintaining proper posture and holding the reins just right, that she was the last to notice the problem up ahead. Her pony stopped suddenly, confronted with the broad and stationary backside of Nyssa's gelding. Shilo looked up. They happened to be alone on the road just then, with no farmers or caravans in sight. The road, almost perfectly straight and neatly paved with crushed white stone, continued on for a hundred paces before falling into a rocky pit. Such a ravine seemed out of place in this landscape, until she realized that the terrain around them had been growing increasingly uneven throughout the day.

"What happened to the bridge?" Nyssa said.

Only then did Shilo notice the splintered wooden posts on either side of the ravine. The road continued on the far side. Such a narrow fold in the earth was too small to feature on any map of Aldria, but with the bridge destroyed, it would be as impassable as any major river or mountain range. They could tell that even from this far out. Still, Nyssa nudged her mount forward, and the others followed.

Near the edge, they stopped again and dismounted—Shilo needed a hand from Thalia for that part. The horses were trained well enough not to wander off. The travelers stepped cautiously toward the lip of the ravine. The split in the earth was thirty feet across and only a bit deeper, with a muddy trickle of a stream along the bottom. The sides were steep and composed of a crumbly, slate-like rock. A person would have a hard time climbing down and up the far side; for the horses, it was impossible. Shattered bits of wood littered the bottom of the ravine. Shilo had seen this kind of destruction once before.

"It appears someone has blown up the bridge," Mina Bellain said.

"But why?" Nyssa asked.

Jayn turned and studied the scraggly woods around them. "One might use such a tactic to set an ambush," she said, "but no highwayman would do that on the busiest road in Aldria."

Mina nodded. "That is unlikely."

Shilo wondered if they could make a shield bridge to cross the gap, but she quickly dismissed the idea. The Weavers could make it across easily, but there was no way the horses could safely cross that way, not without injury. No matter how well trained they were, Shilo doubted any horse could be coaxed to walk off the edge of a cliff, even if they could see the lacings.

Shilo and the others turned away from the destroyed bridge, hearing hoofbeats in the gravel behind them. A lone rider approached. He checked his mount and slowed as he saw a band of Watchkeepers blocking the way ahead. Then he seemed to notice the open ravine beyond them. He stopped and slid from his saddle. He approached with the reins looped over one arm and his hands up, fingers spread to show he was unarmed. The man was tall, with broad shoulders and a light brown complexion somewhere between the darker brown of southern Aldrians like Shilo and the paler pink of northern Aldrians like Jayn. His dense black hair, twisted into stubby braids, showed he had at least some southern blood in his parentage. He wore dark trousers and a loose cotton shirt. He looked older than Shilo and her friends, though perhaps younger than Nyssa and Pavel.

"Hail Watchkeepers," he said by way of formal greeting, his voice just as deep as Shilo had expected but softer. "What happened to the bridge?"

Nyssa stepped forward. "I couldn't tell you," she said. "We've just come across it ourselves."

"It must be recent," Mina said. "Word about something like this would have traveled fast."

"Likely in the night then," Nyssa said, "or early this morning."

The stranger pointed to his right. "It looks like traffic has been diverting this way."

Only then did Shilo notice the dirt lane leading off to the east. Countless paths like it had crisscrossed the road for the past two days. Shilo had no skill at reading tracks, but even she could tell that this lane had seen an increase in traffic, as heavy wagons had turned onto it from the main road, leaving deep grooves in the soil.

Nyssa surveyed the area once more. Off to the south, another caravan appeared, lumbering over a small hill. Nyssa addressed Shilo's Pentad. "We will divert east then. Likely there is another bridge, or the ravine will end, and we can make our way around and back to the main road. We'll still make it to Appencourt with time to spare." Then she turned to the stranger. "You are welcome to ride with us, if you choose."

The man looked at each of them in turn. His eyes widened when he saw that the creature riding on Pavel's shoulder wasn't any sort of bird at all. Most road-weary travelers they'd passed hadn't given Corvus a second glance. A man keeping a pet crow wasn't completely unheard of. Whatever the stranger made of Corvus, he made no comment. Shilo wondered how she herself must have looked to the man. Did he see her as a Watchkeeper with the red pin of a Flame Weaver? Or did he just see a tired and uncertain girl completely out of her element?

Whatever the man made of each of them, he finally nodded. "I would be happy to accompany a group of Watchkeepers and, if I'm not mistaken, one of the Scholars." He made a short bow toward Mina. She merely smiled and nodded in return. The man was sharp, to have picked up on Mina's identity so quickly. "My name is Rav Montare."

They mounted their horses and set off east along the much smaller dirt lane. Shilo's pony was not one to jockey for position, so she found herself near the back of the party, riding alongside Rav Montare. To the right, a low stone wall marked the outer boundary of a wheat field. The yellow grain swayed in the breeze, the stalks not yet bowed over by the weight of their maturity. Shilo glanced at the stranger a few times before he noticed. He regarded her with a friendly smile. She had to say something then.

"My name is Shilo. Shilo Lorn."

"It's a pleasure to meet you, Miss Lorn."

"Where were you headed, Mr. Montare? All the way to Appencourt?"

"If the Maker permits it, that was my intention."

"Are you from there? Or perhaps on business?" She knew she sounded awkward, but she didn't know the polite way to ask why he was going to Appencourt.

He didn't seem to take any offense. "I'm on my way to stay with some friends who are part of the mission there."

"The mission?" She had never heard the word used like that.

In front of her, Pavel turned awkwardly in his saddle to look back at Rav. "You're one of them, then?" he said.

Rav's smile didn't falter, despite Pavel's abrupt rudeness. "One of whom?" he asked.

"The Cult of the Shepherd-King," Pavel said. "Those lot use words like 'mission,' don't they?"

Rav nodded. "We don't call ourselves a cult, of course, but yes, I follow the path."

Shilo had heard of the so-called cult before but didn't know much about them. Her father said that they worshipped the Maker like most people but were stricter in their morality and vocal in their rejection of star guides.

Pavel nodded. "I've read my fair share of holy books, but I've never made it to yours."

"I would be happy to lend you my copy," Rav said, patting his saddlebags.

Pavel shook his head as he turned back around. "Not this time," he said.

Shilo wasn't sure what to say. She was genuinely curious to know more about this man's beliefs, but she wasn't going to push the topic if Pavel was going to continue his condescension. They rode in silence for a while before Rav broke the quiet.

"You look to be a standard Watchkeeper Pentad," he said, "but I couldn't help but notice the extra Wave Weaver." He didn't ask why, but the question was politely implied.

For some reason, Shilo was reluctant to admit that she was a half-trained recruit and not yet a full-fledged Watchkeeper. "Well, we're still new. This is sort of our first outing." She gestured to the woman still leading the party. "Captain Lahmeer is here to… supervise our Pentad."

"Ah, I see. Some of you do look younger than most Watch-keepers I've met."

Shilo didn't know if he included her in that statement. She was the second youngest member of their party after Jayn and barely an adult, but she hoped the stranger didn't see her as a kid. She didn't know what else to say, so she allowed the silence to lull. She wished she were better at holding a conversation. She focused on her posture and holding the reins. To their left, the winding ravine disappeared behind the trees.

They reached the sleepy village of Wydhaven about two hours before sunset. It certainly looked like a sleepy little village, though it had been shaken suddenly awake by the influx of traffic diverted from the main road. A passing farmer had told Shilo's party that Wydhaven would be the best place to turn north. From there they could follow the winding country lanes back toward the main road. Apparently, everyone else had been given the same advice.

Though some travelers pushed through, many decided as Nyssa did to spend the night in Wydhaven. Wagon trains set up anywhere they could find room in the lots surrounding the village, more than doubling its size. One unlucky farmer had gotten his cart hopelessly mired in the mud just off the town green, churned up by the passing traffic. Half a dozen people were trying to help him, but they seemed to be arguing over whether to push the cart forward or backward.

The villagers were making the most of the boom. Everyone seemed to be outside, and on every corner a woman or child was trying to sell whatever spare vegetables or loaves of bread the family happened to have on hand. A dozen men who had likely been tending livestock or crops that day had dug up old flutes or lyres and were set up throughout the town playing as best they could, sometimes with a nervous-looking wife or daughter singing along. Children dodged about everywhere, enjoying a weekday evening that had quickly taken on a festival atmosphere.

Pavel grumbled that they would likely have to pay for over-priced lodging in the house of some enterprising villager, but they tried their luck at the village's sole inn anyway. Nyssa and Mina went inside, while the rest waited out front with the horses. If any rooms could be had, a Watchkeeper officer and a Scholar should have enough influence to secure them.

A collection of mismatched tables and stools had been set up in the yard outside the inn, no doubt borrowed from neighbors. Men and women lounged at these tables, sipping their drinks as the day began to cool, while two overstressed barmaids darted in and out of the main door. Shilo spotted a pair of men slouching against the side of the inn and surveying the madness with sneers on their faces. Likely they were locals who had been hoping to spend a quiet Twigsday evening drinking at their local inn, sitting in their usual spots, and they were none too happy with all these unexpected guests disrupting their routine.

One of the men glanced at Shilo and met her gaze. She looked away, but it was too late. He gestured to his friend and said loudly enough for everyone in the noisy yard to hear, "Thank the Maker and all my lucky stars! The Gray Guard is here." The disdain in his voice was unmistakable, as was the slight slurring of his words. Apparently, he had still gotten plenty to drink, despite the extra competition.

Shilo hunched into herself and tried to be unassuming. She didn't want to create a scene. Pavel had no problem with that, it seemed. He stepped toward the two men. "Good evening, citizens," he said in a weirdly stiff voice.

The two men looked him up and down. Pavel was lean and gangly, with two bladed weapons strapped to his back. He could look intimidating if he tried, at least with people who did not know him. Corvus wasn't riding on his shoulder just then. The Runeform had already darted off to nest in a tree—or do whatever it did each evening when it disappeared. Whatever the men made of Pavel, the one who had spoken was undeterred.

He pushed himself off the wall and took a step forward. "Weaver," he said with a nod. "You got any tricks that could fix that bridge? Of course, if you lot were worth anything, you would have stopped it from being blowed up in the first place."

His friend took a step forward as well, grinning. "My money says it was the Weavers that blew it up themselves, probably on accident of course."

Shilo knew Pavel wouldn't like hearing their insults. She wanted to say something, to stop him from delivering some sarcastic retort and getting them all into some stupid barfight, but she didn't know what to do.

"As a matter of fact..." Pavel began.

Suddenly, one of the barmaids was there, slapping a hand on each man's chest. "Oh, stow it, you two," she said. "You leave my customers alone or I'll cut you off for the night. No more drinks, you hear me?"

Though the men towered over the girl, they staggered back against the wall, as if she really could overpower them. The first one laughed and said, "Oh, come off it, Sara. We were just making polite conversation."

Undeterred, the short but spunky barmaid leveled a finger at the man. "Lem, you wouldn't know a polite conversation if one bit you on the nose. Now do I need to get the sheriff, or are you going to behave yourselves?"

The two men nodded sullenly. "Yes, Sara," they muttered.

Sara turned to regard Shilo and her group with a wide smile, a dimple forming in either cheek. Her long red hair hung over one shoulder in a braid that was quickly coming apart. She couldn't have been much older than Shilo, and yet this girl had gotten the two local drunks back in line with just a few words. She hadn't really bullied them into behaving. It seemed more like they listened out of genuine respect. The formidable barmaid radiated a worldly self-assurance that Shilo could not help but envy.

"The Watchkeepers are always welcome in Wydhaven," Sara said. "Don't pay any mind to those idiots." She whistled and waved through the crowd, summoning a pair of roughly dressed boys, apparently stable hands for the inn. "See to these horses. There should be just enough room in the stables for them. See if Tomas down the road can take the two draft horses for the night." She gestured to Shilo and her group. "Find a seat and I'll get you drinks in a minute."

"Thank you," Shilo said.

"Of course, love," Sara said with another grin and a nod before darting off again.

There were no tables big enough for their whole party, so Shilo sat down between Pavel and Rav Montare, while Ryn, Jayn, and Thalia took a table nearby. Shilo leveled a stern look at Pavel, in what she knew was a sorry imitation of a girl like Sara.

"What were you going to say?" she asked. "No, don't tell me. Remember that pin on your chest. We have to act like real Watchkeepers."

She glanced at Rav, regretting that last sentence. He was politely looking away and pretending not to listen.

Pavel grinned. "Easy, Shilo," he said. "I was simply going to point out the limitations of Weaving and explain how it cannot be used to detonate bridges."

Shilo frowned. "They didn't seem to like Weavers very much."

"Not an uncommon sentiment." Pavel gestured to the town around them. "A little place like this, probably everyone born a Weaver uses that as a ticket to get out of here. The people who are left behind, the ones who can't Weave, well sometimes they get a little resentful. If they don't like how their life turned out, they use it as an excuse. 'If I'd been a Weaver, this would all be different.' And so, some of them end up hating Weavers. Just don't take it personally, kid."

Rav cleared his throat. "Well put," he said. "I don't agree with it, of course, but I've met many people who feel that way. They fail to see that the Maker gives his gifts to everyone, even those of us not born as Weavers."

Pavel rolled his eyes but made no comment. Shilo spotted Nyssa making her way across the busy yard. She stood between the two tables so everyone could hear her. "We've managed to secure the last two rooms," she said. "Mina and I will share one, and the girls get the other."

"Where does that leave us gentlemen?" Pavel asked.

Her lips curved in a slight smile. "The stable hands have graciously offered you and Ryn space in their loft." She nodded to Rav. "There's room in the loft for you as well, Mr. Montare, though you are welcome to look for better accommodations yourself."

Rav shrugged. "I'm sure the loft will be fine. I've slept in rougher spots."

Nyssa nodded. "Good. They will be bringing us out some dinner in a bit, so sit tight." She glanced at Pavel but then opted to sit at the other table, leaving Mina to settle on a stool opposite Shilo. Shilo did her best not to look uncomfortable. Though the Scholar was nothing but nice, Shilo couldn't help but feel the woman was staring into her soul each time she leveled that placid gaze toward her.

Thankfully, Mina directed her attention to the newcomer. "So, Mr. Montare," she said. "If I heard you correctly earlier, I believe you are a… What is it you call yourselves? Scribes of the Truth?"

He nodded. "Some of us use that title. I like to say I am one who is walking the path." He glanced at Pavel. "Others, perhaps erroneously, call us the Cult of the Shepherd-King."

Pavel spread his hands as a sign of concession. "I meant no slight by it," he said. "The world is full of little cults. Mostly, they're nice people, if they sometimes have strange ideas."

"True," Rav said. "There are many different faiths in this world, but they are mostly hollow and bloodless religions."

"Not yours, of course," Pavel said, clearly trying not to grin. "Yours is the one true religion, yeah?"

Rav shrugged. "I certainly believe so."

Mina laughed, making light of the growing animosity, at least on Pavel's end. "The Scribes are rather unique," she said. She looked at Pavel. "Surely, a man as well versed in antiquity as yourself must know how ancient their Book of Truth is."

"It's pretty old, I'll grant you that," Pavel said.

"Older than the Burning," Rav said.

"No book is older than the Burning," Pavel shot back. "They all burned. That's why they call it *The Burning*."

Rav smiled, good-natured as ever. "I would like to tell you a story, if you wish to listen. It's one I believe to be true, and it is somewhat supported and certainly not contradicted by all known historical records."

Pavel leaned back on his chair and scratched his chin. He studied Rav's face carefully, probably in his cynicism looking for some sign of a charlatan behind that earnest smile. Finally, he nodded. "Go on then."

"This story goes all the way back to the Burning," Rav said. "I'm sure you have imagined how chaotic that time must have been. We don't know what exactly happened or how it happened, but everything changed all at once. All books, as you say, were burned. All societies collapsed. All peoples were scattered to the winds. They lost everything, but they did not lose their memories. Those who survived the Burning still remembered everything that had been before and did their best to hold onto it. Yet they also had to survive. They had to relearn how to be a primitive people, to hunt and forage, perhaps to try farming again. They all remembered how to write, but few probably knew how to make paper, and they didn't have time to spend in keeping records.

"Many probably died in that vast new wilderness. Some survived. Then they had children, the first generation with no memory of what had been and no hope of reclaiming it. The parents no doubt tried to teach what they could to their children, everything they remembered about how to be a civilized people. The children listened, but they were still living in that wilderness. They took what was practical, but the rest might as well have been fairy stories and legends—interesting, even entertaining, but not useful. Then those who had survived the Burning died, and their surviving children had their own children. They remembered all their parents had taught them, but what would they pass on to their children beyond the practical? If they'd been taught to write, would they bother to spend hours sketching symbols in the sand for their children? To that second generation, it would all be even more meaningless. It takes only two generations for civilization to be lost entirely."

Shilo shivered, despite the lingering warmth of the evening. She couldn't imagine living in such a time. Rav had an excellent voice for storytelling. Pavel seemed unaffected by it. He shrugged. "Well told," he said, "but not anything I haven't heard before or thought myself."

"Well, I say all that to emphasize how chaotic the times were and how difficult it would have been to preserve any of what had existed before. It would have taken a singular focus and dedication, or perhaps the intervention of the Maker himself." Rav held up two fingers. "We know of only two men who emerged from the Burning with that kind of singular resolve."

"Two?" Pavel asked, sounding genuinely surprised.

"One man you've all heard of." He nodded to Mina. "The wizard Lon who established the Academy of the Ways and preserved knowledge of Weaving."

Shilo had heard many legends about the wizard Lon. He was always referred to as a wizard, though no one knew what that title meant. The meaning had been lost sometime in the past thousand years, but perhaps the Scholars themselves still understood it.

Pavel sighed. "With no disrespect to our Scholar friend, it's hard to say how true that account is and how much of it is legend… Though, I admit, it is possible Lon's life might date all the way back to the Burning."

"We like to think it's true," Mina said. Her good-natured attitude did not come across nearly as genuine as Rav's.

"I'll grant you that," Pavel said with a wave of his hand. "But who's this other fellow then?"

"His name, or hers, has been lost, though we know of the First Scribe through his accomplishments. Probably he was no one special, not of noble birth or anything like that. He was a dedicated man of faith who had studied the Book of Truth. You say you are familiar with many other faiths, yes? Perhaps you have heard of some—often overly fanatical—adherents who will memorize their holy book, word for word."

Pavel nodded.

"Well, the First Scribe was one such man," Rav continued. "He knew the entire Book of Truth by heart. No doubt many learned men who survived the Burning longed for their favorite books. Some may have memorized long passages, entire plays, or poems. Perhaps they even found time to recite these to their children born into that wilderness. The children no doubt appreciated those flowery words and stories, but they had no need to memorize them, and all that was lost within a generation. The First Scribe was different. He knew his mind contained not some literary work of art or now meaningless history, but revealed Truth itself. He knew the book could not die with him. Many others joined him, those who had studied the book before the Burning and knew its importance.

"Despite the ever-present challenges of surviving that wilderness, they dedicated themselves to memorizing the book. They taught the words to their children, and their children understood the value of the book. Where all others failed to pass on knowledge, the Scribes succeeded. The book continued to be passed down orally for generations. When new civilizations emerged and paper was reinvented, they had to create new alphabets, new written languages. The Scribes were the first to push for this. As soon as they could, they wrote the book down again, but they knew how fragile paper could be, so they kept on teaching it aloud, word for word. Many on the path today still memorize the book, though most don't. I myself know several passages by heart, but certainly not all of it."

Pavel's expression was hard to read. After a long silence, he shrugged again. "I'll grant you that your Book of Truth is very old. Even in the ruins of the first city-states, stone tablets have been found containing passages from the book. But no writing was done for at least a century after the Burning. I'm not sure I buy that a book could be passed down orally for that long, certainly not without changing and distorting. But all that aside, even if some version of this book did exist before the Burning, that doesn't mean it contains any Truth with a capital T. As now, there were probably many holy books before the Burning."

Rav was unflustered. "Likely there were, but if only one book out of all of them survived the centuries after the Burning, surely it was the Maker's will that this one did survive. You too can know the Maker's will, if only you read the book."

Pavel smiled, this time with no trace of sarcasm or meanness. "Perhaps I should," he said. "But not tonight, friend."

Shilo wondered at that sudden change in Pavel. He had been suspicious of Rav from the start. Perhaps he believed Rav was only pretending to be a man of faith, using the high-minded words of religion to mask darker, more human intentions. That seemed like the kind of thing Pavel would assume when meeting new people. Apparently, Pavel had concluded that Rav was as genuine as he presented himself and decided that his hostility was unfounded.

The evening meal passed relatively peacefully after that, despite the odd tablemates Shilo had found herself with. Pavel and Rav moved on to lighter topics, with Mina occasionally chiming in. Shilo was content to sit and listen, though her eyes followed the impressive barmaid Sara whenever she emerged from the inn. She knew exactly how to handle all of the locals, cajoling or rebuking as needed, and she made fast friends with all the travelers. Every time Shilo heard bursts of laughter that evening, Sara was right there in the middle of it. The girl was in her element here, more so than Shilo had felt anywhere.

Most of Shilo's life had been spent on her father's boat, but she had never done well as a sailor. Her short time with the Watchkeepers so far had been chaotic and occasionally dangerous. She was learning a skill that she was actually good at, but that skill involved far more violence than she was comfortable with. She didn't know if she would ever feel comfortable as a Flame Weaver. Did that mean she wasn't cut out to be a Watchkeeper?

She shook her head and directed her thoughts away from that existential ravine. She liked Rav's story about the Scribes. If it was true, she found the idea to be comforting somehow. She'd always believed in the Maker and done her best to make right choices, but she felt distant from him. Services she had attended in the Palmoor church and the Rigel temple felt dry and empty. What had Rav called it? Bloodless religion? It seemed to fit. If Rav's Book of Truth really had survived the Burning, if the Maker had seen to that, then it meant he had not given up on his creation, as many skeptics believed. It meant Truth with a capital T was still knowable.

Shilo tried to hold onto those comforting thoughts throughout the evening and as she lay on the edge of a bed—smaller than the last one—crammed in beside Thalia and Jayn. Eventually, she did fall asleep, if only for a few hours. No one in the Wydhaven inn slept through that night.

Chapter 10
A Disturbance

THE SCREAMS EVENTUALLY WOKE Thalia up. At first she thought they were part of the dream she'd been having—something about Ryn and a knife—but as she struggled back into consciousness, the screaming continued. It sounded like two women who were desperately terrified and outside the inn.

Getting out of bed was not easy, with Jayn and Shilo on either side of her, but both girls had awakened to the screams as well and were stirring groggily. Thalia sat up and scooted her way to the foot of the bed. She stumbled over someone's saddlebags in the dark but made it to the window without falling. She threw back the curtains, though the screaming had stopped. Pale moonlight filled the mostly empty yard. A lone woman sat on her knees, her hands clutched to her bosom, and visibly shaking. If there had been a second woman screaming, she must have run away from whatever had terrified them.

Thalia turned back to face the others, who were both out of bed as well. Blue light filtering through the window glinted off the steel of Jayn's drawn sword. Thalia glanced to the corner where her poleaxe leaned against the wall. It was an impressive weapon, with its axe-like blade, the butt of which was shaped like a mallet, and the spear tip on top. It could be used to slash, bash, or stab, depending on the need, but Thalia didn't like the idea of carrying the long weapon through the close quarters of the darkened inn. Probably the thief or whoever had frightened the woman had already fled.

"Come on," Thalia said, leading the way out the door empty-handed.

All three girls wore light linen shifts, sleeveless and hemmed at the knee. They weren't exactly immodest, but it still wasn't a garment Thalia would have willingly worn in public. It couldn't be helped. Pulling on their Watchkeeper trousers and buttoning up their shirts would have taken far too long.

Most doors along the hallway were open now, with half-dressed men and women peering out. Someone had lit a lantern, which they thrust out into the corridor. Thalia squinted her eyes and moved quickly past it, not wanting to ruin her night vision. They met Nyssa at the top of the stairs. The captain wore her Watchkeeper uniform, minus the tabard, which meant she must have slept in it. Only then did Thalia remember the men in her party were sleeping in the stable.

They fell wordlessly in line behind Nyssa. She had strapped on her sword belt but had not drawn her blade. At the bottom of the stairs, they headed for the door. The tile floor of the empty great room felt cool beneath Thalia's bare feet. A plump older woman—Thalia guessed her to be the matron of the inn—stood in the doorway, peering out into the night. She turned as they approached. She started to say something, probably to warn them back into their rooms, but then she recognized Nyssa.

"Captain," she said. She stepped away from the door. "I'm not sure what's happened, but that's Maive, the baker's daughter, out there. She was screaming for her life a moment ago, but she's just sobbing now."

Thalia couldn't guess what time it was. Probably it was hours yet till dawn, but bakers did rise quite early to prepare their morning loaves. Nyssa nodded to the matron and then moved out into the yard, her head swiveling to the right and left. Thalia did her best to imitate the captain's alertness, but she suddenly felt foolish rushing out into the night empty-handed and in a white shift. The cool night breeze seemed to cut right through it. Beside her, Jayn radiated a steely resolve, her sword up at the ready. Shilo followed behind them, trying not to look frightened.

Nyssa stopped when she reached the woman, still huddling into herself on the ground and audibly sobbing. In the dark it was hard to tell how old the woman was, but she seemed young. She wore a plain homespun dress with no visible tears or wrinkling that would suggest some sort of physical assault. Thalia noticed an empty bucket lying beside the woman. That explained what she was doing out in the night then. A well stood on the far side of the inn's yard.

Captain Lahmeer kept turning her head back and forth, scanning the perimeter, even as she knelt to speak to the woman. "What's happened?" she asked.

The woman let out one last strangled sob and then looked up, as if only then realizing she was no longer alone. "I can't…" she mumbled. "It wasn't…"

"Take a deep breath," Nyssa said, patience and warmth in her voice. "You're all right now. Were you alone?" Nyssa must also have heard the second woman screaming.

The woman shook her head. "My Ma… She ran to get Pa… But I couldn't… I couldn't move."

Footsteps approached. Thalia turned to see a man and a woman trotting toward the inn. The woman clutched at the man's arm, pulling him along. The man hefted a rolling pin, peering into every dark corner they passed. This had to be the woman's parents, the bakers. When the woman saw Maive still kneeling where she'd left her in the yard, she broke from her husband and ran to her daughter's side. More voices filled the night then, as people filed out of the inn and nearby houses, all talking at once, trying to figure out what had happened.

Pavel and Ryn came up beside the rest of the Pentad. The men had buttoned on their trousers but were shirtless. Thalia didn't see the other man who had joined their party yesterday, Rav Montare, but probably he was somewhere in the gathering crowd. Pavel moved to stand by Nyssa, showing no regard for his state of undress. Ryn hunched his bare shoulders and looked about as awkward as Thalia still felt. Upper-echelon women often wore dresses that were far more revealing than a shift, especially in the summer, but Thalia still felt overly exposed in what was meant to be a bedroom garment. It didn't really help that most of the men and women around her were equally attired.

It took several minutes before Nyssa could get straight answers out of the mother and daughter, with the ever-growing crowd of noisy inquirers around them. The danger seemed to have passed, whatever it was. Neither woman had been hurt, only terribly frightened. Nyssa ushered the whole baker family into the inn. Lanterns were lit. The fire in the hearth was rekindled. The matron offered the family water or stiffer drinks if they wanted.

The interrogation was delayed by the appearance of the village's sheriff, a lanky older man with an enormous gray moustache and the round copper badge of office pinned to his vest. He introduced himself only as "Wilkes." That led to a brief conversation between him and Nyssa about who should take the lead here. It should have been the sheriff, as there were no signs yet of Weaving being involved, but he deferred to Nyssa after running his fingers through his moustache and muttering something about being no good with hysterical women. By then the baker's daughter had calmed considerably, though her eyes were still glassy with tears and she sniffed continually, running a hand across her reddened nose.

"Tell me what happened, if you can," Nyssa said, offering both women an encouraging smile.

The rest of the villagers and the inn's guests had quieted down and were keeping a respectful distance away from the bakers and the authorities. They still wanted to know the story, of course, so they stood crowded into the far end of the great room or stacked up on the stairs leading to the second floor. Thalia and her Pentad stood behind Nyssa and the sheriff.

The mother took up the story first. She seemed far less rattled than her daughter. "We were fetching water for the dough, like we always do every morning. We were crossing the yard of the inn, when all of a sudden, this heavy fog rolls in, like nothing I'd ever seen before. We get a little fog some mornings in the winter, sure, but nothing like this. It was so thick and heavy, I could hardly see Maive beside me. Then this… wave of fear sort of came over me. I didn't know what was happening. I looked up and saw these red eyes shining at me through the fog. I didn't know what it was, but it scared the soul out of me, so I yelled for Maive to run and I took off and didn't stop till I was back home. Only then did I realize Maive wasn't with me."

The woman wrapped her arms around her daughter and murmured an apology for leaving her behind. The girl had a far-off look in her eyes and ignored her mother. Then a shiver seemed to run up the girl's whole body. She let out a shaky sob and met Nyssa's gaze, a sudden urgency in her countenance. "It was the Wydelk! The Wydelk was here. I swear it!" Her voice quavered with the force of her words.

Chaos erupted in the great room. Several people came forward, all talking at once. "I knew it!" one man yelled, before he was shouted down by his neighbors, all denouncing the Wydelk as superstitious nonsense. Others argued back. Thalia couldn't follow a single speaker in the din of voices, but she gathered that this was not the first alleged sighting of whatever the Wydelk was.

Sheriff Wilkes eventually got everyone to quiet down, mostly by shouting louder than them. Nyssa waited patiently through it all. Even after the room had quieted, she still waited as the mother soothed her daughter, who had started crying again.

Finally, she got the girl's attention and said, "Tell me what it looked like, as well as you can."

The girl shook her head. "It looked just like it, just like the Wydelk… Antlers and everything."

Nyssa turned her attention to the sheriff. "What is the Wydelk?"

The man shrugged. "It's just a fairy story. Every place in the world has their own version of it, a creature that comes on the Solemn Night to punish misbehaving children, or some such thing. Around here that creature is the Wydelk."

Thalia knew what he meant. In Rigel, they had the Light Sprite and the Dark Sprite. The Light Sprite left coins or sweets on the hearth for good kids, while the Dark Sprite carried the bad kids off in a sack, though Thalia had known even when she was little that they were just stories.

"What is this Wydelk supposed to look like?" Nyssa pressed.

Thalia understood why. If the Wydelk looked anything like a Kobold or an owl with a human face, then they were all potentially in serious trouble.

Sheriff Wilkes ran his fingers through his moustache again. "Not here, but in some places further east, they do a little pageant each year where they have a Wydelk. Basically they take the skull of an elk, with the antlers attached, and put it on the end of a stick. Someone carries it around with a sheet draped over themselves, so they look, you know, like a person with an elk's head."

Animals with human faces. Humans with animal faces. It wasn't too much of a leap to think there could be a connection. Nyssa clearly thought so. She gestured to the sheriff. "With your permission, I'd like to take a look around the village. Probably whatever they saw is long gone, but I'd like to take a look all the same."

The sheriff spread his hands and shrugged. "Feel free," he said.

Jayn stepped forward. She had left her scabbard upstairs, so she still held her bare sword down at her side. The blade was an odd counterpoint to her shift, which had puffy bits of lace along the wide straps. "We'll come with you," she said.

Nyssa shook her head. "I'd rather you stay here. Like I said, I probably won't find anything."

Thalia stepped forward then. "Still, you shouldn't go alone," she said. She understood why Nyssa wasn't trying to make a scene. Panicking villagers wouldn't help, even if this was connected to the Kobolds and their ilk, but she didn't want Nyssa taking unnecessary risks.

Nyssa swept her gaze across the group. She sighed. "Talvor can come," she said. "If he finds a shirt first."

It seemed an odd choice, until Thalia remembered that Pavel was the oldest member of the Pentad and had the most experience out in the world. The sheriff ushered all the villagers out and advised the inn's guests to return to their rooms. He escorted the still-shaken bakers back home, as Nyssa and Pavel set out into the dark. Thalia spotted Mina Bellain then, sitting fully dressed at the far end of the bar, sipping a tea she had managed to rustle up, and ignoring everything else. With no other option, Thalia and the girls trudged back up the stairs. She had no plans to go back to sleep, but she wanted to at least put on some clothes.

The room was small, and the girls had not been especially tidy in laying out their saddle bags and undressing for the night. Still, even in the dark, it was immediately apparent that something was wrong. Their spare clothes and belongings lay strewn about the floor and bed. The mattress had been pushed partially off its frame.

"What's this?" Shilo asked, coming in last.

"We've been robbed," Thalia said.

She went at once to her bags, kneeling on the wood floor. She dug through what little had been left inside until her fingers found the carefully wrapped parcel at the bottom. She could tell just by touch that the dagger was still there, the one she had forged two days ago with Master Caston's help. She sighed, only realizing then how worried she had been over possibly losing it.

The room brightened suddenly, lit by a glowing orb of light hovering over Shilo's cupped hands.

Jayn gasped, pausing from searching through her own belongings to look up. "You're making Weaver lights on your own now?"

Despite everything, Shilo smiled. "This is the first one I've managed to make actually."

The light was steady and didn't flicker. For lack of a better place, Shilo affixed it to one of the bedposts.

Jayn sat back on the floor and sighed. "They definitely found my coin purse, but that's all I'm missing."

Only then did Thalia realize she had other possessions of value. She glanced at the corner. Her poleaxe still leaned there, beside Shilo's staff. Then she made a more thorough search of her bags. Her money was also gone, as well as another pouch that had held a dozen copper rings.

She shifted to a seated position and leaned her back against the bed. "They got my money too, and my rings."

"Rings?" Jayn asked. Then her eyes widened. "Thalia, you didn't…?"

"I didn't expect we would need them, but I wanted to be prepared."

Shilo got it then. "Your rings with the luck enchantment? Is that going to be a problem?"

Thalia shook her head. "It shouldn't be. The enchantment doesn't activate unless I directly give someone the rings, and that didn't happen here. They'll just be disappointed to find such cheap jewelry, not worth much more than its weight in pennies."

She became aware of raised voices calling from down the hall. By the sounds of it, the thieves had hit more than one room in the inn. Thalia sighed again and climbed to her feet. "Come on," she said. "Let's get dressed."

Nyssa and Pavel returned just after dawn. Thalia was waiting in the great room with the rest of her Pentad, along with Mina Bellain and Rav Montare. Sara, the red-haired barmaid, kept their teacups full and apologized every chance she could get for what had happened. Most of the inn's guests had cleared out by then, grumbling over lost coins and jewelry but not wanting to stick around in a village haunted by Wydelks and thieves.

Nyssa shook her head as they approached the bar. "No signs of… anything really."

"Something you should know," Thalia said.

She sketched out the details of what they had learned asking around the inn. Most rooms on the second floor had been hit during the chaos and distraction caused by the screaming bakers. Mina assured Nyssa that their room had been spared. Apparently, Mina had been the only one with the presence of mind to lock their door. That was fortunate, as Nyssa had been given the purse for the trip, though the girls had still lost their personal funds. Shilo had also lost the locket she used to carry around a piece of fuel for Weaving. The men sleeping in the loft had been spared. Someone had run and fetched the sheriff again, and he had made a list of everything that had been stolen, muttering promises that he would do what he could to recover the lost coins and valuables.

"Interesting," Pavel said, scratching his chin. He was perpetually in need of a shave. "That certainly changes things."

Nyssa nodded. "We were operating under the assumption that this may have been something related to the… warehouse incident."

She chose her words carefully, as there were still plenty of people up and around, but they all knew what she meant. Thalia had been there with Ryn behind the warehouse that night. She had seen that portal open and one of the creatures emerge, a bear with a human face. She had also seen the owl later that night. Something like a Wydelk would not have been out of place with that group of monsters. But petty thievery didn't seem to fit with anything the Kobolds and their kind had done before. Did monsters need money? Pavel was clearly thinking along the same lines.

"Could just be common thieves, then," he said. "Well, not exactly common with this tactic."

"What are you thinking?" Nyssa asked. "All that outside with the bakers was just a distraction?"

He nodded. "A pretty good one, too. Someone runs around outside with a deer skull on their head to get everyone's attention, while their accomplice ransacks the upstairs."

Nyssa frowned. "I'm still not sure I buy that it was just someone in a costume. What about the fog?" She turned to the others. "We asked around about some of the previous sightings, and every story was consistent. An unnatural mist rolled in each time the creature was seen."

"Weavers, then," Jayn said. "An enshrouding ward looks something like a fog. This could be a modified version of that, maybe even an Etching."

"It's certainly possible," Nyssa said. "We'll report it all to the Appencourt outpost once we get there. They can send a team out to investigate. In the meantime, pack your bags."

Jayn stood up from her stool, though it didn't give her much added height. "Shouldn't we stay and investigate?" she asked. Nyssa opened her mouth, but Jayn cut her off. "We are a Pentad, are we not? It is our primary duty to stop rogue Weavers."

Nyssa gave up on whatever she was going to say. Jayn's challenge was clear. They were supposed to be behaving like a real Pentad, if only for appearances. If they were to present themselves as Watchkeepers in Appencourt, then they had to act accordingly on the road too.

Thalia cleared her throat. "We do have almost a week until the hearing. We can spare a day or two."

Nyssa studied each of them for a long while before responding. "Very well," she said. "We'll stay through today and reevaluate in the morning." She turned toward Mina and Rav, who were seated further down along the bar. "I must apologize. We had agreed to escort both of you, but we would be remiss in our duties if we did not stay to investigate this issue."

Mina smiled. "Not a problem. I am eager to see this Pentad in action."

Thalia did not like the sound of that.

Rav spread his hands. "Truth be told, I did not get much sleep last night. I would welcome another day of rest, and I am loath to give up my escort, times being what they are."

Nyssa nodded. She turned back to the Pentad. "Well," she said, gesturing toward the door. "Go see what you can find."

Chapter 11
The Wydelk

THEY DID NOT BEGIN asking around right away, of course. That early in the morning, most of the villagers would still be in bed after the night's disruption, or if awake, they would not be in a mood to welcome company. So Ryn and the others ate a plain breakfast of eggs and yeasty rolls. Just to be safe, the men moved their belongings up to the girls' room, which could at least be locked. Then around midmorning, they set out, deciding to split up.

Pavel argued that he had already been out much of the night, so he slinked away to the loft to rest. Thalia and Shilo paired up, which left Ryn with Jayn, who would not have been his first choice. Jayn had been giving him a lot more attention than usual over the past two days, but he knew it wasn't a sudden affection that had caused it. She never came out and said it, but she was clearly worried he would embarrass her in Appencourt, so she had taken it on herself to educate him on proper behavior among the upper echelons of society.

He wasn't too bothered by this, as he genuinely did want to learn more and was not looking forward to speaking in front of the most important men and women in the nation. No one in Aen's Hollow had ever used the word "echelon," as far as he knew. Apparently, everyone in his village belonged to the fourth echelon, the second lowest rung of society. The higher echelons were found primarily in bigger towns and cities, while "first echelon" referred to the elite families that passed their ever-growing wealth down from one generation to the next. Like the Eldragors, their ancestors had been nobles under the old Tamor monarchy. The nobles renounced their titles when Aldria separated two centuries ago, but they retained most of their land and all of their wealth. Ryn had learned all this from one of Jayn's many lectures since setting out from Falport.

The inn lay more or less in the center of the village, so Shilo and Thalia would ask around everywhere west of it, while Jayn and Ryn took the eastern side of town. Most of the trade caravans had broken camp and left already, heading north or south, but heavy traffic continued throughout the day. Word traveled fast in such a densely populated place as the Golden Lands, so the proper authorities were probably already making plans to rebuild the destroyed bridge, but that would take time.

Ryn wondered if the bridge and the Wydelk were somehow connected. He also worried that if the rogue Weavers had been part of one of the many caravans already scattered to the winds, then they would never find them. He shared these concerns with Jayn, but she argued that thieves using such a spectacular and effective technique wouldn't be able to stop themselves from trying it again. If the Wydelk visited another village, they would know the thieves had moved on. In the meantime, they still had to search this village, in case the rogues were locals. Ryn could not argue with her logic.

Jayn took the lead as they visited houses and the handful of shops in town. Ryn still felt uncomfortable talking to strangers. Barely three months ago, he had spent most of his time alone, foraging for mushrooms and herbs in the Sylphren Wood, his only friend a pig named Anya. He still wondered what had become of her and sometimes felt a pang of guilt over abandoning her. Had the Kobolds killed and eaten her, as he feared? Last he heard, things had quieted down in the Sylphren Wood. Likely the people of Aen's Hollow had buried their dead and resumed their lives more or less as usual. Perhaps one of the villagers had found Anya and taken her in, hoping to use her as a mushroom pig.

What would they think when they found out she couldn't actually sniff out silverbells? What would they think of him, the herbalist's boy who had vanished on that same day the Kobolds came and killed three of the village's youths? Would another herbalist come to town to take Marla's place? Would anyone move into Marla's cottage, or would the structure be abandoned, left to fall apart over the years and become the subject of countless spooky fairy stories, used to frighten the village kids? Ryn didn't know if he would ever return to Aen's Hollow. Probably, he would not.

While Jayn had no problems striking up conversations with strangers, Ryn quickly realized that she wasn't actually any good with people—not in the easy, friendly way that Thalia or Nyssa could be, nor in the smooth-talking, deceitful way that Pavel operated. She was too blunt and formal, not attempting to relate to the villagers, and with all the tact of an army general interrogating a captured enemy soldier. Ryn saw all that but couldn't do anything to intervene. He certainly didn't know how to talk to people himself, and he had no desire to try correcting Jayn on her approach. That would not have gone well.

Sometime close to noon, Jayn was talking to a woman who stood leaning in a doorway with a baby on her hip. Jayn ignored the child completely, though it cooed and waved a chubby hand at her. Ryn had never before met a woman or girl who would not stop to fawn over a baby if given the chance. Ryn strolled away from them, knowing already that Jayn would get nothing useful from the mother. The villagers had all been polite, despite Jayn's awkward stiffness, but they had learned nothing new.

Nearby, two children, a boy and a girl, were playing a game that involved tossing small stones across the yard and skipping over to them. With each hop, they chanted a different word from a simple rhyme: "Foxes, crows, Drakes, and bulls." The word they stopped on when they reached the stone seemed to have some meaning in the game. The boy laughed when the girl stopped on "crows." Ryn had heard that same little rhyme back in Aen's Hollow, though the game was played differently there. Probably, it was a very old rhyme, passed down as such things were from one generation of children to the next all over Aldria.

Hearing the sound of wood clacking together, Ryn moved further away, around the corner of the next house. Most of the houses in this village were made from wooden boards, with slanted clay tile roofs. In the yard between the house and what looked like a farrier's shop, a pair of young men dueled with wooden practice swords, which looked simple and primitive compared to the practice weapons Mistress Whitcomb used back in Falport. Ryn had only just begun to learn how to fight, but he could tell that this was more a fun sparring match than any serious training.

The two men were probably around Ryn's age. One was thinner and paler, with shaggy brown hair, while the other was a broad-shouldered youth with short black hair and a tan complexion. Both wore dark brown trousers and lighter brown shirts, the typical garb of farmers and villagers in this part of the country. Both smiled as they sparred, and they seemed evenly matched. After a minute, the smaller one broke the fight off. He'd noticed Ryn watching them. He made a mock salute with his sword and said, "Hail, Watchkeeper," though he smiled good-naturedly.

"Hello," Ryn said.

Now that he had a moment away from Jayn, perhaps he could try a different approach to get some answers, though it would not be easy. Two days ago, Ryn had set out from Falport in the company of Pavel and five women. Though Mina Bellain made him nervous, he liked being around the other women—even Jayn, most of the time. It had nothing to do with attraction or a desire to be a philanderer; he simply found that he preferred the company of women over men. He would never be the kind of man that other men flocked to. He was short and skinny, and he would sooner pick up a gardening trowel than a practice sword. He generally found it easier to talk to women, perhaps because they tended to be less intimidating. Still, he had to try relating to these men somehow.

Fortunately, the youth who had spoken first proved to be a naturally gregarious person, so Ryn didn't need to find a way into a conversation. The man dug the tip of his practice sword into the ground and leaned on it like a cane. "So," he said, "were you here for that bit of fun last night?"

"When that girl was screaming, you mean?" Ryn asked. "I wouldn't exactly call that fun."

He shrugged. "Interesting, then. Not much interesting happens around here. The name's Clay, by the way." He gestured to his friend. "This here is Ansel."

Ansel waved his hand. "Hail, Watchkeeper," he said, attempting a grin like Clay's, though he was clearly the more subdued member of the duo.

Ryn nodded. "My name is… Ryn Silverbell. I'm glad to meet you."

Clay pulled his sword from the dirt and tucked it under his arm. "You look a bit young for a Watchkeeper, if you don't mind me saying," he said. "Though I did hear the Gray Guard takes them even younger than the Army does."

"Are you two thinking of joining the Army then?" Ryn had been wondering why two young men were practicing with swords in the middle of a weekday.

"We are," Ansel said.

Clay shrugged again. "It's an option."

Ryn had not realized that Jayn had come up behind him until she spoke. "You two aren't Flame Weavers, are you?" she said, which made him flinch.

Ansel shook his head. Clay's grin broadened when he saw Jayn. "Well, well, well," he said. "Is this your partner, Ryn?"

Jayn's chin shot up as she stiffened. She had a way of making herself seem much taller when she wanted. "My name is Jayn Eldragor," she said.

"Pleased to meet you." He gestured to himself. "You may call me Clay."

She ignored his attempts at charm. "Why do you want to join the Army?"

His smile faltered. "I didn't say we did."

Ansel crossed his arms over his chest, still holding his sword. "So we're not Flame Weavers," he said. "So we won't be officers. It still pays well. It still comes with a pension. That's good money for people like us."

"Ansel is sold on the idea," Clay said. "I don't know why he's so eager to get out of town, when he's got a girl like his right here." He glanced at Jayn and lowered his voice confidingly. "I'm in between girls at the moment, if you were wondering."

Jayn's nostrils flared as she prepared some snappy retort. Ryn had to act fast before the girl's temper derailed the conversation. He loudly cleared his throat and started speaking even before he really knew what he wanted to say. "Last night," he blurted. "Did you two see anything strange? Or hear anything?"

Jayn clenched her jaw and crossed her arms, but she kept quiet. Clay squinted as he looked Ryn over again, apparently reevaluating him. Did he think Ryn was a possible rival for Jayn's affection? Ryn found that laughable, but Clay clearly thought otherwise.

"Maybe," the youth said. "Maybe I did see something." He held his wooden sword by the blunt blade and held it out toward Ryn. "If you can beat me in a sparring match, I'll tell you." His grin took on a cocky slant.

Ryn frowned. He'd had weeks now of formal weapons training, but he still didn't trust himself to win even a practice fight.

Jayn stepped in front of Ryn. "I'll fight you for it," she said.

Clay turned his smile on her. "No need. I'll tell *you* everything you want to know, and it will only cost you a kiss."

"Clay," Ansel grumbled, grabbing his friend's arm. "Come off it. Leave them alone."

Clay shook Ansel off with a shrug, not taking his eyes off Jayn.

Ryn expected a scandalized outburst from her. Instead, she smiled back and said almost sweetly, "I'll give you a kiss, if you beat me."

Clay laughed, but he pressed his sword into Jayn's hands, took Clay's weapon, and ran back across the yard to take up position.

Jayn unstrapped her sword belt and handed it and her actual sword to Ryn.

"Jayn..." Ryn said, but he didn't know what words could stop her now, and she ignored him. She moved out into the yard, hefting the wooden sword to get a sense of its weight.

Ansel sighed, but he moved to take up position between Jayn and Clay. "First to five hits, yeah?"

Clay didn't land a single hit. He was bigger and stronger, but Jayn was faster and far more skilled. She whacked him four times, not pulling her swings at all. On the fifth pass, she feigned to bring him in close. She turned suddenly, kicking his leg out from under him. As he fell on his butt, she struck him on the chest with a flick of her wrist.

He lay on the ground with his eyes screwed shut and wincing for a moment, but then he started laughing. "Jayn Eldragor!" he said. "You are an impressive woman."

Surprisingly, she offered him a hand and helped pull him to his feet. He dusted himself off and then turned his smile back on her. "Now, what would you like as your reward?"

"Just tell us what you saw last night."

He frowned. "You guys really are taking this thing seriously, huh?" He glanced at Ansel and then back at her. "Do the Watch-keepers really believe the Wydelk is roaming the Golden Lands? We're half a year away from Winter Feast and the Solemn Night."

Jayn shrugged. "It honestly would not be the strangest thing I've ever seen. You've no doubt heard of what happened in Falport two months back."

Clay's eyes widened. "You were there then? I heard the Citadel got hit even harder than the rest of the city."

"We lost a lot of good men and women that night, but we drove the Kobolds off. I myself killed a dozen of them."

That clearly impressed Clay. He glanced at Ryn, who did his best to look stoic and competent. Ryn had not killed a single Kobold. Clay let out a long breath. "You must have gone easy on me then. Sorry I doubted you." He paused before asking, "Do you think that business in Falport with the Kobolds and the Drake might be connected to what happened here?"

Jayn raised a reassuring hand. "It's unlikely. There's certainly no need for anyone to panic."

"I don't know. Maive and her Ma clearly saw something frightful. Maybe there really is a Wydelk."

"You heard what happened at the inn, I'm sure. The robbery likely means something more mundane happened. It's probably just common thieves with a flair for the dramatic."

Clay nodded. "I hope you are right about that. Were you staying at the inn? I hope you didn't lose anything too precious?"

She shook her head. "Just some coin. Nothing to cry over."

"That's not bad then."

Ansel grabbed his friend's arm again, lightly this time. "Come on, Clay," he said. "We should get going."

"In a moment," Clay said. "Well, Jayn Eldragor, I hope you find your thieves. Maybe I will see you around later?"

Jayn actually smiled. "Maybe you will," she said.

Ryn didn't know what to make of that. Had the man's ham-fisted attempt at charm actually worked on her?

They reunited with the others shortly after that. Apparently, Pavel had never left the inn, so Ryn and Jayn found him at the bar with Shilo and Thalia. The friendly red-haired barmaid served them each a generous helping of stew made with sliced sausage and boiled beans.

"No leads," Jayn reported. The others hadn't done any better. Whatever had visited Wydhaven last night, only those two women had seen it. No one else had even seen a fog.

Pavel sighed. "I don't fault you for poking your noses around," he said. "Probably it was worth taking a look, but if the thieves are still here, they know the Watchkeepers are definitely looking for them, on top of the sheriff, though he doesn't seem to be doing much. They'll lie low for a while now, I'd wager."

Jayn frowned. "So we should just give up then?" she said.

"Well, the Watchkeepers will keep looking into it, I'm sure, but the five of us have business in Appencourt in a few days. This kind of investigation takes time. Think of how long it took the Watchkeepers to track down—" He glanced at the barmaid hovering nearby and changed his mind on what he was going to say. "That, uh, alleged thief Max Aetherstorm. They, I mean we, were on his trail for months and only found him by accident. These thieves will strike again, I'll bet you, but probably not for a while, not if they're smart. They got away this time, but whenever they come up again, whoever is on the case will have another shot at catching them. That probably won't be us though."

Jayn shook her head. "I'm not so ready to give up yet. Maybe we could get somewhere if you helped out instead of sitting around here eating beans."

"Well, the beans are good. And the company." He nodded to the barmaid and smiled. She was probably used to incessant flirting from customers, so she merely grinned back, her cheeks dimpling.

Just then the door slung open. The room was quiet and mostly empty. At this time of day, most diverted travelers kept pushing through town and few had decided to stay for the night yet. So the opening door was cause to look up. Ryn was surprised to see one of the young men from earlier, not the chatty Clay, but the quieter Ansel, stepping into the inn.

Ansel stopped when he saw Ryn and the four other Watch-keepers in their gray uniforms. Ryn nodded politely to him. Ansel hesitated for a moment before nodding back, a confused expression on his face. Then he looked all around the inn, even leaning forward to see into the far corner. He glanced at Ryn again, shrugged, and left, shutting the door behind him. It seemed like he had been looking for someone in particular, saw the person wasn't here, and then left. But it also seemed like a pantomime of such actions, meant to cover up his true intentions. Weird.

Ryn turned back to the others. Jayn had not looked up when the door opened. Pavel didn't seem to notice the interruption either. "Besides," he was saying, "it sounds like you four have searched the whole village. What else is there to do?"

Jayn stood up. "Maybe we need to widen our search. There might still be some merchant caravans outside the village. We could try asking there."

Thalia shook her head. "Most of the wagons that were here last night have probably left by now."

"Well, we might still get something from new arrivals," Jayn said, standing her ground. "This isn't the first time people have supposedly seen the Wydelk. Travelers from all over the Golden Lands are crossing through this town right now. If we can find another sighting that's connected to a theft, we can start to establish a pattern."

"I don't know," Shilo said. "I think I'm with Pavel on this one."

"Well, I'm going back out there. Protocol says at least one of you should come with me." She looked directly at Ryn.

He sighed. "Fine, I'll go with you. Just let me eat something first."

***

Night had fallen by the time Jayn was willing to give up. Ryn trudged along beside her for hours as they circled through the improvised camps set up around town. As the day waned, the camps only got larger, with more and more new arrivals stopping for the night. The camps ran right up against the fields to the south and east and spilled northward into the sparse sort of woods you could still find even in such developed lands.

They were moving through those trees now, mostly sprawling crown oaks and slender gray ash trees, their bark furrowed into distinctive ridges. Ryn stopped when he spotted a foxfeather bush. He didn't think they grew this far east, but the round alternating leaves were unmistakable. His hand went to his chest, but he'd left his herbalist satchel back at the inn. He'd also traded the small knife he'd used to take cuttings in for a sizable dagger. He could use that, or either of the slender knives he had concealed in his shirtsleeves, but he didn't really have any need for collecting samples anymore. As useful as foxfeather could be to an ordinary herbalist, it was surpassed by even the most rudimentary Rootbalm. His days of being an ordinary herbalist were far behind him now.

Jayn walked several dozen paces before she realized she had lost him. She stopped and looked back at him. "What's the problem?" she asked.

He pointed to the plant. "It's a foxfeather bush," he said, not loud enough for her to hear.

"What?"

He shook his head and spoke up. "It doesn't matter. Look, we're not getting anywhere. Can we call it a night and head back to the inn? Nyssa will probably have us moving out in the morning."

She crossed her arms and tapped her foot, but after a moment she relented. "Fine," she said. "We can go back."

That's when they heard the shouting.

Ryn was running toward it before he knew what he was doing. So was Jayn, and she had a considerable lead on him. The trees parted, and in the dwindling twilight, they could see five or six wagons circled in a clearing. At the center, four grown men stood huddled together and screaming, pointing at something Ryn couldn't see, possibly on the other side of one of the wagons.

Jayn reached the clearing first, her sword drawn. She stumbled when she stepped between the wagons, then she moved forward more slowly, her head swiveling. She got within a few paces of the men, when she must have seen it. Unbelievably, she dropped her sword, sinking at once to her knees. She shuddered and then let out a piercing scream. Ryn stopped running. This was the last thing he had expected Jayn to do. He'd never heard her scream like that before, not even when they faced down Kalo and his army of Kobolds. What could she possibly be seeing? Ryn still saw nothing, though the night grew darker by the second. Maybe it was just there on the other side of that wagon…

Ryn stood rooted to the ground. The men turned as if to run, but they immediately tripped over each other and fell to the ground in a heap. They made no effort to rise but merely covered their heads and mumbled incoherently. Jayn still hadn't moved. Her screams dissolved into a body-wracking sob. Ryn remembered another night, the first time he'd encountered Kalo. He'd stood helpless while the Kobold had cut down Nyssa and Pavel, leaving them to die. He couldn't be helpless anymore. He refused to be.

Knives were in his hands, though he couldn't remember shaking them loose from his sleeves. He willed himself to move. Still, seconds passed before he could take a step forward. He heard shouting from other nearby camps, men calling out to each other and wanting to know what was happening. He couldn't think about it. He just had to act. Whatever Jayn was seeing, it had to have some dark power to inspire such unnatural fear in her. That was the only explanation that made sense. He didn't doubt that he would be just as crippled by fear as soon as he saw the creature. If Jayn couldn't handle the sight of it, then he certainly couldn't.

He had to act as soon as he entered the clearing, before the fear had a chance to take hold. Judging from where the men had pointed and the direction Jayn still faced, he could gauge where the creature must be standing. He'd only have one shot. He ran forward, telling himself he could not hesitate, no matter what he saw.

Everything changed when he crossed between the two nearest wagons. Jayn and the men beyond her vanished into a white mist. It hadn't rolled in suddenly or risen up from the ground. One instant there was no fog, and then it was all around him. He stumbled but did not stop. He moved toward where Jayn had been, until he could see her as a dark silhouette. He turned in the direction she faced. Something was there. He raised his arms and hurled both knives.

The fear struck him like a crashing wave. His knees hit the ground before he knew he was falling. He'd anticipated something like this, but that thought vanished as abject terror overwhelmed his senses. His body shook, his own screams sounding foreign in his ears. The creature towered over him.

The knives had flown true, but they simply vanished into the creature's shadowy body. Sheriff Wilkes had described the Wydelk used in pageants as a man draped in a sheet and carrying a skull. This creature wore not a sheet but a cloak of swirling shadows, inky black as a starless night. The shadowed mass rose seven feet from the ground and filled the bone-white elk skull on top, which tapered into a narrow point, both jaws rimmed with stubby teeth. Above it, branching gray antlers spread into a dozen curved points.

From the deep black eye sockets, red eyes glowed. The creature shimmered like a mirage, but its presence was overwhelmingly real. From the shadowy body, a skeletal arm emerged, pointing a single bony finger at Ryn.

"Be gone!" it said. The alien voice seemed to rattle inside Ryn's skull. "End your search!"

Chapter 12
It Takes a Thief

PAVEL DECIDED THAT HE LIKED Rav Montare after all. Probably, this was surprising to his companions, especially Shilo, who seemed to have taken a different sort of shine to the cultist, or Scribe as he preferred. In general, Pavel distrusted formal religions, as too often they provided shelter and legitimacy to charlatans with evil intentions, but Pavel didn't mind a true believer. He could respect someone who actually sought to carry out the morality he preached, especially if his convictions were reasoned and carefully considered, not just blindly accepted dogma. Rav Montare appeared to be such a person, and he was also intelligent and surprisingly well schooled in history, so Pavel could like as well as respect the man.

They were chatting together over dinner in the great room of the Wydelk inn—Pavel, Rav, and Shilo, though the girl contributed little to the conversation. Nyssa sat at another table with Thalia and the Scholar, probably discussing the events of the day and night before, though Pavel could not hear much of their conversation. The inn was not nearly as full this night, so they were inside rather than out in the yard. A number of the travelers diverted from the main road had evidently opted to push through the night rather than stop in a village rampant with rumors of monsters and thieves.

"Every religion in the world has a moral law," Rav was saying. "There are some notable variations, but most of the core tenets are the same. Surely, that points to a singular origin for morality itself."

Pavel shrugged. He didn't spend much time thinking about such topics, but he was always down for a friendly debate. "Even most non-religious people adhere to morality as well, though. It's part of being human."

"Well, certainly everyone has an ability to distinguish right and wrong actions, and many desire to do what is good, but our natural inclinations are still toward evil."

"That's a pessimistic view."

"It's the truth. Consider the problem of these thieves. The first time a man steals, he knows it is wrong. If he continues to steal, the voice inside that tells him not to do it, speaks more softly. Eventually, he no longer hears that voice, and he tells himself that what he does is good or necessary. He has given himself over completely to evil impulses, and probably he will do more wicked things than just stealing, even if he only began to steal out of poverty or need."

"What could help such a thief then?"

"Only the Maker."

"You mean the Sheperd-King?"

"They are one and the same. Rather, the Shepherd-King is a manifestation of the Maker."

"And that makes your religion better than all the others?"

"Religions are all the same at their root. I walk the path with the Maker, and that has made the difference. I don't pretend to perfection, but I am a better man now than when I first found the way."

"That sounds a lot like religion to me. But I'll humor you. What makes your path better than all the others?"

"True knowledge of the Maker and his will. The religions of man are all counterfeits, pantomime shows meant to reassure the practitioners that they do know the Maker. They perform the rituals and recite the prayers and convince themselves that it makes them better. I'll give you an analogy. Who is the leader of the Watchkeepers?"

"Lahey. Commandant Hiram Lahey."

"What if I told you that I knew him, that he was my friend? What if I read many books written about him and his accomplishments? What if I carried his portrait in miniature wherever I went? What if I knew his habits, his favorite foods, how he took his tea? What if I knew all this from studying and asking other people, but I've never been to Falport, and I've never actually met the man, and he has no knowledge of me? Would you say that I knew him?"

Pavel laughed. "I'd say you were a creep, but no. Certainly, you would know *of* him, but you wouldn't truly know him."

"That's what makes the difference. The leaders of these religions know *of* the Maker, but they do not truly know him or have access to him. That's what makes them dangerous."

"I'm not so sure. Granted, many wolves hide among religious flocks and use them as cover for their misdeeds, but for true believers, don't religions help them to act better? To be more morally correct?"

"On the surface perhaps. Having others around you encouraging you to proper action may make it easier to listen to that voice inside and to suppress your evil impulses, but religion alone cannot solve the problem of evil. It's still in the heart of every man. If you doubt me, then consider that all men, even the best of them, are liars."

Pavel couldn't argue against that. "Granted, but not everyone lies for evil reasons or with malicious intent."

"Men may feel that sometimes a lie is justified or even beneficial, but wouldn't you agree that the world would still be a better place if no one ever had to tell a lie?"

"That would be a very different world. It's hard to say what that would be like."

"I'll acknowledge that in rare cases, concealing the truth may be justified if it stops an even greater evil from being perpetrated, but most lies are told for petty and selfish reasons. Still, we find a way to rationalize them. If we didn't justify our actions, we would end up hating ourselves."

Pavel saw the truth of that statement. In his previous line of work, he'd dealt with all kinds of unsavory men, but none of them saw themselves as wicked or evil. They all had a justification, a way of living with themselves or even seeing what they did as good and right.

"Consider the problem of Tamor," Rav said.

"Which one?"

"They are struggling with the problem of morality right now. Here in Aldria, we generally ignore concepts like good and evil. We say stealing is wrong because it hurts others. If you catch the thieves here, certainly they will be punished, but only as a means of making restitution for the crime, not in order to expunge evil from their souls or from the land. Tamor is different. Under their first emperor and even more now under his son, they have become fixated on good and evil. They preach a strict moral law that no one, not even the emperor, can uphold. The proper response would be to acknowledge their weakness and seek the Maker's grace and forgiveness. Instead, they have doubled down on the law. If a man tries hard enough, then surely he can behave perfectly correct all of the time. So the punishments have become increasingly harsher, as if men can be intimidated into morality. A thief in Tamor, if he isn't killed outright, will have his right hand and left foot chopped off, so everyone will know his moral failings for the rest of his life."

Pavel cringed at the idea. Why did Rav keep harking back to the example of a thief? Probably just because of the recent burglary, unless he somehow knew of Pavel's past reputation. Had one of the kids told him? Pavel glanced at Shilo, who sat listening to Rav with rapt attention. Maybe one of them had.

The conversation went no further that night. Pavel glanced up as the door swung forcefully open and Ryn and Jayn stumbled in. Jayn had an arm slung across Ryn's shoulders, and he kept a hand on her waist as he practically dragged her into the great room. There was nothing romantic in that embrace. Had they made friends among the wagon camps and perhaps had too much to drink? But no, these two wouldn't do that, and their faces were pale, not red. Ryn looked up, and his eyes found Pavel and the others, fear plainly written on his face. Jayn looked up too when they stopped, her expression strangely blank.

Nyssa toppled her stool getting to her feet. She reached the pair just ahead of Thalia and Shilo. She pressed a hand to Jayn's cheek. "She's ice cold," Pavel heard her say as he reached the group. Nyssa touched Ryn's face then. "So are you."

All other conversation in the inn stopped, as the guests turned to stare. These Watchkeepers clearly had undergone some ordeal, and everyone was eager for the gossip. Pavel glanced around the room. The stout matron came out from behind the bar, her mouth agape, but she came on slowly, perhaps not knowing if she should stick her nose in. The lone barmaid stood staring with a full platter in her hands. This was the more homely one, not the pretty and lively redhead who had caught Pavel's attention. Whatever had happened to Ryn and Jayn, this conversation should happen elsewhere. Pavel opened his mouth, but Nyssa beat him to it.

"Let's get her to her room," she said, taking Jayn's other arm, and she and Ryn carried her up the stairs.

None of the curious patrons could follow then, though unfortunately, Mina Bellain did squeeze her way into the crowded bedroom. Under Nyssa's quick instructions, the other girls helped pull off Jayn's boots and remove her sword belt. Then they got her in bed and under the sheets. Shilo ran out to fetch some water and food. Nyssa turned her focus on Ryn, feeling his forehead and looking into his eyes. "Maybe you should lie down too," she said.

Ryn looked at the already occupied bed, and some color came into his cheeks then. He mumbled something about feeling all right and sat on the edge of the bed, his back against the headboard.

Pavel glanced at the still-open door. Rav Montare lingered outside, clearly unsure if he was overstepping his place in the group by being here. Pavel sidled past Mina, who had pressed herself in the corner and was watching everyone. Pavel still wasn't sure why the Scholar had attached herself to their little party, but he knew it wasn't good. He didn't have time to worry about her now. He gave Rav a reassuring smile and said, "Can you keep an eye on the hall? Make sure no one gets close enough to listen in?"

Rav nodded. He turned his back on the room and faced the corridor. Pavel had given him something to do and permission to stay, which he'd clearly been looking for. Pavel turned back toward the others and leaned against the doorframe.

"What happened?" Nyssa asked Ryn. Jayn seemed to be coming back to herself. She blinked up at Nyssa, who sat on the other side of the bed.

Ryn shook his head. It took him a moment to gather his thoughts. "I don't know. We saw it… The Wydelk… Out in the woods in one of the camps, but it wasn't… Something else had to be going on." He balled his hands into fists as sudden conviction came into his voice. "It has to be Weavers."

A confusion of voices rose from downstairs. It sounded like more people were coming inside.

Ryn looked up. "That's probably people from the camps, coming to tell everyone what happened. A lot of people saw the Wydelk this time."

Nyssa turned toward the door. "Someone should probably go down there and hear what they're saying. We need to know if anything was stolen this time."

Thalia glanced back at Pavel. She obviously didn't want to leave Jayn's side. Pavel hesitated. Nyssa was right, but he also didn't want to miss out on hearing what Ryn had to say.

Behind him, Rav cleared his throat. "I can go," he said. "I'll listen to what everyone is saying and come back when I have their story."

"Thanks," Pavel said, offering the man another smile.

Probably, Nyssa would have wanted an actual Watchkeeper downstairs, but just then Jayn gasped and tried to sit up. Nyssa turned her attention to the girl, murmuring assurances and helping her move to a seated position in the bed. Shilo brushed past Pavel, carrying a little tray with a pitcher of water, a clay cup, and a covered dish. She and Nyssa helped Jayn drink some water.

Jayn looked at each of them, her eyes settling on Nyssa. "There was a ward. I didn't see it until I was inside, but it had to be a ward." She shivered and reached for the cup again. Shilo helped her drink.

Nyssa turned her eyes on Ryn, who seemed shaken up but far less affected by whatever had happened.

He nodded. "We heard shouting in the woods and ran toward one of the camps. We saw a group of men in between the wagons, screaming at something. Jayn was ahead of me. As soon as she got up to the men, something took hold of her. She started… I knew it had to have something to do with Weaving. Obviously, she had crossed some kind of barrier, a ward, I guess. Probably, it was dumb to just run in after her. I should have gone for help. If I'd been the first to go in, probably Jayn would have known better what to do…"

"No," Jayn said. She nearly dropped her cup, but Shilo caught it. Jayn tilted her head to look up at Ryn. "You weren't dumb. You did better than me. You actually tried to attack it."

"Well, only because I saw what happened to you. It gave me some idea what to expect. You couldn't have known."

Nyssa raised a hand to get their attention. "Back up," she said. "Tell me everything that happened, as clearly as you can."

Jayn nodded. "At first, I only saw the men. When I crossed into the ward, suddenly there was this dense fog all around me. It really was like crossing into an enshrouding ward, though it was invisible from the outside and not as dark on the inside. I could still see a little bit. I knew the fog wasn't real, just something made by a Wave Weaver, but I still had to find the Weaver. I moved toward the men, but then I saw what they were looking at… The fear I felt then, it wasn't natural…"

Nyssa took her hand. "It's normal to be afraid when you see something like that."

Jayn shook her head and pulled her hand free. "No, I mean… The fear didn't come from inside me. Something else… made me afraid. It forced the emotion onto me. I've seen Kobolds and that man-faced owl. The Wydelk shouldn't have scared me like… like that."

Ryn nodded along, clearly understanding her sentiment. "I saw her drop to the ground and start screaming, just like the men, just like those women last night. I knew it had to be some kind of lacing… Jayn would never react like that on her own."

Jayn offered him a weak smile.

Nyssa looked up, her eyes finding Mina. "What do you think?"

Pavel would not have thought to turn to the Scholar, but obviously the woman had knowledge of Weaving that surpassed what the Watchkeepers studied.

Mina looked around the room at each of them before responding, though her expression and tone remained blandly polite. "Repulsion wards have an effect on emotions."

"Not like that!" Pavel said, not able to stop himself. "Sure, they're good at keeping animals out, but humans only feel a mild uneasiness."

Mina shrugged. "Mild unease can become abject terror, if the ward is strong enough."

"What, like from an Etching?" Pavel asked.

"It's certainly possible."

Nyssa slowly shook her head. "The fear, plus the fog… What are we saying then? Two powerful Wave Weavers with two distinct Etchings working together?"

Mina made no answer. Pavel eyed her suspiciously. Another explanation had come to him, one he had no desire to share with her. They needed to move the conversation forward, past any dangerous speculation. "We haven't even come to the Wydelk yet," he said. "Did you really see it?"

Jayn shuddered, clutching her hands to her chest, just as the baker's daughter had last night. Ryn paled visibly.

Pavel waved a hand to dismiss the question. "Forget what it looked like for a minute, or how it made you feel. What did it do?"

Ryn looked up at him. "It said… 'Be gone. End your search.' It pointed at me when it said that. The fear had hit me too, and I couldn't move."

"But wait," Nyssa said, "Jayn said you attacked it?"

Ryn nodded. "When I saw Jayn go down, I knew some force must have hit her and that probably it would take me down too. I thought maybe I could do something if I was quick, so I had my knives ready when I went in. As soon as I saw it, I threw them. Then the fear hit me, and I couldn't even think."

"Did you hit it?" Nyssa asked.

He hesitated. "I don't think it was real. I think it was part of the illusion, like the fog."

"That's some Etching…"

Pavel heard the wonder and unease in Nyssa's voice. "What happened next?" he asked.

"The creature spoke then," Ryn said. "I don't think it lasted very long. I wasn't under that ward or whatever it was for as long as Jayn, but it felt like ages. One moment it was there, and then it vanished. The creature, the mist, everything. Even the fear was gone, though it took me a minute to recover. I didn't stick around after that. I just wanted to get Jayn out of there."

"Did you see anything?" Nyssa asked. "When the ward went down, did you notice anything or anyone you hadn't seen before?"

Ryn nodded. "My knives… They had passed right through the creature. I saw one stuck into the side of a wagon. I didn't see the other one, but I think… It was dark and I didn't stay to look, but I think there was blood on the ground. I think I hit one of the Weavers."

"Probably," Nyssa said. She looked around at the others. "That's enough for now. Both of you should rest. I'll get us another room so Ryn can sleep comfortably tonight. Let's leave the two of them alone for now and see what we can learn from the people downstairs." She nodded to the tray Shilo had set on a chest near the bed. "Eat whatever's in there, and I'll have some more food sent up." She squeezed Jayn's hand and smiled at Ryn. "Both of you did very well."

Pavel had not spent the day sitting around and eating beans, as Jayn had suggested. While the others had been running around town attempting to investigate, he'd stayed near the inn, making polite conversation with the staff. His gut told him someone working at the inn had been involved in the thefts, and his gut was rarely wrong.

He shared his findings with the rest of his Pentad, shortly after the sun rose on their second day in the blighted town of Wydhaven. He had brought food up for Jayn and the other girls and fetched Ryn from their room. Nyssa had been up and out early that morning to investigate around the village. He had not seen Mina or Rav that morning. He hadn't seen Sara the barmaid either.

"She was a good liar, I'll give her that," Pavel said. "But I could tell she was hiding something."

"Sara?" Shilo asked, clearly doubtful. "The barmaid with the red hair?"

Pavel nodded. "I didn't see her during all the commotion with the baker's daughter, and when I asked her if she'd seen anything that night, she definitely lied. Now that doesn't mean she was part of the theft. Maybe she was off canoodling with a boy or doing something else she wouldn't want to admit."

"But you suspect her?" Jayn asked. She was sitting up in bed, and she looked much better. The normal blush of pink had returned to her face.

"The distraction with the Wydelk outside was good, but it didn't last all that long. Whoever ransacked these rooms had to be familiar with the layout of the inn or know someone who was. That girl is the only one here who seems to be hiding something. Plus, she wasn't around last night when the Wydelk struck again, nor this morning."

"Maybe she was involved," Thalia said. "Could she be a Weaver?"

"Or she's working with them," Pavel said. "Do you remember yesterday when you all came back for lunch, that boy stepped into the inn for a moment and then turned around and left? Well, he came back again later. I saw him and Sara whispering behind the stables. They didn't talk long, but it seemed urgent. She shooed him off before I got close enough to hear what they were saying."

Ryn glanced at Jayn. "The boy you're talking about," he said, "Jayn and I spoke to him earlier in the day."

"So," Pavel said, "maybe you spooked him, and he went to warn his accomplice Sara that the Watchkeepers were still nosing around."

Jayn frowned at Ryn. "Which boy?" she asked. "Clay or the other one?"

"The other one," Ryn said. "Ansel, I think his name was."

Jayn nodded. "Clay did say something about Ansel having a girl in town. If that's Sara… When we met the two of them, they seemed like best friends. If Ansel and his girl were behind the Wydelk, then probably Clay was too, or he at least knew about it."

"Three suspects then," Pavel said. "It could explain what happened last night. Apparently, nothing was stolen from any of the wagon camps, so maybe that little show was just for Jayn and Ryn, to try to scare us off."

"The creature said as much," Ryn said. "It was a dumb idea though. Nyssa is more determined than ever to find the rogues now. I am too, for all that."

Jayn shrugged. "Neither of those boys seemed… particularly bright."

That drew a grin from Ryn, but he didn't say anything.

Thalia sighed. She looked like she would have paced the floor if there had been any room. "Are all three of them Weavers then? The lacings seem incredibly complicated."

"I know," Jayn said. "I've been trying to work that part out. Obviously, Wave was involved. The fog. The illusion of the Wydelk. The fear. Even the way our bodies got colder. It would take at least four different wards layered on top of each other, including two unique Etchings. Unless…"

"A forbidden Blending," Pavel said. He'd had that thought last night, hearing everything that had happened. A silence fell over the group.

Thalia was the first to break it. "A Blending… It has to involve Wave, but what else?"

"Aether," Pavel said. "It makes more sense than Flame. When you add Aether to Stone, it gives it strange properties. Aether can enhance or distort. If you add that to Wave, it could explain the illusions, the fog and the creature. The illusion only affects those inside the ward, which is why no one else saw anything that first night, and you two couldn't see it until you crossed into the ward.

The lacings might not even be visible from the outside, like Jayn's invisibility Etching."

Jayn nodded grimly. "It would make it almost impossible to stop too. Normally, Aether would destroy Wave, but with a Blending like that, maybe not even you could have destroyed it, Pavel."

"I don't know," Thalia said. "I understand how an illusion could make you see and hear things, but to feel emotions? Could one Blending do all that?"

Pavel shrugged. "We won't know anything for sure until we catch these kids and talk to them. We have to be very careful though. The timing is terrible."

"What do you mean?" Thalia asked.

"We're trying to conceal our own forbidden Blending, and now we may have to expose another one. If it was just Nyssa, I wouldn't be worried. We could even let her in on our secret, but not with that Scholar following her around. I don't know if Mina suspects what we really did two months ago, or if she thinks we're part of some star-cursed prophecy, but we can't show our hand around her. We don't want to give her any more reasons to find us interesting."

"What should we do then?" Thalia asked. "Do you have a plan?"

"The beginnings of one. First, we need to figure out if any of these three kids have been stabbed recently."

Chapter 13
Forbidden Blendings

JAYN HAD TO ADMIT that Pavel was very good at what he did. She sat at a table with the rest of her Pentad, while he leaned on the bar behind her, chatting with the other barmaid, a girl named Nance. Jayn and the others carried on a stilted conversation about the weather and the road ahead, but really they were all listening to Pavel and the girl. He made the whole thing sound like a casual conversation, with no whiff of an interrogation, and yet Pavel got so much information out of her, tactfully steering the conversation back to Sara at every turn. He pretended, rather convincingly, that he was interested in a romantic liaison with Sara.

Nance laughed. "Oh, you wouldn't be the first customer to take a run at Sara, but I'm afraid she won't do anything more than flirt with you." The way Nance said it seemed to imply that she herself might do more than just flirt.

Pavel pretended not to notice. "Does she already have a man in her life then?"

"Ansel, the farrier's apprentice. She's quite smitten with him, I'm afraid."

"Sounds like a traveler like me never had a chance then. A little village like this, I'm guessing childhood sweethearts? That old story?"

"Actually, Sara's only been here in Wydhaven about two years." Nance dropped her voice to a confiding whisper, clearly eager to share the local gossip. "She's a bit of a mystery, that Sara. She's cheerful enough and gets along with everyone in town, but no one knows much about where she came from or why she moved here. Maybe she got herself into a spot of trouble with a boy back home, so she came out here where no one knew her. She wouldn't be the first girl to do such a thing. That would explain why she latched onto a safe and dependable fellow like Ansel." Her tone made it clear what she thought about "safe and dependable" men.

"Sounds like you're not too keen on the lad."

"Oh, he's handsome enough, I suppose. Most girls around here prefer his best mate though, a rogue of a boy named Clay. He's too flashy for my tastes though."

Jayn knew what Nance must have meant by "rogue," but it still reminded her of the term Watchkeepers used for Weavers who used their gifts for nefarious purposes. Was he a rogue Weaver? Had he flirted with her yesterday and then used his forbidden Blending to frighten her so terribly hours later?

The fear had faded, but the memory remained vivid. Rationally, she told herself that a shadowed figure with an elk skull for a head should not have frightened her so much more than the Kobolds had, and yet remembering that creature still sent a shiver up her spine. She didn't like that someone could do that—to reach into her soul and make her feel such an intense emotion that was not her own, that had no proper place in her heart.

Clay had claimed that he was not a Weaver, but of course he could have lied. Ansel had only stated that they weren't Flame Weavers. That didn't rule out Wave or Aether. She'd understood Clay right away. Being the most handsome boy in a small village had given him an overinflated sense of confidence. He'd been bluntly transparent and made no effort to hide his interest in Jayn. She couldn't help but find that flattering.

The boys she knew back in Appencourt would never be so brazen. Even if any of them had fancied her—and she suspected one or two of them might have—they would never come out and say it. Politicians were always careful to downplay their true feelings, lest an opponent find an edge over them, and that watchfulness passed onto their children as well, who would never risk a scandal for themselves or their families.

Jayn couldn't help but find Clay's tactless honesty charming, though she would not really have rewarded it with a kiss. Probably she wouldn't have. Certainly, she wouldn't do so now, not if he had anything to do with the theft or creating such terrifying illusions.

She'd been so distracted by her own thoughts that Jayn forgot to listen to the rest of Pavel's conversation with Nance, but he had wrapped it up, and now he was squeezing back into a seat at their table. He waited till Nance had moved further down the bar to speak with another customer, before he leaned in. "Sara and Nance share a room here. Probably Sara isn't in it right now, if Nance is searching for company, which means our thieves went elsewhere last night, after Ryn stuck one of them with a knife."

Ryn frowned. "Do you think I…?"

Pavel shook his head. "You couldn't have done too much damage, if the rogue was able to walk out of there. Someone would have noticed a man or a girl getting dragged along through the woods. Either way, a body would have been found by now.

Probably, they are all lying low somewhere in the village, somewhere they know is safe."

"This village is small," Jayn said. "There can't be too many places like that."

Pavel nodded. "I think I'll take a stroll down by the farrier's shop. See if his apprentice showed up today."

Jayn started to rise, but Pavel put a hand on her shoulder.

"Alone," he said. "I work best alone, and I'll attract less attention. We don't want to show our hand too soon. Once I have a good idea where they are holed up, I promise I'll come back here." He looked around the table. "We'll take these rogues down together, preferably before Nyssa or that Scholar finds them."

Jayn and Shilo strolled through the village, doing their best to look casual. They had changed out of their Watchkeeper uniforms and tabards, under Pavel's advice, to attract less attention. Jayn wore a dark blue riding dress with intricate white embroidery along the hem. It was too fancy for this village—she had packed for Appencourt—but with all the strangers still passing through town, thanks to the destroyed bridge, few of the locals gave her a second glance. Shilo wore brown trousers that were a tad tight in the hips and a loose white shirt with the sleeves rolled up. Like much of Shilo's wardrobe, these were probably clothes inherited from her older brothers.

Pavel had also changed out of his uniform before heading to the farrier's shop. He'd pretended to be a traveling merchant and asked the man how much he would charge to reshoe a horse. Pavel had complained about the quality of his horse's shoes and remarked over how hard it was to find good labor. His approach had been the right one, as the farrier complained unprompted about his lazy apprentice who had not bothered showing up today. Pavel brushed over the rest of the details, but he'd managed to learn that Ansel lived with his parents and their large family in a too-small shack near the center of the village that always had children spilling out into the streets. Clay, on the other hand, lived on the edge of town, near the woods, with only his elderly deaf grandmother.

Jayn and Shilo were making their way toward Clay's house now. Pavel had drawn them a quick map in the dirt behind the inn's stable. Pavel was certain they would find the trio there, lying low and tending to whomever had been injured by Ryn's knife. Jayn and Shilo would approach the house from the back. They had to be getting close now.

They rounded a corner and came face to face with Mina Bellain. She smiled as soon as she saw them. Mina wore a green silk riding dress with vines along the skirt and sleeves. She was the last person Jayn had wanted to run into.

"Jayn Eldragor," Mina said. "I'm glad to see you back on your feet." She nodded to Shilo as well.

Jayn returned the smile as best she could. She focused on slowing her rapidly beating heart. "Miss Bellain," she said. "How are you today?"

"Quite well, but please call me Mina. Have you two gotten anywhere with finding these unusual thieves?"

Jayn shook her head. "Afraid not." She didn't dare to glance back at Shilo, who stood a pace behind her, but she hoped the girl managed to keep her composure. Jayn couldn't say why exactly, but this Scholar made all of them uncomfortable. "We're still looking into it, though," she added.

"I'm sure your Pentad will figure it out. You all seem quite capable for ones so young."

"Thank you," Jayn said. She took a step sidewise, hoping to end the conversation there. The others were probably already waiting for them outside Clay's house.

"I'm curious though…" Mina said. Jayn stopped. She couldn't afford to be rude. "What do you make of these lacings the thieves used? Have you worked any of it out? I admit, I haven't studied Wave much myself."

That intrigued Jayn. The Scholar was of course a Weaver, but she had never told them where her initial talents lay, and it seemed impolite to ask. Apparently, she wasn't a Wave Weaver, and by extension probably not a Root or Stone Weaver either. Unless she was lying and feigning ignorance to draw Jayn into a conversation. Jayn didn't have time to think about all that. She needed to say something. "Not really," she said. "I think there definitely has to be an Etching involved, but we can't really say what until we find them."

"You're probably right. Still, an Etching like that implies a powerful Weaver. If multiple wards were involved, then he or she must have some training. I wonder where they studied and why they're robbing inns now instead of working for a Guild."

"It is strange, yes. I'll have to ask them that too, once we find them."

Shilo cleared her throat, stepping forward. "Excuse us, Miss Bellain," she said. "We really should get back to our search."

"Of course, don't let me keep you." She turned to the side and gestured that they may go. "But please," she added as they walked by her, "call me Mina."

Jayn glanced back once as they made their way to the edge of the village, but the Scholar did not seem to be following them. They needed to capture these rogues quickly and quietly—and then they needed to have an important conversation.

Corvus alerted them to Pavel's presence. The Runeform cawed loudly, perched on the eave of the tile-roofed house just before Clay's. Pavel lay flat on the roof, wreathed in swirling white Aether that was hard to see against the bright noonday sky. Pavel's lacings allowed him to move silently and almost weightlessly across housetops, a handy skill for a one-time thief. Pavel mouthed something and gestured with his hands, clearly asking why they were late. Jayn could only shrug and then nod toward the last house on the edge of the woods. Pavel nodded too and moved to the other side of the roof, out of sight. Probably he would be signaling Ryn and Thalia to move in.

Jayn nodded to Shilo, and they moved quickly around to the back of Clay's house without getting too close. Jayn glanced around, saw they were alone for now, and summoned her own lacing. She stretched the ward out around herself and Shilo and extended it toward the back door of the house. It wasn't a clean half-sphere or box but a curving blob of a ward. It didn't have to look pretty—no one would see it. She set the ward and moved closer to the house. Shilo followed, summoning her own lacings of Flame.

As long as they stayed within Jayn's unique ward, they were completely invisible to anyone outside. Since joining the Watchkeepers, Jayn had mastered her Etching and learned its limits through experimentation with Nyssa and Mistress Bellos. The ward only shielded living things, as well as their clothes and any objects they held. If she were to draw her sword and then drop it, the weapon would suddenly become visible to onlookers. If she sat on a stool, the stool would still be visible, but if she picked it up, it would vanish. For today, it was sufficient that she and Shilo were invisible. If anyone stepped out the back door or peered through one of the windows, open in the midday heat, they would see an empty dirt yard and the woods beyond. Jayn and Shilo did leave footprints behind, but the ground was already covered in criss-crossing tracks.

They got right up beside the door and waited there. Through the open window, they could hear someone, a man, groaning.

"He's not looking good," another male voice said. It might have been Clay.

"This whole thing was stupid," a woman said. "I told you we should never have hit the inn. I work there!"

"I wasn't going to let a golden opportunity like that pass us by! All those rich merchants? Wydhaven never gets that kind of traffic. No, the problem was you and Ansel going after those Watchkeepers. I told you to just keep your heads down."

That overheard conversation confirmed their guilt. It sounded like Ansel and Sara were the ones who worked the Blending, while Clay must have been the thief. Jayn shook her head. That boy must be a more earnest version of Pavel then.

Someone started banging on the front door of the little wooden house. "Watchkeepers!" Thalia's voice boomed over the silence. "Open up!"

"Curse me," Clay swore. "Quick, out the back."

"What about Ansel?" Sara asked.

"Stay if you like," Clay said.

The back door swung open. Jayn dropped to a crouch, though of course Clay could not see her. The brown-haired boy stepped out into the yard and turned, headed for the woods. As he crossed through the ward, Shilo struck. She caught him in the side with a Flame-laced punch. Though he would have barely felt the blow, Clay collapsed, falling flat on his face. He groaned, but with Shilo's numbing blow, he couldn't even turn his neck to get his face out of the dirt.

Sara popped her head through the doorway, her red hair a frizzy mess and dark circles under her eyes from a lack of sleep. Her forehead wrinkled in confusion. "Clay?" she whispered, as the pounding continued on the front door. The boy lay almost completely within the invisibility ward, though one booted foot poked out the side. That must have looked strange to Sara. She took a cautious step out into the yard, eyeing the boot.

Shilo charged. Sara gasped and recoiled, seeing a girl emerge from empty air. Jayn spotted the lines of blue light start to sprout from around Sara's bare feet, but she had no time to form a ward, whatever she was trying to do. Shilo's fist caught her square in the stomach. The barmaid's first thought had been to create a lacing rather than dodge the blow. She collapsed, falling backwards into the house.

"Sara?" a voice inside mumbled, probably Ansel.

Then Ryn and Thalia were there inside the house, standing over Sara, who could do nothing but stare up at them. No locked door could keep a Stone Weaver like Thalia out. Pavel slid off the roof and landed silently in the yard beside Shilo.

"Excellent," Pavel said, glancing around. "Let's get them back inside and warded."

A single hallway ran the length of the house from the front door to the back, with two rooms on either side. They found Ansel in the first room to the right, stripped to the waist and lying on a bed. "What did you do?" he asked in bewilderment, seeing the Watchkeepers drag in his friends' limp bodies. He tried to rise from the bed, but the wound in his side made him too weak. Someone had wrapped cloth bandages around his ribs, but blood showed through and his forehead was beaded in sweat. They dropped Sara and Clay to the ground on either side of the narrow bed.

"Anyone else in the house?" Pavel asked.

"Just an old woman sleeping in the other bedroom," Thalia said. "If she is deaf, probably we don't need to worry about her."

Jayn started to create a sealing ward, which would prevent anyone within it from Weaving.

"Wait," Ryn said, moving to the bed.

Ansel flinched, trying to move away from him.

"Easy," Ryn said. "I'm a Root Weaver. By the look of you, I'd say your knife wound might be turning sour. Maybe your friends didn't clean it just right."

"Leave it," Pavel said. "You can heal him after he talks."

Ryn looked back at Pavel and frowned. "It'll be a lot easier to ask him questions when he's in less pain," he said. "It will only take a moment."

Jayn could tell he wasn't going to back down. Though the Root Weaver was generally passive and went along with whatever the group was doing, he could dig his heels in at odd times. "Careful," Jayn said. "I think this one here might be the Aether Weaver."

"Not a problem," Ryn said, turning back to the man on the bed. "Aether can't hurt me."

Pavel sighed. "Watch the other two, Shilo. If you see any Weaving from them, hit them with something a little harder."

Clay groaned. Probably, he was trying his hardest to get up, but Shilo's lacings would leave him numb for a while yet. "We're not Weavers," he said. "I told you that yesterday. You can't just barge in here like that."

"Stow it," Jayn said. "The girl is a Wave Weaver. She tried some kind of lacing just before Shilo hit her."

Clay fell silent then. Jayn craned her neck to see Sara better on her side of the floor. Tears streamed down the girl's face as she lay staring up at the plaster ceiling, but she didn't say anything.

Ryn murmured reassuring words to Ansel as he sat on the edge of the bed and started undoing the bandages. Ansel winced but didn't try to stop him. "Oof," Ryn said when he uncovered the wound. "Looks like my knife caught you here right between the ribs. I am sorry, but I did think you were a monster. Did you leave it in? Probably better than pulling it out right away, but it must have felt like fire in your guts running all the way back here."

Ryn spoke with the gentle bedside manner of any practiced healer. Jayn had forgotten how he had thrown himself into the work of treating the wounded after the attack on Falport. He'd clearly learned much during those long days.

Ryn glanced back at them. "He's well on his way to a nasty infection. I wish I had some Rootbalm, but I suppose I'll have to blast it all away."

He turned back to his patient as fractured lines of green light formed around him, growing and spreading, assembling themselves into the mosaic shape of an oak tree. He poured the light into Ansel's side, and within seconds the wound puckered and closed. Ansel sighed, laying his head back on the pile of pillows Sara had no doubt placed beneath him. Root healing was remarkably fast, and he looked much better, though he would still need rest.

"Thank you," he said.

"Great," Pavel said. "Now ward them."

Jayn created a sealing ward, molding it to the shape of the room. Shimmering blue light shone along all four walls and across the doorway where Pavel still stood. She set the ward and felt Wave slip away from her. No one in the room, not even her, could Weave now.

"Now bind them," Pavel said. He reached into the satchel he often wore slung across his chest and pulled out three sets of iron manacles.

Thalia's eyebrows rose. "Where did you get those?" she asked.

"Borrowed them from the sheriff," he said with a shrug.

"You see the irony in that, yeah?" Thalia said.

They propped Sara and Clay up to sit against the wall and shackled their hands behind their backs. Ansel didn't put up a fight as they bound him. He just stared glumly at the five Watchkeepers.

"Now that everyone is comfortable," Pavel said, "it's time for a confession."

Clay made a rasping sound in his throat and tried to spit at them, but the phlegm didn't travel far, and he nearly spat on himself. "We didn't do anything, you blighted Gray Guards."

"I heard them talking," Jayn said, "before Thalia and Ryn moved in." She looked at Clay. "We know everything, so there's no use lying." She turned back to her friends. "Apparently, hitting the inn was his idea. Sara didn't want to do it."

Shilo nodded.

Pavel sighed. "We'll tear this place apart in a minute. I'm sure we'll find where you stashed the coins and jewelry. That bit was smart, not taking anything too valuable to fence, but you lot are not nearly as smart as you think."

"It wasn't his idea," Ansel said. "Not him or Sara. It was all me."

"Ansel, stop," Sara said. "It's too late for any of that now. They got us." She shook her head, which meant she was starting to regain feeling in her body. "I knew they would." She sounded more resigned than sad.

"Wait," Clay said, his eyes narrowing. He looked directly at Jayn. "You said Ansel was the Aether Weaver. How could you possibly know that? How did you…?"

"Oh, we know everything," Pavel said. "We know exactly what you idiots did, and believe it or not, we're trying to help you. You're in so much more trouble than you realize."

Ansel turned to look at his friend. "What is he saying, Clay? They couldn't possibly know how we…"

"How you two lovebirds Blended Ather and Wave to create that shadow show? Oh, we know."

Jayn didn't realize till later what Pavel had done. He'd bluffed. They suspected, but they didn't know. Yet the rogues' shocked reactions and nervous shared glances told them that they'd been exactly right.

Pavel continued. "I know what you're thinking. The goods will be returned, and yeah, you'll be fined and jailed, but a year or two of labor and that will be over. You can move somewhere no one knows you and start again. You're all young. This one's done that once already." He gestured to Sara. "But what you fail to see is that there was also a Scholar staying in that inn. If she figures out what you two did, you will all spend the rest of your lives in some dark hole beneath the Academy of the Ways. A trick like that, they'll do anything to get their hands on it, and then they won't want anyone else to know about it."

Sara began to cry. Ansel screwed his eyes shut and muttered to himself. Clay turned his narrowed eyes on Pavel. "How do you know all this anyway? Why do you care?"

Pavel shook his head and laughed. "Just offering some friendly advice, one thief to another. You'll have plenty of time to talk to that Scholar once we haul you out of here. Tell her what your friends can do and see what happens. Or wise up. Decide fast, because we can't stay here much longer."

Clay shook his head. "I don't buy it. There's no way you just… figured it out. I don't know much about Weaving, but I know what these two can do is supposed to be impossible. So impossible that no one would even suspect it. Unless…" He leaned his back against the wall and laughed. "I figured it out, Ansel. This lot can do it too, or they got some other Blending. That's why they want us to keep quiet."

Jayn couldn't stop herself from glancing at Ryn. His face was pale. Even if the others had stopped themselves from reacting—and probably only Pavel had—they'd given themselves away. Clay had bluffed right back at them. He really was like a young Pavel.

"Shut your mouth and listen," Pavel said, no emotion in his voice but a sharp insistence. "My father was a Scholar. I grew up in Lon's Watch. I know how they operate. Maybe you think you know something about us. Maybe you think you can drag us down with you, but that won't keep your friends out of that dungeon. Don't think you'll get off either, even if you aren't a Weaver. The Scholars jealously guard any secrets they uncover, even from each other."

Clay had no retort then. After a long silence, Sara spoke. "What should we do? If we don't want this Scholar to find out our secret, what do we do?"

"Start by telling us everything. Tell us how your Blending works and any other lacings you used. Then we can help you come up with a better story. A safer story."

"Tell us… how you made us afraid," Jayn said. That's what she wanted to know more than anything.

Sara offered her an apologetic smile. "I am sorry for that. I don't really like doing it to people. Clay talked us into trying it at the inn, and then we thought doing it again might scare you off. I see now that was stupid."

"You did that?" Jayn asked. "Is it an Etching?"

Sara nodded. "I used to live down in Farhaven with my Ma. She was a Wave Weaver with the city Guild. When my Etching showed up… Well, it scared her half to death the first time, but she at least understood it. She said it meant I was a powerful Weaver, and she taught me all the wards she knew. She wanted me to follow her into the Guild, and I wanted that too at first. She also tried to help me control my Etching. We thought maybe I could make people feel other emotions, not just fear. But that never worked. I can't feel it myself, but just seeing that look of horror on her face… After a few tries, I didn't want to do it anymore, and she didn't try talking me out of it.

"So I stopped using my Etching, but I still learned all kinds of other wards. I thought my life was on course, but then… Some friends of mine, kids my age, they found out I had an Etching. I told them they wouldn't like it, but they kept insisting I show them. They didn't know how bad it would be. Everyone likes to be a little afraid sometimes, to hear scary stories at night about Drakes and Sprites. I shouldn't have done it, but… I put the ward up for only a few seconds, but even that was too much. They never stopped being afraid of me after that. They wanted nothing to do with me. Nasty rumors started to spread. Everyone, especially the non-Weavers in town, they didn't want me around anymore. They didn't want me to put the fear on them. So I left. I ended up out here, and that's when I met Ansel." Despite everything, she smiled up at him.

"He is an Aether Weaver?" Pavel asked.

Ansel nodded. "Not much of one. I was always climbing trees as a boy, never afraid to go to the highest branches. My folks had heard that was a sign, so they had me tested for Aether. I'm not strong enough to do much with it, and I never really saw myself becoming a dancer or an acrobat anyway, so I just apprenticed myself to the farrier and tried to forget all about Weaving. Until I met Sara." He smiled down at her then.

"We weren't trying to do anything… like that," Sara said, taking the story back up. "He told me he was a Weaver and I said so was I, though I didn't want people knowing about it. He was sweet and never asked me to use my Etching on him, though of course I wouldn't have. His enthusiasm, well, it made me want to try Weaving again. So we would go out in the woods together. I'd practice my Wave, and he'd start practicing his Aether. We'd been taught, same as everyone, that the two couldn't Blend. But one day… they did."

Jayn glanced at the others. They were all listening intently. Even Pavel couldn't fully hide his amazement.

"It took us months to make it happen again," Sara said. "But it was amazing. At first only random flashes of light and shadow appeared within the ward, but then I realized I could make… images. Pictures. Anything I could think of, I could make it appear in the ward." She hesitated. "Of course, Ansel had to tell his best friend about it. It was that one's idea to make the Wydelk."

Clay scoffed. "It didn't take much convincing to do it. These two wanted to rob those rich merchants just as much as I did."

"But why the fear?" Jayn asked.

Sara sighed. "Clay said we had to. Just the image of the Wydelk wouldn't be enough. I am sorry I used it though."

Jayn shook her head in disbelief. "Using an Etching on top of a forbidden Blending, across such a wide area. You really are a powerful Weaver, Sara. You could have joined the Watchkeepers with all that."

"Maybe she still can," Pavel said. "They aren't afraid to sign contracts with Weavers who have… checkered pasts."

"Great," Clay said. "I'm sure she'll love that, but what about your 'forbidden Blending'? That's what you call them?"

No one said anything.

Clay sighed. "Come on, we showed you ours. I bet Jayn and Ryn whipped something up together."

"Clay!" Ansel said. "Don't be rude. Root and Wave already Blend."

Sara looked at Shilo. "You were invisible… Is that…?"

"Silence, all three of you," Pavel said. "You need to forget everything you think you know about us, if you value your freedom. We'll put it all on Sara, the Weaving I mean. We'll say she did it all with her Etching and layers of lacings and this one in a costume." He gestured at Ansel. "We only have one shot at this. We need to make it easy for everyone to swallow.. If you all come with us willingly, if you turn yourselves in and make a full confession, with all the stolen goods in hand, Nyssa—that's our boss—she won't have a chance to ask any uncomfortable questions. She's more eager than any of us to get back on the road to Appencourt. If we bring everything in at once, all tied up nicely with a bow, she won't want to try unraveling it."

"What about the Scholar?" Sara asked.

"If everyone sticks to the story, then there won't be anything she can do, even if she suspects something. If you confess to using Weaving to perpetrate a crime, Nyssa will have no choice but to take you into custody. Don't hide anything—except the one important thing, of course. If we play our cards right, we might even get Sara here a sweetheart deal with the Watchkeepers. The two of you… Well, you'll do time, no way around that, but it won't be your whole life."

Ansel nodded. He looked down at Sara. "If it keeps her safe, we'll do it." He turned to look at his friend on the other side of the bed. "Right, Clay?"

Clay sighed. "It does seem like the best play here." His eyes found Jayn and he flashed that roguish smile that she had found almost charming a day ago. "I'll keep their secret… and yours."

Chapter 14
The Capital

NYSSA STILL WASN'T SURE she understood. She wasn't sure she wanted to know either. Somehow the ever-charming Pavel Talvor had tracked the rogues down and talked them into walking into the Wydhaven inn and making a full confession. After the barmaid and the two young men laid out their version of events, Pavel did ask if perhaps an arrangement like his could be made for the girl. Probably, that offer had been a sufficient incentive to turn themselves in. Hopefully, that was all Pavel had done to convince them.

"I'm sorry," she told Pavel then. "With your deal… To be honest, I kind of went out on thin ice making that kind of offer to someone with your… reputation. I can't make a habit of going around handing out those kinds of deals. Still, she did come forward and confess, and that will be in her favor. We'll haul all three of them along with us to Appencourt. The commander of the outpost there can sort them out. If she continues to be open and honest, then there's a good chance they will offer her a deal, without me having to say anything. That's the best I can do."

Pavel seemed content with that answer, and even after she explained her position to the three prisoners, none of them tried to recant their confessions. They handed in everything taken from the inn, which Nyssa turned over to the grateful sheriff. He allowed Jayn and the other girls to reclaim their lost coins and jewelry first. Nyssa hired a wagon, chained the rogues in the back, and set a sealing ward over them, just in case, though all three were model prisoners, even if they were silent the whole way to Appencourt. Throughout those two days on the road from Wydhaven to Appencourt, Nyssa was reminded of the last time she'd transported prisoners. She told herself this trip would not end in disaster. The roads here were far too busy, the region too populated, for any grave dangers to lurk around the bend. She told herself all this, and she almost believed it.

They took precautions. No inns were built to handle prisoners, so they camped outside of each town where they stopped for the night, and a pair of them would ride in to buy food. They weren't provisioned to camp, but the nights were warming and blessedly it did not rain. Nyssa set a shield over the camp each night, which thankfully no one questioned. Rav Montare continued along with them, though the presence of the prisoners made him more subdued and less talkative. Indeed, the whole Pentad had gone quiet and moody. So the last two days on the road were awkward but peaceful. Only Mina Bellain remained unchanged, neutrally cheerful and always eager to engage Nyssa on one inconsequential topic or another. She seemed to simply ignore the prisoners.

They spent two nights on the road like that. Nyssa could have pushed the group through the second night to reach Appencourt, but with a complicated cargo, she wanted to enter the city in daylight. So early on their seventh day out of Falport they reached the capital. The hearing on Kobolds was set to begin the next day, so they were just in time.

Appencourt was a relatively young city, purposely built to serve as Aldria's capital. Most cities grew up along coasts or rivers or around ancient Runeforms. The wooded hills around Appencourt had once held a secluded fortress but no real town. When Aldria first separated from Tamor, Falport had served as the capital, which was why the Magistrate's Palace in Falport was so large and central to the city. It had once housed the government of the whole burgeoning nation, but originally it had been built by the viceroy of Aldria, serving under the Tamorine king. From the beginning, some of the first lords of the Assembly had wanted a new capital, with no history of foreign rule, but they could not decide on a location. The issue was debated for decades.

Eventually, they settled on the plot of land that would become Appencourt. The city was not built up from any of the marvelous ruins left from before the Burning, but it was as spectacular as modern Stone Weavers could make it. Seen from above, the city of Appencourt would form a five-point star, with the Grand Hall directly in the center. Each section of the star housed a different district. Towering white walls surrounded everything, with a gate at each of the five points.

Though the builders had left plenty of room for expansion within the walls of the planned city, Aldria's prosperity and growing population still overwhelmed the capital within decades of its completion. The poor were forced outside the wall, and five gate towns formed outside the city, each with its own name and personality. The wealthy moved to the hills above Appencourt, building sprawling estates there.

The road from Falport took Nyssa and her party through the gate town of Skalgeld. Hawkers shouted along the street, offering better prices than they would find inside the walls, not mentioning that the quality was also lower. The town also had several inns, offering cheaper rates as well. As guests of the Hall, Nyssa and her Pentad would be housed within the Grand Hall itself during their stay in the capital. Parts of Skalgeld had been built right up against the city wall, and it seemed like it had spread further out since the last and only time she had been to Appencourt. Probably, all five gate towns would eventually meet and merge into one massive slum that ringed the city.

Nyssa glanced back at the others as they neared the towering white walls of Appencourt, which rose as high as the black-spired Citadel back in Falport. Ryn and Shilo craned their heads back to take it all in. Jayn, of course, had grown up in Appencourt. Pavel and Thalia showed less of a reaction, though perhaps they had been here before. Surely Pavel had. Plenty of wealthy people with an interest in "recovered" antiquities had to live here. The three prisoners glanced up but otherwise just sat glumly in the wagon. Perhaps they were regretting their decision to confess, but they were resigned to their fates now.

The guards posted at the open gate waved most people through without comment. Nyssa pulled the wagon to a stop, knowing that transporting bound prisoners would warrant a question or two, despite their Watchkeeper uniforms. Nyssa handed over the papers she'd had the Wydhaven sheriff draw up. He'd been happy to take credit for recovering the stolen money and pass the punishment on to the Watchkeepers, despite one of the suspects not being a Weaver. The papers plus a few brief answers were enough to satisfy the city guards, who all wore white tabards over their chainmail, with conical metal helmets.

White had been the primary color for the designers of the city. Most of the buildings were plastered white and trimmed with dark wood, but no buildings stood within a hundred yards of the gatehouse. Part of this was a functional limitation; since the walls narrowed to a point near the gate, there wasn't room for any structures. It was also practical, as any invading forces that breached the gate would find no shelter within the widening courtyard, while archers on either wall could pick them off. Of course, not once in the hundred years since Appencourt's completion had invaders ever even come close to the city.

The road ahead ran straight into the heart of Appencourt, with an increasing number of buildings and side streets spreading out on either side. The streets here were paved not with rough cobbles like Falport, but with large slabs of gray stone, neatly laid with grooves in between for water runoff. They entered the city through its Foreign Quintant, the district that held the most inns, taverns, and places of entertainment. Most visitors to the city stayed here, so the streets were lively and busy even in the early morning. Musicians were spaced out every fifty paces, performing for coin, with merchant stalls filling the gaps between. They sold everything from produce and cookware to clothes and jewelry. All the finer goods would be found in the Artisans' Quintant to the east, where craftsmen and artists lived and worked.

They passed a pair of acrobats, performing on one corner. Nyssa could see the glow of white Aether around them, though that would be invisible to most onlookers. Even here, only one in five people had any aptitude for Weaving. Nyssa thought about what she would be doing now if she hadn't been a Weaver. Probably, she would still be living in the slums outside Farhaven. Weaving had changed her life and made a way out for her.

The first time her Etching manifested, it had saved her from a possible death and certainly major trauma. She'd thought a lot about that moment since Pavel's casual comment over a week ago when she'd found them holed up in the basement of the Citadel. That first time, her shield had formed instantly around her, without thought or concentration. Why did it take her a full minute to make a shield now? If she could do it in a moment, it would have helped her countless times in the past. When the Kobolds attacked them in the Sylphren Wood, she could have saved her Pentad, or at least some of them. During the few brief moments she had to herself over the course of this journey, she had actually tried summoning her shield without deliberately crafting the lacings. So far, she had been unsuccessful.

Eventually, the buildings of the Foreign Quintant fell away, revealing the massive courtyard that surrounded the Grand Hall. The courtyard itself was not a square but a pentagon, with five rectangular parks built between each of the five converging avenues. These parks were just grassy fields with a few shade trees, and they were nothing compared to the sprawling, ornate gardens found in the Green Quintant. A wide circular moat surrounded the Grand Hall, with five wooden bridges, each painted a different color, arching over it. The moat was more decorative than defensive, with clever fountains hidden beneath the surface, shooting a steady stream of water in arches or fanning it out in domes. Large fish with mottled orange, black, and white scales swam through the gurgling pond.

The Grand Hall itself looked like a solid cube of white marble, resting atop a forest of twenty-foot columns, which though numerous seemed too thin to hold such a weight. A wide free-standing staircase beneath the building rose up into its belly. Window slits along the outside of the Grand Hall marked off three separate levels, though the Assembly Room where the lords and ladies actually met took up a quarter of the interior space and filled all three floors. Banners hanging from the roof displayed the flag of Aldria, a five-colored star on a black field. A dome of shimmering blue light covered the entire structure, built from layer upon layer of Wave. No single Weaver could make a ward that large, but the Wardens of the Hall worked in teams to construct and maintain the wards. No one could enter the Grand Hall without them knowing.

Nyssa pulled the wagon to a stop again near the closest bridge, which was painted red. The colored bridges, and even all the other sets of five within the city's layout, were meant to represent the Five Elements, not necessarily the Five Forces, though they shared the same names, and many people conflated the two.

She looked at Jayn. "You know the city and the Hall, of course," she said. "Can you take your Pentad to the stables and then into the Hall? We are expected and a few days overdue, so I'm sure someone will meet you and show you to our quarters."

Jayn nodded. "Of course."

"I want to unload these three before I do anything." She gestured to the prisoners. "The outpost is in the northernmost Quintant."

Rav Montare brought his horse up alongside Nyssa's seat on the wagon. "I'll be heading off then," he said, adding with a laugh, "My friends are actually back the way we came." He pointed back toward the Foreign Quintant. "Thank you again, for the escort." He looked at Pavel then. "The offer still stands, if you ever want to borrow my book."

Pavel nodded and returned a friendly smile. "We'll only be here a few days I'm afraid. Perhaps next time."

Rav nodded and turned his horse around. Nyssa still found it odd that the soft-spoken Scribe and a man like Pavel had struck up a friendship, but she didn't question it.

Mina Bellain made a sweeping hand gesture that took in the whole group. "I will take my leave here as well," she said. "I'm sure we will all meet again someday." She smiled and rode off to the west.

Though Pavel and the others had all seemed uncomfortable around the Scholar, Nyssa hadn't minded her company. She did wonder why the woman had taken such a keen interest in their group. Probably, it related to their experience with the Kobold Weaver. That kind of thing would fascinate any Scholar.

Nyssa looked over her young recruits again. They were all exchanging quick glances, probably glad to be rid of the Scholar who had strangely intimidated them. "I won't be long," she said. "Get settled into your rooms and rest up as much as you can. The hearing starts tomorrow, and it will probably be a long day, as there will be a lot of sitting around and waiting."

They nodded.

Jayn nosed her pony forward to take the lead, but she stopped when one of the prisoners called after her. "So long, Jayn Eldragor," the boy named Clay said, with a half-smile. This surprised Nyssa. The prisoners had been so quiet and stoic, she'd almost forgotten they were conscious.

Jayn looked back at the wagon. Her expression was hard to read, but a weak smile seemed to cross her lips. Then she squeezed her heels and the pony moved on. The rest of her Pentad fell in line behind her, heading east around the edge of the moat.

Nyssa turned to regard her prisoners. Clay had closed his eyes and leaned back against the side of the wagon. The other two were looking at each other. Nyssa flicked the reins to get the horses moving again. One was her own; the other had come with the wagon. Someone at the outpost would see it returned.

Her path took her west and north along the edge of the Trade Quintant, which housed bankers, wealthy merchants, and warehouses. Then she turned due north into the Civic Quintant, where members of the Hall kept quarters, though many of them owned larger homes outside the city. She passed the court of justice and the capital's main Guild hall, before she reached the Watchkeeper outpost. Appencourt was considered the best assignment by many within the Watchkeepers—close to the seat of power and with little risk of danger. On the rare occasions powerful rogues tried setting up shop within the city, they could count on the city guard and the Wardens for assistance. Nyssa did not find such a posting desirable.

Still, she knew that the man who ran the outpost would be a competent commander who she could trust to take custody of her prisoners, though he was a bit gruff in his manners. She waited in his office while he reviewed the papers from the sheriff and her own written report.

He looked up at her when he'd finished. "It sounds like this powerful Wave Weaver got pressured into committing the crime by these two men," he said.

"That was my assessment, yes."

"You don't think she would have done something like this on her own, then?"

"No, I don't believe so."

He sat back in his chair and studied her beneath lowered eyelids. "We haven't met, but I have heard about you, Captain Lahmeer. You raised a few eyebrows when you offered amnesty to that rogue Pavel Talvor."

She kept her tone level. "I'm sure I did. However, Mistress Agia Bellos did uphold the agreement."

"Yes, that she did. Probably it was the right decision then. You haven't asked for it, but I imagine you might want me to offer a similar amnesty to this girl."

Nyssa shrugged. "That is entirely your prerogative."

He made a sound like the first half of a laugh. "Maybe I will," he said. He leafed through the papers again. "I just might, times being what they are. The Maker knows we could use all the Weavers we can recruit right now." He glanced up at her. "I knew we were expecting you for this big Kobold hearing, but I didn't think you would come and drop all this in my lap."

She did not respond.

He sighed. "The big question the Hall is debating right now, the whole reason for this hearing, is who should be responsible for cleaning up this Kobold mess: the Watchkeepers or the Army."

She nodded. With men like him, she knew it was best to let them talk themselves out.

"My opinion? We let the Army deal with it. The Watchkeepers just aren't equipped for the kind of large-scale operation it will take to crush these star-blighted monsters." He paused. "But of course the decision won't be up to you or me. Anyway, good luck tomorrow."

The head steward himself met Nyssa atop the stairs leading up into the Grand Hall. Laren Stoats was a thin older man with a mane of gray hair and an impeccable white suit. A gold chain hung across his chest and disappeared into a pocket, no doubt connected to a watch. That told her everything she needed to know about the man's position. Clocks were common in Aldria, but small, portable ones were expensive and hard to get. The secret to their production was closely guarded by the Stone Weavers of the Clockwork Guild. Master Stoats was no mere servant; nothing in the Hall of the Assembly happened without his knowledge and supervision.

Master Stoats assured her that the rest of her party had settled comfortably into their rooms. Warm lunches would be sent up shortly, and a servant would fetch them for dinner in the main dining hall. It was a Sunday, so none of the lords or ladies would be present. The Hall could accommodate all fifty of them, but few ever spent the night here. Master Stoats led her down a series of white marble corridors and up a flight of white marble stairs, so starkly different from the black stone of the Citadel. While the Citadel had colorful runners along the floor, the rugs here were all black.

The guest quarters occupied most of the third level, with large suites for ambassadors and other important guests in each of the four corners of the building. Nyssa and her Pentad had been given six small rooms next to the northwestern suite. The girls would be especially glad for their own beds, she thought.

Her room was well appointed, with a large bed against one wall, a plush chair near one of the narrow windows, and two smaller rooms off the side. Master Stoats pointed out a chain hanging on the wall near the door. Pulling that would ring a bell in a central dispatch room and send a servant running to her door, if she needed anything. One of side rooms held a closet with far too much space for the few changes of clothes she had brought. Master Stoats assured her that her bags would be brought up and unpacked shortly. The other room concealed a true marvel: a private bathroom with hot and cold water and a full-sized tub. She had heard a Scholar once argue that indoor plumbing was the greatest accomplishment that Stone Weavers had ever achieved. She had to agree with that sentiment, as she thought about lying in a warm tub and washing away a week's worth of road dust.

They had made it to Appencourt, with only a little excitement and not much real danger. The hearing would take a day or two, and then they would be back on the road to Falport. Nothing bad could happen on this outing. She told herself that, and she almost believed it.

Nyssa was up early the next day. She dressed in a fresh uniform and tabard and moved down the hall, knocking on five doors. They would be punctual, waiting outside the Assembly Room to be called at the appointed time. It took a second round of knocking to roust Pavel from his room, which unfortunately lay right beside hers, but all five members of the Pentad were soon standing in the hallway, freshly scrubbed and in clean uniforms, their loaned pins shining on their chests.

"Good," she said. "It may take some time before they call us in, even after the hearing starts, but we will be there and waiting when they do summon us." She paused, not sure what else to say. "There's no need to be nervous."

She turned, hearing quick footsteps coming down the hall. Here was Master Stoats again, with his white suit and gold chain.

"Oh, I'm terribly sorry," he said, addressing her. He was well informed enough to know she was in charge. "Here you all are, dressed and ready to go. I'm afraid the hearing has been postponed. The Hall will not be calling on you today."

"Postponed?" Nyssa said. "You mean, the Hall will not be discussing the Kobold issue at all today?"

He shook his head gravely. "I'm afraid not. I only just got word myself. Something else has come up, which the Hall feels is more urgent. I am to request that you all remain here in Appencourt, as guests of the Hall, until this matter is addressed. The hearing will still be held, either at the end of this week or the beginning of next. I humbly ask for your patience until then."

Nyssa nodded. "Of course. We await the Hall's pleasure. May I ask, though, what is this more urgent matter?"

"Certainly. You were not the only guests to arrive yesterday. An ambassador from Tamor has come, and it seems he was not entirely expected."

Nyssa understood the meaning behind Stoats' polite wording. The steward ran everything within the Grand Hall, so if he called the arrival unexpected, then everyone had been caught completely off guard. The lords of the Assembly had to be scrambling to figure out how and why an ambassador from Tamor had arrived in the capital unannounced and unanticipated. Nyssa couldn't begin to guess the reason herself, but with the rising tensions on the Tamorine border, she understood why dealing with the ambassador would become a top priority.

"I see," she said. "Well, it's certainly understandable why our hearing would be delayed then."

She saw Pavel stiffen and stand up straighter, clearly seeing something behind her. She turned around. They had been standing near the corner suite, where the hallway turned a right angle. A man had just stepped around the corner. The man wore a cream-colored suit, with a long red coat, trimmed in silver. Wavy black hair framed his face. He had a beak-like nose and an olive complexion. A man and a woman followed him. They were dressed like servants in black and silver livery but carried themselves like bodyguards. Probably they were both. The man they followed took Nyssa and her party in with a sweeping glance. He offered a smile that did not reach his eyes.

"Mr. Ambassador," Stoats said, barely masking his surprise.

"Hail Steward," the man said, in the unmistakable stilted accent of Tamor. "Hail Watchkeepers."

"Ambassador," Nyssa said, nodding.

His eyes focused on her. "I didn't hear everything, but it seems my presence has upset whatever business you have with the Hall."

"It's quite all right," she said. She knew she had to be polite. She could not insult a Tamorine ambassador in any way. The tensions between the two countries were that high.

He studied her a moment longer, before turning to the steward. "Inform the lords that I will be ready to await their pleasure shortly. I took a morning walk around the city, and I must freshen up."

"Of course," Stoats said.

The ambassador's guards moved to the dark-wood door that led into the corner suit and opened it. The man nodded to all of them and then turned and entered his rooms. The steward excused himself and left them standing in the corridor, suddenly having nothing to do.

Nyssa sighed. She did not like that their rooms were so close to the Tamorine ambassador's, but she couldn't ask to move them now. She addressed her recruits. "Looks like we'll be hanging around for now. Remember, we must all continue to be on our best behavior." She looked at Pavel when she said that. "Take advantage of this chance to rest, but practice your Weaving. Stay close in the mornings. If they send for us, it will be early. If any of you decide to go out into the city in the afternoons, don't go alone. You don't need to wear your uniforms though." She glanced at the closed door at the end of the hall. "Avoid the ambassador. We're here to say our piece and then leave. Let's keep our toes out of whatever deep waters are circling here."

Chapter 15
The Bladesmith

BY THE MIDDLE of the second day of waiting, Thalia had grown restless. They'd all kept close to their rooms that first day. Jayn had tried to take them to the balcony level overlooking the Assembly Room so they could sit in on the meeting between the ambassador and the assembled lords and ladies, but two men in blue and white uniforms stood blocking the door. The Hall had been sealed, which Jayn said was not too surprising, given the sensitive nature of the issue. Whatever the ambassador had told the Assembly, the lords and ladies spent the next day in a sealed meeting discussing it.

Thalia didn't know much about the politics that governed Aldria. She knew the name of the lord who sat for Falport and Rigel, a man who had served for six consecutive terms, but she did not know what he looked like. They had few opportunities to interact with the lords and ladies anyway, as most were taking their meals in private rooms, rather than the central dining hall, probably to continue their secret discussions. So despite the air of intrigue that hovered over the building, Thalia and her friends had been shut out of it, and they quickly grew bored.

Thalia had become accustomed to the busy lifestyle of a Watchkeeper recruit and spending what little down time she had working in Master Caston's smithy. She didn't like sitting around being idle. So on that second day after lunch, she proposed an outing into the city to Jayn and Shilo. They were gathered in Jayn's room at the time.

"I want to check out that Artisans' Quintant you mentioned," Thalia said.

Jayn had described the basic layout of the city and what happened in each of the five districts. The Artisans' Quintant housed artists and craftsmen, many of whom were talented Stone Weavers. Thalia also wanted to see more of the city in general. As someone who had grown up comparing Rigel and Falport, she wanted to add a third metropolis to the equation.

"It is worth checking out," Jayn said.

"I'm down," Shilo said with a shrug. "I'd like to buy some nice gifts to send back home."

Thalia smiled at that idea. She sent most of her Watchkeeper income to her own mother, to help support her, but she had amassed some spending money in the last two and a half months, which thankfully they had recovered from those rogues. She still didn't know how she felt about what they'd done, but probably it had been wise to help them conceal their forbidden Blending.

"Great," Thalia said. "We'll make it a shopping trip." She turned to Jayn.

Jayn shook her head. "I know nothing's likely to happen today," she said, "but I still want to stick close. I can't imagine why this Tamorine ambassador has come or what it might mean."

Thalia nodded in understanding. They all knew of the petite blonde's massive ambitions, that she hoped to return to Appencourt someday as an elected lady of the Hall of the Assembly, so of course this international intrigue would fascinate her. Thalia was curious about the ambassador as well, but she was also bored of waiting.

"No problem," she said to Jayn before turning to Shilo. "Should we invite the boys?"

"I don't know," Shilo said. "I've found that men generally aren't interested in shopping."

Though she had suggested it, Thalia was glad they decided not to invite Ryn and Pavel. Out of all the members of the Pentad, Thalia felt closest to Shilo. They had formed an easy friendship from the start. She was glad to spend some time alone with her to deepen that bond. Pavel could be entertaining but also annoying, and Thalia had started to feel weird around Ryn, ever since he saved her life when the Kobolds attacked Falport.

You must trust the boy who saves your life. That's what the Rigel Runeform had told her when she asked it a completely unrelated question, back before she'd ever met Ryn. She was grateful that Ryn had healed her after Kalo had likely poisoned her, but the fountain's prophecy made everything strange. It made the act seem more significant. At the crucial moment back then, when Ryn needed to find a way to heal himself and he landed on the mad idea of trying to Blend Root and Ather, he had asked her to trust him. That simple request, echoing the fountain's words, convinced her they had to try the impossible. If she hadn't told Pavel to try, maybe they wouldn't have. Then where would they be? Ryn would have died, and probably Shilo and Jayn too.

Maybe that was the secret to the Runeform. Sometimes it answered people's questions directly, but sometimes it told them something else entirely, not the answer they wanted, but perhaps the answer they needed. The only other time Thalia had asked the fountain a question, it had told her, "What you seek lies in the third well," an answer which still meant nothing to her, but maybe someday it would.

Thalia had spent plenty of time dwelling on all that over the past weeks, despite her busy schedule. Maybe that moment of trust that saved Ryn's life had fulfilled the Runeform's prophecy, or maybe she needed to continue trusting Ryn indefinitely. Obviously, she had to trust all members of her Pentad if they were to work well together. Yet, a centuries-old enchanted fountain telling her she *must* trust Ryn gave the act of trust an outsized sense of importance. Should her trust be unconditional, even if he proposed doing something seemingly dangerous or unnecessary? She didn't think he would; the shy boy seldom ventured any ideas, and they were all fairly reasonable when he did.

On top of all that confusion, she was genuinely grateful to Ryn for saving her. She'd thought for weeks about how to properly express that gratitude. She'd used her piece of Iscernaen steel to craft a dagger not only to feel a sense of connection to her bladesmith father, but also as a gift for Ryn, who had been training with knives. She still had that knife wrapped up and stashed in the bottom of her saddlebags. She felt weird about it now and wasn't sure how or when to present the gift without making it awkward.

She pushed all those thoughts aside as she and Shilo descended the strange marble staircase set into the middle of the Grand Hall. Back on the ground, they passed through the forest of columns that supported the massive building above their heads and headed for the southeastern bridge. Two days ago, they had passed through the Foreign Quintant, which even on a Sunday had been busy with commerce. They found the Artisans' Quintant to be just as crowded, but it felt like a completely different world.

All of Appencourt she had seen so far had been starkly black and white, all trimmed in mahogany or some other dark wood, the kinds only found deep within Mirkwald's Ever Wood. The buildings in the arts district were just as dour, but they were hard to see beneath the riot of colors on display. Tapestries, rugs, and every sort of decorative covering hung from the walls, showcasing every combination of colors and patterns imaginable. Artists and craftsmen displayed their wares in stalls along the main road, behind the clear glass of large bay windows, and from second-story balconies. Every stray gust of wind set off a tinkling of bells and windchimes. Sculptors displayed their wood and stone carvings, mostly abstract shapes and forms etched with tiny scrollwork, meant to show off the artists' versatility and precision.

No one here seemed to be actively hawking their wares to passersby, yet the din of commerce still filled the air, as wealthy-looking men and women negotiated prices or discussed commissioned work. The vendors let their customers come to them, obviously trusting their displays to do the talking. They all ignored Thalia and Shilo, though the pair frequently stopped to examine one piece or another. Probably their simple clothes set them apart as tourists and not serious customers. Shilo wore her typical loose-fitting shirt over dark trousers, while Thalia wore a sleeveless dress that was well made but certainly not expensive or fashionable. The vendors and artists themselves all wore garishly bright clothes of silk and linen that were even more colorful than the fabrics Iscernaens preferred.

Thalia and Shilo ventured down a side street. The shops there seemed to cater more to the artists themselves. They passed several weavers and a dye shop, which overwhelmed them with its heady and floral but almost putrid smells. Two young women stood loitering out front, seemingly immune to the odors. Their hands and arms, dyed in layers of purple, red, and blue, made them look like works of art themselves.

Thalia and Shilo returned to the main road, passing dressmakers, haberdashers, and leatherworkers. The actual tanning was done outside of the city in the gate town of Rugeld. Thalia was far more familiar with those noxious smells. The girls chatted amicably, laughing at the strange sights of the colorful district. The performers on the street corners here were more outlandish than a simple musician or tumbler. A woman juggled from atop a pair of stilts that made her ten feet tall. A man sat in front of a little booth with an easel, offering to sketch likenesses in under five minutes. Simple canvases stretched over thin wooden frames showed examples of his work, all done in quick but deft brushstrokes using only black ink.

Shilo stopped frequently to admire little ornaments or bits of jewelry, but nothing seemed to catch her eye enough to try to buy it. Thalia, who had no definite ideas of anything she might like to purchase herself, was content to walk along beside her friend, until she began to hear the unmistakable sound of hammers ringing against metal. Then her pace quickened without at first realizing. She glanced back at Shilo, who only smiled and fell into step behind her. Thalia couldn't resist the draw of a smithy.

The fabric, stone, and wooden crafts all vanished, replaced by works of metal. Vendors here sold weapons and armor, as well as decorative metal pieces and functional things such as pots and pans or horseshoes and nails. The smithies filled the alleys behind the storefronts, though the heat and sound radiated out into the main thoroughfare. Iron, steel, tin, bronze, copper, and even gold and silver were on display here, laid out on wooden tables or displayed behind shop windows. Everyone working here would be a Stone Weaver. Stone Weavers made the best smiths, not just because they could enchant their creations, but because they had a natural aptitude for working with metal, in the same way that Wave Weavers made the best sailors and Aether Weavers made the best dancers.

Thalia stopped before a bladesmith's shop. Racks of swords and daggers filled both windows on either side of the open door. No two blades were alike, meant to display the smith's range and skill. Some were plain and practical knives for chefs or hunters, but their lines were still smooth and straight. Other pieces were too flashy to be practical, meant to adorn the waists of upper-echelon men who pretended to be tough but still liked scrollwork etched into the blade and jewels in the handle. Some blades were strange and exotic. One dagger split into three separate points, while another had a blade on either end with a grip in the middle. Though Thalia found some of these weapons silly, they did show off the smith's obvious skill.

Her feet took her not through the open door into the shop but around to the back of the building. There in the open space between the shop and what looked like residential buildings stood the bladesmith's smithy. Six workers were busy making weapons, three men and three women. They shared two fired kilns, which they used to heat rods of steel till they glowed white hot, before shaping the metal over anvils. Three of the workers were quite young, obviously apprentices, who mainly assisted the two older journeymen. The smith herself was a gray-haired woman in a leather apron, who had the most muscular arms Thalia had ever seen on any woman.

The bladesmith wasn't making anything at the moment. She simply moved about among her assistants, handing out compliments or correcting their technique. Her voice was low and husky. She smiled as she moved about her shop, despite the sweat beading on her face. The woman had to be a Stone Weaver, of course, and yet most women with the gift made jewelry or textiles and other delicate pieces. Many people in Aldria still believed a woman had no business swinging a hammer, but here this woman was, and two of her assistants were also women. She saw the branching lines of yellow light flow from their hands into the metal they worked. These weren't enchantments but simple lacings that made it easier to shape the steel.

Thalia wasn't sure how long she stood there watching the work, but eventually the bladesmith looked up. She nodded to Thalia, who dropped her gaze. Thalia didn't want to leave just yet, so she hesitated, lingering beside the smithy.

"Good day," the bladesmith said, stepping away from the smithy and coming toward them.

"I'm sorry," Thalia said. "I was just admiring the work."

The woman's smile broadened. "Are you an apprentice?" She was obviously eyeing Thalia's own arms and broad shoulders, which were far more defined than the average woman's.

"I was," Thalia said. "To a redsmith in Rigel, but now I'm with the Watchkeepers."

"Ah, under Rohan Caston?"

Thalia nodded.

"I've met the man only once, but I've heard good things about his work and his teaching." She nodded to Shilo, who hadn't said anything. "This a member of your Pentad?"

Shilo was a thin girl who could not be mistaken for a smith's apprentice. "Yes," she said. "I'm the Flame Weaver."

"Ah," the woman said, returning her gaze to Thalia. "There's the beauty of Weaving there. This scrawny little thing could take both of us in a fight." Her smile and her friendly tone belied any slight the words might have suggested. "I am Lise Guntrel."

Thalia introduced herself and Shilo. "I've only made one blade," she said, "but I do want to study bladesmithing."

Lise nodded, but a slight wrinkle formed between her eyes. "Moldo, was it? Where have I heard that name before?"

"I'm not sure. My father was a bladesmith, but he wasn't a Weaver."

"Of course," Lise said, brightening. "I've never met your father, but I have heard of him. There aren't too many master bladesmiths in Aldria, Weavers or not. Non-weavers can still make excellent smiths, as I'm sure you know."

"Yes," Thalia said, not sure what else to say. She had no idea her father's reputation had spread so far. She knew he was good, and he had provided a comfortable life for his wife and three daughters, despite all the competition from actual Weavers. She wished he was still around, for many reasons, but also so he could see the smith she would someday become and was already well on her way to being. She hoped he would have been proud of the dagger she had made.

Something of the melancholy mood that had seized her must have shown on Thalia's face. The bladesmith's expression softened. Perhaps Lise also knew what had happened to her father, how he had died shortly after taking a commission with the Standing Army. "Well, Thalia Moldo," she said, "I've got several pieces to finish up today, but if you would like to stop by later on in the week, I'd be happy to show you a thing or two. A Watchkeeper and a bladesmith's daughter. I'm sure you have a lot of potential."

Thalia smiled. "Thanks, I would like that."

Behind them, the noise coming from the main road changed in cadence. The mingling conversations between artisans and even the haggling customers had all sounded friendly and lively. Now those voices shifted to angry grumbling, as shouting and some sort of chanting could be heard further down the street. As Thalia listened, the chanting became louder and more distinct, though she couldn't make out the words yet.

Lise frowned, hearing the noise too. Her apprentices stopped working to look up and whisper to each other. Lise sighed. "Not this again." She gestured to her assistants. "Keep working!"

Lise ignored her own advice and strolled down the short alley back to the main road. Curious, Thalia and Shilo followed her. Faces had appeared in other alleyways and second-floor windows, as the chanting grew louder. A large crowd of people seemed to be moving down the road, coming from near the gate and moving further into the city. Thalia could hear them for a long while before she saw them, but with all the other mingled shouts and voices, she couldn't understand what they were chanting until they were passing before her.

A pair of tall horses pulled a wagon. A man in a black suit stood atop a platform built on the wagon's bed, while two burly men sat on the regular bench, one holding the reins and the other a cudgel. Both eyed the gathering crowd as the wagon rumbled down the street. A group of people, also dressed in black, walked alongside the wagon. They were the ones chanting, "Down with Lacers!" over and over. Those same words had been written on the side of the wagon in black blocky letters. Thalia had never heard that word before, but surely they had to mean Weavers.

A tomato tossed from a second-floor balcony nearly missed the man standing in the wagon, though when it hit the wooden planking near his feet, it did splatter over his boots.

"Curse you, Peniter!" someone shouted over the hum of angry murmurs. If he was denouncing Weavers, the man had picked a bad place to do so. The wagon lurched to a halt, and his crowd of supporters stopped chanting and devolved into their own angry muttering. They looked as though they might attack the gathered onlookers, but the man, Peniter, raised both his hands, and they fell silent. Though a low muttering continued, the artisans quieted as well.

"Peace, friends," Peniter said in the booming voice of a practiced orator. He was a tall and lean man of indeterminate age, with tan skin and straight black hair held back by a leather thong. "We are not here to pick a fight. As you well know, we don't want Lacers to go down for good, but down from their pedestal, for the sake of equality."

The artisans began shouting again then, expressing in colorful language what they thought of this man's ideas.

"Twenty percent!" Peniter shouted. "Twenty percent," he said again, and the crowd quieted. "Only one in five people can Weave, and yet four out of five Pentarchs and half the lords of the Assembly are Lacers!"

Thalia glanced at Lise, who stood with her arms crossed and frowning. "Why does he keep saying 'Lacers'?" she asked.

Lise answered without looking away from the man. "It's a favorite tactic of bigots to intentionally use the wrong word for a group of people."

"We want equality!" Peniter said, and his mob took up the call of "Equality!" When they quieted down, he continued. "Limit the number of Lacer seats in the Hall to ten and let only one Pentarch be a Lacer. That is all we ask! That is only fair. Take the Lacers down to where they belong. Down with Lacers!"

His supporters resumed their chanting, and the wagon began moving again. Peniter smiled and waved to the crowd, as if they were cheering for him and not cursing his name. The artisans shouted after the wagon, but no one moved to follow it, and within a few minutes, the street returned to normal, though it took longer for the distant chanting to fade.

Thalia and Jayn followed Lise as she walked back toward her smithy, shaking her head. Her apprentices and journeymen, who had obviously stopped to listen, took their work back up with gusto, as if to pretend they had never stopped.

"Who was that?" Shilo asked.

Lise turned her head and spit into the gutter that ran along the wall. "You two must be pretty fresh to the city if you haven't had the pleasure of hearing Lucas Peniter speak yet. He's running for a seat in the Assembly on an anti-Weaver platform."

"What?" Thalia said. "How is that a good idea?"

Lise laughed, though there was no humor in it. "You'd be surprised. He's not wrong about the twenty percent part. Despite all the first-echelon types doing their best to breed more Weavers, only twenty in a hundred babies are born with the gift, never more and never less. Well, it averages out that way anyway. We'll always be a minority, and one with outsized influence. He's not the first to go that route, though no one's had his level of success with it in decades."

"Is he likely to win?" Thalia asked. She knew the election would be held at the beginning of next year, still six months away.

"He just might. Plenty of disgruntled people out there who like to blame their misfortune on not being born a Weaver."

Thalia knew what she meant. She remembered those two men back in Wydhaven who had mocked them for being Watchkeepers. She remembered her own thoughts, back before she found out she was a Weaver. She had never hated Weavers, but she had perhaps been jealous of them. It tied into her envy of Falport, which drew all the best and brightest from her hometown of Rigel across the River Aldria. Only a few Weavers stayed in Falport, opting for less competition over better opportunities. She'd heard of plenty of apprentices who, upon manifesting as Stone Weavers, had broken their contracts with non-Weaver smiths to work with the more successful Weavers in Falport. She knew how much harder her father had worked to make a name for himself as a bladesmith. Many wealthy customers would never even consider work crafted by a non-Weaver.

In the end, Falport's allure had drawn her across the river as well, along with her friends Shilo and Ryn, whose ability to Weave had also opened doors for them. Jayn's move from Appencourt to Falport had been a step down for her in many ways, while Pavel had enlisted because his alternative had been prison. All this was true, and yet she didn't think anyone had any business hating Weavers. Jealousy was a petty emotion and not a rational reason to vote for someone. Could someone really win a seat in the Hall on such a platform? She would have to ask Jayn about it later.

Chapter 16
Currents

RYN STROLLED THROUGH a marble corridor beside Pavel and Jayn. Jayn believed if they loitered around the Grand Hall long enough, they would overhear some crucial information. Jayn was dying to know what was going on with the ambassador from Tamor. Though Pavel feigned disinterest, he was clearly curious as well. Ryn didn't know what to make of the whole situation. He knew tensions had been mounting on the border, but he was learning that relations between the two countries were more complicated than he'd thought.

"Take these statues, for example," Pavel said. They were in the broad hallway outside of where the lords and ladies were meeting, and Ryn had been trying to ignore those statues, which depicted various men and women who were essentially naked, covered only by discreetly placed marble leaves. "These are Tamorine-style sculptures, which seems out of place for Aldria, but these were all carved probably three centuries ago, back when Aldria was Tamor.

Most Aldrians can trace their lineage back to Tamor, especially the rich ones, who are basically all descended from Tamorine nobility. So it's complicated. Tamor is not some foreign interloper, but more like an estranged cousin. A cousin who possibly wants to kill us and steal our house."

Jayn shook her head. "A little simplistic, but he is basically correct."

The two of them seemed to enjoy sharing their worldly knowledge with Ryn, and he was happy to accept it. He still felt out of his depth with all this political stuff, so he was somewhat glad the hearing had been delayed. People in Aen's Hollow had never cared much about who sat in the Hall of the Assembly, and while they had worried about Tamor, it was a distant and abstract fear, like the idea that a Drake might swoop down from a blue sky and steal your child. Probably it happened somewhere in the world, but not in Aen's Hollow. Nothing especially bad had ever seemed to happen in Aen's Hollow, not before the Kobolds came down from the Coldreaches.

"Even though Tamor and Aldria seem so at odds," Pavel continued, "the lords still must show this ambassador respect and listen to whatever he has to say."

"I never understood that," Jayn said. "We've never sent an ambassador to Tamor. I can't imagine one would be given a warm welcome."

"True. Aldria prefers using Mirkwald as a go-between for any negotiations, but Aldria has more to lose in the equation. We don't pose an existential threat to Tamor, but they could wipe us off the map if they really wanted to."

"Perhaps, but it would cost them dearly in money and men."

"Which is why we're still here."

Jayn sighed. "I just wish I knew why this ambassador was here."

"Can you ask your mother?"

"No, she wouldn't tell me, not when the session has been sealed."

Of course, Jayn's mother was one of the Pentarchs, though they had not met her yet. The fifty lords and ladies were elected to the Hall of the Assembly by popular vote every five years. The Hall appointed the five Pentarchs, who served until they chose to retire or they died. The Pentarchs were above the Hall in importance, but they weren't directly involved in the creation of laws and regulations, or maybe sometimes they were. Ryn hadn't understood a lot of that lesson, though Jayn had gone into great detail.

Each Pentarch had a specific role in the government, though he could only remember the First and the Fourth. The First Pentarch was essentially the magistrate in charge of the city of Appencourt, and he oversaw the Hall of the Assembly, though he could only vote in the case of a tie. The Fourth Pentarch, Jayn's mother, more or less controlled Aldria's Standing Army. The Army headquarters were not in Appencourt but to the west in Savo. For some reason, the Standing Army was not allowed to cross the River Aldria into the Golden Lands. The generals in Savo oversaw the day-to-day operations of the Army, but the Fourth Pentarch gave the orders anytime forces needed to be deployed. That was all Ryn had managed to remember.

"It's probably one of two possibilities," Pavel said. "Likely the ambassador is delivering some demand from Tamor, which may or may not be reasonable. Changes in trade regulations, or maybe a concession to move the border. Something like that."

"And the other possibility?"

Pavel shrugged. "Something else entirely. Something that no one was expecting, judging from the glimpses I've caught of lords rushing about the halls."

Jayn sighed again. "If it is some demand, I hope the Hall won't just concede."

"I think they probably will, if it's not too onerous."

"What makes you think that?"

"This current crop of lords, they're too… conservative, let's say."

"I don't know about that. Aldria is pretty forward-thinking, especially compared to old relics like Tamor."

"Relatively speaking, sure, but cultures always swing back and forth from one generation to the next. Let's not say conservative; let's say traditional and risk averse. These lords would rather everything just stayed the way it was. None of them are pushing for big social changes."

"What are you basing that on?"

"Well, everything, really. Take these statues, for instance." He gestured to the statuary still around them. They were walking rather slowly, as the goal was to loiter rather than get anywhere. He glanced around and saw that they were still alone, before taking on a wicked grin. "I'll let you in on a little secret I'm sure you don't know, Jayn Eldragor. See these leaves and fronds preserving the dignity of these statues? They're detachable."

"What?" Jayn sounded scandalized.

Ryn glanced again at the statues. He had no idea who they were supposed to represent or why they were so naked. If the covering foliage was not part of the original sculptures, whoever added them had done an excellent job. Probably, it had been a Stone Weaver.

"Oh yes," Pavel said. "Three centuries ago, Tamorine sculptors had no qualms about depicting the human form. The first generation of independent Aldrians found them a bit racy, however, so they covered them up. Every few decades, they take the leaves off or put them back, depending on the social mores of the time."

Jayn laughed, shaking her head. "I do not believe you. If you think Aldria is too traditional, wait till you see how some women dress for the Summer Feast. The way things are going, I'm sure we'll still be here for that."

"Well, again, it's all relative. It's true about the statues, though. Here, I'll show you."

Pavel grabbed one of the statues in a way that would have gotten him slapped had the woman been real. He started wiggling the leaf back and forth, attempting to pry it loose. Jayn gasped and looked around to make sure no one was watching them, a horrified look on her face.

"Probably stuck on with Stone," Pavel said. "Let me summon up some Flame to break the bond."

Jayn grabbed his arm. "You will do no such thing! Stop that at once."

Pavel dropped his hand, laughing. "All right, but you did see it wiggle, didn't you?"

"Fine, you were right about the statues. Let's just move on."

Jayn quickened her pace, moving from the main hall into a narrower corridor devoid of statuary. Pavel fell in beside her, still chuckling. Ryn followed behind. He didn't know what to make of statues with removable coverings, so he pushed all those thoughts aside. Appencourt was a strange place.

"So," Pavel said, "tell me more about the Summer Feast in Appencourt. It sounds delightful."

Jayn scoffed. "It's not as big a deal as the Winter Feast or Solemn Night, of course, but it is still quite the occasion. I don't like that our hearing was delayed, but I'm glad we'll be here for the feast. The upper-echelon women always try to outdo each other with sometimes outrageous dresses, but the food will be excellent. And of course, there will be dancing."

"Dancing?" Ryn said. He'd kept quiet for most of the conversation, having nothing to contribute on the topic of politics or society.

Jayn glanced back at him. "Don't tell me they didn't celebrate the Summer Feast back in Aen's Hollow?"

"They did," Ryn said. "But…" His aunt never celebrated any of the holidays, and he'd always been an outsider among the villagers, never invited to their feast days or barn dances. He didn't say any of that. Though both of them knew how uncultured and removed Ryn had been growing up, he was still sometimes too ashamed to admit it.

Pavel was the only one of them who had caught a glimpse of Ryn's old life. He had been there when that life had come to a bitter end, so he seemed to know why the idea of dancing had startled Ryn. "Don't worry, kid," Pavel said. "We got like four days until then. Their fancy waltzes might look complicated, but you'll get it with a little practice. If you can count to four, you can dance."

Jayn glanced at Ryn again. Apparently, she had never even considered that Ryn might not know how to dance. "Yes," said. "That's a good idea. We can get the whole Pentad together for some dance practice. Probably Thalia knows how to waltz, but Shilo may not. Honestly, I'm surprised that *you* can dance, Pavel."

When they all first met, Pavel and Jayn had been hostile to one another. They were still frequently rude to each other, but it had more of the air of bickering siblings now.

"Of course," Pavel said. "When you work for rich snobs, sometimes you have to act like a rich snob yourself."

Jayn feigned confusion. "What was it you used to do again? You've always been vague on the particulars."

"Let's not dwell on the past."

Ryn smiled along, but he still felt uneasy. He had resolved himself as best he could to speaking before the Hall of the Assembly, though he did not look forward to it, and each day it was delayed, the weight of apprehension in his stomach grew heavier. But now he would have to dance in front of these lords and ladies? And his friends? He'd almost rather have to face Kobolds again than deal with that. Almost.

When they reached the end of the hall, and Jayn and Pavel turned to stroll back the other way, Ryn excused himself. "I think I'll go rest in my room," he said. Jayn and Pavel acknowledged his departure and continued right along. They were back on the topic of the ambassador and relations between the two nations in general. Ryn made his way slowly up the stairs to the third floor.

He wished now the hearing had not been delayed. They could have finished it and been back on their way to Falport already. He didn't mind Falport, though it was a city of equal size to Appencourt. He felt comfortable within the Watchkeeper compound, training with the masters and having Secret Training with his friends. Even the days spent on the road had been fine, apart from the terrifying encounter with the fake Wydelk. He wished they'd had more time to speak with those rogues who had discovered their own impossible Blending. He wondered where they were now. Probably still at the Appencourt outpost, awaiting judgment.

Ryn felt like that now, like he was sitting around waiting for some heavy judgment to be passed down, except he didn't know what he was being judged for. He didn't know what he had done or how he could make it better. Probably he was just nervous and uneasy. Now he had a new reason to be nervous. He definitely did not want to dance.

Knowing Jayn, the lessons would start tonight. He'd rather they just practice their Weaving. They were still going through all Five Forces together, taking one at a time. Ryn had gotten a lot better at Flame and Wave. He had made a Weaver light on his own once and a deflection ward twice. Nothing happened when he tried Stone, and he had summoned only a few puffs of Aether—not nearly enough to be able to Blend it with Root, but he was still convinced that was the best route to recreating the forbidden Blending.

Jayn was still tenaciously trying to master Flame. The others were happy to practice with their opposing forces, but none of them seemed quite as determined to make their own forbidden Blendings. The problem was with creating new metaphors, but also envisioning a purpose for such a Blending. None of them had guessed that Wave and Aether could Blend to create illusions, but it made sense now that they knew it.

Ryn wondered why neither Jayn nor Pavel had suggested trying to recreate the Blending themselves, but of course, Sara and Ansel had made their connection as a result of their romantic involvement, a technique that no one had suggested their Pentad try. Ryn was still pretty sure Pavel fancied Nyssa, though she didn't seem to return those feelings. Jayn seemed far too focused on her future career path, and if Shilo or Thalia had any romantic interest in Ryn or Pavel, Ryn had no way of knowing. He didn't think they did. Maybe that was part of why he didn't want to dance. It did seem too tied to romance, if only tangentially. Whether it was true or not, too many stories involved a woman and a prince falling in love at a ball.

Ryn shook his head, putting all thoughts of dance lessons and naked statues aside. He wondered what Thalia and Shilo had gotten up to. Jayn had mentioned that they'd ventured into the city for some shopping. Then he remembered something else he was supposed to be practicing, instructions from Master Pembrim he'd mostly ignored.

He'd reached the door to his room on the third floor, but he paused before entering. He closed his eyes, deciding to try to detect his friends. He summoned a small Root tree—more of a bush—but he did not draw any energy. He imagined his roots extending outward in an ever-widening circle, but the green tree did not grow any larger.

Master Pembrim had trained him to sense humans, and here in the city there were thousands of people. Ryn became aware of them in a strange way. No images came into his mind; he did not perceive them with any of his senses. It was a little like being in a small room with someone else. Even if you weren't looking at them and couldn't hear them, you could still perceive their presence. Ryn felt he was in a room with a countless number of people, though the impressions were so faint that it wasn't stifling or overwhelming. Mostly, the great mass of humanity blended into a single blob all around him, but a few impressions stood out more distinctly than the rest.

One was close by. That had to be Nyssa, in her room down the hall. He could turn and face straight toward her, but he could only tell that she was close relative to the others. He sensed two more below him and a little to the left. That had to be Jayn and Pavel, still pacing. Much further out, to the southeast, he could barely sense Thalia and Shilo. At least, he guessed that had to be them. He could not tell any of them apart. Those five individuals stood out to him and no one else. He had no sense of Mina Bellain or the rogues or that other man who had briefly joined them on their journey. They had not been together long enough. Or maybe he could only find his friends. Ryn really did see them all as his friends, and after eighteen years with no friends other than a pig, he was grateful for it. Five friends still felt like an embarrassment of riches to him.

Ryn felt another presence looming over him suddenly. His eyes shot open as he turned.

"I'm sorry," the ambassador from Tamor said in his lilting accent that did strange things to the vowels. "I did not mean to startle you."

"No, I'm sorry," Ryn said, trying to hide his alarm. He remembered that he was supposed to be nice to the ambassador but also that he was supposed to avoid him. He glanced down the hall. They were alone. He didn't see the two servants who had been with the man yesterday.

The ambassador raised a hand and offered a reassuring smile. "Oh, I know, I am Tamorine and you are Aldrian, and probably we should not like each other, but I assure you, I mean you no harm."

"All right," Ryn said, not sure what else to say.

"Please forgive me, but were you Weaving just now?"

"Yes, I was—uh, yes."

"I thought so." His smile broadened. "I am no Weaver myself, but I know plenty, and I've seen that look of concentration before. How strange it is to see and do things that the rest of us cannot even perceive."

Ryn nodded. He was never good at conversation in the best of circumstances, and this was strange. He knew he shouldn't be talking to the ambassador, but he didn't know how to get away. The man seemed amicable enough and happy to make his own conversation.

"You know," he said, his tone growing more serious. "I have heard a little of what happened in Falport with those Kobolds and everything else. That could not have been an easy time for you Watchkeepers."

Ryn could only nod in agreement. What did he mean by "everything else"? Did Tamor know about the man-faced creatures and the portal?

"Tamor has been blessed so far," the ambassador said. "No Kobolds have yet crossed into our lands. They have been reported up in the Ever Wood, but people are always seeing monsters in the Ever Wood, so who knows."

Ryn knew very little about the Ever Wood, the massive forest that filled most of Mirkwald, though someone else had told him once before about strange things being reported there. According to Jayn, the Mirkwalders had only been able to establish their own nation in that place because everyone else was too superstitious to live there. Ryn nodded again, which seemed to be all the man needed from him.

"I understand also that you and your fellow Watchkeepers are here in Appencourt because of this business with the Kobolds, yes? I'm sorry my presence has upset all that. I do understand how important it is for Aldria to protect itself from such a threat. That is part of why I am here. Though some may doubt it, I am on the side of peace."

"Oh," Ryn said, genuinely surprised.

"Perhaps I have said too much." The ambassador glanced around now, but they were still alone. "My father says I forget myself too often. I will take my leave now." He made a slight bow while sweeping his hand. "My name, if you do not know it, is Lorenz Savon. I am pleased to make your acquaintance."

"You as well." The man seemed on the verge of leaving, but his eyes lingered on Ryn. He seemed to want something. His name, of course. "I am Ryn Silverbell."

The man nodded, turned, and went into his own room, which was right next to Ryn's, though it seemed to be much larger.

Ryn stood in the hallway for several moments longer. He didn't know what to make of the man, though he had seemed friendly enough. Ryn had heard all his life that Tamor was an enemy of Aldria, but he had never meant any Tamorines before now. The man said he was on the side of peace. Could that possibly be true? Ryn shook his head. Nyssa had been right. There were deep currents circling around Appencourt, and Ryn had no desire to be swept away by any of them.

Chapter 17
Once a Thief

SHILO SAT ON THE EDGE of the moat, dangling her feet over the bubbling water, hidden from the midmorning heat by the Grand Hall that loomed over her. No wall or escarpment surrounded the round island on which the Grand Hall perched; the paving stones ran all the way to the edge before dropping ten feet into the moat.

Her spot was shady and quiet, and she could listen to the burbling fountains and watch the colorful fish. Some of them were quite large, and she wondered what they would taste like, though these were strictly ornamental fish. That was a strange concept to her, but they were lovely to look at, with their golden-orange scales, mixed with splashes of black and white.

This was their third day waiting to be summoned before the lords and ladies. Jayn was convinced that the hearing would not be held until next week at the earliest, which meant they would be in Appencourt for the feast on Moonday. Celebrations would be held throughout the city, but as guests of the Hall, Shilo and her Pentad would join the lords and ladies for their great feast and dance.

Shilo's mother had taught her to dance, but not the stiff, sedate waltzes of the upper echelons. Still, Jayn had wrangled them all into lessons last night—conducted by Jayn and Pavel, of all people—and the steps did not seem particularly difficult.

Shilo still wasn't sure she would enjoy the Appencourt celebration. She missed feast days back in Palmoor, when the whole village would gather together to prepare the meal. They boiled clams, scallops, and little rock shrimp in massive stewpots and made spicy lentil and tomato soup. She imagined the food in Appencourt would be too rich and heavy and not nearly as delicious. She also had not packed a single dress for the trip, but nothing she owned would have been appropriate for an actual ball anyway. Jayn said they needn't worry. Master Stoats, the head steward, was already making arrangements to provide them with appropriate attire, which Nyssa confirmed. Apparently, it was another benefit of being guests of the Hall. A tailor had stopped by their rooms that morning to take measurements. Shilo knew nothing of Appencourt fashion, but she was already certain she would not like the dress they provided.

It couldn't be helped. She would wear the dress, and they would all dance in the Hall. Then maybe next week they could get this hearing over with and be back on their way to Falport. Falport was nothing like Palmoor, but at least it was on the coast. She had never been this far from the sea before. She felt constrained and boxed in here in the city, with no infinite horizon to look upon and find comfort in. Her gifting as a Flame Weaver had taken her off the water, and she had never been a particularly good sailor. Her one attempt to sail on her own, with her younger brother in tow, had nearly gotten them both killed. A storm had swept them within sight of the Rune Lands, a place from which no ship ever returned. Probably they had drifted as close as anyone could and still be able to turn and sail away. She would never forget that long empty stretch of beach, with its ominous gray monoliths spaced out every hundred paces. Still, despite all that, she would always love the sea.

Sitting on the edge of the moat, watching the fish, she could pretend for a time that she was on her father's boat, watching the water rush by. Of course, the ground beneath her did not move. She even missed that feeling of bobbing on the waves, which stayed in your body for hours afterward, so that even lying in your bed back on land, you could still feel the ocean rocking you to sleep.

When she got in these homesick and melancholy moods, she preferred to be alone. Nyssa had told them to take someone along anytime they left the Grand Hall. Shilo didn't think she was violating that order. Technically, she was still on the grounds of the Hall. She just wouldn't cross over any of the five painted bridges.

Traffic circled around her island beyond the moat, though no one crossed the bridges. The lords and ladies had already gathered for another closed-door meeting, and while curious citizens had tried to come and watch on the first and second day, everyone knew by now that the meetings had been sealed. Everyone wanted to know what the Tamorine ambassador was doing in the city. The leading rumor was that Tamor had demanded the right to dock their trading ships in Falport, which would give them direct access to Maer merchants. Shilo did not like the idea of Tamorine ships sailing along the Aldrian coast, a route that would take them past her home village. Those waters were dangerous enough with the Lembalt raiders, pirates who everyone knew were privateers for Tamor.

Adding fuel to the speculation, the Mirkwald ambassador had also arrived at the Hall that morning. According to Jayn, Mirkwald, Iscerna, the Maer, and even Silgaria maintained embassies in Appencourt, as they were all friendly or at least neutral towards Aldria. Mirkwald, wedged between Tamor and Aldria, sat in an awkward but profitable position. Ostensibly neutral, they could send ships to Falport to trade with the Maer, and then profit by selling those goods to Tamor. Obviously, the Mirkwald ambassador would protest any new arrangements that could cut them out of the equation, though they also had to be careful not to offend their much larger and more aggressive neighbor.

Shilo didn't understand all the complicated geopolitics that Jayn had tried explaining to all of them, but she did understand geography. Tamor controlled the whole western coast of the Baston Sea, but that sea was bound by a vast desert to the south and the impenetrable Rune Lands to the east. Though it controlled the entire western half of the continent, with no direct access to the Morro Ocean, Tamor had no trading partners other than Mirkwald. Of course, ships could bypass Aldria by sailing outside the Finger Isles and heading straight for Abyscadis, and sometimes they did, but few sane pilots dared sail so close to the Rune Lands, and crossing the open ocean posed its own challenges. Only the Maer had truly mastered ocean voyages, and they kept that a closely guarded secret. Enterprising Tamorine captains were just as likely to miss the Maer Isles entirely and sail on for weeks until the whole crew died of dehydration or starvation.

Those were grim thoughts. Shilo didn't really need to worry about any of that. They were only here in Appencourt to talk about the Kobolds, which were trouble enough for any mind. She tried not to think about the Kobolds either and just watched the fish. A long-legged green heron stood on a shallow ledge on the far side of the moat, eyeing the fish. They all looked too big to fit down its slender gullet, but the bird seemed determined to try.

Shilo looked up, hearing footsteps.

"I thought that was you," Rav Montare said, smiling.

Shilo moved to stand up and greet him properly, but he motioned for her to stay.

"I'll join you," he said. "If you don't mind."

Shilo nodded, but he was already sitting down. He sighed as he dangled his legs over the edge. Shilo was surprised to see him. She had almost forgotten about him since arriving in the city. He was certainly handsome, though he seemed too old for her. Though he was not a priest, he was obviously devout, and that created another layer of separation. She was only seventeen, and Watchkeeper training kept her too busy to think seriously about boys. Growing up, she had expected her parents would eventually arrange a husband for her, though she of course could object if she found the man unsuitable. Now that she had ventured off into the world on her own, that whole arrangement seemed unlikely to happen. She would visit her family when she could, but Palmoor was no longer her home, in a way she was only now realizing. She couldn't think about that or the prospect of eventually finding a husband on her own now. She had to make conversation.

"How are you?" she managed to ask.

"Well," he said, nodding. "I expected your Pentad would be gone by now, but when I heard that ambassador from Tamor had arrived and delayed everything, I thought I might come check in on you. All of you, I mean."

Shilo smiled. "That's kind of you. There isn't much to say. We are guests of the Hall now, and we'll be waiting here until they have time for us."

"I see."

During the days Rav had traveled with them, Shilo had never had a private conversation with the man. Mostly he had debated philosophy with Pavel, while she had listened in. Still, he was friendly in a disarming way that seemed to make everyone comfortable around him. Shilo didn't mind talking to him now.

"So," she said, "how are you liking the city? You said you were staying with friends?"

"Yes, at the mission here."

"What do they do exactly?"

"Well, our goal is to spread the message of the Shepard-King, but practically, we do charitable works for the community. I've been helping in the kitchens. We offer free meals to anyone in need. Simple stuff, but filling. I kept it to myself when we were on the road together, but I was actually transporting a sizable donation of coin from one of the other missions, so I'm glad those thieves did not find it, though I suppose everything was recovered, and rather quickly, thanks to your group."

"Your people must really trust you. I mean, making a delivery like that on your own seems a little risky."

He nodded. "We try to avoid that situation as a rule, for a number of reasons. I was actually traveling with a friend, but he took sick along the road. I put him up at an inn, but he insisted I continue on my own. Funds were getting low here, so he didn't want the work to stop on his account. I thought it was a bad idea, but I continued on my own anyway, and then I immediately came across you Watchkeepers, and your Captain Lahmeer offered the escort. I thank the Maker for that."

Shilo wondered why he had kept all this to himself before. Probably, he was just being cautious to protect all that coin. Shilo hoped anyone who wore the Watchkeeper gray could be trusted not to turn bandit, but she understood his discretion in front of so many strangers.

"I'm glad we were there," she said, "though perhaps that means the Maker destroyed the bridge so we could meet."

She had meant it as a joke, but she regretted it as soon as she said it. It seemed dismissive of his beliefs. Thankfully, he just laughed. "No, that was down to some foolish or wicked person," he said. "The Maker permits evil to exist in the world, but he works to make good things come from even the worst circumstances."

Shilo had never heard that sentiment before, but she liked it. It sounded optimistic without denying the harsh realities of life. "Our hearing probably won't be until next week," she said. "Perhaps I can come visit your mission."

"You would be most welcome."

Another thought occurred to her then, though she wasn't sure she wanted to share it. Probably, if his disposition had not been so disarming, she wouldn't have. "Do you have plans for the Summer Feast?" she asked. "Or do your people celebrate?"

She knew the Scribes opposed the idea of star guides, so she didn't know how they felt about holidays built around the sun. Feast days were held on the Moondays closest to the solstices and equinoxes.

He made a back-and-forth motion with his hand. "Some don't. Some do. Probably there were strange religious elements when the feast days were first established, but now they're just an excuse to eat a nice meal and spend time with family and friends. That's how I see it anyway."

She nodded. It didn't sound like he had a problem with the holiday, so she pressed on. "Well, as guests of the Hall, my friends and I will be celebrating the feast here. The lords are hosting a ball. It sounds a little intimidating but also exciting. Perhaps, you could join us." After a brief pause, she added, "I'm sure the others would be happy to see you again." She didn't want him taking the invitation the wrong way.

"Hmm," he said, pausing to consider it for a moment before responding. "Well, I do love a chance to waltz. Are you sure it would be all right though? I mean, are you allowed to bring guests?"

"Oh. Well, I guess I should probably check first."

She laughed awkwardly, but he just smiled, good-natured as ever. "Probably you should. I'll consider the invitation in the meantime. I admit, I am a little curious for a chance to see this mysterious ambassador that has the city so stirred up."

"I'll check, and then I can come visit your mission later in the week. I am curious to see that place either way. Where would I find it?"

He described the roads and turns she would need to take to reach the mission in the Foreign Quintant. Shilo wasn't much good at navigating a city, but she thought she could follow his instructions. They fell silent for a time after that. Shilo returned her gaze to the water below.

"This is a lovely spot," Rav said after a minute. "Right in the heart of the city but still peaceful."

She nodded in agreement. The green heron had vanished, perhaps scared off by their conversation. Her eyes drifted to the milling foot traffic beyond that. They were on the western side of the Grand Hall, looking toward the Trade Quintant. Shilo spotted a familiar lanky figure loping his way through the crowd there, angling his steps toward the nearest bridge. Rav saw him too.

"Isn't that Pavel?" he said, pointing.

Shilo could only nod. Why had Pavel gone off into the city alone? What had he been doing in the Trade Quintant, which housed mostly bankers and large merchants? He had changed out of his uniform into a black shirt and brown trousers. He wore his satchel, but he'd left his two blades behind. Shilo didn't know what he was up to, but she wasn't surprised he had ignored Nyssa's order to not go out alone.

Except, he wasn't alone. Another man followed closely behind Pavel. The man seemed to be talking to Pavel, but Pavel completely ignored him and just kept walking. Shilo recognized the man then.

"What's Pavel doing with *him*?" she said aloud.

"Who?" Rav asked.

"I think his name was… Peniter? I saw him in the city yesterday."

"Lucas Peniter? I've heard about him too. What business would an anti-Weaving politician have with a Watchkeeper?"

Shilo shook her head. "Nothing good."

Pavel reached the foot of the arching wooden bridge. This one had been painted white. He started to cross, his eyes focused straight ahead. Lucas Peniter stopped at the foot of the bridge. They'd come close enough that Shilo could hear him now. "You can't walk away from this, Talvor," Peniter said. "You took the oath, same as me."

"Leap into the pit," Pavel said without looking back, his tone perfectly flat.

Peniter sighed, throwing up his hands in a sign of exasperation, but he stopped his pursuit. He turned and headed off the other way. As Pavel reached the midpoint of the bridge, he finally spotted Shilo and Rav sitting on the edge of the moat, some twenty paces away. He froze. Something like genuine shock passed over his face for an instant, before it disappeared behind a mask of indifference.

"Shilo. Rav." He nodded to them.

Rav glanced at the retreating man before looking back at Pavel. "A friend of yours?" he asked, a trace of confusion in his otherwise friendly tone.

Pavel sighed. He crossed the bridge slowly. Rav rose to meet him, and Shilo got up too. Pavel looked at each of them for a moment before responding. "Someone I used to know a long time ago. Not really a friend."

"Lucas Peniter?" Shilo asked.

Pavel's eyes narrowed. "How do you know him?"

"I don't really…" She didn't know what to say. She felt like she had caught Pavel doing something he wasn't supposed to be doing, but she had no idea what that was.

Rav stepped in for her. "Lucas Peniter is making a big stink in the capital right now. He's campaigning for a seat in the Hall of the Assembly, and he's taking a very anti-Weaver stance."

Pavel shrugged. "That's news to me. Like I said, I didn't know him very well even back then." He glanced at Shilo. "We sort of ran in similar circles."

Shilo understood his reluctance. Clearly, he didn't want Rav to know about his criminal past. Pavel used to acquire rare artifacts and Runeforms and sell them to rich clients, in ways that weren't always legal. He'd enlisted with the Watchkeepers as an alternative punishment for his past transgressions. She cleared her throat. "Well, it means you were right to brush him off. Probably, he wouldn't have tried talking to you in the first place if he knew you were a Watchkeeper now."

Pavel offered her a smile that seemed almost genuine. "True enough. I should have led with that." He turned his full attention to Rav then and took on a feigned enthusiasm, no doubt intended to move the conversation forward. "Well, Rav Montare, what brings you here? Come to make converts of us?"

Rav laughed, unruffled as ever. "Just paying a visit to my old friends. Shilo tells me you will be here through the weekend."

"This one and maybe the next one. But really, you give up too easily. I think you nearly had me convinced the last time we spoke."

"Well, it takes more than simple persuasion to find the path."

Pavel glanced back across the city and then gestured to the maze of columns before them. "Come, let's walk and talk," he said. "Maybe we can find a path together."

Rav fell in step beside him, but Shilo stood rooted to the ground. As the two men moved away, Pavel glanced back at her once, his expression unreadable. A heavy weight had started to form in the pit of her stomach from the moment she saw Pavel with Lucas Peniter, and his dismissive words had not persuaded her. Something was going on. Something bad.

She'd learned shortly after meeting him about Pavel's past exploits. She hadn't given them much thought. He really did seem to have left that all behind, giving his full attention to the Watchkeeper training, but had she been too naïve? The kinds of rich men who trafficked in stolen Runeforms probably kept offices in the Trade Quintant. Had Pavel gone to meet an old client? Had he gone to meet Lucas Peniter specifically, despite his denials? Was Pavel stealing again? The Watchkeeper compound housed plenty of Runeforms, though security around them was tight, especially after one had been stolen by rogues.

She didn't like where any of these thoughts were taking her, but Pavel had all but admitted he knew Peniter from back when he was a thief. Should she tell somebody? Should she tell Nyssa? She didn't know what she would say. What had Peniter said? "You took an oath." That had sounded sinister, but maybe she was overthinking things. Maybe Pavel had taken on a job for Peniter in the past but had never completed it. Maybe that was when Nyssa caught him. Peniter must have seen Pavel in the city and tried to make him honor the deal, to fulfill his oath. Obviously, Pavel had wanted nothing to do with the guy, so maybe he wasn't returning to a life of crime after all. Maybe he was still committed to becoming a Watchkeeper, which was why he had brushed the man aside. Both possibilities seemed equally likely, but maybe she was still too optimistic for thinking that. She decided she wouldn't tell anyone what she had seen and what she suspected just yet, but she would be watching Pavel more closely.

Chapter 18
A Change of Plans

PAVEL SIGHED AS HE MADE his way up the marble stairs to the third floor. When he had found the note slipped under his door, he had never imagined he would find Peniter waiting for him at the rendezvous. He assumed it was one or another of his old contacts in Appencourt. He had planned to make nice and offer a few vague assurances, before completely ignoring them. No job was worth the clean slate he would have if he could manage to stick with the Watchkeepers for another sixty-two months and change.

So he went, and he had been blindsided by Lucas Peniter of all people. Pavel had turned and left at once, but the fool had followed him through the very public streets of Appencourt. Shilo and Rav Montare had seen Pavel with Peniter, but he had handled them well enough. Shilo was a trusting girl, and Rav didn't know enough about Pavel to be dangerous.

Still, Peniter's presence in the capital was irksome, and Pavel didn't know what to make of the fact that he'd turned politician. He didn't want to dwell on it too much. Peniter was the last person

Pavel had wanted to meet. The second to last, anyway. Peniter was a bitter reminder of the worst decision Pavel had ever made. He should never have sworn that blighted oath…

He shook his head. He would not dwell on the past. He cast his mind about for something else to dwell on. This business with the Tamorine ambassador, Lorenz Savon, was interesting, but whatever came of it, barring all-out warfare, it would not affect Pavel much. He'd grown up in Lon's Watch, where the Scholars saw themselves as independent from Aldria and above the petty disputes of squabbling nations. The Academy of the Ways had stood for nearly a thousand years, more than twice as long as any nation. Though he disdained the Scholars for several reasons, Pavel had acquired their general indifference for the passing tides of politics.

Pavel reached the third floor and headed for his room, though he wasn't especially tired. The midday meal would be served soon, but he wasn't especially hungry either. He needed some time alone to sit and not think about Lucas Peniter or that oath that still threatened to undo all his plans.

He put his key in the lock and opened the door. His eyes went at once to the comfortable chair by the window. A man sat there. Pavel sighed. This, now, was the last person he wanted to meet.

Pavel shut the door behind him and leaned against it. He glanced at the chain hanging from the wall. "If I pull this," he said, "a servant will come running."

His father laughed. "Always so dramatic," he said. He gestured toward the bed. "Come. Sit."

"I'll stand."

Pavel studied his father. His hair had gone almost entirely gray in the decade since Pavel had last seen him. Deeper wrinkles had set into the corners of the man's tan face. The coloring was genetic;

Pavel was certain his father still never spent much time outdoors. He was amazed the man had come all the way to Appencourt, nearly a week's ride from Lon's Watch.

"Why are you here?" Pavel asked.

"I was in town on business. When I heard the infamous *Pavel Talvor* was here, I knew I had to pay a visit." He said the name with obvious disdain.

"Oh, so you've heard of me?"

His father scoffed. "With a name like that, I assume you were trying to get my attention. Running around stealing Runeforms and calling yourself Pavel Talvor of all things."

"It's just a pseudonym."

"Talvor, I understand. You were always pouring over my maps of the old city-states. Though if you recalled the fate that befell that city, you would have understood why it never became a real second name." He shook his head. "But Pavel? I took that as an insult. That man never liked me."

"Well, you did take his daughter and lock her up in that blighted tower."

"Your mother loved Lon's Watch. You did too once, even if you deny it now."

"You're overthinking it. I picked the name because it had a nice sound to it."

"Perhaps."

A silence fell between them. Pavel knew this was no social visit, but he would not ask again. After a minute, his father sighed.

"How are you liking the Watchkeepers?"

Pavel shrugged.

"Have they at least gotten you to finally take an interest in lacings other than Aether?"

"I may have picked up a thing or two."

His father fell silent for a time. His eyes wandered around the small but comfortable room. They settled on the peg from which Pavel had hung his shoulder harness with his two blades. "Those are interesting," his father said. "Relics, I assume?"

Pavel nodded. "Runeforms," he said, remembering how that other Scholar had described them. Probably his father had the same view.

His father's eyes returned to Pavel. "Have you found anything else of note?"

"What do you mean?"

"Come now. You mustn't think I don't know what you've been doing all these years. What you've been looking for."

Pavel hesitated. It could have been a bluff, but it wasn't. He shook his head. "You spent all those years blathering on about the Five Crowns while never bothering to go look for them yourself."

His father shrugged. "Well, I wanted you to be the one to find them. Why do you think I blathered on as much as I did?"

Pavel scoffed. "You can't have known I would set off on my own. No, you're just saying that now so you can pretend I'm still your dutiful and obedient son."

"Perhaps. You may choose to believe that."

"It doesn't matter. I will find the Five Crowns, but you will never see them."

"You sound confident, but after all these years, you apparently haven't even found one."

"I will. It's only a matter of time."

His father looked around the room again. "Where is your crow?"

"Corvus?" Pavel wasn't surprised his father had heard of the talking Runeform. Corvus was a big part of Pavel Talvor's reputation.

"Corvus?" his father echoed. "How do you know its name?"

"I asked him."

"You asked him? You asked the Runeform its name, and it said, 'Corvus'?"

"Yep."

His father slowly shook his head, a rueful grin on his face. "That certainly has some interesting implications. But where is this Corvus?"

"Nearby, I'm sure. He doesn't really like going inside buildings, especially when they're as heavily warded as this one."

Corvus had not appeared earlier when Pavel made his trip across the city. Corvus must have known who would be meeting him and had decided not to show his beak. The bird was clever, bordering on true intelligence.

"Pity. I would like to meet this Corvus someday." He paused. "What has Corvus told you?"

Pavel wasn't surprised. Probably, his father knew more about Corvus than he did. "I will find the Five Crowns," he said. "It is my destiny." He raised his chin and met his father's gaze.

"So he said…"

"Yes. Exactly."

The old man smiled, and this time it looked almost genuine. "Excellent."

Pavel regarded his father. The man was infuriating, but he was incredibly well informed. If his father wanted to pretend they were on friendly terms, perhaps Pavel could benefit from the arrangement. He did not want to know anything about what his father was really doing in Appencourt, but he could ask about something else, like petty politics of little concern to a Scholar.

"Since you seem to know everything already, maybe you can tell me something," Pavel said. "What's the deal with this ambassador from Tamor?"

His father laughed. "Oh, you'll like this one. But you haven't puzzled it out yourself? You must know he is no mere ambassador. Savon? You've heard that second name before."

Pavel thought about that for a moment. It did sound familiar, but maybe it was just a common second name in Tamor. Then it clicked. "You mean like Savonoy? As in, Lemuel Savonoy, first emperor of Tamor?"

"And his son, the current emperor."

"What are you saying? Lorenz Savon is Lemuel II's son, the crown prince of Tamor?"

"Just prince. His father has not named an heir yet. Rumor is, Lemuel currently favors his eldest daughter."

"What is the prince doing here?"

"Suing for peace." His father chuckled, shaking his head. "It's not half clever. He thinks if he can turn Aldria into an ally and bring an accord to his father, it will finally secure him that 'crown' title. Mirkwald is in an uproar over the idea, of course."

Pavel couldn't believe it. Retaking Aldria through invasion would cost Tamor far too much to be worthwhile, but a true alliance would obviously benefit both countries. Yet it would also mean putting aside decades of built-up pride and hostility. Not much blood had been spilled over the years, but enough had that no one had ever proposed peace without harsh penalties. The Tamor of old would have settled for nothing short of retaking half of Aldria's coast for easy access to the Morro Ocean. It would take quite a diplomat to pull off a negotiation that could please both parties. If Lorenz was such a man, and if he could take the throne of Tamor, that would benefit everyone.

Pavel's father raised a cautioning hand. "It's best to keep all this to yourself. Things are tenuous, but I think the Hall and the Pentarchs will swallow their own pride in the end. Keep your nose out of it. You're here to talk about Kobolds, nothing else."

Pavel raised an eyebrow. "Since you are feeling so generous today, what can you tell me about the Kobolds?"

His father made a dismissive gesture. "Silgarian monsters. They're brutal but ultimately not an existential threat."

His father answered just a hair too quickly. Anyone else would have missed it, but Pavel knew his father better than anyone, though he hated to admit it. The hair on the back of his neck stood up. That had been a lie. The threat of war with Tamor didn't bother the man, but the Kobolds did? All this time, they had been thinking they needed to deal with the Kobold threat quickly, so Aldria could turn its full attention to Tamor. Perhaps the Kobolds were a greater threat than anybody realized. Maybe then it was a good thing the prince had come. If Aldria could make peace with Tamor, then they could devote all resources to the Kobolds.

If Pavel's father feared the Kobolds, that could mean only one thing: He didn't understand them. He was in the dark about the creatures, the same as everyone, and that frightened Pavel. That meant nobody knew their true goals or why they had come down from the Coldreaches—or from another world, as Pavel was beginning to suspect. Pavel, who had been there in Falport when everything went sideways, probably knew more about the creatures than his own father did, though the man would never admit that. Pavel definitely knew more, he realized, as he thought back to the first time he ever saw a Kobold and that star-cursed oath he took alongside Lucas Peniter.

***

Lucas Peniter strolled purposefully through the gardens of the Green Quintant. There were no straight paths here; everything twisted and curved around stands of trees, flowering bushes, and gurgling water features. The water bubbled up from a natural spring, but it had been constrained and guided to flow through a series of streams, little waterfalls, and pools. The whole thing was meant to look natural and untamed, but that was all just an illusion. Imposed civilization masquerading as natural beauty, while beneath all that, a wild river flowed through pipes and underground channels, awaiting its moment to burst free. The whole of Appencourt was like that too, seething below the surface, waiting for the right push to set it off.

The woman was waiting for him on the bench in that secluded corner of the gardens. Here on the edge of summer, it was already too warm at midday for people to venture into the park, so they were alone. Lucas had met this woman only once before. She wore the same voluminous black robe as then. She was a voluminous woman.

He did not sit down. "Talvor resisted," he said. "He'll take some convincing to honor his oath."

"Talvor is no longer your concern," she said, her voice sultry but with a hard edge.

"What do you mean?"

"There's been a change."

"What are you talking about?"

"The test was a success. We're going full scale with that plan."

"I can't be involved with that! I'm supposed to be running for a seat in the Assembly."

"I said there's been a change."

Lucas opened his mouth to respond, but nothing came out. He couldn't believe what he was hearing. He had sacrificed everything for the plan. He was determined to win that seat, not because he really hated Weavers, but because being a lord of the Assembly would make him invaluable to the Reach. He would finally have a seat at the table. That would make it all worthwhile—all the sacrifices, all the horrible things he had done. They could not take that away from him now.

"Will you comply?" the woman asked.

"What?"

"Will you comply?"

"Why? Why do I have to throw it all away?"

The woman glared up at him. "You do not get to ask that question. Your oath binds you. You must comply."

Lucas shook his head, disgusted. "I must comply, yes, so why are you even bothering to ask?"

"For appearances, dearie." Her expression softened slightly. "I know this will not be easy. I've made the same sacrifice myself. I gave up my old life for this, so I can assure you that you will be taken care of, as long as you continue to make yourself useful."

He didn't want to ask what would happen if he ceased being useful. "What would you need me to do? Exactly?"

"I'll put you in touch with our man inside the Lightsmith Guild soon. You've done well gathering in followers. It's time to step up your rhetoric. Tell them the Hall of the Assembly has become too corrupt. It can no longer be changed from the inside. It must be dismantled."

Lucas sighed. "I'll do it. I must."

"Yes, you must." She offered him a smile without a thread of warmth. "We are all bound to the will of the Five."

Chapter 19
Barriers

JAYN PACED THE COURTYARD beneath the Grand Hall, winding her way through the forest of thin columns. This was their fourth day of waiting, with still no news as to what was going on with this cursed ambassador from Tamor. Plenty of rumors were running around the capital but nothing concrete. Jayn's feet took her to the edge of the courtyard, still in the shadow of the great building. Miracles of Stone kept the building perched atop its columns, but it was the lacings of Wave that drew her focus.

A perfect dome covered the entire building. Upon closer examination of its edge, she could see five concentric circles placed so close together that they almost looked like one. The layers of Wave stretching overhead gave the surrounding city a distorted, rippling appearance. Strangely, she had known this place her whole life, but the wards had been completely invisible to her until a handful of months ago. She had known the wards were there, of course, but knowing they existed and seeing them were entirely different things.

For lack of anything else to do, she studied the rippling patterns again, trying to determine the purpose of each ward, but that was not a skill she had practiced much, and the tight layering made it virtually impossible to distinguish one from the next. She knew one of them was a layered sealing ward. Anyone who tried to cross into the Hall while maintaining an active lacing would lose it. Once inside, they could still create a new lacing, but it was meant as a warning. The barrier also included a sophisticated detection ward. Anytime someone crossed into the dome, an image of that person flashed into the minds of all the Wardens who had helped create it. While an Aether Weaver could destroy all the wards in a manner of seconds, the Wardens would still see him, and the destruction of the wards would trigger an alarm sound audible to everyone within the Grand Hall.

"Impressive, isn't it?" someone said behind Jayn.

She flinched. She'd been too focused on unraveling the wards that she had not heard any footsteps. She turned, first recognizing the blue and white Warden uniform and then the young man who wore it. "Jax," she said. "I heard you joined the Wardens."

He nodded. "And I heard you joined the Watchkeepers."

Jax Centillion was the son of one of the lords. He was a few years older than her, and while they had never been close, they had socialized on feast days and at private parties over the years. Joining the Wardens was a common path for Wave Weavers with political aspirations, though not all Wardens were social climbers. Jayn's mother had mentioned it as an option when Jayn first manifested as a Wave Weaver. Jayn didn't think she would have enjoyed being a Warden. The wards they used were complex and interesting, but once mastered, the job probably became tedious. Appencourt had seen its fair share of protests over the years, but nothing approaching an insurrection or revolt had ever occurred.

Jayn gestured to the shimmering wall behind her. "Did you have a hand in this?" she asked.

He shook his head but smiled. "Not yet, though I am learning the lacings." He had been an even-tempered boy, often quiet, but with a steady confidence. He had a large nose and ears but managed to be somewhat handsome despite them. It helped that he was tall, with an athletic build.

"I'm sure you'll be running the place in no time," she said.

"Maybe. My Weaving is only about average."

"The Wardens wouldn't have taken you on if you couldn't handle it."

He shrugged, looking around. "Fair enough. It may not be as exciting as the Watchkeepers, but I do enjoy the work."

"Well, the Watchkeepers can be a little too exciting. I've nearly died a few times already."

He grimaced. "It's crazy what happened. I hear there's still no sign of the Kobolds, even after all these weeks. It seems they vanished as mysteriously as they arrived."

Their arrival had not been so mysterious. Jayn and her Pentad had seen Kobolds in Falport a week before the attack. They kept quiet, at her suggestion, a decision which she had come to regret, even knowing one of the masters had been part of the conspiracy. Still, she told herself not for the first time, she couldn't dwell on the past. She had to keep moving forward.

She didn't respond, and after an awkward pause, he continued. "We've stepped up security here because of all that. There's a sealing ward over the Assembly Room itself at all times now, and we've added extra wards around the vault."

"The vault?"

"We don't have nearly as many Runeforms as the Watchkeepers, but after you all lost so many, someone figured we might be a target ourselves, not that the Kobolds could ever attack here."

If he'd been looking at her instead of up at the dome, Jax would have seen the shock on her face. She had not known more Runeforms than just that mirror had been taken from the Citadel. She couldn't show her ignorance now. If even a new recruit like Jax knew about the missing Runeforms, it had to be common knowledge in the Hall. "Right," she managed to say. "Better safe than sorry, I suppose."

"Exactly," he said, returning his gaze to her. She'd managed to control her expression by then.

She smiled politely. "It was a pleasure to see you again, Jax, but if you'll excuse me, I need to check in with my captain."

He nodded and said goodbye. She turned and walked back through the maze of columns, heading for the marble steps.

Captain Nyssa Lahmeer had to know what the Kobolds had stolen, beyond just the mirror. She couldn't say why, but Jayn felt offended that that information had been withheld from her. Why had no one told her? Her Pentad had spent weeks trying to piece together what exactly had happened that night and why, and now it seemed they did not have all the information.

If raiding the Watchkeepers' collection of Runeforms had been the Kobolds' goal all along, then that explained why they had left so suddenly. The beasts had achieved their goal, which had been more elaborate than just using the mirror to summon those man-faced creatures. The Watchkeepers had not won a victory that night after all. They had not driven off the invaders. The Kobolds accomplished their mission and left of their own accord.

Maybe she was overthinking it. The knowledge could not be too widespread, or she would have heard of it sooner. The Wardens had been told, but they had to be. As protectors of the Hall of the Assembly's collection of Runeforms, they needed to know. One of those Runeforms was used to connect the wards created by individual Wave Weavers into the massive domes that covered the Grand Hall. Jax had mentioned the increased security and the theft to her in confidence, assuming she already knew about it, as a member of the Watchkeepers. The Council of Masters had to be doing their best to suppress the story, not wanting to embarrass the organization any further.

Still, wouldn't the public benefit from knowing that the Kobolds were now wielding any number of Runeforms? What exactly did they take? Only the mirror had been taken from the Gauntlet, and while other Runeforms were used throughout the Citadel—including a special watering can that kept the grass lush and healthy—if any of those had gone missing, word would have gotten out. These missing Runeforms had to have come from a storage room, then. Jayn remembered someone saying that the Watchkeepers had a stash of unidentified Runeforms—objects that were clearly created before the Burning but whose purposes had never been discovered. No one had found a way to use them, so they were all essentially indestructible paperweights. That worried her. The Kobolds would not have taken those if they did not somehow know how to use them.

Perhaps, then, the Watchkeepers had suppressed the information to avoid a panic, as she knew they had done with other facts from that night. If the purpose of the Runeforms was unknown, it meant they could do almost anything. Telling the public that the mysterious and deadly Kobolds had acquired new, unknowable powers wouldn't do much more than incite a panic. Even surmising all that, Jayn still did not like the fact that the information had been withheld from her in particular. She intended to confront Captain Lahmeer and get the full report on the missing Runeforms.

That was her plan as she headed for the back staircase, but she forgot all about it when she rounded a corner and came face-to-face with her mother. Anyse Eldragor, Fourth Pentarch of Aldria, wore a long dress that faded from crimson to black at the hem. It was around midday, so she must have been on her way from one of the private dining rooms back to the Assembly Room. This business with the ambassador must be serious indeed if the Pentarchs were sitting in the Hall. Jayn's mother raised her chin and regarded her daughter with her icy blue eyes.

"Mother," Jayn said, smiling politely.

"Jayn," her mother said, a touch of emotion in her voice.

That surprised Jayn. It had only been a couple of months since they had last seen each other.

"You are looking well," her mother said.

Jayn nodded. "You as well." She glanced over her shoulder. They were alone. "Don't let me keep you if you are needed in the Assembly Room."

Anyse Eldragor shook her head once, a short, clipped movement. "I have a moment," she said.

An awkward silence fell over them. Jayn had never been afraid of her mother, but she did feel strange now. She had left home to make her own way in the world, and she didn't know yet how that had changed their relationship.

"I wanted to see you, you know," her mother said. "When all that business happened in Falport, I wanted to go and visit you. I would have, but as the Fourth Pentarch, I can't just show up at the Citadel, you understand."

"Of course," Jayn said. She didn't know why her mother sounded so worried. "I was fine though. I did write to you."

"Yes, you did." She hesitated, not something her mother often did. "Your father and I thought you would be safe in Falport. We never expected something like this to happen. You had to fight. We never thought you would face combat so young."

"I know I'm young but… You've been training me to fight my whole life. We just assumed it would be with the Standing Army."

"Yes. I know. Still. How was it, fighting the Kobolds?"

Jayn shrugged. "They definitely look fearsome, and they're strong, but they're weirdly bad at fighting. It's like they've never actually practiced with their weapons. Most of them, anyway." She grimaced as she remembered Kalo, but he had been an exception.

Her mother shook her head. "No, I don't mean all that. You had to… kill several of the creatures, I believe?"

"Yes, I did, but…" Jayn trailed off. Her mother searched her face with a strange scrutiny, looking for something. Jayn didn't like that. "I understand your concern, but… They're creatures, Mother, barely more than animals. It would have been different if… if I were fighting people."

Anyse Eldragor had done her best to prepare Jayn for a future career in the Army, but she had not glorified warfare. She had been careful to warn Jayn of the real cost of violence and the weight one would carry for taking a life, even in service of the most just of causes. Jayn didn't feel that kind of weight. She didn't think she did. They weren't people, or they weren't human anyway. She didn't see herself as a killer. Not really. She'd hunted deer with her father before. Kobolds were a lot closer to wild game than people in her eyes.

Her mother searched her face a moment longer. "Perhaps you're right," she said. "Perhaps it's not the same. Still…" She reached out and touched Jayn's arm. This surprised Jayn also. Unlike her father, Jayn's mother had never been overly affectionate. "Don't feel as if you have to be strong all the time. That may sound strange coming from me. Show the world a brave face, that's what I taught you, but it's also all right to be vulnerable sometimes. Do you… Have you made friends?"

That question caught Jayn off guard. Her first impulse was to say yes, of course, but now she wasn't sure. She thought about Jax Centillion again. They'd known each other growing up. They'd been friendly. Cordial. Polite. But they hadn't really been friends. Back then, she'd been too focused on her dream of making it into the Army, and then the Hall, and then the Pentarchy. She had not given much thought to friends and so never realized that she didn't actually have any. All the other upper-echelon kids had seemed the same, playing nice while pursuing their own ambitions and using anyone they could to get there, but they also did seem to have friends.

Jayn thought of that young thief Clay, who'd flirted with her so shamelessly, something no social-climbing boy in Appencourt would dare to do. Maybe Pavel had been right about how conservative the capital had become. She thought about Pavel and the rest of her Training Pentad. Shilo and Thalia had formed an easy friendship from their first day together, which had grown to encompass Ryn and Pavel as well. They were all friendly towards Jayn, though she didn't make it easy on them all the time. She held herself apart and separate, from them and from everyone. They would be together for years, if everything went well with their training. She could maintain the separation for all that time—she'd kept it up for sixteen years—but she didn't think she wanted to.

"Yes," she told her mother. "My Training Pentad and I, we have become friends."

It was a lie but one she desperately wanted to be true. She needed to make it true.

***

Nyssa closed her eyes, concentrating. She'd had a lot of time to herself this week, waiting to be summoned before the Hall of the Assembly. She felt lonely here, so far from Falport. Her recruits were here, and she really did think of them as *her* recruits, but she couldn't socialize with them. She was an officer. It would not be appropriate. She had spent some time with them that week, checking to make sure they were keeping up their practice. She was amused to find Jayn and Pavel giving them all dancing lessons last night. Still, she'd spent most of the last four days on her own. It had given her plenty of time to think, and the thought she kept coming back to was a strange one.

Probably, it had something to do with those rogues in Wydhaven. Only the barmaid had been a rogue, really. The farrier's boy had been an Aether Weaver but an admittedly weak one, who apparently had not used his gift during the crimes. Nyssa couldn't quite understand how Sara had done all that, even with her Etching. The fog and the apparition of the creature were one thing, but there was also the intense fear her ward created and even the cooling effect. It seemed far too complex and sophisticated for just one girl, but Nyssa didn't know what else could have been going on. The group had returned their stolen goods and confessed of their own accord—or Pavel had coerced them somehow—so why would they lie about how they had committed the crime? What detail would they need to hide? Perhaps they had some Runeform that helped them pull off the stunt. It wasn't impossible, but it seemed unlikely. Had someone else been involved in the theft? Someone they were trying to protect? That didn't seem likely either.

Had Pavel been involved? As amusing as that thought was, it wasn't possible. The Wydelk had been seen all over the area for weeks, proof that the rogues had been practicing their lacings well before Pavel arrived in town. Pavel was an Aether Weaver, as was the boy. Neither of them could have done anything to enhance the girl's lacings. They would only have destroyed it. Still, Nyssa couldn't shake the feeling that something more had been going on. That little barmaid had uncovered some secret to Weaving that Nyssa didn't think was possible. It made her wonder what else was possible.

She'd felt that way years ago, when she first joined the Watchkeepers, but now she had learned every lacing she was capable of mastering—Wave and Stone, with tiny bits of Root. She felt like she knew everything she could know about Weaving, but now she was questioning that, which kept leading her back to Pavel's question: Why had her shield Etching been automatic only the first time? Why was Ryn's Etching so automatic that he couldn't even use it willingly, except apparently that once?

Nyssa had an Etching, which set her apart as a powerful Weaver, but did she even really understand it? She felt as if she'd become complacent. Maybe she had not yet unlocked her full potential. Weaving worked, in part, because you *believed* it could work. She'd repeated that mantra countless times, especially since becoming a teacher, but she hadn't really thought about it in years. If she believed her Etching could work differently, then maybe it could.

She wouldn't get anywhere just thinking about it. The key was to *not* think about it. She opened her eyes and threw up her hands, willing a shield into existence. Nothing happened.

Nothing could happen. She was not envisioning ripples of water. She was not shifting her stance to create a circle of blue light. This was not how Weaving worked. The Watchkeepers had taught her that. Agia Bellos had trained her for months until she had gotten her shield down to a minute. A minute was fast. It had taken her much longer to create a shield before that. Except, of course, for that very first time. When those men had cornered her, she threw up her hands, and a perfect shield formed around her. If she had done it once, there was no logical reason she couldn't do it again. She just had to forget everything she had ever been taught about Weaving and find a new way to master her Etching.

She closed her eyes.

Chapter 20
The First Drops

THALIA SAT ON THE EDGE of Jayn's bed and watched her friends dance. Something strange was happening. Maybe several strange things were happening. With three women and two men in their group, someone always had to sit out during dance practice. At the moment it was Thalia's turn to rest.

After multiple nights of waltzing, Ryn had picked up the basic footwork, but he was nowhere near competent. Jayn showed unusual patience, even when he stepped on her toes. Tonight they were all back in their uniforms, not having brought enough changes of clothes for such an extended stay in the capital, though they danced in stockinged feet, as Watchkeeper leather boots were not made for dancing.

"Not bad," Jayn said, as she and Ryn completed one of the lengthy forms used in Appencourt waltzes and paused to rest. "You know the steps. You just need to show more confidence."

Ryn shrugged. "That's never been a strong point of mine," he said, with a sheepish smile.

Jayn returned his smile. "Remember, the man is supposed to lead the dance. You can't keep following my cues." Her tone held no trace of impatience or sarcasm.

"Why is that though? Women can be soldiers or Pentarchs. Why can't they lead dances?"

Jayn shook her head. "It's just tradition. Don't overthink the ball too much. We're not trying to be the center of attention. All this business with the ambassador has made everyone forget why we're even here. We'll blend in with the crowd, dance a few turns, and then it will be over."

Ryn nodded. "If only men can lead, then can I dance with Pavel?"

Jayn actually laughed. "That would certainly turn some heads."

Thalia's eyebrows rose, and she struggled to control her expression. Jayn was being… nice. Jayn had more than once forced herself to be more cordial with her teammates—usually after a rebuke from Captain Lahmeer, but those attempts had always come across as exactly that: forced. There was none of the usual awkward stiltedness now as she chatted with Ryn, whose ignorance of the wide world usually had Jayn's eyes rolling. She seemed to be genuinely enjoying herself this evening.

Thalia studied the pair as they resumed their dance. Ryn smiled and did his best to lead, his ears flushing the usual pink, as they always did whenever a girl paid him too much attention. Jayn couldn't be… flirting with him, could she? It seemed laughable. Still, if Thalia didn't know anything about them or their personalities, if she saw them as a pair of strangers dancing and smiling together, she had to admit, they made a nice-looking couple. Ryn wasn't tall for a man, but he had several inches on the slim and slight Jayn. Both had fair complexions and sandy blond hair, though Jayn's eyes were a sky blue to Ryn's forest green.

Thalia didn't know why that made her stomach feel unsettled. It couldn't be jealousy. She had mixed feelings about the boy who had saved her life, but none of them were romantic. She thought about the dagger still stored in her room, the gift she had made for Ryn that, for some reason, she could not find a way to give to him.

She shook her head and turned her attention to the other pair of dancers. They seemed to be having the opposite problems. Pavel was an impressive dancer. Shilo, though she had been just as ignorant as Ryn about high-society waltzes, had a natural grace and knew how to follow a lead. The pair flowed effortlessly through each step and turn, as if they'd danced together for years. Yet neither smiled or even looked at each other. A palpable tension hung between them. Thalia didn't know why Shilo might be angry with Pavel. She would have to talk to her later. Pavel naturally made people angry, yet something seemed to be bothering him too. While Shilo pointedly avoided looking at him, Pavel's attention seemed turned inward. He didn't even bat an eye when Ryn suggested they dance together. Thalia sighed and lay back on Jayn's bed, staring up at the white scalloped ceiling.

"I talked to him the other day," Ryn said. Apparently, they'd finished another form. "The ambassador, I mean."

Thalia sat up.

"What?" Jayn asked. "When?"

"I just ran into him in the hall. His room is right next to mine. We only talked for a minute. I know we're supposed to avoid him, but I didn't want to be rude either."

Shilo and Pavel had stopped dancing to listen.

"Did he say anything about why he's here?" Jayn asked.

"Not exactly. He told me he was also worried about the Kobolds, and then he said he was 'on the side of peace' or something like that."

"The side of peace? Really?"

"Is that hard to believe?" Shilo asked. In the past two months, Shilo had become a lot more talkative, especially when it was just the five of them alone together.

"Coming from a Tamorine ambassador? That would be a first." Jayn looked at Pavel. "What do you think, Pavel? You have a head for politics."

The lanky Aether Weaver shrugged. "Could be empty rhetoric."

Jayn sighed. "I also learned something interesting the other day. I ran into an old… friend. He's a Warden here now."

"A Warden?" Ryn asked. "Those are the guys in the blue and white uniforms?"

"Yes," Jayn said. Sensing a follow-up question, she explained, "The Wardens are all highly trained Wave Weavers who work to defend the Hall. They're kind of like a city guard, but their only job is to protect the Grand Hall, the lords and ladies of the Assembly, and the Pentarchs. They also protect the valuable artifacts and Runeforms stored here. My old friend Jax told me that they've stepped up security around the Runeform vault, especially after so many were stolen from Falport."

"So many?" Pavel asked. "What are you saying?"

Jayn nodded. "I've thought it over. Jax wasn't lying. Multiple Runeforms were stolen, not just the mirror. If we didn't hear about it before, if the masters were able to keep it quiet, then it had to be—"

"The unsorted ones."

Shilo finally looked directly at Pavel, her forehead wrinkled in confusion.

Pavel glanced at her. "Not all Runeforms have a clear purpose. The Watchkeepers have a bunch they've collected over the years that they don't know what to do with, so they chucked them into storage. I never could figure out where they were kept, but..."

Pavel seemed eager to take on this new puzzle, putting aside whatever else had been weighing on his mind. He mulled it over for a minute before nodding. "I think you are right on the money, Jayn, which explains why the masters kept the theft quiet. It fits a few other pieces, like what happened to the smithy."

"The smithy?" Thalia asked. "What do you mean?"

"Blowing it up was rather dramatic. We assumed it was just so Kobolds could breach the wall. Except the Kobolds also breached the front door pretty easily. The building across from the smithy, the one that got blasted open and where we tried to hide from Kalo, what if that was where they kept the Runeforms?"

"Maybe," Thalia said. "Master Caston never did figure out what they used to blow the smithy. You think they wanted to pulverize the storage building too?"

"It's kind of clever," Pavel said. "The blast destroyed so much of the building, that anything found in the rubble that was still intact..."

"Had to be an indestructible Runeform," Jayn finished.

Ryn frowned. "Why would they want to steal useless Runeforms though? You think the Kobolds actually know how to use them?"

"The Manfaces must," Pavel said.

"Are we really calling them that?" Jayn asked.

"You got a better name?"

"Or the humans know," Thalia said, remembering the strange Pentad she had seen in that warehouse. "We still don't know who these people are who seem to be working with the Kobolds and the… Manfaces."

Shilo crossed her arms and seemed to shiver. "We know Gwen Hinter is one of them."

The group fell silent for a time, as often happened, when they contemplated the various mysteries that still plagued their lives.

"Blowing up the smithy…" Ryn said after a minute. "Do you think it has any connection to blowing up that bridge?"

Thalia had completely forgotten about the destroyed bridge, the one that had forced their traveling group to reroute through Wydhaven. When the thieves had first struck the inn, her group had speculated that the robbers may have blown the bridge to draw in more victims. Having met Sara, Ansel, and Clay, that no longer seemed likely. Thalia shook her head. "They don't really compare. Blowing up the bridge would be easy. To make a bomb, you need some base material that ignites quickly, so quickly in fact that the reaction is explosive. Just pack some blasting powder into a metal or clay container and attach a long enough wick that you can get to safety before the flame hits the powder.

"Whatever blew the smithy was more complicated. Master Caston traced the blast back to the main furnace, which had been fired that day. Tossing a simple bomb into a hot furnace would set it off immediately, so the bomber would have been caught in the explosion. Pavel was right near the furnace when it blew, and he didn't see anyone, so the bomb had to be in the furnace already, for at least a minute, assuming Pavel just missed the bomber, but probably longer. There are substances that on their own don't react to heat, but when mixed together can react explosively. Maybe a two-chambered device with a metal plate in between that eventually melted, causing the chemicals to mix… Either way, compared to blowing the smithy, blowing that bridge was child's play. There also doesn't seem to be any reason why the bridge was destroyed. Probably it was just a bored farm boy with easy access to fertilizer."

Ryn's eyes widened. "You can make a bomb with fertilizer?"

Thalia shrugged. "That and some Stone Weaving."

Jayn sighed. "It's getting late. We still have tomorrow night to practice our waltzes before Summer Feast. We can keep speculating, or we can practice our Weaving, like we're supposed to."

"Sure," Thalia said. "Same routine? All Five Forces? All together?"

Jayn nodded. "Let's start with Flame."

Shilo felt like an idiot as she stumbled through the busy streets of Appencourt, trying not to run into anyone, her cheeks still burning from shame. She should have stayed in the Grand Hall. She almost had. It took all the courage she could muster to track down Master Stoats, the steward of the Hall, and ask him whether she could invite a guest to the Summer Feast. Her dress had arrived that morning, a day before the ball. She was glad to see it was fairly modest, though much fancier than any she had ever worn. The silk fabric was a vibrant red. For some reason, seeing that dress had made her think of Rav Montare.

She wasn't supposed to go into the city alone. Captain Lahmeer had been clear about that. Still, she couldn't bring herself to ask Thalia or Jayn to go with her. After much deliberation, she decided to go anyway. By then, it was late into the afternoon. If she had encountered Captain Lahmeer or any of her Pentad members, Shilo would have turned right around and given up on the idea. But she saw no one on her way down the stairs and out of the Hall.

The courtyard below stood empty, and no one stopped her from crossing over the red wooden bridge into the Foreign Quintant. The bridge looked especially red that day, as if freshly painted, and it reminded her again of the bright red dress hanging in her room.

She'd found the mission fairly easily, though she only half remembered Rav's instructions. The building was small and plastered white like all the rest. She'd asked a woman who seemed to belong to the place about Rav, and the woman directed her to the soup kitchen, where a steady stream of bedraggled citizens stood in line or sat hunched over tables, scraping wooden bowls with wooden spoons. Rav waved when he saw her but was clearly too busy to talk. Shilo asked another Scribe if she could help, and after a few questions, they put Shilo to work in the kitchen. A couple hours later, Rav found her there, scrubbing out a massive pot with the sleeves of her white baggy shirt turned up.

They exchanged a few pleasantries, and then Shilo took a deep breath. She'd rehearsed what she wanted to say but forgot everything as soon as she opened her mouth. She stumbled through her words. "So, I did ask. About the Summer Feast, I mean, and the ball at the Grand Hall. I don't know if you were still interested, but we are allowed to bring guests. I would love for you to come. As my guest."

He smiled, but only slightly. "I am honored, really, Miss Lorn," he said. "As much as I enjoyed traveling with you and your Pentad, I don't think I can make it this time. I hope you understand."

She nodded, mumbled something in response, and then quickly left. She shouldn't have asked him like that. It sounded like she had asked him to go with her as a date. He must have interpreted it that way at least. Rav Montare, ever kind and respectful, had turned her down in the gentlest way possible. Though only a few years separated them, he was a grown and independent man, and she was still just a girl. That's how he must have seen her. Why did she even want him to go to the ball? Had she wanted it to be a date? It didn't matter now. With any luck, she would never see him again.

She stopped abruptly after nearly colliding with a tall man dressed in black who'd stepped in front of her. He glanced at her then quickly moved away down the street. Shilo watched his retreating form. Lucas Peniter. She had no desire to be near that anti-Weaver agitator, but why had he looked so afraid? The expression on his pale face had stopped her in her tracks more than the near collision. His dark eyes had been hard to read. She definitely saw fear there, but also regret and maybe something more.

She was walking again before she realized it, though she couldn't say why. She had thought more than once over the past few days about Lucas Peniter and his mysterious connection to Pavel. *You took the oath, same as me.* What did that mean? What was going on with Pavel? She certainly hadn't asked him about it. She had made a point of avoiding the man. She dared not approach Peniter either; he was a stranger and not someone she would associate with. Still, something about that look on his face compelled her to follow him down the street, his shoulders drooping as he seemed to hunch in on himself. Maybe she just needed a distraction after the disaster with Rav Montare.

Peniter soon turned off the main road, though the side street was just as broad and nearly as crowded. Shilo had no trouble keeping up with him while maintaining her distance. He seemed to drag his feet. He made a few more turns, and the din of commerce faded, as another sound grew louder, the murmuring of a different crowd. Peniter headed toward that sound, and Shilo slowed her pace, letting him disappear around another corner. She lifted her chin and tried to act like she belonged on that street as she strolled forward.

She didn't see Peniter, but she saw the crowd. The street lay otherwise empty, but a crowd of at least a hundred people stood in the large yard of an inn, clearly waiting for something. She hesitated, but nothing too nefarious could be going on here. Though the innyard seemed isolated, they were still in the heart of the capital. She went and stood at the edge of the crowd, hoping no one would challenge her. A few people glanced at her and an older woman nodded, but no one said anything. In her hand-me-down breeches and white sailor's shirt, Shilo didn't look like a Watchkeeper. She more or less fit in with this crowd, which seemed to be mostly laborers and craftsmen. No one wore silk. The majority were men, with only a few women mixed in. Shilo saw boys her age but no girls.

A few minutes passed. Everyone was clearly waiting for something. She began to wonder if she'd been mistaken and Peniter wasn't here at all. Then she saw him. The inn had a simple wooden stage on the other side of the yard, no doubt for musicians or entertainers. Lucas Peniter strode out alone onto the stage. His eyes scanned the crowd as if searching for something. The gathered onlookers fell quiet without him having to say anything.

He seemed to hesitate before he began his speech. "This meeting will be short, and I'll keep my message brief." His naturally booming voice easily carried across the quiet innyard, though it lacked the fire Shilo had heard when he rode that wagon through the Artisans' Quintant. Peniter looked over the crowd again, his gaze focusing on a few individuals. The onlookers waited in anticipation for him to continue. "I thank you all for your support, but I must announce that I will be withdrawing my candidacy for a seat in the Hall of the Assembly."

The crowd began at once to protest. Their confused voices echoed off the whitewashed walls around them. Peniter didn't try to speak over them. He held out his arms and motioned for them to quiet down. Eventually they did, though he let the silence stretch for several moments before he spoke again.

"I know many of you have placed your hard-won trust in me, and I don't want anyone to think I am letting you down here."

"Did they get to you?" an angry voice in the crowd shouted. Shilo wondered who "they" were in the minds of these people. Weavers? The Watchkeepers? She wanted to slip away but didn't think she could without drawing attention.

Peniter held his hand out toward the man who had spoken, as if to restrain him. "No," he said. As he spoke, conviction began to return to his words. It grew stronger with each sentence. "When I began my campaign for the Hall, I believed it could be changed. My platforms were reasonable. That's how I earned your support. I asked only for long-overdue reforms to curb the undue influence of Lacers over our great nation. I have learned… I cannot tell you how, but I have since learned just how deep the corruption goes. I knew the Lacers would fight back. I knew they would resist the necessary changes. No one wants to give up power, even in the name of equality. But I never suspected how deep the Lacers would stoop."

"Down with Lacers!" someone shouted, and Peniter had to raise his hands again to keep the crowd from taking up the chant.

"Most of you have no doubt heard that an ambassador from Tamor is right here in our city. For an entire week, he has been meeting with the Hall and all five Pentarchs, behind closed doors mind you, away from the eyes of the very public the Hall claims to represent. Why the secrecy? Why not let the good people of Aldria know what is happening?" He fell silent again and let the question echo in the minds of his listeners. He shook his head. "Folks, I have it on good authority, from someone placed within the Hall, that this ambassador, Lorenz Savon, is here not to incite another border conflict, but for the sake of peace."

Several people laughed or muttered in angry disbelief. The people of Aldria had been taught their whole lives that Tamor was an enemy.

"I know," Peniter said, as the crowd fell quiet. "I know it's hard to believe. The truth is, this peace Savon seeks is not any kind we could have hoped for. No, he will settle for nothing less than the complete reunification of Aldria and Tamor. Nonsense, I know. But what baffles me, what chills me to my core, if I'm being honest with you folks, is that the Hall of the Assembly is still listening to this man. They are still considering his proposal."

It took a full minute for the crowd to quiet down again after that revelation. "Why?" Peniter asked, once he had their attention again. "What reason could they have? The emperor may not be a Lacer, but we all know the Lacers control him, just as Lacers control the Hall, just as Lacers control the Pentarchy. I have come to believe that this conspiracy goes all the way to the top, to the Academy of the Ways, that bastion of Lacer power. They have never considered themselves citizens of Aldria. The Scholars call themselves 'citizens of the world.' What does that mean, anyway? Hmm? I'll tell you. It means that the Lacers' goal is nothing less than the complete control of the entire world under their puppet emperor, starting with the reunification of Tamor and Aldria."

Angry shouts broke out again. Peniter didn't quiet the crowd. He merely shouted over them. "I don't know about you folks, but I for one will never bow before a king! I will kneel before no emperor! If that's what the Hall of the Assembly wants, then I can have no part in such a corrupt institution!"

"Down with the Hall!" someone in the crowd shouted. "Down with the Pentarchs!"

Peniter made no move to quiet the crowd, as others took up the chant. "Down with the Hall! Down with the Pentarchs!" Peniter did not join in as the chanting grew louder. His eyes moved back and forth across his disciples, as a sinister smile spread across his face.

Shilo turned and ran. No one moved to stop her. She headed for the main street as the chant echoed and rebounded off the white plaster walls of Appencourt. "Down with the Hall! Down with the Pentarchs! Down with the Hall! Down with the Pentarchs!"

Chapter 21
Summer Feast

RYN PULLED ON THE SLEEVES of his new jacket and tried not to look at the guard down the hall. The suit he'd been given for the Summer Feast was a dark shade of green. The shirt and shoes were black, but everything else was green. He loitered in the hall, waiting for the rest of his group to finish getting dressed and emerge from their separate rooms.

He felt the guard's eyes on him. Obviously, the man in the black and silver uniform would be watching Ryn; part of guarding a door meant staring down anyone who got too close. Ryn couldn't help it that his room was right next to the ambassador's. Lorenz Savon must be inside getting ready for the ball, if his servant was standing sentry. Ryn had not seen the ambassador since that one brief encounter, but one of the two stone-faced servants always seemed to be guarding the hall every time Ryn left his room.

Ryn sighed and wished his friends would hurry up. He was contemplating heading down to the ball on his own, when the first door opened. Thalia emerged from her room, wrapped in a satiny honey-yellow dress. Ryn had heard that the women in Appencourt liked to dress provocatively at Summer Feast, but there was nothing scandalous about Thalia's dress. Cinched at the waist, it showed off her ample figure but didn't cling. The neckline dipped only low enough to show the faintest suggestion of cleavage. She wore a simple copper pendant, probably one she had made herself. For once, her long black hair was not constrained to braids but flowed down her back in wavy curls. She smiled when she saw Ryn. Watchkeeper women didn't typically wear makeup, but Ryn could tell she'd done something to redden her lips and darken her lashes.

"You look great!" he blurted without thinking, then felt his face redden.

Her smile widened, and she lowered her eyes. "Thanks, Ryn. You look rather dashing yourself in that suit."

Ryn self-consciously adjusted the lapels of his jacket. Under Nyssa's advice, he'd pinned his green-leaf badge to the jacket. Thalia also wore her yellow pin, stuck on the left side of her dress, near the thin shoulder strap. "Thanks," he said. "The green is a little much, but…"

"No, it suits you. It brings out your eyes."

He didn't know what to say to that. Thalia's yellow dress did nothing for her dark eyes, though it did seem to lend a glow to her light brown complexion. He was saved from saying anything awkward by the next door opening.

Shilo joined them in the hall. She wore a fiery red dress. While Thalia's gown extended to her ankles, Shilo's came only to her knees. Ryn had never seen her bare legs before, but he forced his eyes upward to her face. The skirt of the dress had an added layer of red lace, and the puffy short sleeves were also wrapped in lace. Her hair hung as it usually did in a cloud of tight ringlets.

"That's a lovely dress," Ryn said, managing a more constrained tone this time.

She thanked him and complimented his suit as well, also mentioning that it seemed to be doing something for his eyes. The girls beamed at each other and exchanged a rapid series of praise for their dresses and sparkly sequined shoes.

Jayn emerged next in a surprisingly simple blue dress, with broad shoulder straps, a square neckline, and no added pleats or frills. She wore a silver necklace with little blue gems and a matching pair of earrings. She'd done something to curl her normally straight hair and piled it into an elegant mound atop her head, while two curly strands framed her face. She wore a lot more makeup than the other two girls, but she clearly knew what she was doing. Ryn had always found her pretty, but she looked truly beautiful all done up like that.

Thalia and Shilo showered her with compliments before Ryn could say anything. They all laughed and smiled as they compared outfits.

"That blue dress really brings out your eyes," Ryn managed to say, which set them all laughing again.

The girls exchanged mischievous looks and suddenly all three turned their focus on him. Thalia moved behind him and started to adjust his collar. Shilo fidgeted with the pin on his lapel, as if trying to straighten it, while Jayn pretended to brush lint off his sleeves. All the while, they gushed over the stylishness of his suit and how handsome it made him look. Ryn felt his ears begin to warm and knew his face had to be beet red. They were doing it on purpose of course, knowing how embarrassed it made him feel, yet he didn't exactly want them to stop.

The girls only relented when Nyssa stepped out of her room, wrapped in a long red dress with slashes of black in the skirts. Her hair hung in tight braids, capped with bright red beads. The ladies murmured more restrained compliments to their captain.

Nyssa smiled. "You three all look lovely," she said, before nodding to Ryn. "That's a smart suit."

Jayn patted Ryn on the shoulder. "It really brings out his eyes," she said, which set her and Thalia off laughing again.

Shilo didn't laugh. She frowned as she looked at Nyssa. "Did you… Did you speak with the city guard?"

"Yes," Nyssa said. "No need to worry about that tonight."

"What happened?" Jayn asked, her eyebrows drawing together.

"Oh, she didn't tell you?" Nyssa asked. A faint smile crossed her lips. Shilo stared at the floor. "Our Shilo went out on her own yesterday. She's the last one of you lot I expected to disregard orders, but there you have it. She overheard some rabble-rouser speaking out against the government."

Shilo glanced at Thalia. "It was that Peniter guy we heard speaking the other day."

Thalia frowned. "I did not like the look of him." She turned to Nyssa. "Is the guard doing something about it?"

Nyssa shrugged. "They are well aware of Lucas Peniter. Part of living in a free country is that people can say just about anything without it being illegal. Until he actually does something, all the guard can do is keep watching him. None of that is our concern though. Let's enjoy ourselves tonight, and hopefully next week we can testify and be back on our way to Falport, yeah?"

Shilo nodded, though she still seemed worried.

All heads swiveled as the final door opened.

"You lot look like a blighted rainbow," Pavel said, stepping out into the hall.

"Shut up, Pavel," Jayn said, with a smile and none of her usual bite. "We all look stunning, and so do you."

Thalia laughed. "The color scheme is a bit… on the nose."

Keeping to the elemental theme, Pavel was decked out in pure white. The suit, the shirt, the cravat, even the belt and shoes were all a pearly white, a stark contrast to his jet-black hair that hung almost to his shoulders and framed his tan face. Pavel smiled. "Let's dance."

They headed first to the dining hall, which had been adorned with colorful drapes and bright floral arrangements. The six Watchkeepers kept mostly to themselves, exchanging a few pleasantries with the lords and ladies and their spouses or children. A slim blonde woman in an elegant black dress greeted them briefly before floating away into the crowd.

"Was that your mother?" Thalia asked Jayn, who nodded.

Ryn craned his neck to get a second look at Anyse Eldragor, Fourth Pentarch of Aldria. Anyse and Jayn did look similar. Anyse smiled at everyone she greeted, but in between she surveyed the crowd with a stern, somewhat severe set to her jaw. Ryn recognized that look. It was the same face Jayn pulled whenever she scolded them for not taking their training more seriously.

The feast portion of the evening consisted of at least five separate courses. Ryn lost track of the revolving buffet of food an army of servants set before them and then whisked away, sometimes before he had even finished eating. They had a salad of mixed summer greens, yeasty bread rolls, trout topped with lemon and capers, roasted lamb, and other dishes he didn't even recognize. When the tray of desserts came around, he snagged a slice of flaky pie filled with tart black berries.

Before he knew it, dinner was over, and they were all invited to the dance. Ryn had expected the ball to be held inside the Hall of the Assembly's large meeting chamber. He still had not seen inside the room, but it seemed like the only space large enough to accommodate hundreds of dancing couples. Instead, the servants ushered them all up to the third floor, down a hallway, and then to another staircase that led up onto the flat roof of the Grand Hall. Ryn didn't know the roof could even be accessed. On the far side, a five-piece band was set up and already playing the first waltz. Tables and chairs were arrayed along the edge of the marble roof for those who needed a break between dances. No railings stood between the dancers and the fifty-foot drop over the side, but the roof afforded so much space that no one needed to dance near the edge. The sun had set, but the five points of the city spreading out around them glowed with thousands of lanterns, candles, and even some Weaver lights, as the whole capital would celebrate the solstice long into the short night.

For the partnered dances, Ryn alternated between Thalia, Shilo, and Jayn, dancing only once with Nyssa. Shilo was the best dancer, though all the women were good. Their height difference made the turns a little tricky when he danced with Thalia. Jayn had the softest hands. He liked the way the girls' skirts flared when they spun, like blossoming flowers. The evening passed in a blur of dancing and laughter. He knew he would collapse in exhaustion when he made it back to his room, but it wouldn't be the usual tiredness after a long day of Watchkeeper training or long hours in a saddle. Could a person be exhausted from happiness?

One moment stood out during that evening on the roof of the Grand Hall. Several of the dances involved the whole party and required frequent partner changes. Those were the most complicated. Ryn danced briefly with various women and girls he didn't know, but he didn't speak to any of them, his whole attention focused on not messing up the complex footwork.

At the start of one such waltz, all the men lined up in a row, facing a row of women. Ryn stood opposite Shilo. He glanced to the left. Pavel had paired up with Nyssa again. He seemed to prefer dancing with her over the younger girls in their group. Ryn glanced to the right. Lorenz Savon offered him a smile and a nod. "Mr. Silverbell," he said. "Good to see you again."

"Mr. Ambassador," Ryn mumbled. He'd caught glimpses of the man from Tamor throughout the evening, but he'd never come close until now.

Lorenz wore a black suit with his usual silver-trimmed red coat. He bowed to Jayn, his partner for the start of the dance. "Miss Eldragor," he said.

Jayn's jaw hung open for a moment before she closed it. "Mr. Ambassador," she said, offering a curtsy.

"Please," he said, taking her hand as the band struck up, "call me Lorenz."

Ryn stumbled through the steps with Shilo. She didn't seem to mind. Both of them were focused on eavesdropping on Jayn's brief interaction with the ambassador.

"You know me?" Jayn asked with stilted politeness.

"I've met with your mother more than once this week. She mentioned her daughter was part of the Watchkeeper Pentad here to speak about Kobolds. You have your mother's beauty."

"You flatter me," Jayn said with a short laugh. After a pause, she added, "I hope you didn't try flattery with my mother."

Lorenz laughed, deep and genuine. While Jayn spoke with deliberate pleasantness, the ambassador's words flowed naturally and smoothly. "I think myself wiser than that. I know Anyse Eldragor is a formidable woman, not to be trifled with."

"If you spoke with my mother, then am I to assume your visit here relates to our countries' border?"

"Oh-ho, I see I am not to trifle with you either, Miss Eldragor. I don't know that your mother would want me telling you too much though. The negotiations are at a crucial juncture."

"You told Ryn you are here on the side of peace. I hope that is the case."

"I give you my word. I see a bright future for both our great nations."

Then the song changed and Lorenz moved down the line to the next woman. Ryn gave Jayn a questioning look as he turned to face her. She only shrugged before taking his hand. Ryn cycled through all the women he knew and several strangers before the song finally ended. He nodded politely to his final partner, a rosy-cheeked girl about his age in a clinging black dress he struggled not to look at too closely, and turned to find his friends.

He saw Thalia seated at the edge of the dance floor, trying to catch her breath and sipping water from a crystal glass. He plopped into the cushioned chair beside her. She smiled and opened her mouth to say something, but just then a loud pop sounded overhead. Ryn looked up to see a shower of red sparks illuminate the cloudy sky. For a panicked moment, he worried they would rain down on the dancers, but the lights fizzled out and disappeared. He glanced at Thalia, but another pop and flash of light, this one blue, drew his eyes back to the sky.

Fireworks, he realized. He had heard about fireworks but never seen them before. They were amazing. The dancers all stopped to stare up at the sky and applaud, as more loud pops and showers of sparks filled the night, lighting up the overcast and moonless sky.

Ryn looked at Thalia, her face still turned upward, with a joyful smile on her lips. Her dark eyes might not be enhanced by the colors she wore, but they made excellent mirrors for the bright fireworks.

She looked down and grinned. She leaned over, pressing her shoulder into his so he could hear her over the din of the party. "The Lightsmith Guild, that's what they call themselves," she said. "Master Caston told me about them. They're all Stone Weavers who specialize in fireworks."

"It's amazing," he said, returning her smile.

Shilo found them then. All nearby chairs were occupied, so she stood behind Thalia, resting a hand on her shoulder. Thalia smiled up at her friend and placed her hand atop Shilo's. Jayn drifted over and stood by Ryn. She leaned against his chair and rested her arm on his shoulder.

Touch. Ryn still wasn't used to this kind of friendly affection, which came so naturally and casually to the girls. He had vague memories of his mother holding him as a child, but he couldn't remember if Aunt Marla had ever actually touched him. There had been no slaps, but no comforting pets or hugs either. His friends were quick to pat him on the back when he did well in a training exercise or squeeze his hand when he was struggling. Even Pavel had that silly group handshake he liked to make them do. Still, even after more than two months of exposure, the slightest touch from anyone still made Ryn flush and set his heart to racing.

Just don't overthink it, Ryn told himself. Thalia's free arm and shoulder still rested against him. Slowly, he reached out and took her hand in his. She glanced down but said nothing and returned her eyes to the sky, still smiling. The low clouds must have kept the smoke from rising, and it filled the rooftop, making everything seem hazy and unfocused. The shimmering blue dome of Wave that encompassed the Grand Hall added to the beauty of the scene. Thalia squeezed his hand and shifted to lean more fully against him. Thalia's stature came from her long legs, but sitting down they were the same height.

The rest of the evening passed like a pleasant dream. When it was done, Ryn stumbled back to his room with bleary eyes and sore feet. He peeled off his jacket and shoes before collapsing onto his bed, a smile still on his face. He awoke to a nightmare.

It started like a shiver that didn't stop. Ryn struggled back to consciousness, as a tingling sensation permeated his whole body. It felt familiar, like… Dowsing. A heavy weight settled on his chest. His eyes shot open. A figure towered over him, a man dressed in black, with a cloth covering the lower half of his face. Hands wrapped around Ryn's throat. He struggled to get free, but his arms were pinned at his side beneath the man's knees.

The room seemed to flicker as dark shapes swirled around Ryn. Lacings appeared as streaks of colored light to those who could see them, but unlike real light, they provided no illumination to their surroundings. In the near-pitch-black bedroom, Ryn couldn't even tell what color the lacings were, but he knew it had to be Root, which was… strange.

His attacker was clearly Dowsing him, but why? Dowsing was a precursor to healing. Ryn realized that despite the iron grip the man had on his neck, he could still breathe. The man wasn't squeezing hard enough to actually choke him. What was happening? Ryn's mind raced, yet his body felt strangely subdued. Ryn became aware of his own heartbeat. It should have been thumping madly, but it wasn't. It seemed to be… slowing down.

Ryn had learned a lot about healing during the long week of triage following the Kobold attack on Falport. If a patient's heart beat too quickly, it could sometimes seize up, so Ryn had learned lacings to slow the heart rate. He'd been warned multiple times never to slow a patient's heart too far. Was Ryn's attacker trying to make his heart stop? *When the heart stops beating, death quickly follows.* Master Pembrim's words echoed in Ryn's mind. He remembered something else the Root master had said, about Root Weaver assassins. *Tamorine Death Weavers.*

If this man stopped his heart, could Ryn's Etching start it up again before the rest of his body died? It didn't feel like dying. It felt like falling back to sleep. A small part of his mind told him he had to stay awake. He couldn't fight back. He was too weak. He didn't have any knives on him. Stone trumped Root. He thought it did, anyway. Ryn had tried to practice Stone. They all had. Thalia could wield it, of course, and Jayn and Pavel could do it a little, enough to break Root. It only took a little bit. He and Shilo had yet to make any amount of yellow light spark from their hands, however. He couldn't do it. He was going to die. He listened to his heartbeats, the gaps between them getting longer. He didn't know which one would be his last.

The Watchkeepers kept telling Ryn how talented he was, and how he had this vast capacity for Root Weaving. Yet he was about to die from Root Weaving. It was almost funny. Dowsing a person gave you insight into every aspect of their being—their body, their mind, maybe even their soul. It always felt so intimate. How could this assassin wrap his mind around Ryn's, see the complexity of his humanity, and still want to kill him? Could Ryn do something like that? He tried.

Ryn's body was failing. His mind couldn't focus. That didn't matter. Root Weaving came from somewhere else, a separate place, a reservoir within the body but not affected by the body, and Ryn's reservoir was deep. He knew he was stronger than his attacker.

After months of honing his skill, the Root tree bloomed around him in an instant. It filled the whole room. He wrapped its branches around his killer, not really sure what he was going to do.

He had never Dowsed someone who was Dowsing him before, and the experience was wildly disorienting. First a web of green lights appeared in Ryn's mind, each strand representing part of the man's being. A few flickered yellow. Crouching atop Ryn caused the man some slight physical discomfort. The white glow at the center seemed dimmer than it should, but not like when someone was dying.

Almost against his will, Ryn's attention was pulled to a mass of green threads near the center. This, he realized, was the part only Weavers had, which lit up when they were making lacings. He followed those threads, and the image in his mind suddenly doubled, as another consciousness sprung into view—his own. He'd somehow followed the man's Dowsing back into his own mind. Then it felt like he was falling down an endless stairwell, each floor passing by in a flash of light, or like seeing a million reflections in a hallway lined with mirrors, his Dowsing cycling back and forth between them in an infinite loop.

The man must have felt it too. He groaned and reeled backward, his hands slipping from Ryn's throat and his lacings dissolving. Ryn tried to press his advantage. His Root tree had stayed. He Dowsed the man again. The heartbeat was easy to find, going fast but still a healthy green. Ryn tried to remember the lacings. If he could slow the man's heart, maybe he could get away.

The Death Weaver reared backward and slapped Ryn full force across the face. The sharp burst of pain severed Ryn's tree. Then the hands were at his throat again, and his body tingled as the Dowsing resumed. Suddenly, the pain in his face vanished, the red swelling dissipating. The man had healed him… but why?

Ryn felt his pounding heart already begin to slow again. The few seconds he'd earned of accelerated rhythm had pushed much-needed blood back into his brain, and he could think a little more clearly, though he knew it wouldn't last. He could Dowse his attacker again, but the man would be ready this time and would recover faster. He could prolong the fight, but he couldn't win it that way. Root was out. He couldn't make Stone. That left…

Some forces opposed each other. Normally, Aether would dissolve on contact with Root. Some forces loved to mix, however. He remembered all the times he'd practiced Blending Root and Flame with Shilo. He supplied the Root and Shilo absorbed it into her lacings. He didn't have to try to make them Blend; the Root leapt of its own accord into the Flame, almost eagerly. Ryn envisioned a small flame inside his chest. It took more focused effort than Root to form, but soon streaks of dark fire burst from his torso. The attacker looked down in confusion as his lacings leapt into the Flame. Ryn only knew one lacing that mixed Root and Flame.

He screwed his eyes shut just before a brilliant white light filled the room. Weavers usually created lights from their hands, but they didn't have to. Ryn's light emerged from his chest, flaring up between him and his attacker. The man reeled back again, shocked and blinded. Ryn had anticipated the reaction. Digging his elbows into the bed, Ryn shot up, ramming the top of his head into the man's chest and shoving him back. The man fell away, hit the wooden footboard, and rolled off the side. Ryn's blob of light rose to the ceiling and stuck there.

Ryn scrambled out of the bed, his head still spinning, and stared down at the black-clad attacker, who lay groaning on the floor with his eyes closed. In the light of his orb, Ryn could see the man actually wore black livery, trimmed in silver. Ryn glanced at the wooden footboard again. If the man had fallen on that and hit his neck or back…

"Don't move," Ryn said, holding out his hands. "I think you may have damaged your spine."

The man stopped groaning. He opened his eyes and looked up at Ryn. Then he laughed. "You are a good kid," he said in a clear Tamorine accent. "You think like a healer, but you can't heal everything."

Ryn heard a crunch, like the man had bitten down on something. The man's eyes rolled back in his head, showing only white, and he began gurgling. Ryn dropped to his knees and pulled back the cloth obscuring the man's mouth. He knew already he would recognize the ambassador's bodyguard. The man's mouth hung open, white foam bubbling out. Ryn Dowsed him, but the assassin was already dead. Poison. He'd killed himself. He must have had some kind of capsule in his mouth, maybe even a false tooth, filled with poison, so he could never be captured alive.

Ryn staggered to his feet and looked around the room. He was alone. Everything looked normal, other than the dead body at his feet. Outside the narrow window, rain began to patter against the glass. *Only those who have tasted deadly poison and lived…* His mind ricochetted around his skull, not settling on any clear thoughts. He took a deep breath and sighed. One of Ambassador Lorenz Savon's personal bodyguards was a Root Weaver, a Tamorine Death Weaver, who had just tried to assassinate Ryn in the strangest way possible. He needed to wake someone up. Probably everyone. He would start with Captain Nyssa Lahmeer.

Chapter 22
The Rain

THE POUNDING NOISE ENTERED into Jayn's dream—something pleasant about dancing on clouds with a man in red—and forced her back into consciousness. She groaned. She had no idea how long she'd been asleep, but based on how tired she felt, it still had to be the middle of the night. Someone kept knocking on her door.

"Up and out!" Captain Lahmeer yelled. Nyssa kept knocking on her door.

"All right!" Jayn called as loudly as she could. The pounding stopped, though it picked up again down the hall, on someone else's door. Jayn heard rain outside her window and the distant rumble of thunder.

It seemed to take her a long time to get up and out. She struggled to pull the covers back and sat on the edge of the bed for a moment, her mind still groggy. Apparently, something was happening outside. She stood up, her legs still sore from all the dancing she'd done. She looked around the dark room and then shuffled to the closet. She remembered the last time she'd been forced outside in the middle of the night and didn't want to rush out in just her lacy shift again, not here in the Grand Hall. She found her gray Watchkeeper shirt by touch and pulled it on, not bothering to do up the buttons. She didn't have the wherewithal to manage pants or shoes just then, so that would have to do.

She stumbled out barefoot into the dim hallway and felt as if she'd entered another dreamscape, both familiar and strange. A dozen Wardens in blue and white loitered up and down the corridor, but they didn't seem to be doing anything. She saw Jax Centillion down near the distant corner. Someone still pounded on one of the doors, but it was the steward, Laren Stoats, not Nyssa. She saw Ryn and the other girls huddled together. Something must have happened to Ryn. He stared at the floor with a blank expression. Thalia had a comforting arm draped around him, while Shilo held his hand. Ryn's face was white, rather than the usual red. He still wore his pants and shirt from the night before, while both girls had thrown on their gray tabards over their white shifts.

Jayn shuffled past them. She raised an eyebrow, but none of her friends met her gaze. The servants kept only a few distant sconces lit at night to provide a little illumination to the windowless hallway, but bright light poured from an open doorway near the corner, next to the closed door where Stoats was still knocking. Jayn drifted toward the light, drawn like a moth. She thought it must have been Ryn's room.

Inside, she saw two people crouching over a body on the floor. A strange blob-like Weaver light on the ceiling cast a harsh glow across the room. Nyssa glanced up. Jayn recognized the man with her as Cole Grondor, the head of the Wardens, a lean older man with dark hair and a bushy mustache. The man on the floor wore the dark livery of the ambassador's bodyguards.

Jayn looked left. The steward's insistent pounding finally made sense. That was the ambassador's room. Nyssa and Grondor brushed past Jayn, apparently also alarmed by the unanswered knocks. Stoats gave up on the door and turned to face them, a frown spread across his wrinkled face. "No one is answering," he said. "It's bolted from the inside."

"We may have to force the door," Grondor said, his voice deep and gravelly.

"Wait," Thalia said, coming up behind them. "I can do it."

Grondor glanced at Nyssa.

"She's our Stone Weaver," the captain explained. No lock could keep a Stone Weaver out.

Grondor nodded. He and Stoats stepped aside, while Thalia approached the door. Shilo joined them, leading Ryn by the hand. The Root Weaver still seemed out of it. What had happened to him? Why was there a dead Tamorine bodyguard in his room? If Ryn had been forced to kill the man, that would explain his current state. Ryn had never killed anyone, human or Kobold.

The door popped open with a snap. Thalia stepped aside. Grondor led the way in, but Stoats and the Watchkeepers all followed. Without being asked, Shilo created a Weaver light and sent it up to the ceiling. Jayn's bedroom, closet, and bathroom could all have fit in this first spacious entry room, empty except for velvet couches and an eating area.

Grondor moved quickly to the far side, where a set of double doors hung partly open. He glanced at Nyssa, who drew her sword. Nyssa had to be quite skilled at dressing quickly in the dark, as she wore her full Watchkeeper uniform, complete with tabard and pin. Grondor threw open the door, and Nyssa stepped inside. Her eyes scanned the interior for a moment. Then she sighed and put up her blade. "Light, Shilo," she said.

Shilo stepped into the room and sent another light up to the ceiling. The others filed in after her, including several Wardens who had joined the group. A large four-poster bed dominated the room. The heavily embroidered curtains were all drawn back, and a lone figure lay atop the sheets. Lorenz Savon's mouth hung open, his eyes staring blankly at nothing. The ambassador was dead.

Grondor muttered an oath. He turned toward his Wardens. "Search the rest of the suite. Search the whole building. Look for the other servant or anything else suspicious."

The Wardens nodded their agreement and fanned out. Jayn tried to remember what the other bodyguard looked like. She couldn't quite remember the woman's face, but she'd been tall, with dark hair and the olive complexion common in Tamor.

Grondor turned to the Watchkeepers. "It's time for the lad to talk," he said to Nyssa, while gesturing toward Ryn.

Jayn noticed that Pavel had slipped into the room behind them, wearing his Watchkeeper grays without the tabard. His eyes scanned the room greedily, but he said nothing. Ryn seemed to snap out of his funk. His distracted gaze focused on the ambassador's body. He took a few steps toward the bed. A Root tree sprung up around him, sending branches out toward Savon. Jayn didn't know you could Dowse a dead body.

"No wounds," Ryn muttered. He turned toward Nyssa. "He wasn't stabbed. He wasn't poisoned."

"Then how'd he die?" Nyssa asked, her voice soft. Clearly, she could tell Ryn was still shaken after whatever happened in his bedroom.

"The same way I almost did." Ryn turned to Grondor. "That man, he came into my room, and he attacked me. I fought back. I wasn't trying to kill him. I think he poisoned himself. I pushed him off, and he hurt his back on the edge of the bed, I think."

Grondor held out a hand to stop Ryn's muttered torrent of words. "Slow down. How did he attack you? You don't look wounded."

Ryn's hand drifted toward his neck. Jayn noticed red marks there. "The man was a Root Weaver. He tried to… I think he was trying to use a lacing to make my heart stop beating."

"Stopping your heart with Root?" Grondor asked. "What, like a Death Weaver?"

"Surely that's just a myth," Stoats asked. The steward shook his head in disbelief.

"Apparently not," Grondor said with a shrug. "But why? Why would the ambassador's own bodyguard kill him and then try to kill a Watchkeeper?"

Pavel stepped forward and looked down at the body. "Two corpses without mark or injury," he said. "You stop their hearts and then you can pose them however you like. Probably they wanted to make it seem like you killed Savon and then the guards killed you. That is your knife, isn't it, kid?" He gestured toward a bare blade on the bedside table. Jayn hadn't even noticed it.

Shilo gasped. Ryn's eyes widened. He nodded. "How did they…"

"They're very good at what they do," Pavel said. "It's a good thing they didn't doctor up this body first, or you would be royally cursed, kid." He shook his head, looking down at the corpse again. "It makes you wonder how many politicians who died peacefully in their sleep were actually assassinated. This poor fool probably didn't even know his own servants were Death Weavers, though maybe the woman was a Stone Weaver, if she could bolt the door from the outside. Still, why kill him now?" He turned to Grondor. "Was Savon really here seeking peace?"

Grondor opened his mouth but hesitated. He shook his head. "It's not my place to say, sorry."

"Let's assume he was. Maybe the Death Weaver found out, and maybe Death Weavers don't like peace. Or maybe the emperor found out what kind of stunt Savon was trying to pull here and sent the order down himself somehow. If the emperor doesn't want peace and wants an excuse to start a war, an Aldrian Watch-keeper killing the prince would be a strong provocation, but would Lemuel really have his own son killed?"

"The prince?" Thalia asked in disbelief.

Grondor's brow furled. "How did you know?"

Jayn looked at the corpse again. The ambassador was the emperor's son? She had danced with a Tamorine prince? A dead prince was very bad news for Aldria, even if the two servants hadn't succeeded in framing Ryn. Why had they picked him? Was it just because Ryn's room was next door to the ambassador's? Did Pavel's theory make sense? Lorenz Savon had shown up in the capital, unannounced and unexpected. She couldn't remember the Tamorine prince's actual name, but she knew it wasn't Lorenz. The emperor didn't use a second name, but the first emperor's name had been Savonoy. If the prince entered Aldria in secret under an assumed name, then maybe the emperor hadn't known about it. Lemuel II had yet to name any of his several children as the heir, so maybe the prince had attempted something bold to secure the crown. If he had brokered peace with Aldria, something most parties considered impossible, if he had found a way to restore Tamor's access to the rich Maer trade routes without Mirk-walder middlemen—such a coup would have earned him the love of the people, and Lemuel II would have been forced to name him as heir, even if he privately favored another child. Even if the emperor would have preferred war. He might get one now.

Pavel didn't answer Grondor's question. Clearly, his mind had gone down the same dark road as hers. Grondor shook his head and turned to the only Warden still in the room, standing at attention and awaiting further orders. "We'll need to roust the lords and the Pentarchs. They should all be in the city still."

None of the government officials slept in the Grand Hall. Like Jayn's mother, they all kept apartments in the northern part of the city. Stoats and Grondor followed the Warden out of the room, leaving the Watchkeepers alone with the corpse. Ryn eyed his knife on the table but didn't touch it. Nyssa looked at them. "Right, everyone get dressed. No one is sleeping tonight."

Just then a series of booms sounded outside, as the narrow windows rattled in their casements. It didn't exactly sound like the rumble of thunder or the sharp pops the fireworks had made. Thalia, who stood closest, moved quickly to the window and peered out into stormy darkness. She looked back, her eyes wide. "I think someone just blew up the bridges."

"What's happening?" Jayn asked as Nyssa entered her room. They had all wanted to follow the captain out into the night, but she had ordered them to get dressed and stay put until she had a chance to talk with the head Warden and find out what was happening. They'd all put on their gray uniforms and grabbed their weapons, only to sit and wait in Jayn's room for nearly half an hour before Nyssa returned.

"It's not Kobolds," Nyssa said. No one had suggested that, but they were all thinking it.

"What then?" Thalia asked.

Nyssa shook her head. “Some kind of riot up in the Civic Quintant. A mob of civilians are trying to force their way into buildings. The Wardens and the city guard are on their way to deal with it now.”

“Civilians blew the bridges?” Thalia asked.

“All of them at once,” Nyssa said. “Maybe to try and trap the Wardens here in the Hall. The folks must not have known about shield bridges.”

“The Civic Quintant?” Jayn asked. “They must be going after my mother and the lords of the Hall.” She fought to keep fear from her voice.

Thalia glanced at Shilo. “Maybe it’s Peniter and that crowd you heard him riling up.”

“Maybe,” Shilo said. She turned and glared at Pavel for some reason.

He didn’t notice. He tilted his head, as if listening for something. “Blowing bridges… It’s too coordinated to be random mob violence, and it can’t be a coincidence that this is happening the same night the prince was killed. No, there’s something more going on here.”

Jayn shot to her feet. “I’m going to find my mother,” she said.

Nyssa still stood in the doorway. She raised a restraining hand. “Wait. It’s dark. It’s raining. The guards and Wardens can handle whatever this is.”

“What if Pavel’s right though?” Jayn fired back. “What if something else is going on here? Six Watchkeepers might make a difference out there.”

Nyssa shook her head. “You’re wearing those pins, but you’re not even halfway trained. It’s too chaotic out there. We’re talking about fighting civilians, not Kobolds, but you could still get killed by a randomly thrown brick. Worst yet, if one of you killed a citizen, even one who is rioting, it would still tarnish the Watchkeeper name. Going out there is not the smart play. If these are anti-Weaver agitators, then it's definitely not our place either. There won't be any rogues out there."

Jayn wouldn't back down. "My mother is out there."

"Your mother is a combat-trained Flame Weaver. She'll be fine."

"Wait," Thalia said, stepping between them. She cast an imploring look at Jayn that told her to stop arguing, then she turned to Nyssa. "What if I could guarantee that nothing bad will happen to any of us out there and none of us will cause any accidental harm?" She reached into her pocket and produced a small velvet purse.

Nyssa frowned. "What are those? Did you bring luck charms?"

Thalia nodded. "I didn't think we would need them, but…"

Nyssa sighed. She screwed her eyes shut and massaged her temples. "That… might actually work."

It wasn't a yes, but Jayn would take it. She held out her hand toward Thalia. The Stone Weaver gave her an unadorned copper ring, which she slipped over her finger. The others crowded in to get one too, even Ryn, who seemed to have recovered from his previous shock. The others had reassured him more than once that he was not responsible for the assassin's death. Thalia put a ring on her own finger and held another out toward Nyssa. "Captain?" she said.

Nyssa stared at the ring for a long moment before shaking her head. "I make my own luck," she said with a half-smile. "We stick together. You do everything I tell you, without question. Disarm and disable. Don't get in the way of any of the guards or Wardens. Am I clear?"

"Yes, ma'am," they all said, nearly in unison.

***

Jayn made a shield bridge with Thalia's help, and they all slid over the ornate moat. Forming such a lacing beneath the Grand Hall would have normally been impossible with the layered sealing ward, but the Wardens had taken the whole dome down to make their own exit. That left the Hall vulnerable, but no one seemed to be trying to attack it. The broad parks surrounding the city center all looked deserted. Sounds of fighting came only from the north.

All five bridges had indeed been destroyed. Bits of wood floated in the water, still somehow burning, despite the steady rain that continued to fall. Had the bridges been sprayed with some kind of flammable or explosive compound? The floating bits of flame in the bubbling moat added to the surreal feeling of that whole night. Jayn wondered if she was perhaps still dreaming. She gripped the hilt of the sword at her waist. This was real.

She crossed the shield bridge last, sliding silently over the water and climbing quickly back to her feet. She reached back and dissolved the lacings with a touch. She nodded to the others, and they followed Nyssa into the darkness.

They advanced at a quick walk. Running in the dark would be reckless. Some Summer Feast parties could last until daybreak, but the rain must have put a damper on them, in the Civic Quintant at least. All the buildings they passed stood quiet and dark.

A Warden standing in the middle of the street heard their footsteps and turned, raising a stout baton in challenge. It made sense they wouldn't be using blades against citizens. He saw their uniforms and lowered his weapon. "Hail Watchkeepers," he said.

Beyond him, half a dozen other Wardens stood over a row of men and women in commoners' clothes, all lying face down with their hands bound behind their back. A man in a white city guard tabard dragged another rioter out of the shadows and threw him down with the others. The rioters' weapons lay strewn across the ground, mostly broken pieces of furniture or lengths of pipe, with a few knives and even a blacksmith's hammer.

Nyssa surveyed the scene. "We wanted to see if we could lend a hand," she said, "but you seem to have things under control here."

The Warden shrugged. "This sector anyway. You should find Commander Grondor. I heard they might have breached some of the houses further down."

Nyssa nodded and led her team down the road. They caught the tail end of another fight. Half a dozen city guards were taking on twice as many rioters. One guard was down, but most of the rioters had already been subdued. Following Nyssa's lead, Jayn didn't draw her sword. The only one in their group who didn't have a bladed weapon was Shilo, who carried her staff.

One of the rioters broke free and tried to rush past the Watchkeepers. Shilo lowered her staff and reached out as if to grab him. Her fingers just barely grazed his arm, but it was enough. The numbing lacing dropped him like a sack of potatoes. A guard jogged over and nodded in thanks. "That one got away from me," he said. "Lucky you were here."

Jayn smiled. Lucky indeed.

Ryn stopped to quickly heal the injured guard, and then they pressed on, but everywhere the fighting seemed to already be over. The rioting citizens had broken into some of the houses. They didn't know if any of the lords of the Hall had been hurt, but it seemed like the attackers had all fled or been arrested. They found Commander Grondor with ten of his men, standing before a narrow building with a broken front door.

Jayn knew the building. "That's my mother's apartment," she said, jogging forward to reach the commander. "What's going on?"

He turned and sighed when he saw her. Of course, he knew who she was. Before she could ask another question, he grabbed her arm. He squeezed too hard and looked her directly in the eye. "Do not go in there, Jayn. Lucas Peniter is in there with two dozen of his cronies. They've taken your mother hostage."

"What?" Jayn couldn't believe what she was hearing. "That can't be. My mother is a Flame Weaver. They couldn't have taken her."

"They could if they hit her over the head while she was sleeping. Weavers are still human."

Nyssa came up beside her, the others in tow. "Commander?" she asked.

He looked at her but kept his tight grip on Jayn. She resented it. "I spotted Lucas Peniter in the crowd. He seems to be the one giving out orders. We tried to capture him, but he and his group fell back into that building. The door was already busted open. We tried to follow, but then Peniter stuck his head out the second-story window and said they had Anyse Eldragor inside. He threatened to kill her if we got any closer. That was maybe ten minutes ago. We haven't heard a sound since."

Jayn shook his grip, but she didn't head for the building. She took a few stumbling steps away, trying to clear her head. Who was this Peniter guy? Apparently, he hated Weavers. He wasn't a Weaver then, and none of his followers could be Weavers. How had they overpowered her mother? What was happening? Did this have anything to do with the ambassador? Weavers killed the prince. If Peniter hated Weavers, then he couldn't be working with them, could he? She thought about the two dead bodies she'd seen already that night. Her mother had to be all right. Powerless lower-echelon filth like Peniter couldn't harm Anyse Eldragor, a general in the Standing Army and Fourth Pentarch of Aldria.

Someone put a hand on Jayn's shoulder. "It will be all right," Thalia said.

"They have my mother," Jayn said and hated the fear she heard in her own voice.

"Exactly," Thalia said.

Jayn turned to her, frowning.

"If something bad happened to your mother, well, that would be very unlucky for you."

"Oh," Jayn said, realization dawning. "It would, wouldn't it?"

Thalia pulled her in for a hug. "Trust the luck," she whispered.

Jayn didn't hug her back, but she believed the words. She pulled free, nodded, and turned back to Grondor. "What's the plan?" she asked, surprising herself with how calm she sounded.

He studied her face. "They're dug in. We may have to wait till morning and see if we can negotiate something. The sun should be coming up soon."

They both looked up at the gray sky. Was it getting lighter? The heavy rain clouds made it hard to tell. The rain hadn't been strong but was steady enough that it had soaked through her clothes. She shivered, staring up at the dark three-story building where Lucas Peniter was holding her mother hostage.

Grondor sighed again. "Listen, I get how you must be feeling right now, but the truth is, your being here for this, it's not going to help. Cool heads are called for. I need you to trust me. Peniter is dumb, but he's not an idiot. He knows it's treason to kill a Pentarch. He knows he can't do something like that and make it out of the city alive."

"I understand," Jayn said. She turned and walked away.

"Jayn?" Nyssa said. They all must have been shocked that she'd backed down so readily. She heard five pairs of boots splash through the wet street behind her. Nyssa caught up first. "You're giving up?" she asked.

"Commander Grondor told me to stand down. You heard him."

"I did," she sputtered, "but I also know you better than that. What are you doing?"

"Would you agree, Captain, that my Pentad, with our currently enhanced luck and our skill as Weavers, stands the best chance of getting my mother out of there alive?"

"Yes, exactly. I was willing to make that argument to Grondor."

"I'm glad to hear that, but I'm assuming Peniter or someone else was watching and listening from one of the upper windows. It's better they think we left."

"So you do want to go after your mother?"

"Of course. I've stayed in that apartment plenty of times, so I know there is a back entrance."

Jayn led them down a narrow alley. She got as close as she dared before creating an invisibility ward, forming a tunnel through the air that they could all follow. She couldn't see far enough to take it all the way to the back door, but she could make a second ward when they got closer. It reminded her of the tactic they'd used to approach that house in Wydhaven with the rogue Weavers. And Clay. She shook her head and told herself to focus. They stepped lightly, hoping the constant drumming of rain on stone would muffle their footsteps.

Soon she reached the edge of the ward and could see the back of her mother's apartment. A set of narrow steps led to the door. Probably, it was locked, but Thalia could handle that. Jayn wondered if Pavel had picked up enough Stone yet to open locks. Surely, mastering that skill was a top priority for the one-time thief.

She began to form the lacings to create another ward all the way to the door. In theory, they could keep this up all the way until they reached whichever room held her mother, but things would get tricky once inside, with narrow spaces full of rioters. Anyone who crossed through the ward would be able to see the Watch-keepers. The plan stood little chance of succeeding without dissolving into a fight, unless they got very lucky.

The back door opened. Jayn quickly released the half-formed ward and dropped to a crouch, even though she was still invisible. Someone stepped out into the dark alley. "Quiet," he whispered back into the building, as he moved down the steps. Another rioter followed on his heels, and then another. An entire line of people emerged from the building, all hunched over and moving fast. They were making an escape, apparently. Jayn didn't see her mother in the crowd. She didn't know what Lucas Peniter looked like and couldn't make out any faces in the dark.

Her hand went to the hilt of her sword. If the mob turned left, they'd blunder right into her ward. Luckily, they turned right. She tried to count the retreating figures but lost track at twenty. That had to be nearly the whole mob. Why were they sneaking out now? Had they already killed her mother? Surely the Wardens and city guards had set up a perimeter just out of sight. They wouldn't get away. Trust the luck.

She turned to the others. "That had to be nearly all of them," she whispered. "My mother wasn't with them. It'll be easier to get in now, though I'm sure they left someone to guard her. I don't know what Peniter looks like. Did anyone see him in that crowd?"

"He wasn't there," Pavel whispered. She could trust his Aether-enhanced night sight.

Shilo turned to look back at Pavel. "Are you really not going to tell them?" she said, anger in her voice—something Jayn had never heard from the meek Flame Weaver.

"Tell us what?" Nyssa asked.

Pavel sighed. "Nothing. Now is not the time, anyway."

"They're friends," Shilo said.

"What?" Jayn asked.

"No, we are not," Pavel said, frustration in his voice. "This has no relevance, but if you really have to know, I did a job for Peniter one time, years ago, and I haven't had anything to do with him since."

"I saw them together, just a couple days ago," Shilo said.

"You really think that little of me?" Pavel shook his head. "I swear I didn't know Peniter was even into politics, and I certainly had no idea he was going to do something crazy like this. Yes, he did reach out to me last week. I assumed he wanted to hire me for some other job. I told him I was a Watchkeeper now and shut him down before he got any of the details out. I had no clue. I swear."

Jayn tried to study Pavel's face, but the darkness and the rain made it impossible. Sunlight probably wouldn't have helped; Pavel was a master liar. She either had to trust him or not. She looked at the back door, still hanging open. She knew she could trust the luck, but she still wanted to do everything she could to guarantee success.

"If it's just Peniter and a few others, then not all of us have to go in. Six people, even if invisible, make a lot of noise. I know the layout. Shilo can disable Peniter. Maybe just the two of us then?"

"No," Nyssa said, "I can't send you in alone. I'm coming too."

Jayn nodded.

"The rest of you stay out here and watch the back," Nyssa said, her eyes fixed on Pavel.

He didn't say anything. Ryn and Thalia nodded in agreement.

Jayn formed an invisibility ward that snaked up the steps and stopped at the door. She led the way, with Nyssa and Shilo right behind her. They stopped to stare into the dark house, spotting no signs of movement and hearing nothing. Jayn stretched another ward across the room to the far side. She motioned for the others to step into it, then she dissolved the ward behind her. She didn't want to leave a maze of wards crisscrossing the house. She paused to take a long sip from the waterskin that hung on a strap at her side, glad she'd had the foresight to bring it. Nyssa had one too; it was standard issue for a Wave Weaver in the field, just as Shilo wore her locket with a fresh lump of coal. Jayn had not drunk enough water at the ball last night, and her throat was already dry. It didn't matter.

They made their way through the house, one room and one ward at a time, like earthworms burrowing tunnels through dirt, which collapsed behind them. They cleared the first floor, seeing no one. Aside from some overturned furniture, the place was exactly as Jayn remembered it. They headed for the stairs.

Jayn stopped herself just before her foot touched the third step up. It squeaked. She looked back at the others, pointed at the step, and then took an exaggerated step to avoid it. They nodded. They moved silently to the top of the landing. Jayn angled her next ward toward the open door that led into her mother's bedroom. She hesitated, fearful what she might find there.

She felt Nyssa's hand on her back and knew she had to keep going. She edged toward the dark doorway. A dull gray light filtered in through an open window. The sun must have finally dawned behind the clouds. Anyse Eldragor sat alone in the corner, still in her nightgown, her knees up and her arm wrapped around them. She swayed a little. Jayn heard a sob. Her mother was… crying.

Jayn froze in the doorway, as a cold fear gripped her heart. She didn't think anything could make her mother cry. What happened? Jayn couldn't see any visible injuries. Nyssa touched her back again. Jayn forced her eyes away from her mother and swept the room. Empty. Where was Peniter? Why had he left her mother alone? What did he do to her? Dark visions of vile deeds threatened to overwhelm her mind, but Jayn forced them all back.

She stepped out of the ward. Anyse didn't look up. Jayn crossed into the middle of the room. "Mother?" she said.

Anyse's head shot up, her eyes wide and wild. "No!" she screamed.

Lucas Peniter had been hiding in the shadows beside a large wardrobe. Jayn could not have seen him from the doorway. She realized all this too late, spying a blur of movement from the corner of her eye. Peniter grabbed her from behind, wrapping one arm around her chest and placing something cold and metallic against her throat.

Peniter spun, turning her to face the door. Nyssa materialized from thin air, stepping into the room with her sword drawn. Shilo stepped out beside her, her hands beginning to glow.

"That's far enough, ladies!" Peniter said. "Stay where you are."

"Please, no," Jayn's mother cried, rising to her knees and reaching a wavering hand out. "Not her! Please, not her."

Her mother's behavior terrified Jayn more than being grabbed by Peniter. Anyse Eldragor did not beg. "What did you do to her?" Jayn asked. She kept her arms down at her side and made no move to resist him.

"What is that?" Nyssa asked Peniter. "What did you do to the Pentarch?"

Jayn frowned. What did Nyssa mean? Jayn couldn't see what Peniter held to her neck. She assumed it was a knife, except it did feel more like something blunt.

"Only what she deserved," Peniter said, and Jayn could hear the edge of madness in his voice. "What all Lacers deserve."

Anyse screamed again, unable to restrain her fear. "Please, not her! Don't take it from her!"

"Shut up!" Peniter said.

Jayn felt the object lift from her neck as Peniter turned slightly to yell at Anyse. It was the opening Jayn had been waiting for. She still didn't know what Peniter was holding or what he had done to her mother, but Jayn had to trust her luck, and the years of combat and self-defense training her mother had given her. Peniter had the height and weight advantage, but Jayn knew how to use that against him. Jayn's right leg shot out, as she bent forward and settled into a wide stance. Turning back into Peniter, her left leg snaked behind him. She dropped her weight further onto her bent right knee but kept her left leg out and straight. She wrapped her arms around his knees and threw herself backward onto the floor. He stumbled, tripping over her leg, and landing hard on his butt. He dropped whatever he was holding, which clattered and rolled across the floor.

Jayn scrambled out from under him and took a few stumbling steps away before turning to face him. He regained his feet much faster than she'd expected. He pulled something from his side and lunged toward her. She saw the flash of an actual knife this time. She easily sidestepped the reckless charge as he barreled past her and almost smacked into the wall. She turned to face him again, drawing her sword. Nyssa and Shilo stepped up beside her.

Peniter turned back toward them, brandishing the knife, a grim smile on his face.

"Drop it," Nyssa said. He had to know he was outmatched now.

Peniter's wild eyes darted around the room before settling on Anyse Eldragor, still crouched on the floor, still overcome by some unfathomable grief.

"No!" Jayn gasped, but it was too late.

Jayn surged forward, even knowing she could never close the distance in time. Anyse Eldragor made no move to defend herself, staring up at Peniter like a dumb animal, awaiting the swing of the farmer's axe. Time seemed to slow as his blade snaked out toward her.

The dagger stopped a few inches short, as first it and then Peniter smacked into an invisible wall. He fell forward but didn't land on Anyse. He hit a dome and then slid off the side. Only then could Jayn see the rippling Wave shield that had enveloped her mother. She looked down, tracing the line of blue light to the toe of Nyssa's boot.

Peniter groaned and struggled to get back on his feet again. Shilo got to him first, not bothering with a numbing blow but swinging her staff down to crack him across the face. He collapsed into an unconscious heap.

Shilo looked at the shield and back at Nyssa. "How did you make it so fast?" she asked, nearly breathless.

Jayn didn't hear if Nyssa responded. She didn't care how miraculous the shield had been just then. She dropped to her knees in front of her mother and pressed her palm against the dome, wanting to touch her. Anyse did not look at her. Her eyes wandered across the floor. Idly she fingered the hem of her nightgown.

"Are you all right, Mother?" Jayn asked as softly as she could. "What happened?"

Slowly, Anyse's eyes found her daughter. They meandered upward until they reached Jayn's face. "He took it," she said. She looked old now, wrinkles etched around her mouth and eyes. Her hair looked thin and almost white in the gray light of morning.

"What?" Jayn asked, her voice hardly a whisper. "What did he take?"

Anyse closed her eyes, her lips moving wordlessly for a moment. Jayn could hear Shilo and Nyssa moving around the room, securing Peniter and his weapons, whatever they had been. She dared not look away from her mother. Anyse's eyes opened again, her expression gone distant and hollow. She breathed a single word. "Flame."

Chapter 23
The Lucky Ones

NYSSA SAT WITH HER BACK straight and her gaze steady. A silence filled the massive, mostly empty Assembly Room. None of the lords or ladies sat on their benches. No faces peered down from the two levels of viewing galleries. The meeting had been sealed. Probably few people in Appencourt knew this meeting was even happening, still early on Sunday morning, hours after the riot. Nyssa sat at a long table in the center of the room, with Ryn and Pavel to her left and Shilo and Thalia to her right. The whole Pentad was present, save Jayn Eldragor. Four of the five Pentarchs looked down on them from the highest bench, all present save Anyse Eldragor.

The mother and daughter had been spared from this initial interrogation, given time to rest in a secure suite within the Grand Hall. The Fourth Pentarch had not said much before Nyssa left her, slipping into a nearly catatonic state. She'd said enough though. The bizarre device lay on the table in front of Nyssa. Barely a foot long, it consisted of a thin metallic rod the color of copper, with two stubby silver prongs on one end—the end Peniter had held to Jayn's throat. They'd all been hesitant to touch it, not knowing how it was activated. Apparently, Peniter had used it on Anyse to somehow seal—or sever—her ability to Weave. She claimed she could no longer create any lacings.

The four remaining Pentarchs communicated with one another by writing notes on bits of paper and sliding them back and forth on a table that stretched between them. Nyssa had just finished giving her account of everything that had happened during the night, starting with Ryn banging on her door, waking her up to tell her there was a dead man in his room. She decided not to mention the fact that Pavel and Peniter had some past connection. Now that Peniter was in custody, that truth would eventually come out, if it had any relevance. It took several minutes for the other Pentarchs to write down their thoughts and pass them to the First Pentarch, Morace Prentley, a gray-haired man with an angular face, who seemed small in his voluminous black robes of state.

Prentley read the notes and shuffled them together, before raising his eyes to regard the Watchkeepers. "Thank you," he said. "We will wish to hear from you again when the full Hall can be assembled. Thankfully, no one seems to have been killed, but many of the lords and ladies are understandably still shaken up." He glanced to his left, at the empty spot on their bench. He shook his head. "That device. Do you have any idea how Lucas Peniter got his hands on it?"

"No, sir," Nyssa said. "I have never heard of any device capable of disabling someone's ability to Weave." The other Pentarchs visibly cringed or squirmed in their seats. All were Weavers themselves, except for Prentley. Nyssa hesitated. She wasn't quite sure if she should say what she was thinking. She wished Agia were there. Nyssa had no head for politics. She sighed and said it anyway. "I have to wonder… I would advise sending a messenger to the Citadel in Falport with a description of this device. They can check it against the archive."

Prentley arched a white eyebrow. It stood out like a fuzzy caterpillar against his dark skin. "Are you suggesting this may be one of the Runeforms stolen during the Kobold attack?"

Her recruits shifted in their seats beside Nyssa, but no one spoke. They had not been told about the theft, though Nyssa would not be surprised if Pavel had sussed it out.

"I admit, I don't know how it could have ended up in Peniter's hands, but… Let's call it a hunch."

Prentley slowly shook his head. "It's as good of an explanation as any at the moment." He paused to look over his notes again. "We've sent for the best Root Weavers in the city Guild. With any luck, they can find some way to reverse what's been done to Anyse." He sighed. "I'm afraid I must ask all of you to remain on as guests of the Hall. You came here to talk about the Kobolds, and we haven't even gotten to that issue. Then there is the matter of the dead ambassador… Still no sign of his missing servant… We require your discretion in all these matters. Please don't breathe a word about anything that happened last night to anyone outside of the Hall."

"Yes, sir, of course," Nyssa said, and the others mumbled their agreement.

Prentley waved his hand. "That's all for now. Go and get some rest."

Nyssa and the others began to rise. Thalia cleared her throat. "I'm sorry," she said. "There is another issue."

All eyes turned toward her. Nyssa heard her gulp, but the young Stone Weaver kept her chin up. "I admit it is minor, in light of everything else, but it does need to be addressed."

Prentley glanced at the other Pentarchs, then gestured to Thalia. "Go ahead, young lady."

Thalia nodded. "As Captain Lahmeer mentioned, when we set out to help last night, we made use of my Etching. I have the ability to enhance a person's luck for a short time."

Prentley nodded. "We read up on you and your Pentad before you arrived."

"Right. Then you may also know that my Etching has a pretty severe recoil. For the rest of today and tomorrow, the five of us—the captain didn't take a ring, but Jayn did—we will have uncommonly good luck. But sometime late tomorrow night, the recoil will hit, and something very unfortunate will happen to each of us. It won't be anything super catastrophic. Normally, when someone uses my Etching, we send them out to a remote location—"

"I'm sorry," Prentley said, holding up a hand to stop her. "We cannot permit any of you to leave the city right now. We'll need you on hand for when the Hall is ready to assemble again. How much of a risk does this recoil pose to other people? I mean no offense, but you five chose to take on the risk when you used your Etching."

Thalia nodded. "I understand. Yes, we all accepted that we would have to deal with the recoil. As far as other people… Well, if you were walking down the street, and you saw a stranger fall and get hurt, that would be unfortunate, but not unlucky, not for you. The recoil shouldn't affect strangers or people we have only just met, but it might affect those closest to us." She glanced at Nyssa. "We'll need to be kept apart from Captain Lahmeer, and Jayn can't be near her mother. Ideally, we would go somewhere isolated, but sturdy enough that we don't have to worry about the roof falling in on us."

The Third Pentarch, a dour-faced woman who oversaw the courts, scribbled something on a page and passed it to Prentley. He glanced over it and nodded. "That would work," he said. "What if you used the cells beneath the Hall?"

"Cells?" Thalia asked.

He waved a hand. "It's not like a dank dungeon or anything. They're actually quite comfortable. When Appencourt was first built, Aldria was not as settled as it is now. The cells were intended for mainly political prisoners—high-profile dissidents, captured spies, and the like. They haven't seen much use in recent years. We won't lock you in or anything."

Thalia shrugged. "It sounds like that would work. We need separate cells, if possible, preferably spaced apart from each other."

Prentley nodded. "I'll have Commander Grondor make the arrangements. Like I said, they're mostly empty. We've only one prisoner at the moment."

Nyssa knew whom he meant. Lucas Peniter.

The Pentarchs dismissed them, and Nyssa led her recruits out of the hall. Halfway to the stairwell, Thalia cleared her throat again.

"Yes, Moldo," Nyssa asked, not looking back.

"Well, I am of course dog-tired right now, and I plan to sleep for at least ten hours, but..."

"Uh-huh?" Nyssa had an idea where this was going.

"It seems the five of us still have a day and a half of good luck left..."

"What do you have in mind?"

"Nothing definitive... They told us not to leave the city, but they didn't confine us to our rooms."

"That's true." She stopped and turned to look over her recruits. They tried to keep straight faces, but she saw the barely suppressed smiles. "I would tell you to be careful, but... Remember, just because you are lucky, doesn't mean you should be reckless. Be up and dressed at dawn tomorrow. It's unlikely, but the Hall may send for us. If we are not needed, then I will give you the rest of the day to yourselves. Just be back before dark and ready to spend the night in those cells." They nodded and thanked her. She turned to keep walking but stopped. She leveled a finger at Pavel. "Oh, and no gambling."

He rolled his eyes. "Come on, Captain…"

She poked him in the chest. "No gambling!"

"I mean, would it technically even be gambling if it was a guaranteed win?"

"No gambling. Nothing illegal. Remember the uniform you are wearing. None of you should do anything to make us look bad, especially right now."

"Fine," Pavel said with a wicked grin. "No gambling."

Thalia swung the hammer, and bright sparks flew from the red-hot metal. Blended lines of Stone and Aether swirled along the steel rod. Sweat beaded on her forehead from the heat of the nearby furnace. They'd all been up at dawn, as Nyssa had ordered them. Once it was clear they would not be sent for, Thalia changed quickly into a sleeveless dress and headed for the Artisans' Quintant. Lise Guntrel, the master bladesmith, had offered to give Thalia a few pointers, and when Thalia explained her Etching and how Master Caston had found great success himself using it, Mistress Guntrel had been eager to put Thalia to work in the smithy.

"Take a quick break," the bladesmith said, coming up beside her.

Thalia nodded. Using a pair of tongs and insulated gloves, Thalia put her rod of steel back into the furnace. Mistress Guntrel handed her a rag and a canteen. Thalia wiped her face and took a long sip of water. "Thanks," she said. The work was exhausting and backbreaking, but she couldn't help but smile.

"This is really only your second blade?" Guntrel asked.

"Yes, although I used to watch my father in his shop when I was a girl."

"I'm impressed. I like your idea for incorporating a lasting lacing into the sword. I've only seen that one used in boots, but the way you are lacing the blade, it should help its wielder keep swinging longer."

Thalia shrugged. "Call it a lucky hunch."

Guntrel shook her head. "No, luck is only a part of it. You have natural talent." She glanced around to make sure none of her assistants were nearby and lowered her voice. "Even my journeymen still struggle to lace an enchantment and swing a hammer at the same time."

Thalia beamed at the compliment. Objects could be enchanted after the fact, but for the best results, the lacings had to be applied in layers as you shaped and molded the piece.

Guntrel patted her on the back. "Keep it up. I know a few lords who play at being swordsmen who would pay top price for this piece. I'll be sure to send your cut of the commission down to Falport."

"Thank you," Thalia said, as she turned back to the furnace. She didn't really care about the money. She reveled in the simple joy of creation. She used to love making copper kettles with Master Foster, but getting a chance to work on a real sword was something else. She hoped her father would have praised her work.

***

Shilo took a deep breath and stepped into the soup kitchen, nearly empty this early in the day. Rav Montare was there, wiping tables with a rag. If he hadn't been there, or if he'd been preoccupied and hadn't looked up when she walked in, she might have turned right around and left.

She smiled as he came to greet her. "How was the Summer Feast?" he asked.

"Oh, it was…" she stammered. She had forgotten about the party itself, given all the chaos that had followed that night. The Hall really had managed to keep the ambassador's death a secret, at least so far. News of the riot in the Civic Quintant had to have swept the city, but Montare couldn't have known Shilo and her friends had gone to help stop it. She still wasn't sure what she could safely say, but she had to say something. "The ball itself was lovely. They had fireworks… You may have heard there was a riot early yesterday. Someone blew up the bridges around the Hall. My Pentad and I, we helped… restore order, I guess. It was a little crazy."

He nodded. "I heard something about fighting. Are the rest of your Watchkeepers all right?"

"Yes… mostly. Well, you see, Thalia—you remember Thalia, our Stone Weaver? Well, she has this Etching that can temporarily increase a person's luck. We didn't know how bad things would get with the rioting, so we used her enchanted rings." Shilo held up her hand to show the copper band on her finger. She didn't have to wear it to have the luck, but it would break as soon as the recoil hit, the only warning they would get. "The way it works… Well, for the rest of today I'm still going to be very lucky." She laughed, realizing how strange that must have sounded.

He stared at the ring and slowly shook his head. "That is astounding…"

"Anyway," she pressed on. "I wasn't sure what I wanted to do with all my extra luck today—I'm pretty sure Pavel is off gambling somewhere, even though Nyssa told us not to—but then I remembered you and the Scribes, and all the things you do to help people. I thought I could come and offer up the rest of my luck…"

He smiled. He really was handsome. "I don't know what to say. I've never really been sure if I believed in luck, as like a cosmic force, I mean. Good luck, bad luck… I always saw that as a sort of superstition. We do of course believe that when we follow the will of the Maker, he himself will intervene in the world to ensure our success."

"Well, now you will have the Maker on your side and the advantage of my luck. Whatever good deeds you might want to do today, if you take me with you, I can guarantee you will accomplish them."

She tried not to sound too eager, but she was. It wasn't just about spending time with Rav. She knew he was too old for her, and she'd dismissed her feelings as a childish infatuation. She really did want to do something to make the world better. Violence came too easily for her now. She still couldn't believe how she had whacked Lucas Peniter over the head like that. She could have killed him. She hated the man. She hated him for what he said about Weavers. She hated him for threatening Jayn and for what he'd done to Jayn's mother. Still…

When her Etching first awakened, Shilo had knocked a pirate off her family boat, into the ocean. She had doubted it for a long time, but she was now certain she had killed that man. She was a killer. She'd done it to save her family. She would do it again if she had to. She would kill to protect her new friends or innocent people. The Maker had given her a powerful and deadly Etching, and she could no longer deny that. Still… More than ever, she needed to find ways to do good, to help without hurting.

Rav mulled it over for a few moments. Then an idea seemed to dawn on him. "The people we serve here at the mission, many are the poorest and most vulnerable members of society. We have our regulars, people who come in almost every day, but sometimes they just vanish. It's a transient population. Sometimes they might get word about a chance to work somewhere else and take off. We worry, though, because sometimes they get sick, but they can't afford a healer. Or there are unsavory types out there who will exploit or hurt these vulnerable people. Sometimes they end up in real bad situations. My friends and I, especially if we suspect something is wrong, we go out and look for these missing people. We haven't had much… luck lately."

"Are there missing people right now you are worried about?"

He nodded. "Two or three come to mind, and I can ask the others for more names. But… How exactly will your luck help here? I've no idea where to start a search."

"That's exactly a situation where luck can help. If we went out and just sort of… wandered, I think we would eventually stumble across your missing friends or someone who knows where to find them."

He shrugged. "I guess if nothing else, it will be good exercise."

"Trust the luck," she said with a grin.

He nodded, returning the smile. "And trust the Maker."

Jayn carefully set the teacup and saucer on her mother's bedside. "Careful, it's hot," she said.

Her mother glanced at it but didn't touch it. "Thank you," she muttered. A night of sleep seemed to have restored Anyse

Eldragor's senses, but she still had dark circles under her eyes and a vacant cast to her gaze. She sat up in bed, propped by pillows, with blankets over her lap. Jayn sat on the edge of the bed, wanting to say something, but not sure where to start.

Her mother glanced at her again. "Are you sure you're not needed with your Pentad?"

Jayn shook her head. "We've been given the day to ourselves. I don't even know where the others are. Possibly, they're off gambling." She forced a half-hearted laugh.

Anyse looked briefly confused but said nothing.

"Oh, I forgot to mention, we used Thalia Moldo's luck Etching. I've written to you about it, I believe. We still have the luck for the rest of today. I'll have to leave you tonight. We need to be isolated when the recoil hits, so they're moving us to the cells under the Hall." Jayn had never been in the prison before, but she knew how to get there. A narrow staircase built into the side of the moat led down to the entrance.

Anyse nodded. "I'll be fine without you." She started to say something else but stopped short. Jayn waited patiently, hoping her mother would open up more. Jayn wanted to comfort her, to help her in any way she could. After another long while, Anyse glanced at her, before dropping her eyes to the coverlet. She spoke in a low voice. "It's funny, you know. I keep thinking about it, trying to be rational. I'm not a general anymore. My days of fighting with the Standing Army are long behind me. You're out of the house now and on your own. My role as the Fourth Pentarch, well… It's mostly just meetings and reading reports. My body is still healthy; my mind is intact. My life will go on, essentially unchanged, now that I can't... even though I'm not a Weaver anymore." Her eyes found Jayn then. "So why does it feel like half my soul has been ripped out?" she asked with a sob, her eyes wet with tears.

Jayn scrambled up onto the bed and embraced her mother, in part to offer comfort, but also because, with her face buried in her mother's neck, she would not be able to see the great Anyse Eldragor crying again. She couldn't stand that. She didn't understand her mother's defeatist attitude either. There had to be a cure, a way to undo what Peniter had done. Sealing wards placed on rooms prevented anyone inside from Weaving. This had to be just some kind of advanced sealing ward placed on a person. Wards could always be broken eventually. Still, she could understand the sense of loss Anyse must be feeling. It wasn't really the same, but when Jayn had failed the test for Flame, she'd felt as if her whole future had been torn away.

They stayed like that for a long time, embracing one another. Jayn felt her mother pull away eventually, so she sat back on the coverlet. Anyse reached for the teacup then and took a sip. She glanced at her daughter. "I'll be fine really. I have to get this out of my system before your father gets here. He'll fall to pieces if he sees me moping like this."

"Mother…"

Anyse waved her hand. "You really should go. I don't need you playing nurse. You said you still have a day of luck? Go take advantage of that." She shrugged. "Why not place some bets?"

Jany shook her head. "That's why I'm here, Mom." She felt the tears welling up in her own eyes now. "I want you to have all my luck."

Pavel walked through the Appencourt Civic Library, scanning the rows of books. "Luck, luck, luck…" he repeated under his breath like a mantra. Despite Nyssa's direct order, the others must still think he'd headed straight for the nearest gambling hall. Good, let them think that. If his gambit paid off today, it would open the door to more riches than any day of playing cards.

A gray uniform and pin could open many doors. It got him into the largest private library in Aldria, a place normally closed to men like Pavel Talvor. He'd visited here last week, only to realize the vast collection of tomes would take months to search properly. He could ask a librarian for help. Surely, they could pull up a list of all texts referencing the lost and legendary Five Crowns. But no one could know what he was looking for, especially not if his father was still in town. He couldn't resume his search in earnest until he finished serving out his five years with the Watchkeepers, but he could still look for clues, especially if luck was on his side.

"Luck, luck, luck…" he mumbled.

He reached the end of the row. None of the books had caught his eye. Maybe he was going about this the wrong way. If he wanted to take full advantage of the luck, he needed to introduce a bit of randomness. He looked around, seeing no one. The tall bookshelves spread out in all directions. He closed his eyes and began to spin. He counted to five and stopped. He walked forward, his hands outstretched. It took longer than he'd expected to touch something. He must have been moving down the broad aisle between rows. His hand touched wood. He felt along the edge until he found the leathery spine of a book. He walked along the shelf, still with his eyes closed, letting his fingers slide along the books. "One… Two… Three… Four… Five."

He stopped, pulling the last book he'd touched off the shelf. He opened his eyes. He held a thick tome with a black cover. Gold lettering along the spine read, *Bellevue's Encyclopedia of Subtropical Plants, Volume II.* He leafed through the pages, glancing at the blocks of small type and simple illustrations. There was absolutely no way this book had anything to do with the Five Crowns.

He sighed and put the book back, slotting it in between Volumes I and III. The book went in halfway but then caught on something. He pushed harder. It wouldn't budge. He pulled it back out and peered into the dark gap. Something was back there. He pulled out Volumes I and III, dropping all three books onto the floor. A small, thin book had fallen behind the encyclopedias somehow. He pulled it out. The cover, which may once have been white, looked filthy, completely covered in overlapping yellow stains. A single word in tiny red lettering had been scrawled across the cover: *Poetica.*

Pavel opened the book. The pages were brown and tattered. Apparently, it was just a book of folk poems. The first page held a familiar children's rhyme, though with more verses than Pavel had ever heard before.

Foxes, Crows, Drakes, and Bulls
Stand against the Darkened Foes.
The Bulls all die, the Drakes all fly,
The Crows betray the Darkened Sky.
Foxes alone without a home
Stand against the Darkened Throne…

Pavel shook his head. He glanced around. This whole section of the library seemed filled with dry scientific texts and treatises. Finding this tiny book the way he had felt like the stroke of luck he'd been seeking, but how could this flimsy pamphlet help him? He turned a few more pages, finding more folk songs and children's rhymes. The author, who had not bothered to put his name to the text, had added a paragraph at the end of each poem, offering some cultural context or explaining the meanings behind each song—where one was known. No one really knew what the Foxes and Bulls rhyme was talking about.

Pavel kept turning the pages until a name caught his eye: the Cobalt King. He stopped and read the whole poem. It was a ballad he'd heard a thousand times before, portraying the Cobalt King as a wise and generous ruler. No one knew the meaning of the title—most historians assumed the king had simply chosen a cobalt blue flag as his standard. Most people who knew anything about King Aldous used a different title: the First Emperor.

First came the Burning. Obviously, a lot of stuff happened before that, but it had all been lost to history. Next came the Dark Century, a hundred years of chaos, when mankind struggled merely to survive. Sometime after that, the first city-states formed, including Talvor. Most of those lasted less than a few decades before dissolving into chaos again. Eventually, they began to stick. Trade started. Roads were built and maintained. The Academy of the Ways, which had been working in isolation since the Burning, began to share its hoarded knowledge with the world, though most people back then still saw Weavers as evil witches.

Sometime around 400 AB, King Aldous came to power, starting as the ruler of a small city, but eventually conquering the entire continent, except of course for the Rune Lands and the Maer Isles. Accounts of the Cobalt King varied widely. Some portrayed him as a great uniter of the masses; others, as a brutal and oppressive dictator. Probably, he was a little of both. The First Empire barely outlived him. His successor did not have the same talents to hold so many people groups together. The empire split apart into warring factions, and another century of chaos followed. During his reign, King Aldous had collected the Five Crowns, legendary and powerful Runeforms that helped him maintain power. They all vanished soon after his death.

Pavel had no aspirations to be a king. Truthfully, he didn't exactly know what he would do once he collected the Crowns. If the legends were true, he could do anything he wanted. He would have time to figure it out once he had the Crowns. All he knew was that it was his destiny to find them. Corvus had told him as much.

The blurb at the end of the mythologizing ballad told him things he already knew about the real historical King Aldous. Then the last few lines caught his attention:

According to the legend, when Aldous knew his life was drawing to a close, he entrusted the Five Crownes to his closest adviser. This man, a powerful Weaver, hid the Crownes and placed a mighty enchantment upon them, to ensure only a worthy successor may find them. All of the Crownes were sealed from the eyes of mortal men, save the first, the Ring Crown. Whosoever finds the Ring Crown, if he be worthy, will receive a vision of the second, and in this fashion, he will be led to all five.

Pavel looked up from the page. He'd read countless accounts of King Aldous, the First Emperor. None had ever mentioned a Weaver adviser or an enchantment placed upon the Crowns. He'd heard that they'd been cursed, but that was just superstition. Apparently, they also had to be found in sequence. Months ago, Pavel had asked the Rigel fountain where to find the First Crown, simply because that seemed like a good place to start. He wished the fountain had actually told him, rather than returning a nonsense answer, as now he definitely had to find the Ring Crown first. He'd never heard the First Crown called that name before either, but now he could search for references to it. Of course, this was all assuming a random book of poetry could be trusted. He shook his head and told himself to trust the luck.

***

Ryn dragged the blade across the back of his arm, making a shallow cut. He'd wasted most of the day trying to figure out exactly what he wanted to do with his enhanced luck. He'd found a gold coin in the corner of his room. Maybe the assassin had dropped it. Maybe it was part of his good luck. The last time he had used a luck charm, he'd discovered a way to Blend Aether and Root and save his friends. Maybe luck was what he needed to make it work again.

He held a cloth to his arm to staunch the bleeding. Then he closed his eyes. Root was the easy part, so he decided to start with Aether. He imagined a hole opening up in the ceiling and a cool breeze shooting down, touching the top of his head. Aether formed at the crown of one's head of all places. He sensed something begin to form. If he'd had a mirror in front of him, he would have seen swirls of white light hovering around his ears. Even the simplest Aether lacings were still beyond his grasp, but he didn't need the Aether to do anything, other than Blend.

He kept his mind focused on pulling more Aether from the cosmos and reached for Root with a tiny fraction of his awareness. Root Weaving came second nature to him now and didn't require much focus. A tree sprung up around him, the trunk reaching up to his chin. He brought the branches up, slowly, toward his head. The green tendrils brushed up against the white swirls—and the Aether vanished. He felt it slip away like something yanked from his hands.

Ryn sighed. Maybe he still needed more control. He'd hoped the luck would give him an edge. He opened his eyes and looked at the knife, laid out on the bed beside him. It was one of the small ones he kept in his sleeves. He had not yet asked if he could have his main knife back. He assumed the Wardens still needed it as part of their murder investigation. Someone had once suggested that Ryn should stab himself to force his Etching to work. Maybe he could force the Blending to work as well, if he had a more serious wound than just a small cut that could heal on its own. It seemed like the sort of reckless thing Nyssa had warned against, but then again…

He wouldn't be putting himself in real danger; he didn't think the luck would let him. He knew where to sink the blade into his torso, away from the really important organs. The wound would bleed a lot, and he could pass out. Even if that happened, his Etching would activate on its own, as it always had, and he'd wake up in an hour or two, completely fine. It was drastic, sure, but nothing else seemed to be working.

He picked the knife up, turning it over in his hands. He lay back on the bed and pulled his shirt up, exposing his belly. He held the knife tightly with both hands, the blade pointing down. He closed his eyes and took a deep breath.

Someone knocked tentatively at the door. Ryn shot up. He'd forgotten to lock the door. What if he had passed out and someone came in and found him unconscious and bleeding? They would have raised an alarm for no reason. He scrambled off the bed, feeling foolish. He didn't even want anyone to see the cut on his arm. He glanced down and smiled. His Etching had set a new record for activating on its own. The cut had vanished. That was lucky.

"Just a second," he called to whoever was outside.

He used the rag to wipe the last smear of blood from his arm and shoved the knife and the bloody cloth up under the bedspread. He ran a hand through his hair and moved to the door. He was still in his uniform, though he'd removed his tabard and boots.

Nyssa nodded to him when he opened the door.

"Captain Lahmeer," he said. He stepped back and gestured awkwardly for her to enter.

"I just wanted to check up on you, though I'm surprised you are still here. Jayn is still with her mother, but the others are out doing the Maker knows what."

Ryn shrugged. "I just couldn't think of something to do with my luck… You know, since you told us we couldn't gamble." He tried for a sheepish smile.

She laughed. "Oh, I didn't know you were a gambler, Ryn."

"Big time, yeah. It's kind of turning into a problem…"

She shook her head. "It sounds like you're hanging in there though. With everything else, we just haven't had much of a chance to talk about what happened the other night." Her gaze dropped to the spot on the floor where the dead body had been.

"Oh, that." Ryn plopped down on the edge of the bed. He stiffened for a moment, remembering what he'd just put there, but luckily he had not sat upon the knife. "I'm doing fine."

She didn't seem to believe him. "You did good, fighting back like you did. I'm proud of you. I'm glad you're not dead. We wouldn't have believed it, you know, if they had killed you and framed you for the ambassador's death. No one would have believed it for even a second."

"I know." He stared at his stockinged feet. "I'm no killer."

"You say that like it's a bad thing."

"It's strange. I didn't want that man to die. When I pushed him off and he fell back, I think he hit his neck on the edge of the bed. He was on the ground, disabled, and my first instinct was to try and heal him, even though he'd been trying to kill me the moment before." He forced a laugh, though he didn't find it funny.

"You're a healer, Ryn. Of course that would be your instinct."

"The guy said the same thing too, right before he bit down on that fake tooth. He said… 'You are a good kid. You think like a healer… But you can't heal everything.' And I know, the Root Weaver isn't supposed to fight. The rest of the Pentad is supposed to protect him, and then he heals their wounds. But it doesn't always work out that way."

"You *can* fight, Ryn. You fought him off. What about when we were on the road? When those rogues hit Jayn with their fear Etching, you charged in after her. You threw your knives and got them to stop. You saved her."

He frowned. "Yeah, and I was sick to my stomach afterwards, thinking I might have killed one of the rogues. Even if they were criminals."

Nyssa dropped down to sit beside him on the bed, luckily not on the knife either. "You're being too hard on yourself. Killing is never going to be easy. During my time with the Watchkeepers, I've killed… three rogues. Each time, it was because they were trying to kill me or one of my teammates. Each time still hurt me. Hopefully, you never find yourself in that situation, but if you do, I think you will find the strength to do what you must."

He kept his eyes down. "I didn't."

"I'm sorry?"

"I didn't find the strength to do it. When he attacked me, when he was on top of me… He was using Root. I knew exactly what he was doing. It was a modification of a lacing I learned in the triage tent back in Falport, after the attacks. I knew what he was doing to me, and I knew I was stronger than him. I Dowsed him back, and that broke his concentration. Then I had the advantage. I had him wrapped in Root. I could have stopped his heart right then, but I… hesitated. Then he slapped me and broke my focus. He healed me right after, which seemed insane, but I guess he really did want an unblemished body to pose.

"Even after that, I knew I could still fight back again. I could overpower his Root with my own and kill him. But I didn't. Sure, I came up with another way, by summoning Flame to syphon off his Root and blind him. If that idea hadn't come to me though, if stopping his heart had been my only option… I don't think I would have done it. I think I would have let him kill me. I don't think I have what it takes to be a Watchkeeper. I honestly don't know if I could even kill a Kobold, as much as I hate them."

A long silence elapsed before Nyssa responded. Ryn didn't look up. "I guess you're right," she said. "You're not a killer… But maybe you don't have to be."

His eyes found her then. "What do you mean?"

She sighed. She stood up and paced the room for a moment, mulling something over. Finally, she stopped and looked back at him. "I know what I'm supposed to say here, about 'necessary evils' and 'the greater good,' but I'm not going to. I've been keeping tabs on you and your Pentad, Ryn. Of course, you know that. I've spoken to all of your teachers, and I know I'm not supposed to say this either… It's the kind of thing that would give people a big ego." She waved her hand in a dismissive gesture. "Other people anyway, not you. Every master who has worked with you tells me the same thing. You are the most powerful Weaver any of them have ever seen, and that's saying an awful lot."

He dropped his eyes again. "I don't feel powerful."

"You said yourself you were stronger than a trained Root Weaver assassin. That heart-stopping lacing probably took him years to master, and you picked it up in a second, while fighting for your life. You're nowhere near your full potential. That trick you pulled using Flame against him was genius. If you stick with your training and you master Root and Flame and Wave—maybe even Stone or Aether while you're at it—and you train your mind… there's no telling what you'll be able to do. I think… and I really do believe this… If you set your mind to that goal, if you decide in your heart that you are not a killer… then you'll never have to become one. You will always find the second option. Come Kobolds, come the whole blighted Tamorine army, it won't matter. If anyone can find a way to fight back and still keep blood off their hands, I believe that person is you, Ryn Silverbell."

He smiled and tried not to cry. "Thanks, Nyssa." He almost broke down right then and told her all the secrets his Pentad had been keeping from her—the forbidden Blending, the poison prophecy, what really happened in Wydhaven—everything. Almost.

Chapter 24
Recoil

PAVEL LAY ON THE LUMPY straw mattress, staring up at the stone ceiling. Before they went into their separate cells for the night, Pavel had asked Thalia if they could delay the recoil by getting a second luck charm. Apparently, she had already tested that strategy with Rohan Caston, and it didn't work. Giving out additional charms did nothing to extend the luck window, and the recoil still hit.

The cells were cold, but he didn't mind that. He'd gotten a couple hours of sleep, spaced out between long stretches of wakefulness. He just didn't like being in a cell, even if the door wasn't locked, even though he could get up and leave if he desired. He tried to focus on other things, but his mind kept wandering. He thought now of a strange connection his drowsing mind had made, which felt like some sort of clue, though he couldn't make much of it.

Aldous, the First Emperor, the Cobalt King… Did it mean anything that Cobalt sounded an awful lot like Kobold? That was exactly the sort of little linguistic shift that could occur when a story was passed down for half a millennium. Had Aldous originally been called the Kobold King? What could that title possibly mean? Aldous surely had been a man, not a literal monster. That sort of detail would have survived any number of centuries. Had Aldous used Kobolds to help his conquest? That seemed equally unlikely, as Pavel had never heard a single story involving both the First Emperor and those little gray monsters.

Kobolds, at least in myth, had existed since the Burning, a part of local folklore like Drakes and Sprites. Real flesh-and-blood Kobolds had only stepped into the world very recently. Pavel saw his first Kobold nearly four years ago. He didn't know what it was at the time. That was back when he was working for that fool Lucas Peniter. He didn't like to think about the choices he'd had to make back then. It didn't help that Peniter was somewhere nearby, here in this dungeon, in the only locked cell.

Pavel sighed and sat up, knowing he wouldn't get to sleep again that night. He played with the copper ring on his finger. The ring was a little too big, so he could spin it easily. The luck charm snapped in two. He caught one piece; the other clattered to the stone floor. He didn't know what form the recoil would take, but he didn't have to wait long to find out.

"Pavel Talvor," a voice said from the dark.

A central hallway ran the length of the dungeon, lit by a few guttering torches. Each cell sat at the end of a long side corridor. Pavel had snuffed out the lantern he'd been given, so he could only see a shadowy figure, lit from behind by the distant torchlight. The hooded stranger looked short and broad like a Kobold, but her sultry voice had been distinctly human.

"Who might you be?" he said, trying to play off his surprise. Not many people could sneak up on him like that. He had excellent hearing.

He squinted his eyes, as a sudden light flared up. A black cloak swathed the woman's ample figure. A smile spread across her pale face. A round Weaver light floated above her outstretched hand.

"Don't you recognize me?" she asked. She did look vaguely familiar, but he couldn't place her immediately. She sighed. "I suppose we never really interacted back in Falport. What a shame." That last bit held a suggestive undertone, as her eyes traveled up and down Pavel's body.

He had it then. He'd been in Falport hardly two weeks when the Kobolds attacked. He remembered a woman in a voluminous green robe stooping to heal him after he'd been caught in the smithy explosion. "Mistress Hinter," he said, again trying not to sound surprised.

Her smile broadened. "No one calls me Mistress anymore. I do miss that."

His mind raced, trying to figure out what exactly was going on. The Watchkeepers had kept Gwen Hinter's betrayal a secret, but she had been reported as missing. If she'd shown up in Appencourt out of the blue, would the Wardens have let her down into the cells without asking questions? Even if she had used her Watchkeeper credentials to talk her way past the guards at the entrance, at a minimum, someone would have woken up Nyssa. Or maybe Hinter had used more than words to get past the guards. She couldn't have taken them all out, not alone, not without setting off an alarm.

She laughed. "I can see the wheels turning in that clever mind of yours. Don't worry. Your Pentad members are all asleep in their cells. We'll all be gone before they awake."

He arched an eyebrow. "We?"

"Lucas told me you haven't been honoring your oaths."

A memory flashed through Pavel's mind. An old wooden barn in the foothills of the Coldreach Mountains... Him and Lucas Peniter kneeling in the dust before a hooded figure… A creature watching them from the shadows. The Kobold had been cloaked, but Pavel had known even then it wasn't human. He had no choice but to swear that blighted oath, to serve and obey the Reach. At the time, he thought it nothing more than an overly dramatic criminal syndicate.

Pavel shrugged. He kept his voice calm. "I've never been great at keeping my word."

Hinter glanced over her shoulder. "Maybe we should wake up your little friends. Do they know anything about you, Pavel Talvor? Do they know your real name?"

"You've been gone two months, Gwen. They've grown a lot. You may regret bringing them into this."

"I don't doubt it. That Ryn Silverbell… He's an idiot, but he has amazing potential."

"What does the Reach want? Why did they have Lucas attack the Hall and Pentarchs? That device he used… Was it one you stole from Falport?"

"My, my, so many questions." She sent her Weaver light floating to the right, where it stuck on the wall. She stepped closer to his cell, running her fingers along the iron bars. "I promise I'll answer every one of them… if you come with me."

"Where? To do what? Attack the Hall again? It didn't work last time."

She shrugged. "Maybe that's what we wanted you to think. Use that pretty head of yours. We blew up the bridges. Why do you think we didn't just blow up those bureaucrats while they slept in their beds? Or we could have killed everyone when they were all together at the Summer Feast."

"You used Peniter and his mob as some diversion then?"

Why had they blown the bridges? If Hinter was behind that, she had to have known how easily the Wardens could have made shield bridges. Except they had to take the dome down first…

"You were watching, is that it? You watched them take all their fancy wards down and then put them back up the next day. You saw how they built it, so you could have a Wave Weaver pick it apart, huh? That's how you got in tonight without setting off any alarms."

She smiled. "Full points for you, Mr. Talvor. Now, the Reach has need of you. Will you honor your oaths? Before you answer, know that they will always take care of you."

"Just like they took care of Peniter? Looks more like they used him."

"But he walks free again tonight. The Reach has far more resources than the Watchkeepers. They can even help you with your little quest."

What did she mean? Did she know he sought the Five Crowns? He thought about going with her then. Not because he cared about some stupid oath, not because he actually wanted to work with Kobolds and men like Lucas Peniter again, but because he thought he might be able to use them. If he could discover their true goals and find out who else was working with them—and yes, if he could learn more about the Five Crowns—then maybe he could also work from the inside to take them down. He could learn their dirty secrets and expose them. He almost said yes. He almost went with her. Three months ago, he would have done it without a qualm. Now, however, there were people he would not betray, even temporarily.

Maybe he could get more information out of her still. He ignored the bait about his quest. "What are the Manfaces after this time? Stealing more Runeforms?"

"Manfaces?"

"Those creatures you summoned in Falport. We assume they're your masters?"

She laughed. "The Five would *not* like that name. Enough questions, though. Are you coming or not?"

He shook his head. "Sorry. You have to know I have no intention of honoring that cursed oath."

She sighed. "You can't blame a girl for trying." She kept running her fingers along the iron bars that made up the cell door. Her actions seemed casual, but before Pavel had a chance to react, she'd swung the latch closed and snapped the padlock into place.

He kept his composure. He shifted his feet slightly, letting his body coil like a snake. He threw himself at the bars, but she must have anticipated it. She danced back, just out of reach of his grasping fingers. He wasn't sure what he would have done if he had gotten hold of her.

She laughed. "Easy, Talvor. I'm not that kind of girl." She winked. She turned and sauntered away. "Give my love to Nyssa," she said over her shoulder with a casual wave.

Pavel waited a full minute after she disappeared around the corner before he fumbled for the lock. Reaching his hands through the bars, he could just barely touch the padlock. Hinter must not have known he'd been studying Stone. Handy with a lockpick, Pavel had never envied Stone Weavers' ability to break locks. Still, he set himself to mastering the skill as soon as he started to pick up Stone. He'd known better than to ask Rohan Caston or Thalia for help with it, but he'd figured it out eventually.

He closed his eyes and let the branching lines of Stone extend from his fingers, giving him a strange awareness of the iron that comprised the lock. It took him a minute to twist the pins into place and pop the lock open. He cloaked himself in Aether, a much easier feat, and silenced his footsteps.

He glided first to the entrance and found the door still open, the two Wardens crumpled to the floor, their throats slit. He poked his head out into the night. The fountains burbled in the moat at his feet. He craned his neck to look up the narrow staircase. He heard no noises overhead. He moved back down the corridor, turning down the first side passage. Peniter's cell hung open, another dead guard slumped against the wall. He sighed. It was time to wake up the kids.

Pavel sighed again. "Yes, Gwen Hinter was here," he explained for the fourth time.

He'd woken Ryn up first. The kid had asked a lot less questions than the girls. He hadn't been sure which cells the other kids had selected for themselves, so it had taken some stumbling around. They found Shilo last, and now it was her turn to sit on the edge of her cot and blink up in confusion at Ryn's Weaver light.

"Peniter?" she asked.

"Gone," Thalia answered for him.

"And the guards outside are dead," Jayn added.

"We need to find Nyssa," Pavel said, gesturing toward the exit.

Shilo didn't stand up. She studied Pavel with narrowed eyes. "Why you?"

Pavel didn't look at her. "Come on," he said. "I've wasted enough time explaining this to each of you."

"We have to be careful," Thalia said, holding her broken ring in the palm of her hand.

"Why you?" Shilo asked again. She had not moved.

Pavel sighed for what seemed like the hundredth time that night. "What do you mean?"

"Gwen Hinter shows herself for the first time in over two months in order to get Lucas Peniter of all people out of prison, but she stops on her way out to talk to you? Why not Ryn or Jayn? They actually trained with her. Did you ever even talk to her back in Falport?"

"Yeah, that is weird," Ryn said.

They all turned to look at Pavel, awaiting some explanation. Ever since Shilo had seen that idiot Peniter following Pavel through the streets, the girl had been suspicious of Pavel. He'd seen it but hadn't known how to get her back on his side. He didn't want to waste time pacifying her now, but he had to say something.

"She knew that I used to work for Peniter years ago, acquiring artifacts. Peniter wanted to recruit me for some job the other day. He must have told her to come ask me one last time if I would help. She didn't explain anything, but she wanted me to go with her. I declined."

"So she just left?" Shilo asked.

"She locked my cell, but… I've been studying Stone."

Thalia sighed. "Of course you learned that lacing."

"It's a good thing I did," Pavel said. "Now come on, we really need to get up there and figure out what's happening. I haven't heard an alarm. They must have disabled the wards."

"I don't believe you," Shilo said. "None of this makes sense. Hinter is a Weaver. Peniter hates Weavers, or he says he does. If he is working with Weavers… Thene is working with Kobolds…

Then everything he said was a lie. We don't know the real reason why he did the things he did. We don't know anything."

Jayn spoke up before Pavel could think of a response. "We won't figure it out down here," she said. "Either we trust Pavel or we don't. Let's just go."

"Wait," Thalia said. "I understand the urge to rush out there. I want to do that too. But don't forget, we're all at the height of the recoil right now. We may not be able to help anyone. We might trip over our own feet walking down that hallway. We don't have any weapons... Maybe we should just wait till daylight."

"I can't just sit here," Jayn said. She crossed her arms. "My mother is up there alone right now."

"I know," Thalia said, "but she's surrounded by Wardens, all on full alert after that riot, all not currently experiencing abysmal luck. You rushing up there... That might be the thing that gets your mother hurt."

Jayn gritted her teeth. "We can't let Peniter get away, not after what he did. We won't go up into the Hall... I'll stay away from my mother, but we can sound the alarm."

"Wait," Ryn said. Heads swiveled toward him. He had his eyes closed, a green Root tree spreading around him. He didn't seem to be forming any actual lacings. "Kobolds," he said, and the light vanished. "I can't tell how many, but there are Kobolds above us."

"You can detect them?" Jayn asked.

He nodded. Apparently, it was a new Root skill he had picked up.

"All the more reason to alert the city guard," Jayn said. "I don't care if I break my neck doing it."

Pavel didn't wait. He knew Jayn at least would follow him. He turned and bounded for the door. "Don't run!" Thalia called after him. He knew he was being reckless. He didn't care. Jayn was worried about her mother. He was worried about Nyssa. He felt guilty, though he had no reason. He hadn't done anything for the Reach in years. He hadn't been involved in anything Hinter had done. He'd done nothing to help Peniter with whatever mad scheme he was pulling here in Appencourt. He'd never directly or knowingly helped the Kobolds. Despite Shilo's doubts, he really was trying to do the right thing here. Still, he'd sworn that blighted oath…

He reached the entrance and leapt over the dead guards. His foot landed in slick blood. He fought the skid. His arms windmilled. He turned halfway back around but couldn't stop his forward momentum. His foot slid off the edge, down into the moat. *This is so stupid*, he thought, as he plummeted into the cold water. He didn't even try to use Aether, thinking only of the idiocy of what was happening. His head smacked against the stone ledge and he blacked out.

Pavel gasped as he awoke, feeling the tingle of Root, as Ryn healed whatever injuries he'd sustained falling into the moat. They'd fished him out and dragged him up into the broad circular courtyard beneath the Grand Hall. He glanced around but saw no one else among the sea of columns. The kids were all wet and bedraggled. "Right," Pavel said, sitting up, though his head still spun. "Now that I've gotten my recoil out of the way…"

"Us too," Thalia said with a bitter laugh. "I told you this was a bad idea."

Jayn rubbed her neck, as if feeling for soreness. "She and Ryn fell in the moat trying to pull you out before you drowned. Shilo and I tripped coming up the stairs."

Pavel glanced at Ryn, sitting on the ground beside him with his legs stretched out.

The kid shrugged. "Twisted my ankle," he said.

So Ryn had healed whatever injuries the girls had sustained and woken up Pavel, but he still couldn't heal himself. "Sorry, kid," Pavel said. "I'd offer to lend you some Aether, but there's no way we could get that Blending to work right now."

"Right," Jayn said. "Some of you stay here with Ryn. I'm going to find the city guard."

"I'll go with you," Shilo said.

The two turned and set off across the courtyard at a brisk walk, everyone having learned their lesson about running. The five bridges had not been repaired yet, but two improvised wooden platforms had been laid across the moat on opposite sides. The girls only made it a few paces. Pavel caught a blur of movement from the corner of his eye. Something huge stepped out from the maze of columns directly in front of Shilo and Jayn. The girls stopped short, staring up at the towering monster.

"Oh-ho, what's this?" the creature asked in a high, inhuman voice.

The girls backed up slowly. Pavel staggered to his feet. Ryn tried to stand but fell back onto his butt. Thalia moved to stand beside him, placing a protective hand on his shoulder. Pavel crept closer to the beast, trying to make sense of what he was seeing.

The creature stood at least eight feet tall. Wiry gray hair covered its body. It looked like a monkey, though not a species Pavel had ever seen. It swayed on its hind legs, but clearly it could move on all fours. A long fluffy tail, banded in streaks of black and white fur, swished across the ground behind it, like a restless serpent. It had tufted white ears and a white belly. Its all-too-human face dispelled any doubts what it might be. Thin lips peeled back into a smile, revealing small white teeth. Its eyes were large, shaped like a man's, though completely black. It made a strange clicking sound, what might have been a laugh.

"All five," it said, making that sound again. "Ts-ts-ts."

No one answered. Probably no one knew what to say. Pavel formed a quick Aether lacing that would let him dodge if the creature made any aggressive moves. Red Flame flared up around Shilo, though she hadn't moved. Jayn had her fists clenched.

"You all bear the Mark. Kalo really has been careless, ts-ts-ts."

"What do you mean?" Ryn asked. "What mark?"

Pavel hadn't expected the kid to be the first to break the silence. The Manface cocked its head, looking at Ryn. It moved sideways around the girls, circling their little group. It stayed upright, a slight hop in its step as it walked.

"It asks a question?" the creature asked. Despite how alien it looked and sounded, Pavel felt it was a male. It seemed to notice Ryn's bad ankle. "What, little Root Weaver? Is it hurt? Ts-ts-ts." The strange sound it kept making seemed less like a laugh now and more like some kind of verbal tic.

"You're one of them, aren't you?" Ryn asked, no fear in his voice. "You're with the owl and the bear?"

"It knows the Five?" the creature asked, looking over the rest of the Pentad. "The five know the Five, ts-ts-ts."

"What do you want with us?"

"Want? The Five want you to die. Unless…" It squatted down on its haunches, studying Ryn. Its arms dangled at its side, its long gray fingers curling slightly. "Is it the one?"

Pavel remembered that question. The Kobolds back in the Sylphren Wood had asked it in their own garbled speech. What did it mean? Who or what were the Kobolds and the Manfaces looking for? Did it have anything to do with Rigel's prophecy about the Rivening? The "Mark" had to be the Kobold poison that they had all survived, something which the Kobolds and the Manfaces could still sense in them, apparently. *Only those who have tasted deadly poison…*

"What is the Rivening?" Pavel asked, taking a gamble, though the odds were still stacked against him.

The creature turned to Pavel, cocking its head again. "Has it been Seeing? Too clever, ts-ts-ts."

"Is that your goal?" Pavel pressed. "You want this Rivening to happen and you don't want us around to stop it?"

"Not clever enough, ts-ts—" The creature stopped talking mid-tic and closed the distance between itself and Pavel in a fraction of a second. Aether gave Pavel a fast reaction time, but this creature was faster. White light surrounded Pavel, but before he could form a single lacing, the creature's long gray fingers wrapped around his torso. In one fluid motion, the Manface lifted Pavel up and threw him over its shoulder like a discarded rag doll.

Pavel spun end over end and saw the ground rush up to meet him. Anyone else would have broken their neck. Pavel tucked his chin and made a hasty cushion of Aether. He still landed hard on his back and lay panting for breath. The creature's brief grip around his chest had been crushingly strong. He couldn't sit up yet, but turning his head to the side, he could see the others.

Shilo charged the creature, her hands aglow. The girl's curly hair lifted up off her head and Pavel could almost feel the static crackling in the air. She was using her Etching and pulling no punches. Still, none of her blows landed. The creature casually evaded each swing of her fists, moving around her like a dancer. No lacings swathed the man-faced ape, but Pavel couldn't help but think it moved with the grace of an Aether Weaver. Actually, the way it floated and flowed like a leaf on the breeze made Aether

Weavers look like lead-footed oafs. This creature seemed less like a Weaver and more like the living embodiment of Aether itself, if that made any sense. Like a Sprite. Was it a Sprite? Physical descriptions of those elemental creatures varied wildly, but they were supposed to be vaguely human-shaped.

Shilo didn't stand a chance. She may as well have been fighting the wind. The creature's long banded tail, which it held upright like a squirrel as it moved, suddenly snaked out and wrapped itself around Shilo's waist. With a flick it tossed her a dozen paces, sending her plummeting into the moat. Pavel heard the splash. It was better than landing on stone, assuming she didn't black out.

Pavel looked to the others. From the moment the Manface showed aggression, Jayn and Thalia had begun working their own desperate gambit. Maybe they sensed intuitively a direct attack would be worthless. Thalia stood behind Jayn, her hands on the Wave Weaver's shoulders. Ryn still crouched at their feet. The creature stopped its attack and merely stared down at them, as if fascinated by the shield they were trying to finish. They didn't stand a chance of setting it in time… Except the creature stopped attacking. It let them finish. The girls formed a dome over themselves and Ryn and set it. Thalia dropped her hands, and they all stared up at the monster looming over them.

Only an Etching like Nyssa's could form a truly impenetrable shield—though Aether could still destroy hers. A determined attacker, even a non-Weaver, could eventually force his way through a lesser shield like Jayn's. Maybe the Manface knew that, and it was just toying with them by letting them finish.

A long silence filled the night, punctuated only by splashing sounds from the moat, probably Shilo swimming back to the ledge near the jail entrance. She wouldn't make it back in time to save them. She couldn't help even if she did. This monkey clearly outclassed all of them, especially without any weapons. As if to prove that point, the Manface extended a creepy long finger and popped Jayn's shield like a bubble. Pavel's jaw dropped. Only Aether could do that, but the beast had not formed any lacings that Pavel could see. Maybe it really was the living embodiment of Aether.

The creature's head bobbed up and down, as a high-pitched wheezing sound escaped its lips. This then was how the creature laughed. Pavel found the noise deeply unsettling. The laugh stopped short as a low boom sounded overhead. It seemed to have come from within the Grand Hall. The creature tilted its head, maybe hearing something they could not.

"No more time to play, ts-ts-ts." Ignoring the Watchkeepers completely, it turned and bounded off. It had a strange way of moving, hopping sideways rather than forward. It slipped into the shadows beneath the Grand Hall. They saw it disappear up the stone steps, into the belly of the marble cube.

"What happened?" Shilo asked. She had just managed to make her way out of the moat and back up the stairs. Her boots squelched as she moved toward them, water streaming from her uniform. They had all slept in their Watchkeeper grays, minus the tabards.

"He went inside," Pavel said. He managed to stand back up. "I shudder to think what's happening in there."

"That thing was a monster," Thalia said, shaking her head in disbelief. "How could it move like that?"

"Don't think about that right now," Jayn said. She looked at the others. "Rousting the city guard is still our top priority." She hesitated but then clenched her fists and continued. "Shilo and Pavel, you two should go."

"What?" Shilo began to protest. Apparently, she still wasn't over not trusting Pavel.

Jayn cut her off. "There might be Kobolds out in the city. I'm useless without a weapon, but you're not. Worst case, Pavel can outrun anything and find help. It's the right call." She glanced down. "Thalia and I can stay and shield Ryn if we have to, assuming that… Manface doesn't come back."

Pavel shook his head. "I love that you're using my word, but I'm not just going to run away here."

Jayn must have read his mind. "Captain Lahmeer can take care of herself. You charging up there won't help. We might still be weathering the recoil. Getting the guard is the best way to help right now."

Pavel stared up at the Grand Hall. "Fine," he said through gritted teeth. He knew Nyssa was tough, but she would need all the help she could get. He turned to Thalia. "Do you have more luck charms?"

"Up in my room… on the third floor."

"You should go get them."

"They won't work for us, not until the recoil wears off fully."

"I know, but you can find anyone who's still alive inside and start handing them out."

"Oh," she said and nodded. "I can do that."

They should have moved then, but they all hesitated, staring fearfully around. He forgot sometimes they were still just kids. Kobolds. Evil Weavers. Monsters. It was a lot.

"Right," he said, stepping forward. He held out his fist with his pinky finger extended. "We can do this."

No one laughed or protested. Thalia helped Ryn to stand and kept an arm around his waist. They all held out their hands and grabbed each other's little fingers, forming a circle with their fists.

Pavel counted them off, "One, two, three…"

"Pentad," they said in unison. They spoke the word not as a shout or a battle cry but as a soft and solemn declaration of who they were and what they were capable of.

Chapter 25
The Storm

NYSSA LUNGED FORWARD, driving her sword into the Kobold's belly. She pulled her blade free as the creature collapsed to the ground. She flicked her wrist, shaking drops of bubbling blue blood off the sword. She knew from experience that getting it on her skin would cause an annoying rash. She turned to see Anyse Eldragor dispatch her foe. Nyssa scanned the corridor, but all the Kobolds were dead. So were half a dozen servants and two Wardens.

The screaming had awoken Nyssa from restless dreams. She'd thrown on her uniform, grabbed her sword, and stepped out into a nightmare she thought she had escaped. It seemed impossible that Kobolds could be in the very heart of Aldria, but here they were. When the first Kobold swung at her with its spiked club, she almost didn't get her blade up in time. Maybe she was getting rusty, but something else had changed too.

The last time she fought hordes of Kobolds, she only survived because the creatures tended to ignore her, at least until she swung at them. Pavel reasoned that because they had previously been exposed to Kobold venom, the beasts could smell that stench of death on them. Expecting Nyssa and the others to drop dead at any moment, the creatures had treated them like low-priority targets. It was just a guess, but it made sense at the time. Now these Kobolds hadn't even hesitated to attack her. Maybe the taint of poison eventually wore off. Or maybe…

Something else had happened the night Kobolds attacked Falport, something she had never been able to explain. There were many events beyond explanation that night, but this one applied specifically to her. A giant owl with a human face had appeared above her when she was slaying Kobolds in the streets. "Great fools!" it had shouted. Perhaps the insult had been meant for the humans for fighting back or the Kobolds for dying; Nyssa couldn't say. Then the owl's gaze focused on Nyssa. "She is Marked, but she lives," it said.

Though less human-like, the owl seemed far more intelligent than the Kobolds. Nyssa assumed the owl had also been able to sense the poison in her blood but had been smart enough to realize she wasn't dying. The owl attacked her then, driving its talons into her flesh. In that moment, Nyssa believed it was trying to kill her. She had not expected to live. Yet, hours later, Agia found her lying in the street and healed her wounds. The talon marks had been shallow and superficial, Agia said, which made no sense.

The creature was powerful. It knocked Nyssa down with ease, and later her recruits saw it lift the black-clad Kobold known as Kalo into the air and carry him off. Nyssa could not understand why it had not simply killed her. She reasoned that perhaps it had done something more subtle to her, suspecting that like Kalo, it may have had strange, Weaver-like powers. She went as far as having multiple Root Weavers examine her, to see if anything detectable had been done to her body. They found nothing. She wondered now if perhaps the owl had somehow used its claws to drain the taint of poison—the "Mark"—from her body, leaving her vulnerable to the next Kobold attack.

She shook her head. Now was not the time to speculate. "Are you hurt?" she asked Anyse. "Did any of them scratch you?"

The Fourth Pentarch checked her bare arms and twisted to look down at her body. She wore a plain linen nightgown, now splattered with acidic blue blood that would eventually eat through the material. "I'm all right, I think." Despite having lost her ability to Weave, the former general was still formidable with a sword.

"Watch their claws. We think they might carry a sort of toxin that can be deadly."

Anyse bent to look at one of the gray corpses. "So these are Kobolds? Ugly little things. Jayn was right. They're strong, but it doesn't seem like they've had any combat training. How did they get inside though? What happened to the alarm?"

Nyssa had been wondering that herself. She shook her head. "I don't know, but if they made it up here to the third level, the whole Hall has to be crawling with them. We'll need to be careful." She looked at Anyse again. "Are you…?"

"Yes, I'm fine," she said with an impatient toss of her head. "I've moped around long enough. If this is how Kobolds fight, I'll have no problem helping you clear the lower levels, even without Flame. Do you think Jayn and her Pentad are all right, down in the cells?"

Nyssa shrugged. "The timing is awful. They must have hit the recoil from Moldo's luck charms by now. Still, they're a competent group. I wouldn't count them out."

If Anyse was worried for her daughter, she kept fear from her countenance and voice. "Ready when you are."

"Right."

Nyssa led the way down the hall. She didn't think they needed to clear the rest of their floor. No other guests of the Hall had been staying in the rooms here, and the noisy fight should have drawn in any lingering Kobolds. She headed for the main stairwell, trusting Anyse to watch her back. They reached the second-floor landing, stepped out into the wide central corridor, and found a horror show.

Bodies lay everywhere, a mix of Kobolds, Wardens, and servants. Red blood mingled with blue, causing a strange chemical reaction that bubbled and smoked, filling the air with a noxious odor. Nyssa saw Thalia first, standing protectively over Ryn, who sat in a pool of blood—not his own. The Root Weaver had a young Warden wrapped in green light, working some healing. The man's right leg ended in a bloody stump just below the knee. Nyssa didn't see Pavel or Shilo, but she spotted Jayn, moving through the tangled mess of bodies, searching for something.

"Hurry up," Ryn called, not taking his eyes off the Warden, who appeared to be unconscious.

"I'm trying," Jayn said. "This isn't easy… Ah-ha!" Crouching down, she lifted a dead Kobold, rolling it over onto its side. She reached under it and held up a white boot in triumph. Nyssa realized it wasn't just a boot.

The recruits looked up when Nyssa and Anyse approached.

"Captain," Thalia said with a nod.

"Mother," Jayn said, smiling. She stepped her way back through the bodies, laying the severed leg down by the Warden's stump. Searching the bodies had bloodied her uniform a little, but she and the other seemed unharmed. They must have missed the fight, arriving in its aftermath, though they were all wet.

"What are we doing?" Nyssa asked, scanning the room again for any more survivors—friends or foes.

"I'm going to reattach his leg," Ryn said, not breaking his concentration. He must have been using lacings to stop the man's blood from pouring out of the wound without fully healing it. Doing so would have left the man with a smooth stub.

Nyssa sighed. "Didn't you learn your lesson doing triage back in Falport? This man can live without a leg. A reattachment will drain you completely. If Kobolds are still here, we'll need you for the fight or to heal others."

He shook his head, already beginning to form the elaborate lacings necessary to stitch a severed limb back onto a body. When had he learned them? Normally, a team of Root Weavers would have to work in tandem for such an elaborate healing. "I may be out of the fight. I can't walk right now. I turned my ankle pretty bad. Thalia had to carry me up here. And it won't drain me."

Nyssa remembered the words of encouragement she'd shared with Ryn yesterday. Maybe she shouldn't have said everything she had. Maybe the kid did have a big ego now. Still… Though Root Weavers could boost their abilities by draining nearby vegetation, they all had a limit, and when they reached it, they usually blacked out. Nyssa had seen Ryn push himself past the limit more than once in the few months she had known him. Still, he had a deep reservoir, and weeks of strenuous Watchkeeper training had only made it deeper.

They all watched in fascination as Ryn laid crisscrossing lines of Root between the leg and the foot. Carefully, he reached out with his hand, lifted the foot, and held it in place, lining up the two severed bones. Those knit together first. Though Root was complementary to Wave, Nyssa had never been able to master healing. Even she knew that causing bones to grow took a tremendous amount of energy.

Ryn tilted his head, looking down and to the right. "It's a good thing the kitchens grow their own herbs," he said, almost to himself. Nyssa's eyes widened. She knew where the kitchen lay. The roots of Ryn's spectral tree disappeared into the ground, but it seemed impossible that they could reach down to the kitchens. If the cooks came in tomorrow, they would find their potted herb plants shriveled to brown husks.

As Ryn painstakingly stitched each tendon and artery back together, Nyssa pulled her gaze away, turning to Thalia. "Where are the others? Pavel and Shilo?"

Thalia turned to her, though she didn't answer right away. She blinked her eyes, trying to refocus. Apparently, Ryn's healing had also enthralled her—or made her queasy. "Sorry," she said. "They're fine. They went out to find the city guards and sound the alarm. Somebody disabled the dome."

"Did Kobolds attack the cells?"

Thalia shook her head. She glanced at Anyse and hesitated. Whatever she wanted to say, she apparently didn't want to say it in front of the Fourth Pentarch. "Someone, uh, did kill the Wardens down there, and they busted Lucas Peniter out of his cell, but they left us alone. We'd still be asleep down there if Pavel hadn't woken us up."

Nyssa knew there had to be more to that story, but it could wait. She looked at Thalia's hands. None of them were wearing their copper rings anymore, which meant Nyssa had been right about the timing. They were all walking magnets for bad luck right now.

Thalia saw Nyssa checking their hands and must have figured out what she was thinking. "We all, uh, tripped over our own feet coming this far. None of us would be standing right now if Ryn hadn't healed us. It's possible the recoil has passed."

"It was smart to send the other two out for help, but the rest of you might have been better off staying in your cells."

She nodded. "I know. We thought we could at least make it up to our rooms to grab more luck charms and hand them out to anyone still standing."

Nyssa glanced down at Ryn, still focused on his healing. "It's not a bad idea, under the circumstances. Anyse and I can stand watch over Ryn. The third floor is clear. You and Jayn should go up and grab your weapons and rings. Just try not to trip and break your necks coming down the stairs."

Thalia nodded. Jayn glanced at her mother, seeing the blue blood stains and the sword in her hand. "Are you all right, Mother?" she asked.

Anyse waved her hand. "Listen to your superior officer. Don't worry about me. You were right about these Kobolds. They're vicious but terrible fighters."

"Still, they make up for it by traveling in packs." Jayn glanced back at Ryn. "When he finishes healing Jax, have him check for Kobolds again. Ryn can detect them. It's how we knew we were safe to make our way up this far." She pointed down the corridor, away from the stairs. "He said there were a bunch down that way still. We assume they're breaking into the vault to steal more Runeforms, like they did in Falport, but we don't know."

"Thanks," Nyssa said. "Now hurry up, and someone get a knife for Ryn."

Jayn nodded. She turned and hurried toward the stairs. Thalia followed but stopped at the exit, turning back to Nyssa. "Something else you should know," she called back. "There's another one of those human-faced creatures around here somewhere. This one is like a giant monkey. Be careful. It would have killed us, except it was in a hurry to get in here."

Nyssa glanced down the hallway in the direction of the vault, as fear gripped her heart again. Another beast. Was it like the owl? Nyssa closed her eyes and tried to deliberately *not* think about Weaving. She threw up her hands and instantly a shield formed over her, Anyse, Ryn, and the still unconscious Warden. What had Jayn called the young man? Jax? Nyssa still didn't understand how she had been able to make her shield work instantaneously again, but she had. She glanced back at Thalia, who still lingered in the entryway. "Go," she said.

Thalia hesitated. "That, uh, might not work. Jayn and I put up a shield when the monkey-thing attacked us. It reached out and touched the shield. That's all it did, just touched it, but the shield vanished. I don't know how."

Nyssa sighed. At this point, she was willing to believe anything they told her, no matter how preposterous it should have sounded. "Hurry up then. I think I will take a luck charm this time."

Nyssa turned back to the long, silent passageway strewn with bodies. She raised her sword and squared her stance. She didn't know what to expect. Literally anything might come charging down the corridor toward them at any moment—an army of Kobolds, a whole menagerie of man-faced creatures, maybe even a Drake. Whatever fresh nightmare awaited, she would face it, on her feet and swinging.

Shilo moved down the empty street as quickly as she dared, still fearing to run, lest she trip over her own feet again. Her boots squelched with each step, still wet from when the Manface threw her into the moat. She glanced at Pavel, realizing only then that he wasn't wearing the standard-issue gray leather boots.

"Are those your dancing shoes from Summer Feast?" she asked.

He shrugged. "They're more comfortable than my boots, and I wasn't really expecting all this to happen."

"Did we do this? I mean, did our collective recoil of bad luck cause this?"

He shook his head. "Don't think like that. Sure, the timing is unlucky, but tonight's attack still would have happened. Whatever this is, the Reach had to be planning it for a long time."

"The Reach?"

He winced but didn't look at her. "Years ago, when I did that job for Peniter, he was working for a group that called themselves the Reach. I always thought they were just petty criminals, and maybe they're not the same group of people working with the Kobolds now, but… we don't know what else to call them, so I've been thinking of them as the Reach in my head."

"Why didn't you say any of this before?"

He sighed. "Listen, Shilo, I know you don't trust me, and I don't blame you, but you can't think I have anything to do with Peniter, or Hinter, or those monsters."

Shilo didn't respond. They trudged on in silence. When Jayn sent them off to get help, they hadn't really picked a direction. They ran toward the nearest makeshift bridge, which happened to face north toward the Civic Quintant, so here they were. Shilo regretted that now. After the riot two nights ago, this section of the city lay essentially deserted. According to Jayn, most of the lords and ladies had fled to their country estates. They had not seen a single city guard or anyone else. The eastern sky had begun to brighten, though the sun had not yet risen.

Could she trust Pavel? She knew he wasn't telling her everything, but she couldn't fathom that he would knowingly work with Kobolds. She knew he'd fought their leader, Kalo, on two separate occasions, nearly dying both times. From the time they'd spent together, she knew Pavel to be a natural liar with questionable morals, but he wasn't evil. Only truly evil people like Lucas Peniter and Gwen Hinter could work with Kobolds. She didn't have to like Pavel, but for the moment, she had to at least try to trust him.

Something swooped down from a nearby rooftop, a small dark shape with glowing blue eyes. Corvus landed gracefully on Pavel's shoulder. Shilo had seen no sign of the Runeform since they'd reached Appencourt some ten days ago. It cawed in greeting, an uncanny imitation of a real crow. Then it spread its wings and took off. "Everything's fine!" it called as it vanished from sight.

Shilo and Pavel stopped in their tracks. Lacings of Flame burst from her chest as she prepared to defend herself. A glance told her Pavel had made similar preparations with swirls of Aether. She wished she had a weapon. She gritted her teeth. Her frustration with Pavel had boiled over into irritation at his pet Runeform. "Why does he always say that?"

"Huh?" Pavel asked, sounding distracted. They'd shifted to stand back-to-back, scanning the dark streets for signs of danger.

"That stupid sarcastic crow. Why does he always say, 'Everything's fine,' when something bad is about to happen?"

"He, uh, thinks it's funny, I guess."

Shilo sighed. She wondered if a Runeform could pick up mannerisms from its owner.

"On your left," Pavel said.

Shilo turned. Three Kobolds had just emerged from a side alley. They paused, seeing Shilo and Pavel. The closest one studied them. Its ugly face wrinkled as it seemed to sniff the air. It grunted, then gestured with its head toward the Grand Hall. The Kobold and its companions turned and loped off down the street, completely ignoring the two Watchkeepers.

"What are they doing?"

"Ignoring us," Pavel said. "That's how they treat anyone who's been poisoned by a Kobold."

Shilo understood then. She had heard the others describe how Kobolds tended to ignore them. She too had been scratched by Kalo's claws, but she had not encountered any other Kobolds since that attack. She thought about just letting them leave. She didn't want to fight them, not empty-handed. Still, she knew where they must be headed—toward the Grand Hall, where her friends and Captain Lahmeer still were. Along the way, they might also kill some random citizens who stumbled upon them. She was also still a little bit mad at Pavel, and maybe she just needed to hit something. She clenched her fists and charged.

"What are you—" Pavel started to say. She didn't hear if he finished the question.

She caught the rear Kobold unawares. She jumped, bringing her glowing fist down onto the creature's back. The Kobold crumbled under the full brunt of her Etching. She knew to blink so the sudden flash of light wouldn't blind her. Her Etching imparted a strong static charge and a great deal of force. The downward angle of her punch had smashed the Kobold into the paving stones. Its ruined body looked like it had been thrown from the top of a tall building.

She leapt over it. The second Kobold turned back toward her, swinging wildly with its wooden club. Shilo planted her feet. She let go of her Etching and formed a different lacing, remembering something Jayn had said about how a talented Flame Weaver could stop an arrow in flight. Summoning vines of Root, she reached up and grabbed the club as it came down toward her. She barely felt it, as her lacings absorbed all the energy from the swing.

The snub-nosed monster blinked in confusion. Shilo snatched the club from its hands, tossing it over her shoulder. Then she hit it in the stomach with an uppercut that sent it flying backward. The last Kobold, who had also turned back around, barely dodged the flying body of its companion. Then it charged Shilo, slashing with its sword. Shilo danced back, wary of the blade. She knew she could stop the momentum again but worried it might still slice her hand.

Shilo took another step back and tripped over the body of the first Kobold. She fell backward, landing awkwardly on top of it. She put her palms down, trying to scramble back onto her feet. Her right hand splashed into a pool of blood. The last Kobold raised its sword and prepared to bring it down and split Shilo's skull.

The Kobold flinched and froze, with its arms still up over its head. Its eyes left Shilo as it looked down at its own chest. The metal tip of an arrow bloomed there. A trickle of blue blood ran down its gray skin. The creature's yellowed eyes rolled up into his head. He began to fall forward onto Shilo, slowly, like a tree that had just been felled.

Pavel reached her then. He planted one foot and hit the Kobold with a roundhouse kick, sending it sideways so that it collapsed onto the street and not onto Shilo. He offered her a hand and pulled her to her feet. They both turned to see a dark-haired woman in a blue dress, still holding up a crossbow.

"Miss Bellain?" Pavel said, clearly incredulous.

She nodded, lowering her weapon. "Pavel Talvor. Shilo Lorn. It's a pleasure to see you again."

"What are you doing out here?"

"I'm an early riser. I was just out taking my morning constitutional."

"With a crossbow?"

"A woman can never be too careful," she said with a smile. "And please, I told you to call me Mina."

They all turned, hearing boots clatter against the paving stones. Two city guards, with white tunics over their chainmail, approached at a run. "What's all this?" the first said. The two men stumbled to a halt when they saw that the bodies in the street weren't human.

"Curse me…" the second guard said, eyes wide.

"Watchkeepers?" the first guard asked, recognizing Pavel and Shilo's uniforms, though they weren't wearing their tabards or pins.

Pavel nodded. "Listen, the Grand Hall is being attacked. All the alarms have been disabled. My friend and I are a bit… cursed right now, so we're trying to keep our distance. We need to roust the city guard. All of them, preferably."

"Are those Kobolds?" the second guard asked, clearly still distracted by the sight of the bodies.

"Yes," Pavel said, a touch of impatience in his voice. "More Kobolds are attacking the Grand Hall, as we stand here. What's the fastest way to alert the whole city guard?"

The first man blinked at Pavel in confusion. "You said the Hall's alarms are down?" He glanced back toward the north. "We have our own bells. The fastest way to sound the alarm would be going north to the Melgeld Gate guard house. From there, we could also send runners to the other four gates."

"How did Kobolds get into the city?" the second guard asked, still incredulous.

"We need to move," Pavel said. He crouched down and picked up the sword the Kobold had dropped. "Blight, I got blood on my white shoes."

Shilo saw the flecks of blue, as the first rays of sunlight broke over the city. She looked back at Mina Bellain. "The streets aren't safe," she said. "You should find somewhere to shelter."

She didn't wait to see what the Scholar would do. Pavel had already set off at a trot. Shilo picked up a club and followed at his heels.

"We'll come with you!" the first guard said belatedly.

Shilo sent a silent prayer to the Maker that her friends could stay alive until help came, even if they could no longer trust the luck.

Chapter 26
The Vault

THALIA TOOK HER TIME going down the stairs. She nearly tripped once, but she didn't know if it was from bad luck or being nervous. The marble steps she'd taken up and down for over a week seemed suddenly steep and precarious. She was extremely aware of the sharp blade at the end of her poleaxe. Jayn went just as slowly and said nothing. By the time they reached the second level, Ryn had finished healing the young Warden. The youth, whom Jayn had called Jax, had to be about the same age as Thalia. Jax was awake now, taking a long sip from a waterskin, while Ryn examined his leg. A jagged red line ran around his calf where the limb had been severed.

"Damage like this needs time to fully heal," Ryn said. "I did my best, but… Well, I think this leg is going to be slightly longer now. You may have to wear corrective shoes."

Jax stopped drinking and barked a laugh. "Better than using crutches for the rest of my life. Thank you… Ryn, was it?" His voice sounded hoarse.

Ryn nodded.

Nyssa glanced back as Thalia and Jayn approached. With a wave of her hand, she dropped her shield. Jax tilted his head toward Jayn. "You have an impressive Pentad, Jayn. You guys saved my life."

Jayn smiled. "We did set a new record for the training Gauntlet."

"I wish we could have saved the others," Ryn said, more to himself.

Thalia looked over the carnage again. They had missed the fight. The first time they'd reached this hallway, Thalia had been carrying Ryn. They stopped so he could try to detect if any Kobolds were nearby. If they hadn't, they would have missed Jax. The already unconscious Warden looked like just another corpse at first glance, until Ryn sensed his life force.

"Here," Thalia said, crouching beside Ryn. She pulled the knife from her belt and handed it to him.

He examined the blade with interest, a puzzled look on his face. "Where did you get this? It's not one of mine."

She glanced away and tried to keep her tone casual. "I, uh, made it actually, back in Falport. It's Iscernaen steel. I wanted to give it to you actually, as a sort of thank you for saving me back when we were behind that warehouse. I just, uh, never got around to it."

"Wow, you did a good job," he said, running his finger along the blade's edge. He looked up and smiled. "The way I remember it, we saved each other that night."

She couldn't help but smile herself. Ryn was sweet.

"Right," Nyssa said, stepping past them to peer down the hall. "Now the question is, do we wait here for the city guard, or do we try to stop the Kobolds from breaching the vault? I hate to think what they will do with more Runeforms."

"They're already inside," Jax said.

All eyes turned toward him. He sat leaned up against the wall.

"How do you know?" Nyssa asked.

"My Etching," he said. A coughing fit seized him then. He glanced at Anyse Eldragor.

"Of course," she said, stepping forward. She gestured to the young Warden. "Jax Centillion is a family friend. His Etching is why the Wardens recruited him. He can place a small ward in any room, and then when he closes his eyes, he can see what's happening in that room… like he's actually there."

"Wow," Jayn said, clearly impressed. "I hadn't heard that."

Thalia knew Wave Weavers could create security wards where if anyone crossed through or tampered with them, an image of the trespasser would flash into the Weaver's mind. Jax's ability to always see through his wards was unique and clearly valuable.

Jax nodded and took another long sip of water to suppress his cough. "When we stepped up security last week, the commander had me place a ward inside the vault. The commander…" He craned his neck to look around.

"He's not here," Nyssa said, understanding his concern. She must have checked the bodies when Thalia and Jayn were getting their weapons.

Jax nodded. "All the other wards are down. I don't know how they did it. They missed my Third Eye though… That's what I call my Etching. I made it really small and stuck it up in the corner."

Nyssa crouched down to look Jax in the eye. "What do you see right now?"

Jax closed his eyes. His forehead wrinkled in confusion. He kept them shut as he spoke. "There's a lot of Kobolds. They have these… burlap sacks, and they're filling them up with all the small Runeforms. There's people in there too. Weavers. Five of them."

"What are the Weavers doing, Jax?"

"I don't know… I've never seen anything like it…"

"Describe it."

"They're standing around the Viewing Glass, and they're all sending lacings into it. It's all Five Forces… How are they doing that?"

"What's the Viewing Glass?" Nyssa asked.

A cold chill ran up and down Thalia's spine. She locked eyes with Ryn. This sounded all too familiar. Jax opened his eyes and glanced at Anyse. Maybe he didn't know what secrets of the Grand Hall he could share with the Watchkeepers.

Anyse frowned. "The Viewing Glass is just what we call it. It's one of our most valuable Runeforms. It looks like a large mirror… Kind of like the one used in Falport, I think." She had made the same connection, having read the initial reports from the Watchkeepers.

"What does the Viewing Glass do?" Nyssa asked.

"There's another part to it, a little hand-held mirror. We can give it to an ambassador, or anyone we want, and they can take it anywhere in the world. If both mirrors are activated at the same time, we can see and speak to our agent, no matter how far away they are. You can't walk through the mirror though. I'm not sure… I think a representative we sent to the Tamor border has the small mirror now."

"They may not need that part for what they're doing."

"You don't really think they can turn this mirror into a portal too? Can they?"

Nyssa shrugged. "It would seem so. We can't let them finish." She returned her attention to Jax. "The Weavers, the humans in there, do you recognize any of them?"

Jax closed his eyes. He kept them shut as he shook his head. "The Wave Weaver… It's a girl wearing a Warden's uniform, but I don't know her."

Thalia glanced down the corridor. The vault was back there somewhere, just a few hallways away. They still couldn't hear anything. "Jax," she asked, again fighting to keep her voice level. "The Root Weaver in the group, how would you describe her?"

"She's… I guess you could say she's big for a woman. Wide, I mean, with brown frizzy hair."

Thalia stared at Nyssa and tried to impart a significance to her look. Nyssa's forehead wrinkled in confusion for a moment, but then she nodded in understanding. Pavel really had seen Gwen Hinter down in the cells, and now she was here in the vault. Anyse had not missed the silent exchange, and though she looked puzzled, she didn't say anything.

"Jax," Nyssa said, returning her attention to the boy. "Are there any… creatures in the vault, other than the Kobolds?"

Thalia could see Jax's eyes moving beneath his lids, as if he really were peering around a room. "They all look like Kobolds to me. I've never seen a Kobold before tonight, but… they all pretty much look the same. That gray skin, like a dead body…" If the ape-like Manface wasn't there, Thalia wondered where it could be.

"Do any of the Kobolds stand out to you?" Nyssa asked.

"Yeah, there's a really tall one. He…" Jax hesitated for a moment, confused by whatever he was seeing. Then he gasped. His eyes shot open and he stared up at Nyssa, a touch of madness in his gaze.

"What happened?" Nyssa said, her voice still surprisingly calm.

"I don't believe it…" Jax said. "When I focused on him… It was like he could sense me looking at him somehow. He turned right around and stared up at my ward. It was like he could see *me*. Then he raised his hand and something shot out of it. He destroyed my ward."

"Kalo," Jayn said. They could all hear the dread in that single word.

"What?" Anyse asked, staring at her daughter. "How can you know?" Jayn didn't meet her gaze.

Nyssa sighed, rising from her crouch. "Kalo is the Kobold who wears black leather armor. We think he leads the other ones. And he is a Weaver."

"What?" Anyse asked again, clearly aghast.

"We don't think the other Kobolds can Weave, but Kalo seems able to create some kind of lacings, though they look like… black shadows."

"A Kobold Weaver?" Anyse asked, shaking her head. "Why was this information kept from your reports?"

"The masters decided it was too… controversial and potentially inflammatory to put into writing. If we'd been able to testify last week, I would have told the Hall."

Thalia didn't know if that was exactly true. She remembered Commandant Lahey saying Nyssa would use that information as a secret bargaining chip, only if the Hall didn't respond appropriately to the Kobold threat. None of that mattered now. The Hall would have no choice but to turn its full attention to the Kobold threat now—assuming there would still be a Hall at the end of the day. Thalia assumed the sun had risen outside.

Anyse shook her head in disbelief but didn't say anything further.

Nyssa looked down at Jax. "How many Kobolds could you see inside the vault?"

"I didn't count them, but… maybe twenty."

Nyssa sighed. "Twenty Kobolds. Five rogue Weavers. Kalo. A giant monkey…" She looked around at their group. Thalia did too. Jax looked too tired to even stand. Ryn's Etching could activate at any moment and heal his twisted ankle, but given their luck, it could also take hours. That left three Watchkeepers and the Fourth Pentarch, who had just lost her ability to Weave. Nyssa shook her head. "We don't stand a chance against all that."

"You suggest we retreat?" Anyse asked.

"No. We cannot allow them to open another portal. We still don't know everything that came through last time, or where they even came from. They also don't need any more Runeforms. I've seen the vault, from the outside at least. There's only one way into it, down a narrow passageway. If we can make it to that passage… We won't be able to force our way in, but we can also use that bottleneck to keep them trapped inside. Maybe it will be enough of a distraction to break the Weavers' focus… If we're lucky."

She held out a hand toward Thalia, palm up. Thalia nodded. She reached into her pocket and pulled out the velvet bag. She fished out a copper ring and handed it to Nyssa.

Nyssa clutched the ring into a fist and looked around again. "I can't ask any of you to come with me."

"You don't have to ask," Jayn said, placing her hand on the pommel of her sword, which hung at her waist.

"I'll take one of those rings," Anyse said, holding out her hand. "I won't let them destroy my home."

"We still need to be careful," Thalia said, handing rings out to each of them, even Ryn and Jax. If the recruits were still experiencing the recoil from last time, the luck couldn't help them yet, but it was worth a shot. "Last time we faced Kalo using luck charms, he used some kind of lacing to break them, and then he nearly killed us."

Anyse's eyes widened. "A lacing that can destroy Stone enchantments? Does that make this Kalo a Flame Weaver?"

"Maybe," Nyssa said. "He's strong and formidable in a fight, but the lacings he uses… It may not even come from any of the Five Forces."

Anyse shook her head, but she still slipped the copper ring onto her finger. "Let's get moving then."

Ryn reached up and touched Thalia's hand. She looked down at him. He met her gaze, a frown on his face. "Be careful," he said. "All of you," he added, looking around.

She nodded, slipping a ring onto her own finger. "Trust the luck," she said and forced a smile, but she couldn't shake the feeling that death was waiting for each of them inside that vault.

Even from inside the first floor of the guardhouse, Pavel could hear the massive bell tolling five stories up, atop the massive white wall that surrounded Appencourt. Pavel and Shilo were in a small interrogation room, seated at a table opposite an officer. He had believed enough of what they were saying to sound the alarm and send runners along the walls, but he still wasn't convinced.

"Kobolds?" he said. "In Appencourt?" The man was built like an oak barrel, and he was completely bald. He turned and looked at the two guards standing near the door, the same two Pavel and Shilo had met in the street. Pavel hadn't caught any of their names.

"Yes, sir," one said, bobbing his head. "We saw the bodies ourselves. Course, I've never seen a Kobold before, but they matched the description."

"They certainly weren't human," the second one said, nodding in agreement.

"They were Kobolds," Mina Bellain said. She stood behind Pavel, where she'd positioned herself in the corner. She had ditched her crossbow at some point. He didn't know why she had come along. He didn't like it, but there was nothing he could do about it.

"And you are?" the officer asked Mina with narrowed eyes.

She smiled, pleasant as ever. "Mina Bellain, of the Academy of the Ways."

"A Scholar?" he said, his thin eyebrows crawling up his red face. He nodded, apparently willing to take a Scholar's word over his two men. He looked back to Pavel. "But these Kobolds are dead now?"

"The ones who attacked us are, sure. But there are more attacking the Grand Hall right now."

The officer frowned. "Why? This time of day, with so many lords gone after that riot, there's nobody in the Hall."

"We don't know," Pavel said. "Maybe they wanted the Hall to be empty. It's possible they are trying to steal the Runeforms kept in the Grand Hall's vaults. If it is just a smash and grab, then we need to seal all exits to the city."

"I'd advise you to do as he says," Mina piped in from the corner.

The officer nodded. "We've shut our gate. The other guardhouses will have heard our bell and done the same. It's standard procedure." He glanced upward. "The runners may be back by now." He sighed and pushed himself up from his chair. He staggered to the door and left without another word.

Pavel exchanged a glance with Shilo. She shrugged. They got up and followed the officer. The two guards gaped at them and seemed like they might tell them to stop, but the officer hadn't ordered anyone to stay put. Maybe the guards were intimidated by Watchkeepers and Scholars. In the end, the guards stayed mute, falling in line behind Pavel and Shilo. Pavel didn't know if Mina followed or stayed behind. He didn't want to look back. He hoped the less attention he paid to her, the less she would study him. He still wasn't sure why she had taken such an interest in his Training Pentad, but it couldn't be good. Did she know Pavel's father was a leader among the Scholars? That seemed unlikely, unless she knew Pavel's real name. Or maybe she had noted their physical resemblance. He could unravel that puzzle later.

They followed the officer up a tightly spiraling staircase to the top of the wall. Stepping out into the light of dawn, they could see the whole Civic Quintant spread before them in a widening V. They could make out the square roof of the Grand Hall. From this distance, nothing seemed amiss. Looking back, Pavel saw the gate town of Melgeld hugging the base of the wall. A broad road emerged from that mess of ramshackle huts and squat brick buildings, winding its way north and disappearing into the wooded hills that sat above Appencourt, where the wealthiest citizens kept their estates. From atop the wall, the sounding of the bell was nearly deafening. In the lulls between gongs, Pavel could hear answering bells from other points in the city.

"A runner!" one of the guards shouted between peals. They could all see a man making his way along the broad wall that ran south and east. Pavel could just make out the point where the wall turned and ran due east along the edge of the Green Quintant. The man could not have made it all the way to the Walgeld Gate and back in such a short time, but he must have met someone coming from that gate. The runner stopped short in front of the officer, panting to catch his breath.

"Come on!" the officer said, grabbing his arm and pulling him back inside. The ringing bell would have made a debrief nearly impossible. They only descended one level, and the officer pulled the runner out into a hallway. Despite the thick layer of stone overhead, the bell was still quite loud. The guards had to shout to hear each other.

"Sir!" the runner said, saluting.

"What's the report?" the officer said, waving his hand, clearly impatient.

"I met a runner coming from the Walgeld Gate. The man had been off duty, asleep when he heard our bell. He and the other guards woke up. They went down to make sure the gate had been sealed. They found it standing open. All the guards on duty were dead! Their throats had been slit. He doesn't know how it happened. He says there's no way they should have slept through an attack on the gate. He doesn't know why no one set off their alarm either…" His voice faded out as if exhausted from shouting and running. "They must not have had a chance," he added, fear in his eyes.

The officer let loose a colorful string of oaths—some Pavel had never even heard before. He looked back at Pavel and Shilo. For a moment, it seemed like he had completely forgotten they were there. Pavel glanced over his shoulder. He didn't see Mina anywhere. The officer shook his head. "That's how your Kobolds got in then," he said. "They overran the gate somehow. The Green Quintant is mostly parks and museums and the like. They would have had no problem ghosting through it at night, all the way to the Grand Hall." He turned to another guard standing at attention. "Let's send reinforcements to the Walgeld Gate. Help them seal it and defend it. From this point on, no one gets in or out of the city."

The officer barked out a few more orders. White-clad guards began running about like someone had kicked an anthill. Pavel nodded to Shilo. "We should get out of here," he said. "We've done what we can."

She nodded and turned back to the stairwell. He followed her down. They had to stop more than once to press against the wall and let guards charge past, some heading up and some heading down. Near the bottom, Shilo glanced back at him. "Do you want to try heading back to the Hall?"

"I'm not sure. I don't know if the recoil is over yet, but… I don't want to just stay on the outskirts either."

"I feel the same way. Maybe we can get a little bit closer and see what's happening."

He knew they probably wouldn't be able to do anything. Whatever the Kobolds and the Reach were doing in the Grand Hall, they had probably already finished. Nyssa and the kids had either made it out, or they were all dead. Nothing Pavel did now could change that. He knew that. He also knew the luck was probably still against them. He had no good reason to go charging back out into the streets. Getting attached had been foolish. Pavel Talvor didn't need friends. In less than five years, Pavel Talvor would cease to exist, and the man behind the name would set out on his own to fulfill his destiny of finding the Five Crowns. He knew all that but—blast the stars—he didn't want to lose any of them yet!

Chapter 27
Wave and Flame

JAYN AND THE OTHERS made it to the vault entrance unchallenged. Two heavy metal doors stood on either end of a narrow corridor. Both had been left wide open. Rows of Weaver lights set high up on the wall illuminated the marble hallway. A single Kobold stood sentry at the second door, but when he saw them, he called over his shoulder to the others inside. A dozen Kobolds spilled out into the hall. Thankfully, Nyssa had been right about the bottleneck. The broad-shouldered Kobolds could only come out single file, but the women could fight two abreast.

Nyssa took on the first Kobold. It held a large knife and slashed wildly with it, but Nyssa deftly deflected its blows and lashed out with her sword. The creature howled and stumbled backward, into the Kobold waiting behind. The second Kobold, clearly impatient to join the fight, shoved its companion forward—right onto the spiked tip of Thalia's poleaxe. The Stone Weaver had used the superior reach of her polearm to thrust past Nyssa. The weapon snagged inside the dying Kobold. Thalia tried to wrench it loose, but she was stuck slightly behind Nyssa. Seeing her dilemma, Nyssa stepped forward and kicked the Kobold square in the chest, dislodging it from the poleaxe. The second Kobold now had to clamber over the dead one to join the fray. Thalia jabbed at it with her poleaxe.

Jayn glanced at her mother, standing beside her with her sword ready. As soon as Nyssa or Thalia began to flag, one of the Eldragors would be ready to take her place. The four of them could hold this passageway for a long time, but they also stood little chance of advancing forward into the vault. Jayn couldn't see much of the vault's interior beyond the milling line of Kobolds. She began to hear a faint humming sound.

Nyssa dealt a fatal blow to the second Kobold. Before it could fall, a third Kobold seized it from behind. The beasts were strong, and this one had no trouble lifting the dead weight and tossing it back over its shoulder. The creatures waiting behind caught the body and passed it backward. The third Kobold then leapt over the first body, swinging its shortsword in a downward arch. Holding her sword with both hands, Nyssa blocked the blow, but it did force her to stumble backward. Jayn caught a flurry of movement behind the third Kobold as the others dragged the first body back, sliding it between their legs. The Watchkeepers could try to block up the corridor with dead bodies, but the Kobolds would work just as hard to clear it.

As Nyssa fell back, Thalia stepped in, lunging with her poleaxe again. The Kobold howled in anguish as the spear-like tip of the poleaxe entered into its side. Thalia's weapon caught again. The Kobold grabbed the poleaxe's shaft and threw itself against the wall, trying to wrench the weapon from Thalia's hands. She staggered but didn't let go. Another Kobold grabbed the injured one from behind and threw itself backward. Thalia couldn't hang on then. The weapon slipped from her fingers, still speared in the dying creature, which fell to the ground as its companion slid past it. The butt of the poleaxe stood upright like a flagpole.

Jayn grabbed the now unarmed Thalia by the shirt collar and pulled her backward. Anyse stepped in to take her place. Nyssa recovered and surged forward, going on the offensive. The two swordswomen fought shoulder-to-shoulder, lashing out with their blades and keeping the Kobolds at bay, for now anyway. Jayn rested a hand on Thalia's shoulder, who leaned against the wall, panting to catch her breath.

"You did well," Jayn said, knowing Thalia had not killed before.

"You hear that sound?" Thalia asked.

Jayn nodded, though she had been ignoring the low humming, all her attention focused on the fight, waiting for her chance to step in.

"It's the same sound the other mirror made. They're opening the portal."

Jayn craned her neck but still couldn't see what was happening in the vault. "We're too late," she said.

Whatever came out of this new portal, if it was anything like the man-faced creatures they had seen already, then the four of them would not stand a chance. That monkey-thing had danced circles around Jayn's Pentad. It seemed to be toying with them. If it had really been trying to kill them, they would be dead. Jayn glanced over her shoulder. She saw no sign of reinforcements coming up behind. She strained her ears. She couldn't quite tell with the low droning and the echoing clangs of steel swords, but could she hear distant bells?

Pavel and Shilo probably had reached the city guards by now, but they wouldn't just come storming into the Hall. No, they would seal the city first. Patrols would then sweep their way through each Quintant, converging on the Grand Hall at the center of Appencourt. Few of the city guard members were Weavers, but they were all trained fighters. When monsters came pouring out of the Hall, they would face a hard battle to leave the city. Of course, none of that would help Jayn and the others here and now. Jayn didn't want to die, but she would not turn and run. Her mother still fought, despite having had her Weaving snatched from her a mere two days ago. Jayn would make her mother proud, even if it killed her.

She turned back to the fight. The Kobolds waiting in the back began shouting in their garbled speech. Ryn had said they spoke a broken dialect of the King's Tongue, but Jayn still couldn't understand them. Suddenly, the Kobolds were falling back. The last one turned to run, but Anyse didn't let it. She slashed the back of its neck, nearly decapitating it. The beast fell flat on its face, revealing an empty stretch of hallway all the way to the vault.

Not questioning it, Anyse and Nyssa surged forward. Jayn followed behind. Thalia stooped to wrench her poleaxe from where it had been left, still stuck into a dead Kobold. Anyse and Nyssa stopped short, just a few paces from the door. Looking between them, Jayn could see a tall figure standing in the doorway.

Kalo stood seven feet tall. A jagged white scar traversed his broad face. His thin lips peeled back to reveal pointed yellow teeth. He wore a full set of black leather armor, with lots of straps and buckles, but no helmet. In one hand he held a massive scimitar; in the other, he held a short copper rod. Jayn's eyes widened. How did he have that device? She only wondered for a second. Nyssa had handed over the cursed Runeform to the Pentarchs, so of course, they had stored it with all their other Runeforms, here in the vault.

The pieces began to fit together in her mind as she thought of the riot two days ago. Had it been designed to fail? Had they wanted Peniter to be captured? Using such a horrific device on one of the Pentarchs had all but assured it would be placed inside the vault. Had Kalo given it to Peniter directly, knowing he would be taking it back today? Or maybe Peniter hadn't known he was working for monsters. Maybe Gwen Hinter had told him what to do. Jayn had not forgotten that that loathsome woman was right there, just out of sight within the vault, opening a portal to another world.

"Careful," Nyssa called. They all recognized the device.

Anyse took a step forward, raising her blade. "That rod can't do anything to me now."

"He's not like the others," Nyssa said, not taking her eyes off Kalo. "He knows how to fight and he's faster than you think."

Anyse did not back down. She squared her stance, staring up at the gray-skinned giant. Jayn had not moved since she recognized Kalo. Fear had frozen her in place. Seeing that brute stare down at her mother did nothing to assuage that fear. She remembered the brutal fight her Pentad had waged against Kalo two months ago. Kalo was clever. The same trick would not work against him twice. Jayn's eyes went to her mother's hands, clenching the sword. The copper ring on her finger glinted in the harsh overhead lights.

Jayn knew what Kalo would do next. If he was using the Five Forces, then he would strike out with Flame. Kalo raised his hand, palm out. He held the Runeform with his thumb and forefinger, his other fingers splayed. Jayn shifted her foot and threw up a wall of Wave. She pushed it forward, trying to protect Nyssa and her mother. She wasn't fast enough. Four streaks of shadow shot from Kalo's chest like arrows. Two hit Nyssa and Anyse. The other two shafts, aimed at Jayn and Thalia, vanished when they touched the wall of Wave. Jayn hadn't formed an actual lacing, but it didn't matter. Wave always consumed Flame.

She heard two plinks as Nyssa and Anyse's broken rings clattered to the ground. Jayn and Thalia still had their rings, but if the recoil still hadn't faded from last time, then those rings were worthless. Jayn's mother glanced down as her ring fell, but she kept her sword up. "I don't need luck to stop a creature like you," she said, her voice steel.

Kalo's lips peeled back further in what may have been a smile. Then he attacked. The narrow hallway limited the broad beast's range of movement. He couldn't get full swings in, but he still slashed and stabbed with his scimitar. Anyse Eldragor looked like a princess from a fairy story in her white nightgown, her long blonde hair flowing down her back. She met each blow with her sword, though each powerful strike forced her backward. Nyssa stepped back too, giving Anyse space, so Jayn and Thalia also had to retreat. Jayn couldn't breathe. She watched in horror as Kalo bore down on her mother.

The Fourth Pentarch's decades spent honing her skills with the blade kept her alive for now, but she was clearly outmatched. Kalo had more speed, strength, and reach. Anyse could only parry and move backward, with no chance of a riposte. She would not win this fight. Jayn could only watch, helpless to do anything. She glanced at Thalia, who held her poleaxe at the ready. One of them might be able to get a thrust in with the polearm, but Jayn didn't want to risk distracting her mother for even a second. One false step and Kalo would kill her. Jayn had to do something to help her mother, but what?

Thalia came up with an idea first. She raised her arm and threw the poleaxe like a javelin, using all the strength her brawny arms could impart. The weapon sailed over Anyse's head, arcing toward Kalo's face. The creature reeled backward, bending at the waist, away from the projectile. He almost avoided it. Jayn saw a spurt of blue blood as the edge of the poleaxe's blade sliced through Kalo's pointy ear. Anyse took advantage of the moment. She threw all her weight into the next swing, knocking back Kalo's sword.

Anyse raised her blade and swung it downward toward Kalo. It was a desperate tactic that left her completely exposed, but Anyse must have known she was outmatched and could only win by trying something reckless. It didn't work.

Rather than fight to regain his balance, Kalo let himself fall flat on his back. His body dropped faster than Anyse's blade, as she slashed empty air. Kalo hit the ground and seemed to rebound like a rubber ball. His scimitar shot back up. He buried it in the Fourth Pentarch's stomach.

Jayn screamed. She saw the metal tip emerge from her mother's back with a bloom of blood that stained the white nightgown crimson. Jayn's knees buckled. Thalia grabbed her and kept her from falling to the ground. She could not look away. Her mother fell backward, crumpling to the ground. The scimitar slipped from Kalo's fingers, still buried in Gen. Anyse Eldragor, who'd been Jayn's hero all her life. If she wasn't already dead, she would bleed out in seconds. Jayn couldn't save her now. Jayn couldn't stop Kalo.

Nyssa surged forward, swinging on the unarmed Kobold. Kalo parried with the Runeform he still held in his left hand. Sparks flew. The device was not any kind of weapon in the traditional sense, but as a Runeform, it was indestructible. Nyssa's blade couldn't even scratch it.

Kalo held the device like a knife and lunged at Nyssa. She jumped back, wary of the silver prongs on the end. They didn't know how quickly the Runeform worked, but they knew they didn't want it to touch them. Kalo stepped easily over Anyse's ruined body, pressing forward. Nyssa stepped back several paces, lowered her sword and threw up her left hand. A wall of Wave rose between her and Kalo, hardening into an impenetrable shield.

Nyssa looked back at her two recruits. "Get her out of here!" she yelled to Thalia.

Jayn tried to surge forward, but Thalia still had hold of her. She wrapped her arms around Jayn's waist and began pulling her backward. "No!" Jayn yelled, too wracked with grief to think straight. She dropped her useless sword and beat at Thalia with her fists. The big Stone Weaver was too strong. She practically carried Jayn backward down the corridor. Jayn couldn't leave. Her mother was still there, trapped on the other side of the shield with Kalo. Jayn couldn't lose her, not like this.

Nyssa turned back to Kalo. She staggered backward another step, as dark shadows swirled around Kalo's head. It looked nothing like Aether, but that was where Aether formed, which meant… The shadows shot forward, hit Nyssa's shield, and shattered it. So Kalo could use Flame and Aether. That thought came to Jayn like a whisper heard from another room. She still fought desperately to break Thalia's grip on her.

Nyssa spun back toward them. "Run!" she yelled. She took two steps forward, before shadows wrapped around her, freezing her in place. Jayn knew that lacing. Kalo had used it on her all those weeks ago. It froze its victim in place, rendering them unable to move and barely able to breath. In all of her nightmares now, she felt that paralysis again, fighting to move but unable to lift a finger. Jayn couldn't lose Nyssa too. She used her nails now, scratching at Thalia's arms, but still the fool wouldn't release her. They stumbled backward into the doorway at their end of the hall.

Jayn stopped fighting, frozen in sudden horror as she finally realized how Kalo did it. Before, Kalo's Weaving had always seemed an inky black. They had all agreed on that detail, even Nyssa. Maybe it was because they had only fought him at night before, in the dark, or maybe Jayn's eyes had not been attuned to see the impossible then, but now in this brightly lit corridor, Jayn suddenly saw the lacings differently. They were composed of shadow instead of light, but they weren't solidly black. She saw a slight tinge of color. The shadows emerging from Kalo's chest were the color of dark red wine. That *was* Flame. Other shadows seemed to rise up from the ground below Kalo, tinted the deep blue of a summer night. It didn't move anything like Wave, but that was Wave. The intermixed shadows that enveloped Nyssa were distinctly purple. A Blending.

Here then was what Jayn had been seeking so eagerly all these weeks, a lacing that could Blend Wave and Flame. Wave, the gift she hadn't wanted, and Flame, the one she'd always coveted. Together, they created this abomination, the lacing that had nearly killed her, a nightmare that still caused her to wake in a cold sweat. They had called what Ryn and Pavel had done—and what the two youths in Wydhaven could do—a "forbidden Blending," but that had just been a silly, dramatic way of describing it. It seemed apt now, as she watched Kalo pervert the Five Forces for such an end. She could never create such a Blending now.

Jayn watched, helpless, knowing what would happen next. Kalo would pry his sword from her mother's corpse and plunge it into Nyssa, her mentor, her teacher. Jayn couldn't save her mother, and she couldn't save Captain Lahmeer.

Kalo didn't go for his sword. Instead, he raised the Runeform, pressing the two silver prongs into Nyssa's neck. Nyssa could only stare straight ahead, horror clear in her eyes that couldn't even blink. Of course. Kalo, that villain, would never just kill somebody if he could inflict some vile cruelty upon them first. Kalo twisted the Runeform. Jayn didn't see anything happen, but apparently the device had done its job. Kalo pulled it back and released his lacings. Nyssa's eyes rolled up into her head as she collapsed onto the ground.

Kalo stepped over her. He didn't go back for his scimitar, but stooped to pick up a different blade, the sword Jayn had just dropped. It looked small in his hand. He locked his eyes on Jayn and began advancing again. Behind him, the constant humming from the vault grew louder.

Thalia yanked Jayn back again, and they stumbled out into a broader hallway. Jayn heard footsteps coming up behind them, but she didn't take her eyes off Kalo. Someone charged past her, through the open doorway. The figure seemed blurry and out of focus. Jayn recognized the deflection ward, a blending of Root and Wave. A transparent doubled image trailed behind Ryn, as if his own ghost chased him. His hands were empty but glowing.

Kalo answered Ryn's reckless charge with a high slice, intended to lop off the Root Weaver's head. The blade hit Ryn's neck and bounced like a wagon wheel hitting a rut. The sword slid over the top of Ryn's head. Jayn thought she saw a few strands of blond hair fly off, catching the light. Ryn kept charging, hitting Kalo in the gut with a Flame-laced uppercut. Its power didn't come near Shilo's Etching, but it was enough to send Kalo staggering back several steps.

Ryn squared his stance and raised his still-glowing fists. Jayn almost didn't recognize the expression that flashed across Kalo's distorted features: surprise. Ryn pressed his advantage, lashing out not with his fists, but with a massive Root tree that suddenly bloomed around him. Jayn remembered that Ryn had Dowsed Kalo the last time they fought, and the Kobold had not liked the experience.

Kalo dropped the Runeform, slashing at the spectral tree with his clawed fingers. Dark shadows dissolved the green branches. Was that Stone? A truly gifted Weaver could gain proficiency in as many as four different forces, but it was not easy. Ryn's response was equally miraculous. Normally, contact with the right opposing force would destroy any lacing, completely and almost instantly. While the branches of Ryn's Root tree did vanish, the trunk held, and Ryn immediately sent out another torrent of branches. He must have anticipated Kalo's defense. The deflection ward still swirled around him, and his fists still glowed with Flame.

Root, Wave, and Flame—sure, someone else, probably Jax Centillion, had to have placed the ward on Ryn—but seeing him so deftly juggle three forces still left Jayn gaping in awe. Ryn, the scrawny little backwoods idiot, now appeared to her like a hero from a storybook. Even Thalia had stopped trying to pull Jayn away, though her grip had not loosened.

Jayn didn't recognize the Root lacings Ryn unleashed on Kalo. It wasn't Dowsing or healing but something decidedly different. Kalo raised Jayn's sword to swing at Ryn again, but this time he was too slow. The blade slipped from his fingers as the massive Kobold fell backward, landing with a thud on the marble floor. Whatever Ryn had done had completely incapacitated him. Was that the lacing the Death Weaver had tried to use on Ryn? Had Ryn stopped Kalo's heart?

Ryn wasn't done performing miracles. The light faded from his hands and the deflection ward dissolved, but he held onto the

Root tree. He glanced at Nyssa, who still hadn't recovered from whatever the Runeform had done to her. Leaving her for the moment, Ryn crossed over to Jayn's mother, who lay motionless in a rapidly expanding pool of blood. From this distance, Jayn couldn't tell if her chest still moved. Green light swathed Anyse's body. Ryn grabbed the hilt of Kalo's scimitar. Anyse convulsed as a violent wave of healing surged through her body. Ryn knit her insides back together even as he pulled the sword out. It was like Anyse's stomach spat out the blade. Ryn's healings were never gentle.

Jayn still remembered the moment this amazing boy had saved her life. Kalo had brutally beaten her in a fight then left her lying in the rubble of the destroyed smithy, his powerful venom coursing through her veins. She and Shilo had both blacked out from their injuries. She didn't know long she had been out, before she was suddenly awake, gasping for breath, as a powerful tingling cascaded through her body. She had to just lie there panting for a moment, not seeing anyone. Then she heard Thalia's amazed whisper: "No, Ryn, *what* did you *do*?"

"Someone grab Nyssa!" Ryn yelled, an unfamiliar command in his tone.

Jayn snapped back into reality. Ryn had scooped her mother up, carrying her with one arm under her back and the other in the crook of her knees. He staggered as he stepped forward, but he held onto her. Thalia let go of Jayn and ran back into the corridor. Nyssa was awake but didn't seem quite able to stand. Thalia half-dragged, half-carried her out the door. Jayn stood helplessly watching it all. Ryn stumbled out into the hallway, dropping to his knees as he lay Anyse down on the ground. Jayn's mother seemed lost in a daze of confusion, perhaps amazed to still be alive. She peeled open the slit in the front of her nightgown to stare down at her blood-smeared but unblemished stomach.

They all looked up as the dull humming from the vault rose to a sudden crescendo. An inhuman roar echoed down the corridor. "Thalia!" Ryn shouted. "The door!"

Ryn threw his weight against the heavy metal door. Thalia rushed to his side. The door closed slowly. They could hear the thudding of heavy boots on the other side, as Kobolds or something worse moved into the narrow corridor. The door shut with a rusty squeal but almost immediately began to swing open again, as something on the other side pushed back.

Ryn and Thalia groaned, fighting to keep the door shut. Jayn ran forward then, finally seeing a way to help, though her admittedly small body didn't add much weight to their side. She felt something slam against the other side of the heavy door. The three Weavers inched backward. Jayn saw light begin to pour through the widening crack in the door.

Beside her, Ryn's hands began to glow with Flame again. How had he gotten so good with Flame all of a sudden? She saw the copper ring on his finger. Maybe their luck had returned. Ryn drew back his arm and punched the door, which had to hurt. A wave of Flame washed over the metal frame as it slammed shut. "Seal it!" Ryn yelled.

Thalia understood what he meant. Lines of yellow Stone arched from her hands, spreading through the door. She grabbed the wheel stuck in the center of the door and turned it, driving the heavy bolt into place. It was more of a latch than a lock, as another wheel on the other side could easily open it. The actual locks, near the top and bottom of the door, had been disabled somehow. Just as Stone Weavers didn't need a key to open a door, they didn't need a lock to close one either. Jayn heard a series of metallic shrieks and pops as Thalia's lacings jammed and then broke the internal mechanisms of the door.

If a full Pentad had opened a portal inside the vault, then they had at least one Stone Weaver of their own, but undoing Thalia's work would take a while. They would have to take the whole door apart to escape. Thalia had bought them some time. She released her yellow lacings and in unison the three of them slid down onto the floor, landing in an exhausted heap. Immediately, the creatures on the other side began pounding on the door. *Thud, thud, thud!*

Ryn sighed. He looked around the room. He sat wedged between Thalia and Jayn, who were both still breathing heavily. Across from them, Anyse had managed to sit up. Her focus was not on them, but on Nyssa, who was awake but had made no effort to get up. Instead, she had curled herself into a ball. Ryn still wasn't quite sure what Kalo had done to her.

Ryn flexed his hand, seeing if he could still make a fist. Punching the door like that had bloodied his knuckles, but nothing seemed broken. Jayn placed her soft white hand atop Ryn's. Their eyes met. "Thank you," she said, with a softness he'd never heard from the fiery Wave Weaver. "You saved… all of us."

He smiled, in spite of everything.

Thalia groaned and staggered to her feet. "Come on," she said, offering a hand to Ryn. "We're not out of it yet."

The pounding still continued on the other side of the heavy door. Ryn grabbed Thalia's forearm, allowing her to hoist him back to his feet. He took hold of Jayn's hand with his free one and pulled her up with him.

Jayn seemed to notice the others then. "Mother?" she said, taking a few steps forward, though not letting go of Ryn's hand.

Ryn followed her, his other hand slipping from Thalia's grip as she stayed by the door.

Anyse Eldragor looked up as Jayn placed a hand on her shoulder. "Oh, I'm fine," she said with a feeble smile. "Thanks to Mr. Silverbell." She gave him a polite nod. She dropped her gaze as she noticed Jayn still clinging tightly to Ryn's bloodied hand but said nothing, her attention returning to Nyssa. Ryn felt awkward but didn't try to free his hand. Jayn seemed to need the contact right now.

Nyssa appeared to have come back to herself, at least a little. She stared up at them with wide eyes. Her lips moved silently for a moment. "I can't…" she managed to say. "He took it!"

"Shh," Anyse said, reaching down to touch Nyssa's shoulder. "I know, oh, I know, darling." Ryn didn't think a woman like Anyse Eldragor often used such a gentle tone, yet her voice was also tinged with an immense sorrow.

Jayn let go of Ryn's hand then, only to turn and throw herself against him, so like a frightened child seeking comfort from a parent. Not knowing what else to do, he wrapped his arms around her and held her as she sobbed.

"Oh, it's awful, Ryn," she whispered. He felt her hot breath against his ear as she buried her face in his neck. "Kalo used the device on Nyssa… He took her Weaving…"

Ryn tightened his grip on Jayn as blood drained from his face. He hadn't recognized the device in Kalo's hand. He'd seen Nyssa fall, and then he'd just charged in blindly. He was glad Kalo had only used that sword instead of turning the device on Ryn. He didn't know what he would do if he lost his ability to Weave. What would Nyssa do now? The Watchkeepers had been her whole life. There had to be a way to fix it.

He looked at the others over the top of Jayn's head. Nyssa was still curled on her side. Anyse sat rubbing her back and whispering soothing words, like a mother comforting a child. Thalia moved and crouched down on the other side of Nyssa, her forehead wrinkled in concern. She kept glancing up at Jayn and Ryn, probably also concerned with Jayn's unusual behavior.

Ryn loosened his arms as he felt Jayn pull away. She moved back only enough to peer up into his face. Tears still filled her beautiful blue eyes, but the usual steel had returned to her gaze. "Did you stop his heart?" she asked, her voice shaking with sudden anger.

He knew exactly what she meant. He shook his head. "I thought about it, but that would have taken too long, so I, uh…" He couldn't really explain what he'd done to Kalo. He had no plan when he charged the Kobold, but after his Etching finally healed his ankle, he had just rushed in after the others. "It's hard to explain, but basically I switched off his brain."

"What?" she gasped.

He shrugged. "I don't think it killed him, just knocked him unconscious." He knew for a fact it hadn't killed Kalo, but he didn't think Jayn wanted to hear that. He was right.

He dropped his arms as she pulled away completely. She took a step back, wiped the tears from her eyes, and shook her head. "You should have killed him," she said, turning part of her anger on Ryn.

He winced, but he didn't know what to say to that. Behind him, the cadence of the pounding changed. Before it had been the dull thud of fists or bodies, but now they were swinging something metal against the door.

"The door won't hold forever," he said. "We need to get out of here."

"Come on," Anyse said to Nyssa. She and Thalia helped Nyssa stand and began to lead her away.

Ryn placed a hand on Jayn's back, but she stepped away. She was over needing comfort now. She looked back at him only once, as they made their way slowly out of the Grand Hall. They were passing through the room with all the dead Wardens and Kobolds. "Where's Jax?" she asked.

"When my ankle healed, he wanted to come with me, but he couldn't do more than hobble, and he was still weak from the healing. I told him he was better off going downstairs to meet the city guard and tell them what was happening in here."

She nodded. Thalia glanced back. "That deflection ward you had, did Jax make it?"

"Yeah, I asked him if he could set one on me. I didn't know what I would find when I caught up to you."

They stumbled down the stairs to the first level, moved down a short hallway, and then descended the final set of stairs, emerging from the belly of the Grand Hall. They reached the courtyard below and paused amid the forest of marble columns to look around. The sun hung just above the buildings to the east, casting long shadows. Outside, they could clearly hear ringing bells from several different directions. Pavel and Shilo had alerted the city guards, but no one had moved in on the city center yet.

Turning in a slow circle, they could see the five main boulevards radiating out from around the Grand Hall, but the city appeared deserted. The citizens must have decided to stay indoors rather than go out and see why the alarm had been raised. Ryn glanced at the others again. Nyssa stared straight ahead, seemingly unaware of the world around her. Jayn's mother had taken two days to recover from the trauma of losing her Weaving, but she seemed to be keeping it together now. Jayn and Thalia stood back-to-back, alert for any sign of help or danger. The women had all lost their weapons inside the vault's passageway. Ryn still had his knife strapped to his belt, the one Thalia had gifted him, but a knife wouldn't help much against Kobolds.

They all froze, hearing a familiar rasping sound overhead: "Ts-ts-ts."

Chapter 28
The Flood

THALIA LOOKED UP, knowing already what she would see. The massive monkey-like Manface crouched overhead, hiding among the columns near the base of the Grand Hall. Its wide gray hands and feet clutched the marble columns, while its banded tail wrapped around a fifth. She had seen apes before in a traveling menagerie. A monkey's face was similar to a man's—more similar than an owl's or bear's anyway, but this creature's visage still looked unnatural. Maybe it was the solid-black eyes or just the uniquely human nose, but its face appeared decidedly uncanny.

The Manface slid down the columns, dropping closer but stopping well out of reach. Anyse gasped. Nyssa didn't even seem to notice it. Thalia wished their captain would snap out of this funk, though she supposed she couldn't blame her. Thalia clenched her fists, wishing she had her poleaxe. Her arms still burned from where Jayn had scratched her. The girl still hadn't apologized. Thalia could have asked Ryn to heal them, but she knew that he had to be close to his limit after two major healings. She also didn't want to seem petty by calling out Jayn for hurting her.

Thalia didn't understand the pang of jealousy she'd felt watching Ryn and Jayn embrace back inside the Hall. Thalia and Ryn were just friends, and that was all she wanted. Besides, she didn't think he would be interested in a girl who was taller and more muscular than him. Still, when Ryn kept saving her life in such dramatic fashion, and with Rigel's admonition that she must trust him echoing in the back of her mind, Thalia couldn't always think rationally. She pushed all the confusion aside to focus on the immediate danger.

"Five again," the Manface said in its high, almost musical voice. "But not all the same. Three who are Marked and two who are sealed, ts-ts-ts."

Thalia glanced at the others. The creature had described her Pentad as "Marked" before, so it was calling Nyssa and Anyse "sealed"—but hadn't Nyssa also been marked by Kalo's poison, back before Thalia had met her and the guys?

Thalia took a step away from Nyssa, who seemed capable of supporting herself now, at least when they stood still. "What do you want?" she said to the Manface.

It cocked its head at her. It shifted fluidly through the columns, grabbing onto just one with both hands and feet and spinning in a lazy circle around it before stopping to stare down at her. "We want much from you," it said, "if you are the one. Time will tell, ts-ts-ts."

Thalia frowned, not understanding but not liking its words. "Why did you open another portal? Are you bringing more creatures like you into our world?"

The creature made a strange trilling sound that might have been a laugh. "No creatures are like the Five, and this is our world now, ts-ts-ts."

"So you're taking over, is that the plan?"

"It has been Seeing, but not enough."

"Tell us what you want," Anyse Eldragor said, stepping away from Nyssa but still keeping a hand on her back. Nyssa finally seemed to have noticed the Manface, but she stayed silent.

The creature shifted its gaze to Anyse but did not answer.

Jayn's mother stared up at the monster, undaunted. "I am the Fourth Pentarch. I represent Aldria in all military matters. If you want something from our country, you may negotiate with me."

The creature laughed again, its long tail swishing like a cat's. "We want nothing from you, little sealed Weaver. You think it yours? This land belongs to the Reach." The Manface swirled itself around the column again and stopped, dangling upside down with it headed tilted toward them. Its musical voice took on a harsher edge. "We want chaos. We want madness. We want to bring about the Fall." It turned toward the stairs leading into the Grand Hall, as if hearing something inside that they could not. "Here they come."

Thalia turned toward the stairs. The Kobolds must have escaped the vault. Any second now, they would come spilling down the steps, and Thalia was powerless to stop them. They had to run, if the Manface would let them.

"If the Marked survive," the creature said, "then we will know. Then we will come for the one, ts-ts-ts… But we've no need of the sealed."

Before any of them could react, the Manface dropped into their midst. It sent Anyse sprawling backward with a swipe of its massive paw, slamming her into the side of a column. It turned and trotted off on all fours. Just as Thalia wondered if it was really leaving, its snake-like tail shot back and wrapped around Nyssa's waist. She made no effort to fight it, as the tail pulled her from her feet and dragged her across the courtyard.

"No!" Thalia shouted, as the others echoed her. They all ran after the Manface, who seemed intent on taking Nyssa along, wherever it was headed. Jayn and Ryn easily outpaced her, but even they could not keep up with the beast. The creature barreled toward the edge of the courtyard. It could probably leap across the moat with ease.

A massive Root tree sprung up around Ryn even as he ran. He sent a dozen green branches arcing toward the Manface. Would he try the same trick he had used on Kalo? The creature stumbled, falling flat on its belly, although Ryn had only just touched it. There was no way Ryn's lacings could have done anything to the beast in that split second. Mere contact with Root seemed to have disabled the creature, at least for a moment.

Jayn and Ryn almost closed the distance to the prone Manface before it recovered. Its tail had not lost its grip on Nyssa, who lay limp like a doll. It climbed back onto its feet, turning its head to snarl at Ryn. The Root tree vanished, as Ryn drew his knife from the sheath at his waist, Flame flowing down his arms, making his hands glow and wrapping the blade in streaks of red light that seemed especially vibrant in the morning sunshine.

Ryn raised his arm and hurled the knife with Flame-enhanced strength. The knife spun end-over-end, faster than an arrow, and buried itself up to the hilt, not in the creature's broad gray flanks but in the narrow tail, near the base. The creature howled. Its tail went slack and dropped its hold on Nyssa, who fell flat on the ground. It bared its teeth in anger, reached back, and pulled the dagger from its tail. The blade seemed miniscule in its large gray hand.

Ryn and Jayn stopped their charge. The creature seemed to look back and forth between them. Its eyes locked on Ryn as he summoned another Root tree. With a casual flick of its wrist, it tossed the knife back at Ryn.

"No!" Jayn said, throwing herself against Ryn. She was too slow. Thalia saw Ryn flinch, and his Root tree snuffed out. He turned halfway back around from Jayn's shove and fell on his back, the leather-wrapped hilt of the knife Thalia had made for him sticking up from his stomach.

The Manface reared up onto its hind legs. It glanced back at them, anger written across its uncannily human face. It snarled but made no move to attack them. Instead, it hopped away, moving sideways, which seemed to be its natural gait, though its tail did drag uselessly behind it. It crossed the moat in a single bound, scurried up the side of a three-story building, and disappeared.

Thalia stared after it for a moment but then ran toward Ryn. Jayn was already kneeling at his side. She glanced up at Thalia, her eyes wide with concern. "He's unconscious," she said.

"That might be good," Thalia said. "He blacks out when his Etching activates, at least when it's something major."

They both glanced at the knife in his gut. "Should we…?" Jayn asked.

Thalia hesitated for a moment. She knew pulling the blade out would increase the bleeding, but he also couldn't heal himself if they left it in. With a sigh, Thalia grabbed the knife and pulled it out in one fluid motion. Ryn flinched but didn't wake up. She tucked the knife into her belt and pressed both palms to the wound, hoping to staunch the bleeding. His hot blood warmed her fingers. She looked up, surveying the courtyard again.

Nyssa was sitting up, her legs splayed out in front of her. She seemed to be staring at them, though her gaze still looked hazy and unfocused. Anyse stumbled slowly toward them. She clutched one arm, which hung limp at her side. A trickle of blood ran down the side of her face from a small cut. She stopped when she reached them and stood staring down at Ryn for a moment. She cleared her throat. "Jayn… could you…?" She gestured with her head toward her limp arm.

Jayn looked up from Ryn, blinking in confusion for a moment until she saw how Anyse carried herself. "Dislocated?" she asked. Anyse nodded.

Thalia's eyes widened. She had never dislocated anything herself, but she knew it was supposed to be extremely painful. Anyse handled the pain with admirable stoicism. Whatever training the Fourth Pentarch had given her daughter in preparation for a planned military career, it apparently included instructions on how to pop a dislocated arm back into place. They were at the edge of the forest of columns beneath the Grand Hall. Anyse positioned herself against the nearest column, while Jayn took hold of her mother's arm and gave it a violent twist. That seemed to do the trick. Anyse closed her eyes and released a sigh as her arm popped back into place. Thalia winched, imagining the pain.

She glanced back toward the Hall, seeing movement on the stairs. A tall Kobold in black armor descended the steps toward them. Apparently, Kalo had recovered from whatever Ryn had done to him. The Kobold had abandoned his signature scimitar for a stranger weapon, like an oversized farmer's scythe, with a long black handle and a wicked curved blade. He flowed gracefully down the steps with the litheness of a big cat. A cold chill gripped Thalia's chest despite the summer air. That wasn't Kalo. Even from a distance, she could tell this Kobold was different. This one lacked the scar across the face, and it had only one beady eye, opposite a puckered and empty socket. She saw another pair of black leather boots appear at the top of the stairs, and then another. Suddenly, dozens of giant Kobolds in black leather armor were descending the steps. This was what Gwen Hinter's rogue Pentad had summoned through the portal—not more Manfaces but more Kobolds like Kalo. Kobolds who could Weave.

"Run," Thalia said to the others, needlessly.

She bent and scooped up Ryn into her arms, carrying him again like she had carried him up into the Grand Hall after he twisted his ankle. Jayn ran to Nyssa, grabbed her arm, and pulled her onto her feet. Nyssa seemed to have recovered enough to understand their need to flee. Anyse stumbled along beside Thalia.

Thalia glanced over her shoulder. The black-clad Kobolds had stopped at the bottom of the stairs, spread out in a loose circle, apparently getting their bearings in the city. A few looked with interest at Thalia and the others but made no move to pursue. Maybe they wouldn't. She remembered when the Kobolds had attacked Falport. After doing what they'd intended, they left the city. Maybe these creatures were just trying to leave now.

First, they would have to cross the moat surrounding the Grand Hall. Two temporary bridges led off the round island. Thalia and the others were headed for the southern bridge now. She couldn't move very fast, not while carrying Ryn. If the Kobolds meant to flee south, they would easily overtake her. Even if they were just trying to leave, she knew they wouldn't hesitate to cut her down if she got in the way. She needed to make herself as unobtrusive as possible and too inconvenient for them to pursue.

"Go left!" she shouted to the others. Anyse and Jayn looked back at her, confused. "The water!" she added, angling her steps toward the edge of the moat.

They slowed down, not quite understanding, but as she barreled toward the edge, they fell in beside her, Jayn dragging

Nyssa along by the hand. Not pausing to look, Thalia clutched Ryn's still bleeding body to her chest and jumped. The bubbling water rushed up to meet them.

Shilo walked along the empty boulevard, just behind the guards. She and Pavel had both wanted to charge directly back to the Grand Hall, but upon reconsidering, they decided to stick with the city guard. They still couldn't be certain their bad luck had worn off. Shilo still had the stout club she'd scavenged from a Kobold, and Pavel had his sword. They walked behind a pair of guards carrying spears, the sturdy kinds meant for thrusting not throwing. A line of guards spread out behind them, fanning out to check side streets before returning to the group. The farther they went, the wider the quintant became, and the slower they progressed. They crested a slight rise in the road and the white marble block of the Grand Hall came into view—along with a row of Kobolds marching north.

One of the guards lifted a horn slung under one shoulder, pressed it to his lips, and sounded the alarm. More guards rushed forward. Shilo stopped in her tracks as she got a good look at the Kobolds. They were taller than the ones she'd seen before, all wearing black leather armor, each carrying a weapon more bizarre than the last. There had to be fifty of them, walking in two lines.

She turned to Pavel, who'd also frozen in place. "They all look like Kalo," she said.

He understood her fear. "If they're all Weavers…" He grabbed her arm and yanked her to the side. "We got to go."

She hesitated. She had no desire to fight an entire squadron of Kobold Weavers, but she didn't want to just run away either.

Pavel sighed. "Those things are going to mow right through these guards and us, if we wait here. We won't help anyone if we're dead."

Maybe it was the cowardly choice, but he made a lot of sense. She nodded and fell in step behind him. They hurried back toward the gate. They made it a few paces before she heard the crash of steel on steel behind her. A moment after that the screaming began. The only voices she heard were human. She and Pavel broke into a sprint. He glanced over his shoulder and then swerved to the right, toward a side street. Shilo stopped, sparing one look back, as she turned to follow him. The lines of Kobolds marched on, right down the center of the road. The two in front carried massive weapons—one a two-handed axe that looked carved of black stone, the other a mace of similar size, studded with ridges that looked like thick green glass. Both weapons were spattered in blood. Half a dozen guards lay dead in the street behind the Kobolds, and the rest were in full retreat, charging toward Shilo.

She hoped the Kobolds would continue north in pursuit of the guards and none would peel off to run down Shilo and Pavel, but she didn't look back again. Pavel led them down the side street for one block before swerving left into an alley. Shilo listened for the sound of pursuit but couldn't hear anything over the pounding of her own feet and the blood pumping in her ears.

Pavel turned into a small yard, dashed up a set of stairs, and threw his weight against a wooden door. Thankfully it had been left unlocked. It swung open, and he disappeared inside. Shilo didn't know how much she should trust the former thief, but she could trust he knew how to evade capture. They seemed to be inside an apartment building. A long hallway ran the length of the first floor, with numbered doors on alternating sides. Pavel tried an unmarked door near the entrance that opened onto a stairwell.

He ran up. Shilo tried to keep up, but she was winded by the time they reached the third floor. Few of the buildings in this quintant went above three stories, but Pavel kept climbing, reached the final landing, and pushed through the door.

Daylight poured in. Shilo caught up, stepping out onto the flat roof of the building. A squat lip ran around the edge of the roof, with holes in the base for drainage. Some resident had built raised wooden beds along the far end for growing vegetables. Pavel raced down the rows to the edge of the roof and jumped onto the low wall. Shilo skidded to a halt behind him, not trusting her balance to jump up next to him.

Three stories below, the city guards were still in full retreat. The black-clad Kobolds continued at a steady march, unbothered that the humans were getting away. Shilo saw a guard stumble. He dropped his spear and seemed overcome by panic. He scuttled forward on his hands and knees. The foremost Kobold lowered his massive axe and raised an empty palm toward the guard. A mass of shadows sprung up around the creature's feet, rose to chest height, and shot out, wrapping around the guard. Shilo knew that lacing. She had seen Kalo use it on Jayn what now seemed like a lifetime ago. The guard froze in place, still on his knees, one hand reaching forward. In the morning light streaming between the buildings, the dark lacing looked slightly purple.

The first Kobold held the man frozen in place, while the second one continued its steady advance, hefting its giant mace with both hands. Pavel hopped back off the wall, grabbed Shilo's sleeve, and pulled her back from the edge. She let him. She felt like a coward, but she didn't want to see the guard die. She still heard the dull thud and a sickening squelching sound. She heard a muffled scream. Maybe someone was watching from a window.

"Come on," Pavel said, moving toward the north side of the building.

"Where are we going?" she asked.

"To the gate."

"You want to just run away? Leave the city?"

He glanced back at her. "The gate is well fortified and defended. If we join the fight there, we'll stand the best chance of making a difference. The two of us on our own can't stop that."

Shilo looked south, along the rooftops. She could see the top of the Grand Hall. "What about the others?"

"Those creatures are coming from the Hall. Probably, they busted into the vault, took whatever they were after, and now they are retreating. Whatever fight happened in the Hall, it's over now. Either Nyssa and the others are dead or they were spared. Hopefully, they had luck on their side, but whatever shape they're in, we can't help them. Or have you learned healing?"

Shilo shook her head. She could make enough Root to Blend in with her Flame and make Weaver lights, but healing was still beyond her grasp.

Pavel shrugged. "Well, I know you can use Aether." White light sprouted from the top of Pavel's head, cascading down over his body. He took a few running steps toward the north edge of the building, vaulted over the low wall, and sailed easily across the alley onto the roof of the next building.

Shilo stood rooted to the ground.

"Come on," Pavel said, waving toward the distant gate. "We need to move fast if we want to reach the wall before the Kobolds."

"I can't make that jump!" Shilo said.

"Yes, you can. I showed you the lacings right before we left Falport."

"One time!" Even then, they had jumped across level ground, not a three-story drop.

"You got this. Come on, just like I showed you." He swathed himself in light again, by way of demonstration.

Shilo moved toward the edge. The alley was relatively narrow, maybe ten paces across, but still more than she could jump on her own.

"Remember," Pavel said. "Aether isn't like Flame. It's not about making your legs stronger. Focus on making yourself lighter and your muscles… springier. You can do this."

He didn't wait to see if she actually could do it. He turned, dashed across the rooftop, and bounded to the next building. Shilo sighed. She tucked her club awkwardly into her belt. She had to loosen it to make it work. She moved back a few paces. She imagined a cool wind coming down on her, and white light sprung around her head. She was getting decent at summoning Aether, though it did not come as naturally as Flame. She tried to recreate the lacings exactly as Pavel had shown her, letting them settle into her legs. She rose onto the balls of her feet, willing herself to become lighter and… springier. The fall would break her legs, but it probably wouldn't kill her. She tried not to think about that.

She ran forward, planted one foot on the wall, and jumped. She couldn't help but scream as she sailed out over empty air. Still, the lacings held, and she made it to the next roof. She landed too hard and fell forward. The energetic Trevor Flint, the Aether master, had made her and Pavel practice tumbling for weeks. She understood why now. She turned the fall into a roll and bounced back onto her feet. Pavel was already two buildings ahead of her.

She pushed him out of her mind, as well as the Kobolds below filling the streets with death. She focused solely on forming the lacings again. She didn't scream on her next jump, and she landed on her feet. She kept running.

She lost count of how many jumps she made. She jumped, she landed, she paused to reform the lacings, and then she jumped again. It seemed to take hours to reach the gate, but it had to be mere minutes. Halfway through, she came to the widest crossing, the last main side street as the quintant narrowed to its point. She almost didn't make it across. She packed as much Aether as she could manage into the huge jump. She watched as her outstretched foot clipped the edge of the far rooftop. It took her weight for a fraction of a second, then slipped. She lunged forward, throwing out her hands. Her chest slammed painfully into the edge of the roof. She grabbed the lip as she fell. Her whole body jarred as she hung onto the narrow ledge that rimmed this roof, just like the first one. Her feet scrabbled against the white plastered wall as she hoisted herself up and over the edge.

She rolled onto her back and lay panting for a moment, staring up at the peaceful blue sky. Her chest ached. She wondered if she had broken her collarbone when she slammed into the roof, but careful probing with her fingers told her she would just have a nasty bruise. She climbed back to her feet. She couldn't see Pavel anymore, but he had to have reached the gate already. She re-formed the lacings and leapt the next gap. The landing jarred her whole body.

She didn't know if she could keep going. She avoided looking down with each jump, but the occasional scream told her she was not outpacing the Kobolds. If she descended to the streets now, she would have to contend with the monstrous Weavers on her own. She could stop and just wait here until it was all over, one way or another. She wanted to. She really did. When Kobolds attacked the Watchkeeper stronghold in Falport, she had run and hid. That's how she had seen Gwen Hinter kill another Watch-keeper. True, she had later stood up to Kalo, but she'd had her friends at her back then. Now that she was alone, the temptation to hide returned.

She ignored it. She could not be a coward again. She would keep going, even if it killed her. She gritted her teeth and made the next jump. She pressed on, even when she thought she couldn't. With each leap, she expected the lacings to fail. She expected to fall to her death. But she didn't. Suddenly, there wasn't a next roof to jump toward. The high city walls closed in on both sides, with only a narrowing stretch of paving stone between her and the gate.

Pavel glanced at her from his spot crouched at the far corner of the roof. "We're too late," he said.

She heard the thwack of bowstrings then and saw the blur of movement coming off the tops of the walls. Archers lined the parapets on both sides, raining down arrows. Shilo joined Pavel, grateful to stop moving for a second. A row of spearmen stood before the closed wooden gates. An iron portcullis had been lowered in front of the massive doors. The guards had their spear butts planted against the ground with the tips up. It seemed like a formation intended to stop a line of charging cavalry, but it still made sense against their current foes.

The advancing Kobolds had formed a phalanx of sorts, though none held shields. Instead, they hoisted up the dead bodies of slain guards to catch most of the arrows. The occasional shaft still made it through, striking a Kobold, who let out an inhuman groan, but none of the monsters seemed to have fallen. That would change as they drew closer to the gate. The archers, though positioned fifty feet up, would not miss at such close range. Even if all these Kobolds were Weavers, Shilo couldn't see how they could possibly break through the gate without suffering heavy losses.

She leaned over the edge of the roof to look south. Several yards behind the black-clad Kobolds and well out of arrow range, a group of smaller Kobolds wearing the familiar brown vests and breeches stood in a clump. Most carried heavy burlap sacks stuffed with irregular-shaped objects, likely the Runeforms they had stolen from the vault. Behind them stood a group of a dozen humans. Some carried weapons, but none seemed bothered by their close proximity to monsters. Shilo recognized Gwen Hinter in a voluminous black robe and another man who might have been Lucas Peniter.

She glanced at Pavel. He'd been telling the truth about seeing Hinter in the cells at least. Pavel's gaze was focused on the black-clad Kobolds. Shilo looked back at them, just in time to see a mass of shadows stirring in their midst. She couldn't tell which Kobolds were Weaving, but it seemed to be multiple ones. She gasped as the swirling shadows suddenly rose and settled into the familiar rippling dome of a shield, a Blending of Stone and Wave. The dome looked darker than what human Weavers would make, composed of shadow rather than light, but it had a distinctive blue tinge.

The arrows stopped in midair, hitting the dome and then rolling uselessly off the side. After another unsuccessful volley, someone atop the wall bellowed a command, and the archers stopped. Silence filled the streets, as the guards waited to see what the monsters would do next. The Kobolds threw down the pin-cushioned bodies they'd been using as shields. She saw the injured Kobolds rip the arrows from their arms and shoulders, grunting as blue blood poured down their sides. Three Kobolds whose hands were empty, though weapons hung at their waists, moved through the crowd, sending out green-tinged shadows to heal their injured companions. All fifty-something Kobolds Weavers were still alive.

The crowd seemed to part as one Kobold stepped to the forefront, standing just inside the shield. This one seemed to be missing an eye, and it carried a wicked scythe. He raised his weapon and made a sweeping motion. "Gropen up!" he bellowed in the strange, garbled way all Kobolds spoke. "Gropen the grates!"

Shilo wondered if Kalo was there in their midst, but from this distance, they all looked more or less the same. She didn't see any with a scimitar at least. She remembered the strange blue sparks that had flown when Pavel had fought Kalo with his ancient Runeform weapons. Kalo's scimitar had not shattered against Pavel's bladebreaker, which meant it was likely also a Runeform relic. She wondered if all these Kobold Weavers carried Runeform weapons. It seemed unlikely that they could have so many, but maybe, if they did come from another world, it was a place where they still knew the secret of how to make new Runeforms—a place that had never Burned.

For a while, it seemed like no one would answer the Kobold's command to open the gates. The creature seemed content to wait, staring defiantly up at the archers and ignoring the spearmen in front of him. Finally, a bald head appeared atop the wall, the officer Pavel and Shilo had spoken to earlier, what now seemed like hours ago. "Lay down your arms!" the officer shouted down. To his credit, his voice did not shake.

The Kobold ignored the man. Its single eye swept across the whole wall. Then it grunted and turned away. It walked back toward the south, with most of the other black-clad Kobolds falling in line behind it. Five stayed behind, probably to maintain the shield. The rest retreated. Shilo realized that they had not formed a perfect dome but left an opening in the back. The Kobolds filed through that opening, walking calmly back into the city. A few archers opened fire, but at that range, they were unlikely to hit anything. The horde of Kobolds disappeared from view.

Pavel turned to Shilo. "Do you know the lacings to soften a landing?" he asked.

"What? No."

Pavel turned his back to her. "Come on, then. Possum ride."

"What? Are you crazy?"

"Climb on."

"I'm not doing that."

"If we go now, we can get inside the guard house. We may not have another chance."

Shilo sighed. Trying not to think too much about what they were about to do, she grabbed Pavel's shoulders and hopped up onto his back. She wrapped her legs around his waist, and he wedged his hands under her knees. Without warning, he leapt up and over the edge of the building, wrapping himself in Aether. She thought she was through screaming. She was wrong.

She felt the jar as they landed, but it was like he'd jumped off a curb into the street rather than a thirty-foot drop. She hopped off his back, managed to stay on her feet, and looked around. They had landed much closer to the Kobolds and their shield than the guards and their gatehouse.

"Run!" Pavel said. He lunged toward the Kobolds, throwing his hands up. Aether Weavers could only apply lacings to themselves, so they didn't often extend their light outward—unless they were trying to destroy a ward.

Shilo wished he had warned her he would try that. She didn't wait to see the shield go down. She turned and sprinted toward the line of spearmen. "Fire!" Pavel yelled up to the archers. She heard the twang of arrows raining down. There was no way the five Kobolds could survive that barrage, but they might still pull off some counterattack. Shilo half-expected not to make it to the gate. With every step she waited to be frozen in place by a lacing or struck down by a thrown weapon.

She made it. The line of spears parted to let her pass. The side door leading into the guardhouse was shut, but a pair of eyes watched her through a narrow slit. Pavel overtook her and stumbled to a halt in front of the door. "We're Watchkeepers," he said. "Let us in."

Shilo looked back then. Five armored Kobolds lay in the street, each pierced with a dozen arrows. After Kalo had survived a blow from her Etching, Shilo hadn't been sure these Kobold Weavers could be killed. They could. Their blue blood ran in rivulets between the paving stones, flowing towards the gutters at the edge of the road.

She heard the door swing open on rusty hinges. She followed Pavel inside. The door slammed shut behind them. Pavel headed straight for the stairs. She followed him up five winding flights. As they stepped back out onto the wall, she realized the bells had stopped ringing some time ago. She supposed it didn't do much good to deafen the archers.

The bald officer spared them a glance as they joined him at the inner parapet. He didn't seem surprised to see them. "What was that?" he asked, staring down at the five dead Kobolds. "Since when can Kobolds Weave?"

Sometimes she forgot that most people could not see the light—or shadow—of Weaving. Most of these guards would not have seen the shield dome, but they would have seen the arrows catch on thin air and would have understood.

"Most can't," Pavel said. "We don't think so, anyway, but the ones in black armor, they seem to be a different breed."

The officer nodded as if that made sense. Pavel spoke calmly, despite the fact that before today, they thought Kalo was the only Kobold who wore black and could Weave. Now there were at least fifty—less five. The officer glanced at them again. "Couple months back, when the beasts hit Falport, were you there?"

"Yep," Pavel said.

"How did you lot beat them off back then?"

Pavel glanced around, then lowered his voice confidingly. "Keep this to yourself, but… we didn't, not really. Sure, we killed lots of the regular sort of Kobolds, but the rest got what they were after, and they fled the city." Pavel pointed. "You see those ones there?" From this angle, they could see all the way to the Grand Hall. The black-clad Kobolds had disappeared somewhere into the city, but the smaller ones and the humans with them still stood in the street.

"With the big sacks?" the officer asked.

"Yeah. I can't be sure, but I think they attacked the Hall in order to loot the not-so-secret vault where the Pentarchs keep all their valuable Runeforms. I think they succeeded. That's what they got in the sacks. I don't think they want to do anymore killing or looting. They wanted you to open the gates because now they just want to retreat." Pavel turned and looked to the north. "Maybe they'll hit the estates on their way north, but I don't think so. I think they will hightail it all the way to the Coldreaches, if they can leave."

The officer scoffed. "They won't be leaving. It's true, they slipped into the city without setting off any alarms. Maybe they could have made it out if they'd finished before sunrise, but our hackles are raised now." He seemed to have forgotten that Shilo and Pavel were the ones who told him to sound the alarm. "I've sent runners to every gate, telling them what we're up against. I know they busted through the city wall back in Falport, but our walls are much thicker, and we have archers all along the length of it, just in case." He shook his head. "No, we'll put an end to this today, no matter how they try to bust out."

Pavel scanned the city. "I don't know," he said. "I don't think they're trying to find another exit. They gave up on this one too easily. Something else is going on."

"Like what?"

Pavel shook his head. "Nothing good."

Then they heard the screams.

Chapter 29
Hostages

NYSSA REACHED THE TOP of the steps and shuffled forward. She shivered as water ran down her back. They were all soaking wet from jumping into the moat. She didn't know why they jumped, but it seemed to have worked out. She had allowed Anyse Eldragor and Jayn to hold her up as they treaded water and waited, listening. They couldn't see anything, but they could hear heavy footsteps on stone. A whole army seemed to have emerged from the Grand Hall and then charged off to the north. Then silence.

She'd let the others pull her along as they swam around to the narrow ledge in front of the prison entrance and then trudged up the stairs, back into the courtyard. The others were talking now, discussing their next move. Nyssa didn't bother listening. She planted one wet boot and slid it forward. Then she slid her other foot, shuffling slowly along. The others ignored her. Probably they assumed she was in some sort of daze or stupor. She wasn't. Her mind was intensely focused.

"Close your eyes," she remembered Agia Bellos telling her, what now seemed like a lifetime ago. "Imagine a still pond. Imagine a single rain drop falling into the center of the pond. See the ripples spreading out. Feel the tiny waves flowing outward. Take a step forward. Step into the pond."

Nyssa forced herself through the exercise again and again. Step. Flow. Step. Flow. It didn't work. Her legs moved well enough, but nothing more happened. Since Kalo had used that Runeform on her, she'd been focused on a single task: summoning Wave. She couldn't. She ran through every visualization exercise she could think of. A raindrop on a pond. A leaky faucet dripping into a full sink. A boat swaying on the surface of a stormy sea. Her imagination still worked, but it never left her mind, never spread outward from the soles of her feet. She could not Weave. Still, she tried.

Even when they dragged her out of the Grand Hall, even when that giant ape grabbed her with its tail, she had done everything she could to Weave. If she could touch it, if she could form a single lacing, then she could help. If she couldn't, then everything was doomed, and she might as well let the monsters kill her.

She did her best to ignore the others, but she still caught bits and pieces. They seemed to be arguing.

"There's a reason we jumped in the moat," Thalia said. "Why would we chase after them now?"

"We'll keep our distance," Jayn said. She may have been responding to Thalia or to someone else.

They all fell silent for a moment, then Ryn said, "They're only to the north, not in any other direction."

Nyssa remembered Ryn getting stabbed, but he seemed fine now. Ryn was always getting stabbed. She didn't quite understand what they were discussing, but she didn't care. None of it mattered if she really was sealed. Anyse Eldragor put a hand on Nyssa's back. She cringed. The Fourth Pentarch had also been sealed, days ago, and she still couldn't Weave. But maybe she wasn't trying hard enough. Maybe the device affected Flame Weavers more than Wave Weavers. There had to be a way through. She had to find it. She didn't know what Anyse said to her. She didn't care. Step. Flow. Step. Flow.

"Captain," Jayn said, raising her voice as if Nyssa's hearing had been damaged. "We're going to head north. We think the Kobolds are trying to escape the city. Ryn says it should be safe to stay here. Just wait and we'll come back for you, all right?"

Step. Flow. Step. Flow. Nyssa paused and looked around. The others were gone. She was alone now. Where were they? She tried to remember what they had said to her. The road before her ran straight, but a slight rise and dip prevented her from seeing all the way to the gate. She remembered the Kobolds, all in black armor like Kalo. Her hand went to her waist. She felt the empty scabbard. She didn't remember dropping her sword. Foolish. Why did she leave it behind?

She heard a distant scream, a shrill woman's voice. Nyssa couldn't Weave. She had no weapon. She couldn't even think clearly. She was worse than useless right now. Still, when she heard another scream, she didn't hesitate. Her boots squelched across the courtyard, over the rickety temporary bridge, and into the Civic Quintant. She passed between two little parks, noticing that the short swathes of grass had all turned brown and died. Ryn was always killing grass.

She crested the low rise. To her left, a door fell off its hinges, clattered down stone steps, and landed in the street. A massive Kobold in black armor stepped backward out the door, dragging a woman in a yellow dress by the hair. The woman screamed and fought back, with all the success of a toddler throwing a tantrum. The Kobold let her squirm as it pulled her into the street.

Nyssa heard screams and shouts coming from all sides now. A doubled image flashed into her mind of another attack on this part of the city, that one at night and carried out by mere humans. Nyssa froze. Her hand pawed uselessly at her waist again. She didn't know how she could have left her sword behind. The Kobold ignored her, dragging the woman north.

Nyssa planted her foot and envisioned a wall of Wave forming in front of her. Nothing happened. She remembered unlocking the full potential of her Etching, how she'd been able to form a shield without envisioning anything. She threw her hands up and willed a shield into existence. Nothing happened. More Kobolds emerged from busted doorways, dragging shrieking or unconscious citizens along.

Need. There was often an aspect of need when it came to Weaving. Her shield had first come to her when she'd been just a girl, cornered in a blind alley by a mob of boys with wicked intentions. Maybe she could force her Weaving to work again, if she placed herself in a hazardous situation. The danger increased with each step she took north. The Kobolds were all around her now, too preoccupied with taking people captive to notice her. She would force her Weaving to work again, or the Kobolds would kill her. Either way, it would put an end to her nightmare. Step. Flow. Step. Flow.

Nyssa looked up, catching sight of a familiar gray uniform. Despite how tiny Jayn Eldragor was, it had apparently taken two towering Kobolds to subdue the scrappy girl. One creature held her wrists, while another had her by the ankles. They carried her between them like a sack of grain, while she squirmed and writhed like an insect caught in a web. Spurts of red Flame emerged from the girl's chest. She seemed to be trying to channel them into her fists, but they kept sputtering out. Some small part of Nyssa was impressed that a Wave Weaver could summon even that much Flame, but why had Jayn been practicing Flame?

Nyssa stumbled forward, not knowing what to do. A moment before she'd been ready to die, but the sight of her student caught in the grasp of these monsters awakened something in her. She ran forward, all thoughts of Weaving vanished from her mind. She threw her entire body against the nearest Kobold. The brute stumbled, dropping Jayn's legs. The other Kobold continued onward, dragging Jayn by the wrists. The girl planted her freed feet on the ground and tried to stand, but she was still overmatched. The Kobold Nyssa had shoved grumbled as it turned back toward her. She took a few steps back. The creature reached up and in one fluid motion unsheathed a massive broadsword from a scabbard on its back. The shining blade looked like it had been forged from silver.

Nyssa danced back again as the creature swung on her. The Kobold carrying Jayn disappeared into the milling crowd. Nyssa couldn't stop them. Even if she'd held onto her sword, even if she could still Weave, it would not have made a difference. They were too strong, and she was too weak. This was a fight she could never win.

Nyssa dodged another swing, even as she saw the futility of it all. She should just give up and stand still. The creature could probably take her head off in a single stroke. She'd be dead before she even realized it. Still, some small part of her mind forced her limbs to jump back each time the silver blade flashed toward her.

She stepped back again, the blade passing just inches from her face. She smacked into something solid and immovable. She spun around, staring up into the hideous face of another Kobold. This one had a nose like a lumpy gray potato. It grabbed her head with both its massive hands, though it didn't scratch or squeeze. Instead, a wall of swirling shadows blotted out her vision. She didn't even have a chance to scream as the lacings pulled her down into darkness.

"Line them up," someone said.

Jayn awoke as someone grabbed her roughly by the shoulders and lifted her up. She tried to stand but was forced to her knees. She blinked, looking around. She didn't remember blacking out. An image flashed through her mind of a gray-skinned Kobold with a bulbous nose, but nothing more.

She looked down. Gray hands with pointed black nails gripped her shoulders. She looked left. Thalia and Ryn were there, also on their knees. The Kobolds that held them were the smaller kind, without armor. She looked right and saw Nyssa and her mother. Everyone seemed to be rousing from unconsciousness along with her.

She looked up. Gwen Hinter smiled down at her. The one-time Root master was an ugly woman. Jayn had trained with her for only two weeks, but she had hated every minute of it. When Hinter disappeared in the wake of the attack on Falport, Jayn's dislike for the woman had only deepened.

"Look at all my old friends," Hinter said. "Though we're missing two."

It took Jayn's muddled mind a moment to realize she was talking about Shilo and Pavel. She hoped those two were faring better than her. She looked around again, trying to get her bearings. They were in the street, some four hundred paces away from one of the city gates. If they were still in the Civic Quintant, that would be the northern Melgeld Gate. A line of guards with spears defended the gate. Archers lined the walls above, but no one was firing.

A rippling dome shield covered a large swath of the street, sheltering a mob of creatures and humans. The shield looked like a normal Blending of Wave and Stone, except it was nearly black in color. The Kobold Weavers had made it. Those black-clad beasts were all here, standing near the front of the dome. Jayn guessed their number to be around fifty.

There were just as many humans under the dome. Most seemed to have been taken as hostages like Jayn and her friends, but a few stood unrestrained behind Gwen Hinter, clearly at ease in the presence of monsters. Most seemed at ease anyway. She spotted Lucas Peniter to the left, his arms crossed tight across his chest as he shot nervous glances all around.

"Hello, Gwen," Nyssa said. She seemed to have recovered from her malaise following Kalo's attack and met Hinter's gaze without wavering.

Hinter shook her head. "It's a shame it's come to this, Nyssa. You were a troublesome student, but you made an excellent Watchkeeper."

"You were a good Watchkeeper too, before you betrayed us all."

Jayn glanced at her mother. If she seemed surprised to see a member of the Council of Masters working with the Kobolds, she hid it well.

Hinter shrugged. "It was no betrayal from my perspective," she said in her raspy voice. "I swore my oaths to the Reach long before I joined the Watchkeepers."

"The Reach? Is that what you and your friends call yourselves?"

The name sounded familiar, but it took Jayn a moment to remember. *We are bound for the Reach.* That's what the owl-like Manface had said to Kalo. The monkey one had used that word too. Jayn's Pentad assumed it was a location, possibly the Coldreach Mountains, but it must be an organization instead. Jayn looked around at the people again, trying to get a sense of who would willingly work with Kobolds. The group looked diverse in dress and appearance, men and women from all echelons of Appencourt society. Two men stood with their backs turned to Jayn and her friends. She couldn't see their faces, but they did look familiar.

Anyse saw the men too. "Master Stoats?" she said, amazement in her voice. "Commander Grondor?"

The steward of the Hall and the leader of the Wardens both turned around. The gray-haired Laren Stoats seemed embarrassed to be recognized, but the gaunt Cole Grondor offered a rueful grin and a nod. "My lady," he said.

Jayn's mother scoffed. "That explains how they breached the Hall so easily." She turned her focus back to Gwen Hinter. "The Watchkeepers? The Hall? Just how far does your reach extend?"

Hinter laughed. "There is a reason we call ourselves the Reach."

Jayn couldn't keep quiet any longer. "But what do you want?"

Hinter narrowed her eyes at Jayn. "You wouldn't understand."

Nyssa scoffed this time. "She doesn't know. She's following orders just like the rest of them. Look at poor Peniter over there." Jayn hated Lucas Peniter for what he'd done to her mother. She could never have sympathy for him, but he did look wretched and frightened now. "Before today, I doubt he had any idea he was working for literal monsters."

Maybe Nyssa was right. A group as secret and widespread as the Reach seemed to be probably kept its members separate and in the dark, only telling them what they needed to know.

"He'll get used to it," Hinter said. "We take care of our own and reward their loyalty. He's smart enough to honor his oaths, unlike a friend of yours."

"You mean Pavel?" Jayn asked. It was a guess, but Pavel's story about how he knew Lucas Peniter never sat right with Jayn. She didn't know much about Pavel's criminal past, but it seemed likely he could have fallen in with a shadowy group like the Reach, if the pay was good, maybe without even knowing their true purposes.

Hinter nodded. "He's a naughty boy, that one. He was happy to take the oath when it benefited him, but now he'd rather die in the dirt with the rest of you. He will die, rest assured. Oath breakers will not go unpunished."

Nyssa shook her head. "Sounds like Pavel is the smart one from my perspective."

Hinter shrugged. "I wonder. Is he still smitten with you, Captain Lahmeer? That explains why he wanted to stay with the Watchkeepers. He's not the loyal kind, but men will do all kinds of foolish things for a pretty face."

Nyssa ignored the taunt. She looked past Hinter and the members of the Reach, to a group of normal Kobolds holding overstuffed burlap sacks. "Stealing Runeforms again, huh?" she asked. "What do you need all of them for anyway?"

"Enough talk," Hinter said, a hardness in her voice now. "The show's about to start, but I want to have my own bit of fun first." She reached into her pocket and pulled out a short copper rod. Jayn froze. How did that horrid Runeform keep falling into the wrong hands? Hinter's smile widened. "Well done to you lot for taking out Kalo. I don't know what you did to him, but we had to leave that poor fellow behind in the vault." Hinter swept her eyes across their group before settling on Jayn. "Let's start with your little protégé, eh?"

Jayn fought the sudden fear that gripped her. She didn't want Hinter to see her panic, but she couldn't stop her heart from beating wildly in her chest. She couldn't breathe. Hinter took a casual step toward her, waving the Runeform back and forth. Jayn tried to stand, but the Kobold behind her forced her back to her knees. As selfish as the thought felt, she didn't want to end up like her mother or Nyssa. She saw how the device had affected them. If Jayn lost her Weaving… her life would be over. She saw no future for herself as a regular person. She had to fight back. If she couldn't escape, she could at least force them to kill her. She resolved to die before giving up her Weaving. But what could she do? What ward would help her now? Maybe if she made herself invisible, it would confuse the Kobold behind her for a moment, and she could break free. The creature wouldn't see the lacings forming, but Hinter would. She had to be quick.

"Wait!" Nyssa shouted. "Don't touch her."

Hinter glanced at Nyssa. "Why shouldn't I? She's just a little first-echelon brat."

"Exactly," Nyssa said. "She's sixteen. She's barely had any training. She's no threat to you or your group. If you want to have your fun, if you want to use that thing… use it on me."

Hinter's eyebrows rose in amazement. "Such nobility, Captain Lahmeer. You know what this device will do? Look at poor Anyse over there. She couldn't Weave if her life depended on it. If I use this, your Watchkeeper career will be over. Are you really prepared to give all of that up for this blonde little idiot?"

Nyssa stared up at Hinter, defiance writ across her face. "You talked about loyalty… You've chosen these monsters as your friends, but my loyalty is to my recruits. I will die for them if I must."

It was a brilliant bluff. Apparently, Hinter didn't know that Nyssa had already been sealed. Jayn wondered if Nyssa would still have volunteered if the rod could harm her. Jayn wouldn't have done it, if someone else were under threat, no matter who they were.

Hinter made a big show of considering Nyssa's request. "Hmm…" she said, tapping a finger against her lips. Then she tapped the rod against Jayn's forehead. Jayn winced with each touch of cold metal. She held her breath, refusing to look up, not wanting to give any sign that Nyssa was playing Hinter.

Finally, Hinter sighed. "Very well," she said. She pivoted quickly, pressing the silver prongs against Nyssa's neck. The captain flinched and gritted her teeth. That wasn't acting. Even though the rod could no longer harm her, Nyssa still must have hated feeling it against her skin again. "So long, Captain," she said, sounding almost regretful. She twisted the device and then pulled it away. Nyssa dropped her head, but the Kobold holding her arms kept her from falling.

Hinter stepped back. She glanced to the left, toward the gate, where some commotion seemed to have started. "We'll have to finish this later." Her hand slipped back into her robe and the cursed Runeform disappeared.

Jayn stared at the ground in front of her. She fought to control her breathing and stop her heart from pounding so rapidly. She felt like she had just been spared from an execution.

"Gropen the grates!" someone shouted in a voice distinctively Kobold and not human.

A long silence followed. Jayn got her breathing down to an almost normal rate. She looked up, craning her neck to see the front of the group of Kobolds. One black-clad beast stood apart from the others. He held a long black scythe. A woman in a yellow dress, torn at the neck and threatening to slide off her shoulders, crouched on her knees beside him.

Jayn wondered at the weapon. While scythes looked menacing, they were farming tools, meant for mowing grass, and seemed totally impractical as a weapon. For starters, the cutting edge was on the inside of the curved blade. A wielder had to swing the blade toward himself—great for reaping vegetation but not useful against people. Few opponents would be foolish enough to step inside the reach of such a blade, and while the wielder could then hook the fool in the back, he would leave his front open and exposed.

The woman in the street was an easy target, however. After another minute, when it became clear that the guards would not open the gates, the Kobold pressed a knee against the woman's back, hooked the scythe around her neck, and pulled. The motion seemed slow and casual from where Jayn knelt, but the blade sliced cleanly through. The woman's body fell forward into the street, and her head rolled off to the side. Jayn winced. People all around, other hostages, screamed or shouted in horror, but not the members of the Reach. They stood in stony silence. Gwen Hinter smiled.

The Kobold with the scythe gestured to the others. They dragged another hostage forward, a man in the homespun clothes of a laborer. They forced him to his knees beside the dead woman. The lead Kobold raised his scythe. "Gropen the grates!" he shouted. Then he waited.

The message was clear. They would continue executing hostages until the city guard let them leave. Jayn looked around, trying to count how many hostages were left. She and her friends were near the back of the group, but the scythe-wielding Kobold would get to them eventually. She didn't know if the guards would ever open the gates. Probably, they would send forces out from the other guard houses and close in on the Kobolds from behind. The battle would be bloody and casualties would be high. Jayn didn't know if she would live to see it. She closed her eyes. At least beheading would be a quick death.

Shilo averted her gaze, as a third hostage lost his head. Beside her, the bald officer stood completely still with a grim expression on his face. She didn't know what she would do in his shoes. Would she open the gate? Her eyes swept over the group in the street below them, skipping over the growing pile of headless bodies. She froze, seeing four figures in gray uniforms near the back of the mob.

"Pavel—" she started to say. He grabbed her arm and shot her a warning look. Her brow furrowed in confusion. Pavel fixed his gaze on the officer. Did Pavel not want the man to notice the Watchkeepers? Even from this distance, Shilo recognized Ryn, Thalia, Jayn, and Captain Lahmeer. The blonde woman beside them may have been Jayn's mother. She decided to follow Pavel's lead.

A runner approached the officer. He glanced at the man but said nothing, returning his gaze to the scythe-wielding Kobold as a fourth hostage was forced to kneel. The runner hesitated but then delivered his report to the officer's back. "We just got word from the Aethgeld and Walgeld gates. They've begun their sweeps of the city. We're still awaiting runners from Skalgeld and Rugeld."

The officer nodded. The runner saluted his back and retreated.

"How many?" Pavel asked. The officer did not respond. "How many people have to die before you open the gate?"

"Gropen the grates!" the Kobold shouted below.

"We're not opening the gate," the officer spat the words out. "We won't yield."

"It's your job to protect the citizens. Are you just going to let all those hostages die?"

"You heard the report. The rest of the city guard is closing in on this spot as we stand here. We will avenge the dead."

"There will be plenty to avenge. I know how you lot work. The other guards will have to sweep their whole quintants first, in case more Kobolds are hiding in the city. How long will that take? It'll be an hour, maybe two, before any of them make it here. Then the Kobolds won't just lay down their arms. The fight will be bloody and vicious. There might not be a city left for you to protect before this is over."

The officer turned on Pavel then, his face red. "Curse you, ya Gray! You think I don't know all that? What do you want from me? If you want to help, why don't you jump down there and destroy their shield again?"

Pavel took a step back and raised his hands. He seemed calm, but Shilo caught a hint of desperation in his eyes. She knew he would play every angle and do whatever it took to convince the officer to open the gate, if only to save Nyssa and his Pentad. That's why he had silenced Shilo a moment ago. He didn't want the officer to know how personally invested he was in letting the Kobolds escape. Shilo still wasn't sure if that was the right choice. She also still didn't know the officer's name. In the silence that followed the officer's outburst, they heard two dull thuds below, as another civilian lost his head.

"I could," Pavel said. "Your boys would get a few shots off, maybe kill a few of them, but then they would kill me, and the shield would go right back up, and you would still have a problem. Let's think this through. That crazy sickle that Kobold has? That's no kind of weapon, unless it's a relic, a Runeform from before the Burning. Look at the rest of them. None of those weapons are normal. Those are all Runeforms, all unbreakable, and maybe they have other deadly properties. Then there's the piles of other Runeforms they've pillaged from the Grand Hall. Some of those have to be weapons, if they wanted them so bad. I haven't even gotten to the fifty black Kobold Weavers holding those weapons. I've seen one use a lacing that will paralyze you where you stand. You won't be able to move or even breathe, and then they'll kill you at their leisure. I've seen that."

Pavel hadn't raised his voice, but in the silence atop the wall, all the guards nearby could hear him. Shilo looked around at the fearful faces. They all looked so young, barely more than boys. The officer stared at Pavel a long while before he spoke again. Down below, the Kobold bellowed once again for the gate to be opened. "What would you have me do?" the officer asked, a slight tremble in his voice.

Pavel looked around at the audience he had drawn. He focused on the officer, but he clearly addressed the entire guard now. "You could do the noble thing here, the honorable thing. Hold the line, wait for reinforcements, and then charge down there. These beasts are strong, but they're not unkillable. We can take some of them down with us, make sure they bleed for what they're doing down there right now. How many civilians will die first? Dozens? Maybe hundreds, at the rate they're going. These monsters will not give up. They'll burn this whole city to the ground if they must. We'll die, everyone of us, and then the Kobolds who are left—and there will be plenty left—will dust themselves off, gather up their Runeforms, and walk through whatever rubble remains of the gate we're standing on." He paused for emphasis, looking around at all the guards again. "We can certainly do that and take solace in the fact that we will be remembered forever in legend and song, the heroes of Appencourt who fought to the last man. Yes, we can do the noble thing… Or we can do the smart thing and save countless lives." His voice dropped to a whisper. "Open the gate."

The guards all looked to their commander. Pavel had convinced them. He was always convincing, even when he lied. A wild thought came to Shilo. What if Pavel hadn't betrayed his oath to that group? What had he called them, the Reach? What if he was working with Peniter and the Kobolds? Of course, he would want the gates opened then. Shilo studied Pavel's profile. She wished she were a better judge of character. She didn't really think he could work with monsters, and even if he was… opening the gate still seemed like the right decision. It would save lives today. It would save Thalia and the others.

Of course, the Kobolds would not disappear forever. They would likely attack again somewhere else. Maybe the Academy of the Ways? The Scholars probably had more Runeforms than anyone. Still, letting them go now would give Aldria time to prepare. The Hall would not take the Kobold threat lightly, as Commandant Lahey had feared. They could call in the Standing Army and hunt these monsters to the ends of the earth if they had to. Shilo decided to keep quiet.

"Sir?" one of the guards said. The officer silenced him with a wave of his hand. The man appeared to be deep in thought, his eyes shut and his lips moving silently. They heard another thud as another hostage died.

Finally, the officer let out a world-weary sigh. He turned and looked at all his men and their frightened faces. He strolled toward one man, positioned near the door. He had a horn swung under one shoulder. The officer grabbed the horn and yanked it so fiercely that the leather strap tore. The guard made no protest, watching his commander. The officer moved back to the inner wall, raised the horn to his lips, and released a three-note call. He leaned over the edge. "Open up!" he yelled to the men below. Shilo rushed to his side. Some of the guards below dropped their spears in their hurry to fall back to the guardhouse. She heard a metallic grinding noise as the portcullis began to rise.

The lead Kobold had been preparing to behead another woman who wore a ruffled servant's uniform. The Kobold raised his scythe, staring up at the men on the wall. The woman on her knees looked up. The Kobold ignored her. Tentatively, she crawled away from him, and when no one stopped her, she climbed to her feet. She rushed toward the guard house, smacked into the shield, and fell flat on her back. Panic seized her then. She screamed and curled into a ball. Still, no one made an aggressive move toward her.

All throughout the crowd, still protected by the black rippling dome, hostages began to stir, realizing that their captors were now ignoring them. Slowly at first, they began to move away, back toward the city. The Kobolds had once again left an opening at the rear of their shield, and maybe some of the hostages could see that. The poor servant at the front was back on her feet, feeling blindly along the shield, trying to find a way out. Eventually she would circle back to the rear. The Kobolds seemed content to let her.

Shilo searched the crowd for any sign of a gray uniform, but she'd lost sight of her friends in the milling mob. Frightened citizens stumbled away, while the rest of the Kobolds and a few humans pressed forward, ready to charge through the gate as soon as it opened.

"I'm no Weaver," the officer said. "Will you tell me if they drop that blighted shield?"

It took Shilo a second to understand he was talking to her. She nodded and then said, "Yes," realizing he wasn't looking at her.

"It looks like they're making a new shield," Pavel said, on Shilo's other side.

Below, a new wall of shadows rose from the mob, extending forward toward the gate and merging with the base of the wall. The first shield dissolved, and the Kobolds charged forward toward the gate. The new shield had no rear exit, and a few of the slower civilians had been caught inside. They panicked, screaming and throwing themselves against the shield, but the Kobolds still ignored them. It seemed they really did just want to escape the city.

Shilo turned and ran to the outer wall. She had completely forgotten about the gate town there. A few citizens had ventured out of their homes, but when they saw the monsters emerge from the city, they screamed and fled, unpursued. Shilo glanced at the officer, who had followed her. She shook her head. "They're making another shield." The web of shadows stretched across half of the gate town.

The officer sighed. He turned and leaned his back against the parapet. "I hoped we could at least get a few shots off as they ran." Archers stood ready along the wall, waiting for the command to fire. The officer shook his head as Pavel joined them again. "I pray to the Maker and all the stars we made the right decision today."

Pavel didn't respond. Shilo watched the black-clad Kobolds march forward in two orderly lines. The regular Kobolds came next, hefting their bags and looking puny behind their towering brothers. Then came a dozen humans, members of the Reach. Shilo recognized Hinter and Peniter. More Kobolds took up the rear, shoving five humans with their hands bound behind their backs. Four wore gray uniforms and another wore a blood-stained nightgown.

"Blight," the officer said. "I thought they'd dropped all the hostages. That looks like the Fourth Pentarch—and some friends of yours."

Shilo looked at Pavel. His eyes were fixed on the retreating hostages. The foremost Kobolds stopped to form their next shield. Shilo turned to the officer. "Have your men ready to open fire. We'll take out their shield."

Pavel quirked an eyebrow. "What's the play?"

"Possum ride."

His eyes widened. "That's a fifty-foot drop."

"You can't do it?"

"I didn't say that."

She didn't let him say another word. She grabbed his shoulders and turned him forcefully toward the wall. She jumped on his back, and he reluctantly took her weight. Pavel sighed. "Jump," she ordered.

She managed not to scream this time as he hopped up on the edge of the parapet and stepped out into space. They dropped straight down, while Aether surrounded Pavel. His feet hit the shield dome. It took their weight for a fraction of a second before it shattered like a glass ceiling and the ground rushed to meet them. The landing was harder than the last one. Pavel collapsed to his knees. Shilo hopped off his back and nearly fell over. She looked down the road. Dozens of Kobolds and humans stared back at her in surprise. Then the arrows began to fly.

The Kobolds cried out with their inhuman voices and ran, weaving between buildings to avoid the archers but still fleeing the city. Shilo saw a man in a white uniform. He looked like the steward of the Hall. She charged toward her friends and the Kobolds who held them, as Flame enveloped her. Her hands began to glow.

The rearmost Kobolds took one look at Shilo, charging toward them with death in her eyes and in her hands, and they released their hold on the hostages and fled. Shilo stumbled to a halt and released her Etching.

"Shilo!" Thalia said, smiling in spite of everything.

Shilo took a quick head count. Thalia, Jayn, Ryn, Nyssa, and Anyse were all there, all looking haggard but relieved. "Come on!" Shilo said, gesturing back toward the gate. She waited until they stumbled past her. They still had their hands tied behind their back, but they could be unbound later. She looked back to the north. The Kobold Weavers had formed another shield, and the arrows now dinged uselessly against it. A few Kobolds lay dead in the street, including a couple in black, but not enough. The new shield was only a hundred paces away. The Kobolds clearly only wanted to leave. Shilo could wrap herself in Aether and charge the shield again. She began to form the lacings.

"Shilo!" Pavel called. She glanced back. The heavy wooden gates were closing. Probably, the officer didn't want to risk the Kobolds turning back and reentering the city. Her friends would make it inside before they closed.

She looked back at the dome shield. She could still take it down, even if it would trap her outside. The Kobolds would keep fleeing, and more would die. She would only be taking a small risk.

She flinched as someone grabbed her arm. Pavel had come back for her. “Come on!” he yelled. “We’ve had enough heroics for today!”

She hesitated only a moment longer. They had to sprint to make it back into the city before the massive gates closed with a final thud.

Chapter 30
Before the Hall

IT TOOK THE HALL of the Assembly a full week to recover from the attack and send for Jayn and her Pentad. Overall, the casualties were less than what Falport had experienced some two months before. Thirty-two people died within the Grand Hall, a mix of servants and Wardens. Another dozen citizens and twice as many city guards were killed as the Kobolds fled the city. A comparable number of Kobolds died, including nine who wore the black armor. Six members of the Reach were killed, including Laren Stoats and Cole Grondor, but Gwen Hinter and Lucas Peniter escaped. None of the Runeforms stolen from the vault had been recovered.

The officer who ordered the Melgeld Gate opened had been stripped of his rank and demoted to the lowest rung of the city guard, but the citizens of Appencourt seemed to agree that he had made the right decision. The Tamorine Ambassador Lorenz Savon and his two personal guards were also listed among the dead in the official report. Jayn wondered if that story would hold up to scrutiny, especially since one of the bodyguards hadn't actually died, as far as anyone knew. Shifting the blame to the Kobolds, a common enemy of all mankind, was a savvy move, though it still meant that the Hall had failed to protect the emperor's son while he was in their care. It could still be a provocation for war, but only if the emperor acknowledged that Lorenz was actually the prince, which would raise potentially embarrassing questions about why he slipped away to Aldria in secret. Time would tell, and Aldria would deal with Tamor eventually, but their top priority was now the Kobolds and the Reach.

Jayn, Thalia, and Ryn had been permitted to leave the city to weather the recoil after their second round of luck. They didn't know for certain the luck had even activated—that night and morning had been horrible, but of course none of them had died, and they didn't want to take any chances after the last disastrous recoil. They were all put up for the night in separate farmhouses and were each served completely different dinners. Yet all three awoke just before sunrise with the overwhelming urge to vomit. Food poisoning, a nasty sickness Jayn had never experienced before, kept them at their farmhouses another three days. Jayn was glad no one she knew had seen her in that wretched state. When they recovered enough to return to Appencourt, Ryn made a joke about "tasting deadly poison," and she laughed in spite of everything.

The first day the Hall reconvened, Jayn and her Pentad were up at dawn, dressed in freshly laundered uniforms, tabards, and pins. Captain Nyssa Lahmeer, in light of what Kalo had done to her, had been excused from testifying before the whole Hall, but the recruits still expected that she would show. They waited for her outside their rooms. Pavel knocked on her door. She didn't answer. She had barely left her room all week. Jayn didn't blame her. Her mother seemed to have recovered faster, but as she had said, the Fourth Pentarch of Aldria didn't need to be a Weaver. A Watchkeeper who couldn't Weave… That had never happened before, and no one knew what would become of Nyssa when she returned to Falport.

The five recruits waited in the lobby outside the sealed Assembly Room all day, but they were never called. Other people did file in and out to give testimony, mostly Wardens and members of the city guard. Jayn spoke briefly with Jax Centillion on his way out. He walked with barely a limp now. Jayn's Pentad was up at dawn again the next day. Pavel knocked on Nyssa's door again, but she did not answer. They waited outside the Assembly Room for an hour before they were finally called in.

The five Watchkeepers sat at the table in the center of the floor. Five Pentarchs and fifty lords and ladies looked down on them from their ring of benches, listening to their testimonies. The First Pentarch led the questioning, but several lords and ladies chimed in during the hours-long meeting. A couple weeks ago, Jayn's Pentad had been so worried about having to lie to the Hall, to cover up the secret of the impossible Blending Ryn had created. Now that hardly mattered. The Hall asked few questions about the attack on Falport, their attention on more recent matters. Ryn's Etching never even came up, nor did the topic of Kobold poison.

They also didn't have to dance around the thorny issues Commandant Lahey had warned them about—Gwen Hinter's betrayal and Kalo's ability to Weave. The whole city knew about the Reach and Kobold Weavers now. Jayn had shared her revelation about Kalo's paralysis lacing, a Blend of Wave and Flame, with her friends, but that was an easy truth to keep to themselves. They told the Hall quite truthfully that the Kobolds' lacings appeared as dark shadows and didn't resemble human lacings, an unsettling answer but one the Hall accepted.

They discussed their limited interactions with the "Manfaces," a name everyone in the Hall quickly adopted. They described the owl and the ape, as well as the bear Thalia and Ryn had briefly seen, but they shared no speculations about the creatures. Pavel had cooked up a new theory that while the monkey Manface had not done any Weaving, it still had the intrinsic traits of an Aether Weaver, or possibly Aether itself. The way it moved, the way it popped Jayn's shield on contact, and even the way it collapsed when touched by Ryn's Root all seemed to fit that theory. Pavel kept his many theories to himself before the Hall, for the most part.

Near the end of the long meeting, the First Pentarch began asking questions about the Reach. They had all agreed beforehand that Jayn would take the lead during the meeting, and she had spoken more than any of the others, though each had answered their fair share of questions. Here, she glanced at Pavel. Despite being knocked out for half a week by food poisoning, Jayn had had plenty of time to discuss everything with her Pentad, including the Reach. They decided that they could not keep Pavel's connection to the group a secret. Jayn's mother had been there when Gwen Hinter talked about Pavel swearing an oath, though the Fourth Pentarch did not mention it now. Anyse Eldragor had been silent throughout the meeting, looking regal, if a bit weary, in her black robes of state, with a practiced neutral expression on her face.

"Do you know anything else about this group calling itself the Reach?" Morace Prentley had asked.

Pavel cleared his throat. "I once worked for the Reach, four years ago."

Murmurs broke out all around the Assembly Room, but only the First Pentarch questioned the Watchkeepers now. "Explain yourself," he said.

"It is likely common knowledge now that my service to the Watchkeepers is a condition of a deferred sentence for… alleged criminal activities. I used to work in the recovery of antiquities and Runeforms, and I had a number of well-connected clients, including"—Pavel glanced around the room—"some here in Appencourt."

Pavel had wanted to call out the specific lords he'd done jobs for, but Jayn had cautioned against that. The more subtle insinuation still had the desired effect. There was more murmuring and a number of lords shifted uncomfortably on their benches.

"Four years ago," Pavel continued, "I was contacted by a man named Lucas Peniter. He recruited me to work for a group he called the Reach. At the time, I assumed they were a… well, a crime syndicate, black-market smugglers, something like that. I only did one job for them. They hired me to break into an unmarked barrow up in the Hollow Mountains and recover a relic—which is perfectly legal under the Law of Salvage, of course."

"What was the relic?"

"It was a glass sphere. I assume it was a Runeform. I don't know what it did. I didn't ask."

"If they hired you for a legal job, why did you believe they were a criminal group?"

"Well, they were shady, and way too dramatic. Before they agreed to hire me, I had to kneel and swear an oath."

"What sort of oath?"

"Loyalty. Secrecy. I was never to speak of the Reach to anyone outside of the group or talk about anything I did for them." He looked around at the assembled lords again. "I freely break that oath now."

"Is this sort of oath standard in your… former line of work?"

Pavel shook his head. "Not at all."

"Then why did you take it?"

"Taking the oath came with several promises. The Reach paid better than any of my other clients, and they guaranteed my protection. If I stayed loyal to the group, they said they would always come to my aid, even if I got arrested. I didn't put much stock in that promise, but Lucas Peniter also took an oath, and he's certainly not in prison today."

More murmuring. Prentley raised a bushy eyebrow. "If your work for the Reach was 'perfectly legal,' as you say, then why did they promise to bail you out of trouble?"

"The salvage job was sort of an audition. I assume they would have moved me onto more sensitive, less-than-legal work after that. The whole oath thing made me uncomfortable. I was supposed to deliver the relic directly to my contact with the Reach—a man whose name I never learned and face I never saw—but I reached out to Peniter instead and arranged a dead drop. They had given me half the gold up front, and I decided that was payment enough, so I skipped town."

"So you never worked for the Reach again?"

"No, sir."

"They never tried to contact you again?"

Pavel shook his head. "Not until about two weeks ago, right after we arrived in Appencourt. Peniter approached me on the street, but I took one look at him and turned the other way. I still don't know what he wanted from me. Maybe he was trying to recruit me for his attack on the Hall, though I've never done that sort of job before."

Prentley considered Pavel's testimony for a moment. "If you'll forgive the question, how do we know you are telling the truth? How do we know you aren't still working for the Reach?"

Jayn sat up straighter in her seat. They had anticipated this response. "If I may?" she asked the First Pentarch.

Prentley nodded to her.

"When Kobolds attacked Falport, I fought alongside Pavel Talvor. Ryn Silverbell can tell you about fighting Kobolds with Pavel in the Sylphren Wood. Shilo Lorn can tell you about how Pavel fought to defend this city last week. The truth is, Pavel Talvor has killed as many Kobolds as anyone. That fact alone should clear him of suspicion."

Pavel nodded. "I admit to having worked for the Reach. I admit that that was a mistake, but I have never knowingly worked for or alongside Kobolds."

"Knowingly," Jayn said, looking around the room. "That's the key word here. When the Reach and the Kobolds were fleeing the city, they took most of my Pentad hostage, along with Captain Lahmeer and the Fourth Pentarch." She nodded to her mother. "I saw Lucas Peniter then. He looked truly frightened. I don't think he had any idea who he was really working for."

"I agree," Pavel said. "Peniter stayed loyal to the Reach because they paid well and they guaranteed his protection. The Reach told him to denounce Weavers and run for a seat in the Hall, so he did. Then the Reach told him to rile up a mob and attack the lords and ladies of the Hall, so he did. He allowed himself to be arrested and kept his mouth shut, trusting that he would be taken care of. The Reach came through and broke him out of the cells beneath our feet, but I think Jayn Eldragor is correct. I think Lucas Peniter is regretting his oath now." Pavel looked around the room again.

"Think about it," Jayn said, just as they had rehearsed. "The Reach thrives on secrecy. We believe they keep their own members isolated and in the dark, telling them only what they need to know, when they need to know it. They have been operating undetected for years, and they seem to have infiltrated every layer of Aldrian society and government. Gwen Hinter sat on the Council of Masters in Falport. Cole Grondor was head of the Wardens. Laren Stoats oversaw everything that happened in this very building."

"The truth is out now," Pavel said. "The Reach is public knowledge, and it has been inextricably linked to the Kobolds and the Manfaces. How many people now find themselves in Lucas Peniter's position? How many now regret swearing an oath to the Reach? I am here today to tell you that it is not too late for anyone to break that oath."

Once again, Pavel allowed his gaze to sweep across the room. The meaning of those looks was now crystal clear. Jayn scanned the crowd. Some glowered at Pavel in anger or indignation, while others began to regard their fellow lords with suspicion and even fear. Suddenly, dozens of people spoke all at once, denouncing the insinuation.

"Quiet!" the First Pentarch bellowed, silencing the lords and ladies. He regarded Pavel with narrowed eyes. "What exactly are you implying?"

Pavel opened his mouth but hesitated.

"Do we need to say it?" Jayn asked, rising to her feet. "If the Reach has infiltrated the highest ranks of the Watchkeepers and the Wardens, then we must consider that it is possible—I would say almost certain—that members of this Hall have also sworn that oath."

When Jayn was a girl, sitting in on meetings of the Hall, they had mostly been dry and tedious, but occasionally the debates could get heated. Nothing she saw before could compare to the chaos her words unleashed. Half the lords were on their feet, shouting down at the Watchkeepers or at each other. Others eyed their colleagues with open suspicion. Some moved slowly toward the door, as if expecting a member of the Reach to reveal himself by drawing a concealed weapon and attacking the other lords—or maybe transforming into a Kobold on the spot. The First Pentarch was also standing and shouting for order, but no one listened.

Jayn looked to her mother. The Fourth Pentarch regarded her daughter with an unreadable expression. Then Anyse Eldragor rose to her feet. "Listen to me!" she shouted, and the words echoed through the Assembly Room with all the authority of a Standing Army general. The lords and Pentarchs fell silent. All eyes turned to Anyse. She took her time before she spoke. She seemed to regard each member of the Hall in turn, before fixing her gaze on Jayn. "I must agree with my daughter and her Pentad. It would be pride and foolishness to assume no one within the Assembly has been compromised by the Reach." Some lords muttered to themselves, but no one challenged Anyse. "You all know by now what Lucas Peniter did to me… What the Reach did to me. Still, I have no wish to see our government collapse under paranoia and suspicion." She turned to Prentley. "I propose an amnesty. If anyone present here today wishes to come forward, confess their ties to the Reach, and denounce their oath, then I say, they should be given the benefit of the doubt. We will assume they did not know what they were really working toward. No one would lose his or her seat in the Hall."

Jayn suppressed a smile. They had hoped something like this would happen, but she had not expected her mother to be the one to suggest it. What the Reach had done to Anyse cleared her of any possible suspicion and gave immense weight to her words.

A quiet fell over the room, while the First Pentarch considered her request. Finally, he nodded and addressed the Hall. "I second the suggestion. If anyone here has sworn to the Reach, I ask you to place your loyalty to Aldria over whatever payments and promises you may have received. Now more than ever, we must be united. Confess now and there will be no penalties."

The silence that followed seemed interminable. Feet shuffled. Men and women exchanged nervous glances. No one spoke. No one stepped forward. Jayn frowned. She had been certain someone would confess. Pavel had agreed to her plan, to denounce his own oath and call for others in the Hall to do the same, but he had predicted that no one would confess. Jayn had dismissed his pessimism, but he was right.

Still, it was all in the open now. Maybe no one would step forward today, but they might still denounce their oaths, at least to themselves. Peniter and the Reach had gone after all of the lords in the Civic Quintant after all, even if it had been just a distraction, meant to fail. The Reach had finally been exposed. Within a month, the whole nation would know that name and what they had done in Appencourt. Hopefully, silent support would be broken within the Hall, and the hidden members inside the government would not hinder Aldria's efforts to eradicate the organization. But maybe Jayn was being too much of an optimist. Regardless, no one gathered here would ever forget Jayn Eldragor's first appearance before the Hall of the Assembly.

The meeting adjourned shortly after Anyse Eldragor's call for amnesty. No one wanted to ask many more questions, now that they were all suspecting each other of being secret Kobold collaborators. The Watchkeepers were asked to remain as guests of the

Hall through the end of the week. It was certain they would be called for again. They spoke a little over dinner, but they were all exhausted after a full day of testimony. They trudged upstairs and retired to their rooms.

Pavel lingered in the hall. He found himself standing before Nyssa's door again. She'd refused to speak to him all week. He understood. What Kalo had done to her would be devastating to any Weaver, but Nyssa had taken it especially hard. Maybe he should keep giving her space, but he didn't want to. He didn't know what he could do, but there had to be some way for him to help her.

He knocked. She didn't answer. "It's me, Nyssa. Please open up. We need to talk."

Silence. He tried the handle. It was locked. He sighed.

"Blight, Nyssa, I'm coming in, so you better be decent."

He gripped the knob and filled the door with lacings of Stone. It was strange how different metals had a different texture in his mind. The knob and lock were all brass. It took him nearly a minute of fumbling to pop the lock open. She had to have heard him, but she said nothing.

He hesitated before opening the door. "All right, I'm coming in," he said.

She lay atop the sheets in a rumpled white nightgown, staring up at the ceiling. She'd taken all the little braids out of her hair, turning it into a mass of frizzy curls. For a minute, he thought she might actually be asleep. "What do you want, Talvor?" she asked, her voice hoarse. She still didn't look at him.

He sighed, shut the door, and crossed the room. Light from the setting sun spilled in from the narrow window, but the room was otherwise dark. He sat on the edge of the bed and spoke without looking at her. "I hate to see you like this."

"Then go away."

"The Hall finally called for us today. The kids did pretty good, although…" He forced a laugh. "I don't know how Commandant Lahey will feel about it."

She said nothing. He let the silence stretch for a minute.

"You should join us tomorrow. I'm sure the lords will want to hear from you."

"The Hall sent for Watchkeepers. I'm not a Watchkeeper."

"Don't say that."

"Only the best Weavers can be Watchkeepers. I'm not any kind of Weaver now."

"We don't know what that Runeform did to you. There's no reason to believe the damage is permanent."

"I've been trying. Every minute of every day. It's gone."

"If there's a Runeform that can seal a Weaver, it stands to reason there's another Runeform that can unseal you."

"I'm sure there is, and I'm sure the Kobolds stole it."

"Then we'll get it back. I'll kill all the Kobolds and Manfaces there are if I have to, but we'll get it back."

"Why are you here, Pavel?"

He looked at her then. She still lay with her head on a pillow, but she studied him. Her big brown eyes glistened, but she didn't cry.

"What do you want from me?"

"I don't want anything."

"You want my gratitude? You want me to throw myself at your feet and call you my hero?"

He rose to his feet, staring at the opposite wall. "You're upset. You've been hurt."

"Whose fault is that?"

He felt her angry eyes on his back. He said nothing.

"I've been thinking. You know what I've decided?"

He clenched his jaw. He knew she would want to lash out. He just wished she wouldn't lash out at him.

"I've decided that you are cursed, Pavel Talvor."

He fought to keep his voice even. "Why do you say that?"

"Because my life has been cursed since the moment I met you. You bring death with you. First, my entire Pentad dies. Then my home gets attacked. Now this. I wish I had never met you."

Pavel didn't respond. He kept his back to her and waited until he could control the emotions flashing across his face. When he turned around, she had rolled over onto her side, facing away from him.

Maybe he should leave. Maybe he should let her push him away. He didn't want to. He leaned against the wall and watched her still form, the slight rising of her side as she breathed. He looked down at his feet. A single red bead lay on the floor. Silently, he bent down, picked it up, and put it in his pocket. He couldn't say why. He didn't know how to help her, but he wasn't going to give up.

He heard a faint tapping at the window. He glanced toward it. Something like a crow perched outside, tapping the glass with its beak.

"Look," Pavel said, though Nyssa continued to ignore him and the sound. "Corvus is here."

Pavel moved to the window. Corvus cocked his head and regarded Pavel with a single cerulean eye. "Hey, buddy," Pavel said. "I'm glad to see the Kobolds didn't snatch you with the other Runeforms." He looked at Nyssa's back. "Captain Lahmeer isn't feeling well, but I'm sure she will be glad to see you."

The window could be opened by turning a small crank at its base. Corvus flew off as the glass pane swung open, but he came back a moment later and alighted on the inner windowsill.

"Well," Pavel said, "what's the report? How's the city?"

Pavel's affected cheerfulness finally got to Nyssa. She groaned and rolled over onto her back again. "I don't get it, I really don't," she said. "Why do you keep that thing around? Why do you keep asking it questions? All it ever does is spout silly nonsense and lies. Watch. I bet it's going to say something ridiculous now."

The man who called himself Pavel Talvor smiled. He'd been around for thirty years and considered himself a good liar, but the Runeform that called itself Corvus had been flying the earth for over a millennium, and it was the greatest liar in existence.

Corvus squawked. "Your mother is here!"

Epilogue
Prophecies and Poisons

TERRON LAITH GHOSTED down the stairs at the back of the tea shop. A hallway ran the length of the basement. He stopped by the first door, not seeing anyone. A tea service rested on a rolling cart. He lifted the lid on the ceramic teapot. His noise wrinkled. It was some complicated herbal blend. He had never been here before, but he knew it was one of hundreds of secret outposts the Academy of the Ways operated across the continent. The old Iscernaen couple who ran the tea shop upstairs had no idea what the Scholars did below, but they were paid well for their discretion.

Terron Laith didn't know what went on down here either, but he wouldn't admit that. He hefted the satchel he carried under one shoulder and heard the rustle of the loose papers inside. He considered knocking on the door, but before he could, it swung open, and Mina Bellain stepped out into the hallway. Terron caught a glimpse of another woman inside, seated at a table. She had straight black hair and wore a black and silver servant's uniform. He didn't recognize her or the livery.

He still wasn't quite sure how he had gone from spying on Mina for Rense Gilhart to working with her, but here he was. Mina was also a member of the Sanctum, so perhaps she could nominate him to that illustrious rank. Terron had assumed Rense would be his ticket into the Academy's inner circle, but he liked to have options. If Rense found out he was working with Mina, Terron could still spin it, play the triple agent, and tell Rense everything Mina had been doing.

He'd learned a lot already working with Mina. She had put him to work unlocking the secrets of the Runeform fountain in Rigel and then disappeared for two months. Four days ago, he got word to meet Mina here in Appencourt. Once again, he found himself traveling to a city in the wake of a Kobold attack. Once again, he'd missed all the fun.

Mina locked the door behind her and turned to Terron with a smile. "You made good time," she said.

He nodded. "I wish I got here sooner. Were you here for that bit of fun last week?"

"Indeed. I killed my first Kobold, in fact."

"Well done. I still haven't even seen one of the blighters."

"You may regret wanting to."

Terron placed a hand on his satchel. "I have the Rigel report here."

"What's the highlight?"

Terron considered the question. He knew it was some sort of test. Every conversation with Mina Bellain felt like a test, and he wasn't always sure he passed. Still, she kept him around, so he must be doing something right. Terron considered himself a good judge of character, good at reading people and knowing how they thought. He still hadn't quite cracked the riddle that was Mina Bellain, but he knew she liked to be surprised.

"I had to alter your oath," he said.

"Really?"

"I swear that after I ask this Runeform fountain one question, I will never again attempt to ask it any other questions, for any reason, under any circumstances," Terron quoted. "We wasted our first candidate because Rigel refused to answer her *one* question. I changed the oath to say, 'After I receive one more answer…'"

"Sounds like you picked a bad question."

"There's another rule."

"Oh." Her smile widened.

He knew she would like that. The Runeform fountain was simple, once you knew its secret. Terron wasn't vain enough to think that he and Mina had been the first to crack that nut. Doubtless many Scholars had worked it out over the centuries, but all had kept the secret of the fountain to themselves. Terron loved a juicy secret, but even he wondered sometimes if the Scholars were hurting themselves by hoarding knowledge. How much more could the Academy learn if they all worked together?

The Rigel fountain answered any question asked of it, with some exceptions, but it didn't dole out the answers in the same order as the questions. A man might ask the fountain, "Does my wife really love me?" and Rigel might say, "A heart defect." It wouldn't really make sense, until ten years later, when the man might return and ask, "Why did my wife have to die?" and the fountain would say, "With all her heart." It gave the right answers, but in the wrong order. The more questions you asked, the more muddled the answers would become to sort out, but if you only asked a single question in all your life, you would get a simple answer. The fountain would not answer hypothetical if-then questions and did not give advice. Terron had found another exception.

"It took us a while to find our first candidate. It seemed like everyone within a hundred miles of Rigel had asked the fountain a question at one time or another. Then we found a little old lady in Falport who had lived her whole life in the city and never once crossed the bridge into Rigel. She was happy to come along, like it was some kind of adventure. She used the Keeper's Bracelet and swore your version of the oath, and then I had her ask directly: 'What is the Rivening?'"

"And Rigel didn't answer."

Terron shook his head.

"So what's the rule?"

"As near as I can figure, it's a matter of personal relevance. If I asked Rigel, 'What color undergarments does the queen of Iscerna wear?', it probably wouldn't answer me, because that information has no bearing or personal relevance to me, the questioner."

"But the Rivening should be relevant to everyone."

"I did say she was an *old* lady."

"I see. I assume you're keeping tabs on her?"

"Of course. She'll be our canary. As long as she's still kicking, we don't have to worry, but the moment she croaks…"

"That's helpful," Mina said. "But please tell me you have actually figured out what the Rivening is?"

He nodded. "It's all in the report." Rigel's answers were always brief, never more than a single sentence, but he had worked out the broad strokes of the coming cataclysm. He shook his head. "It's nothing like we thought." He had no idea what Mina Bellain had been expecting, but he spoke the truth for himself.

"I look forward to reading it." Mina glanced at the tea cart. "Go upstairs and get something to drink. I'll join you in a minute. I need to finish making my rounds down here before this tea cools."

***

Clay heard muffled voices through the door, but he couldn't make out any of the words. His mouth was dry, and his stomach grumbled. He didn't know how long he'd been locked in this basement, but it had to have been several days. There were no windows, so he didn't know if the sun was even up outside. A single guttering candle illuminated the cell.

He and Ansel had been cooling their heels in the Watchkeeper prison for a week. Two guards woke them in the middle of the night and told them they were being transferred. They didn't answer any of Clay's questions, but they put bags over their heads and forced them into a carriage. The ride had been short, so Clay knew they were still somewhere in Appencourt. They were pulled from the carriage, led into a building and down a staircase, and shoved into separate cells. Sara had been kept in another part of the Watchkeeper jail with the other lady prisoners, if there were any. He didn't know if she'd been moved too. He hoped the Watchkeepers really had cut a deal with her.

The conversation outside stopped, and then the door swung open. A woman in a blue dress with shoulder-length black hair came in, walking backwards and pulling a little silver cart. She shut the door behind her and shoved the cart up against the bars. Clay had limited experience, but this room didn't seem like a standard prison cell. It looked like a regular basement room, with a dusty stone floor, a wooden roof, and plaster walls. A row of iron bars with a locked door cut the room in half, trapping Clay in the back section. He didn't even have a bed, just a blanket and a wooden chair.

The woman sat on the other chair on the opposite side of the bars and offered him a friendly smile. He recognized her then. It was the Scholar who had been traveling with the Watchkeepers that had convinced Clay and his friends to turn themselves in. Clay had long come to regret that decision. Mina, he thought the woman's name was. He remembered the older Watchkeeper's warning about what would happen if the Academy of the Ways found out what Ansel and Sara could do, how they would all be thrown into a dungeon forever. Here he was. In a dungeon. With a Scholar.

He fought to control his expression, but she must have seen the fear in his eyes. Whatever she saw, she ignored it. That bland smile stayed plastered on her face. "My, it's dark in here," she said. She raised her hand and an orb of light emerged from her palm. It rose up and stuck to the ceiling. Clay shivered and squinted up at the sudden brightness. His best friend was a Weaver, but it still made him uncomfortable seeing Weavers do such unnatural things.

"That's better," the Scholar said. She leaned over toward the cart, lifted a tea pot, and filled a small porcelain cup. "Please, help yourself."

Clay looked at the cart. Tea did not sound appealing to him. He really just wanted water. A tray of spongy yellow cakes also sat on the cart. His stomach rumbled again. He reached through the bars, grabbed a little cake, and shoved it into his mouth. It was the driest thing he'd ever tasted. He coughed, fumbling for the teacup. He took a big gulp, wetting his mouth enough to swallow the rest of the cake. Fortunately, the tea had cooled enough to not burn his mouth. He took another long sip. The cake was awful, but the tea wasn't bad. It was an herbal blend, with lemon and bergamot and a tangy aftertaste he couldn't quite place.

His thirst partially quenched, he looked up at the woman. How had the Scholar found out about Ansel and Sara? They had all agreed to keep their mouths shut about that weird "forbidden Blending." Had the Watchkeepers ratted them out? He didn't think that pretty blonde girl, Jayn, would have betrayed them, but maybe that shifty older guy or Ryn had. It didn't matter now. He resolved to admit nothing.

"Let's have a little chat," Mina said.

"Got nothing to say."

"Oh, I know, you'll never betray your friends and all that. Don't worry, I don't need you to tell me anything. I know all about that Wydelk scam. Very clever."

Clay didn't answer.

Mina kept on smiling, chatting away like they really were having a casual tea. She didn't take a cup herself. There'd only been one cup on the cart, though Clay noticed now there were three empty saucers. "Yes, you robbed the rooms while Sara and Ansel made the illusions outside, a Blending of Wave and Aether, which everyone knows is impossible, but those lovebirds found a way."

He gritted his teeth, thinking of the Watchkeepers again. "Who told you?"

She laughed. "Oh, don't be mad. No one told me." She leaned forward, and her pleasant mask slipped for a moment. Her voice took on a harder edge. "Come on, do you really think a couple of backwoods idiots figured out a Blending that the Academy of the Ways didn't already know about?"

Clay shook his head, wishing he had just run when he had the chance. "So turning ourselves in, lying to the Watchkeepers, that was all just a waste of time…"

"It might have worked, if I hadn't been there. A stroke of misfortune, I'm afraid."

"So that's why I'm in this hole now? Your Academy doesn't want the world finding out about these forbidden Blendings?"

"Forbidden? Is that the word the Watchkeepers used? We say 'contrary,' but I like that phrase. Forbidden…"

Clay clamped his mouth shut.

"Oh, don't worry," she said with a laugh and a wave of her hand. "You still haven't betrayed anyone. Those young Watchkeepers showed their own hand when they lied for you. I'm still not certain what contrary Blending they stumbled on, but I have my theories." She sighed. The pleasant mask was back. She sounded like a farmwife complaining about moles in the garden. "My gut tells me it's that Ryn Silverbell. It's always those unusual Etchings that give it away."

Clay wanted to scream, but he kept his cool. "How many people have stumbled upon these secrets you're so intent on keeping? What do you do with them all? How many dungeons do you have?"

"Oh, we mostly just kill them."

Clay's throat felt dry again. He took another sip of tea. Was there any way he could get out of this jam? The tea tasted sour now. What was that aftertaste, anyway? He looked again at the three empty saucers. The cup slipped from his hand and shattered on the floor. The tea splashed on his bare feet.

Mina's smile never faltered. "Don't worry, darling, you won't feel a thing. It's like falling asleep."

Clay fought the panic for a moment. *Never show them fear.* That's what his rotten father used to say, when he was still alive and wasn't beating on Clay or his mother. Clay hadn't learned much from his father, but he had hung onto that lesson. If he was already dead, he wouldn't give this evil woman the satisfaction of seeing him squirm. He forced his mouth into the shape of a smile. "Do me a favor then, will you? When you dump our bodies into some hole in the woods, would you tip me in next to that pretty blonde Watchkeeper?"

Mina laughed. "Oh, I'm afraid Jayn Eldragor will not be joining you in the next world."

He attempted a shrug. Was his vision getting blurry, or was that his imagination? "I'm not mad, but it doesn't really seem fair."

"I know. We've had to make an exception for Jayn and her Pentad, for now at least. There's a pesky little prophecy involved."

"Oh," he feigned sympathy. "You hate a prophecy."

"Yes, we may need those kids around, in case a little old lady dies."

Was she not making any sense, or was Clay's mind starting to slip? His eyelids had begun to feel heavy. He forced them open and focused on the Scholar.

She sighed again. "I'm doing my best, but they don't make it easy, now do they? It's fine by me if Rense Gilhart wants to assassinate a Tamorine prince, but why does he have to try to pin the murder on my Watchkeepers?" She shook her head.

Clay had no idea what she was talking about anymore. She didn't even seem to be speaking to him really. A woman like her, doing the things she did, she probably had to keep secrets from everyone around her all the time. A moment like this, alone with a dying man, that was probably the only time she could let her guard down and be honest. The realization came to Clay in a final moment of clarity. Then he slipped from his chair and collapsed to the dirty floor, sending bits of broken porcelain skittering across the cell.

~

ABOUT THE AUTHOR

Michael Hardcastle teaches high school English and writing in Tampa, Florida, and has an MFA in Creative Writing from the University of Tampa. His fiction has been published in The William & Mary Review and West Trade Review, and his poetry has been published in Common Ground Review and Torrid Literature Journal.

If you enjoyed reading, please rate and review *Wave Weaver* on Amazon and Goodreads.

The Five Forces series will continue with *Stone Weaver*. Visit www.hardcastlewrites.com for more information and to sign up for the newsletter.

www.ingramcontent.com/pod-product-compliance
Lightning Source LLC
LaVergne TN
LVHW100501110826
845146LV00002B/480

* 9 7 9 8 9 9 4 2 5 1 7 2 0 *